A WILD COLONIAL GIRL

A WILD COLONIAL GIRL

JEAN HARRINGTON

Kenmore, WA

A Camel Press book published by Epicenter Press

Epicenter Press
6524 NE 181st St.
Suite 2
Kenmore, WA 98028

For more information go to:
www.Camelpress.com
www.Coffeetownpress.com
www.Epicenterpress.com
www.AuthorJeanHarrington.Weebly.com

Cover design by Scott Book
Design by Melissa Vail Coffman

A Wild Colonial Girl

ISBN: 978-1-94207-866-1 (Trade Paper)
ISBN: 978-1-94207-867-8 (eBook)

Printed in the United States of America

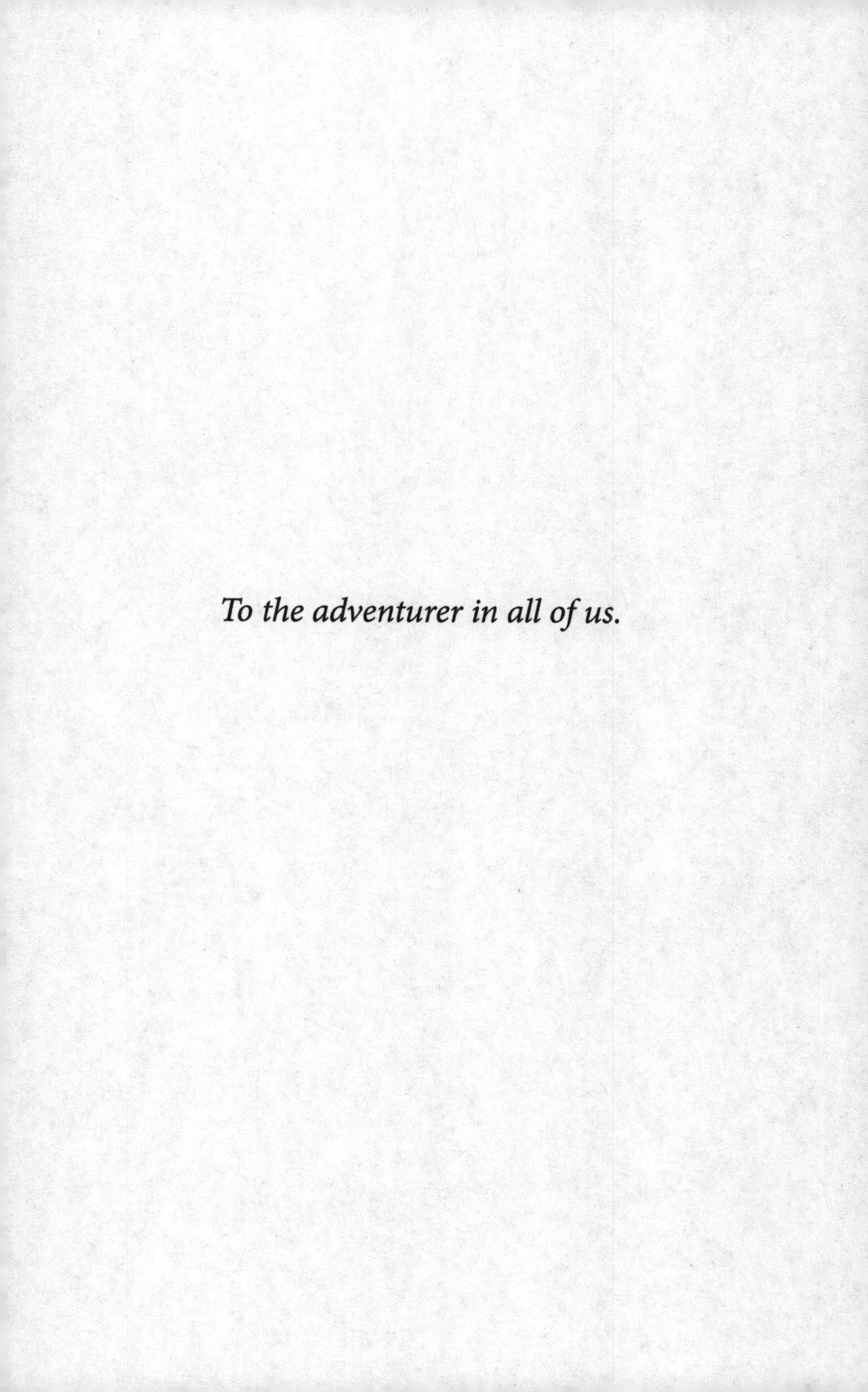

To the adventurer in all of us.

ACKNOWLEDGMENTS

CURRENT ACKNOWLEDGEMENTS MUST GO, happily, to my fine editor, Jennifer McCord. For inspiring the three books in my Irish/Colonial series, I am indebted to Mary Ann Harrington for her Irish lilt, and to John for his. Acknowledgement also to my hero in history, Roger Williams, who though a man of God understood that church and state had to be separate.

CHAPTER ONE

HARTFORD HALL, ENGLAND, 1686

WITH A CASUAL EASE HE WAS FAR FROM FEELING, Harry Rushmount leaned as far back as the hard seat would allow and crossed one booted leg over the other. "What if there was no duel?" he said. "What if father was murdered?"

Lady Anne Rushmount stiffened and clutched the arms of her tapestry chair, her knuckles as prominent as the ruby gems on her fingers. "You're asking that now, Harry? Nigh on twenty years have passed since your father died."

"Exactly." Harry reached into his doublet and removed a sheet of yellowed parchment. "Why was this report of his death never shown to me?" A hiss of sparks from the fireplace then silence. "Well, Mother?"

She flicked at lace on her wrist before looking toward the mullioned windows. "Where did you find that wretched document? I thought it had been destroyed."

No doubt she was lying, but he wouldn't challenge her. The time for challenges was long past. "Not destroyed, well hidden among the estate papers. I came across it a fortnight ago, purely by chance." He slipped the parchment back into his doublet. "I don't believe a word it contains and intend to discover the truth for myself. In the colony where this so-called duel took place."

"You'll discover nothing new there." She brought her gaze back to him and thrust up her chin. "I forbid you to embark on such a quest."

She forbids. Although he had no intention of giving in to her wishes, sympathy welled in Harry's heart as he studied her, old now and entrenched in wrong-headed beliefs.

"I have another purpose in going on this voyage. I'm about to—"

"Ah yes." She cut him off with a wave of a hand, her rubies a quick flash of fire. "Indulge in trade, of course. That does not surprise me. I thought it would come to this. You understand you risk destroying your name and that of your entire family?"

"That's a risk I'm prepared to take."

Her fingers drummed on the arm of her chair.

Harry groaned silently. What next? Something else he could never agree to?

The drumming stopped. "While I hate the very idea of trade, under the circumstances I understand your decision."

Her quick surrender to his plan stunned him, and he sent a darting glance her way. Were those tears welling in her eyes? An appalling idea, one he stifled the instant it sprang to life. How absurd. He had never seen her cry.

"Without a dowry, your sister's marriage to Sir Sydney was doomed. You do understand, my boy, why she received what was left of the—"

"Say no more, Mother. Elizabeth's well being is everything to me. As long as she is happily married, I am more than content to make my own fortune. In fact, I would have it no other way. With the estate in Ireland, run down though it may be, and knowing you are safe here in Uncle Richard's care . . ." his arms swept wide at the high-ceilinged drawing room with its magnificent stone fireplace and mahogany paneling, its carved furnishings and porcelain treasures ". . . I am doubly content."

She smiled, her glance moving over him, from the top of his head to the soles of his boots. "There is another way. You're a handsome lad in more ways than one, and you have an illustrious name. Why not use *that* to make your fortune? Entice a well-connected woman into matrimony. After all, you *are* related to King James." Another flick at her lace. "On your maternal side, of course."

Harry suppressed a temptation to scoff. "Marriage? Not for a while yet, and truth be told, our relationship to the king is a tenuous thread at best."

Lady Anne flushed to the very edge of her décolleté. "How dare you."

That he had upset her distressed him, but he could not bend to her demands, nor could he let her know how they affected him. She would seize upon any show of emotion as a sign of weakness. He had learned that lesson well as a child.

God, he couldn't pretend to be at his ease any longer. The chair was harder on his ass than a pub stool. He rose to pace before the fire. He had dressed in his finest for this visit in fawn breeches, a cascade of lace at his throat, a bottle green doublet smooth over his shoulders. His mother had no realization that this—his one and only suit of decent clothes—was still unpaid for. Nor that he had donned it today rather than his usual attire of linen shirt and workman's breeches to save her from the anguish of seeing her son for what he was, a down-at-heels aristocrat. A circumstance he intended to change by any means, preferably legal, he could employ.

As if he were no longer present, Lady Anne stared past him at the paneled wall behind his head. Though his stomach rumbled at the hint of pheasant on the spit wafting in the air, he wouldn't stay and dine with her this evening. At best, it would be a stilted, awkward meal.

Rather than retake his seat, he bowed. "Would you be so kind as to inform Uncle Richard I'm sorry to have missed him? We sail at the first suitable tide, so I'd best get back to London." In a final attempt to bridge the chasm between them, he added, "I didn't want to leave without saying good-bye."

Her glance met his, but the glittering in her eyes failed to warm them. "A pity. If you had, you would have spared me this sad realization. While I deplore having you chase after a fortune, I understand it. This other . . . this seeking after a dead man's secrets, I have no patience for."

He blew out an exasperated breath. "Why not, Mother? Don't you want to know who killed your husband?"

Chapter Two

The tide was low, the sun high, a perfect time for shell fishing. Abby O'Donnell stripped off her shoes and stockings and waded into the ankle-deep water, its coolness a blessing on such a hot day. She wiggled her toes in the sand and soon felt the hard back of a quahog under foot. They made a fine stew, quahogs, and within minutes her wooden bucket was filled to the brim. Mam would be pleased. Abby plucked a last one out of the water, straightened and gasped.

A ship loomed on the blue horizon. An ocean-going vessel, a trimaster, its sails billowing in the salty breeze, coming closer and closer to shore like a vision in a dream. Quahogs, clams, stews all forgotten, she cupped her eyes against the sun's glare and stared at the wondrous sight. Was it real? Sudden shouts from others along the shore gave the answer: *Yes.* As she watched, the ship's sails were furled tight against the rigging. They had anchored. They were staying.

Abby grabbed her bucket and waded through the surf to the patch of dry sand where she'd left her shoes and stockings. She rolled the stockings up to her thighs, buckled on her shoes and dashed back to the water's edge. Mam would probably skin her alive for not hurrying home with her catch, but she couldn't bear to leave, not with a skiff being lowered from the ship's side and then another one. *They were coming ashore.*

Footsteps crunched on the sand behind her. Emma Harris, a round little robin in her brown, linsey-woolsey frock, came racing over, her face pink with effort. "The minute Nate told me, I ran all the way."

Nate? Abby glanced around quickly, but Emma was alone, her brother Nate nowhere in sight for once. Good. Lately, he kept popping into view whenever she and Emma were together, what he had in mind clear on his broad, oily face each time he looked Abby's way.

"They're here!" Emma pointed to the shallow surf. "Look, Abby!"

The first skiff had reached shore, and a sorry-looking crew of bearded men climbed out, their grins at the welcome party revealing mouths full of rotten stumps. They're all old and well nigh toothless, Abby thought, her excitement dimming a bit.

Hard to believe they had come from a ship so beautiful. Even with her sails furled and weighted with cargo, she rode the harbor waves gracefully, gleaming black, her name, the *Lady Anne*, emblazoned on her hull in gilt lettering, her brass fittings polished and glowing in the sun.

For as long as she could remember, Abby had longed to sail away on such a ship. Like her Irish ancestress, Granuaile, the legendary pirate queen, had done so long ago. And like her own mother who had crossed the wide ocean to seek a new life here in Providence colony.

A sigh escaped her. But that was then and this was now. She had no way of sailing off on such a ship. No way at all. Still . . . life surely had more to offer than marriage to a dullard like Nate Harris. More than walking the same narrow paths in the same narrow village day after day, year after year, until there were no more days left, and no more years. If only, for the memory alone, she could go aboard the *Lady Anne* just once to see what—

"Lookie, Abby, the other skiff."

"Ship oars!"

The sudden shout caught Abby's attention and held it fast.

The skiff hit the beach with a thump, and the young man who had shouted at the oarsmen stood up, frowning. He leapt onto the wet sand, his frown melting into a brilliant, white smile as Elder John Thayer, the most prosperous man in the village, came forward to greet him.

Emma ran a sleeve across her damp forehead. "Lordy. Have you ever seen the like of him?"

Abby's breath caught in her throat. "No, never."

She couldn't pull her gaze away and stared at him, from the top of his dark, cropped hair to the heels of his high, polished boots. None of the village men wore such boots, nor had their hair clipped so close to the head. Was it cut short to better accommodate a wig? Whatever the reason, she liked the neat, trim look of it. She liked the white shirt, too, flowing smoothly about his broad shoulders. Could the fabric be silk? Was that lace at his wrists?

She forgot all about the lace as his breeches caught her attention. Unlike the shapeless garments of the townsmen, they fit close to his body, outlining his thighs and, when he turned, his backside, so thoroughly she gasped.

Her mouth half open, her pulse pounding in her temples, she followed his every move, the gestures of his arms in the flowing sleeves, the way he held his head so high, his erect bearing, his long-legged stride in those polished boots. In all her eighteen years, she had never dreamed a man like this existed anywhere in the world.

With catcalls and raucous shouts, the seamen unloaded the boat, wading through the shallow surf to stack the bales and boxes on the shore. Paying no heed to the seamen's efforts, the stranger kept on speaking to Elder Thayer. What could they have to talk about so long? She burned to know. Was he the ship's captain? Was he the owner? If so, he might allow visitors on board, even a female like herself.

"I'm going to move closer to him, Emma. I want to hear what they're saying."

Emma grasped her arm. "No. It's not seemly. What would Nate say?"

"Pish." Abby lifted Emma's hand away. "Wait for me. I won't be long."

"But Abby . . ."

"Shhh, I'll be back in a trice."

After a quick curtsey to Goody Baxter, Abby inched past Thomas Wayland and his da and eased around a knot of children frolicking in the sunshine. A few more steps and she stood behind the stranger and Elder Thayer. The sun beating on her head, her pulse throbbing in her ears, she stayed still and listened.

"You'll find our hospitality warm in the colonies," John Thayer said, jamming his cane into the sand for support and rocking back on his heels. "Though I must warn you, Providence is a small market for a ship full of English goods."

Harry Rushmount eyed the man with open curiosity. The red veins marking his face testified to a love of spirits and his belly to a love of dining. Amazing how well these colonists managed to live.

Thayer cleared his throat. "The English goods, my lord . . ."

"Ah, yes, of course. We're less than half full now. Boston was our first destination. We did much trading there, but I have a listing of

what's left for sale. Or barter. Furs would be welcome. If your townsmen wish—"

"Undoubtedly they have needs. I'll ask about."

"Excellent." Harry withdrew a sheet of paper from his breeches pocket. "This is what we can spare from our cargo. Perhaps it could be posted
in the village square."

Thayer tucked the list inside his doublet without reading it. "Of a
certainty. And how else may I help you?"

Harry pulled out a kerchief and mopped his dripping forehead.
Damn, but this New World was piercing hot. A momentary pang shot
through him at the thought of his family's London home with its cool,
manicured gardens. The longing faded quickly. He'd be back there again
soon enough then off to his Irish estate. In the meantime, his purpose
for being here in the middle of nowhere was about to be realized. He
pocketed the kerchief. "Tell me what you know about my father's death."

Thayer gripped his cane as if without it he'd fall to the sand. "I know
only what the original report stated."

"The one Governor Williams signed? I've read it. It leaves many questions unanswered."

"What more can be learned? The governor's dead now, and it's near
twenty years since your father died."

"Since he was killed."

"Yes, killed," John conceded, gazing off into the distance as if a gull
riding the currents had captured his interest.

Harry's eyes narrowed. "Tomorrow, I intend to meet with the witnesses the report mentions. They may recall something left unsaid at the
time. This Canonchet, for one. A chieftain, I take it."

Thayer's attention snapped back to him. "Dead. Long ago. In King
Philip's War."

"The report mentioned other witnesses. What of them?"

"All gone. Only a man and wife remain."

Harry drew in a shocked breath. "A woman was involved? I had no
knowledge of that."

"Governor Williams thought it best to keep her name clear of the matter."

"Why tell me of her now?"

"It's widely known about the colony that she witnessed your father's
death. And that, young sir, is all I know of the matter."

Unconvinced, Harry eyed him askance. There had to be more, much
more. "Who is this woman?"

"One of great beauty and firm mind. Not a female to trifle with."

"I haven't ventured all this way to be easily put off."

"Out of me way! Out of me way!"

At the shouted warning, Harry glanced up quickly. One of his crewmen was staggering across the sand, a heavy sack precariously riding his shoulder.

"Look out, I say. Look out!"

Harry touched Thayer's arm. "You'd best step aside, sir."

"Aye." With a grunt, Thayer pulled his cane out of the sand, swiveling out of harm's way without a moment to spare.

The other villagers in the seaman's path leapt to obey as well, but engrossed in her quest, Abby didn't hear the warning. She was so close to the handsome stranger she could reach out and touch him—if she dared. She extended a finger, just one . . . Panting, ready to drop his burden, the seaman slammed into her back, knocking her off balance, straight into the stranger. Her knees buckling, she reached up and grasped him about the waist.

"What the—"

He twisted around, the swift move taking away her support. She fell, landing on her rear in the wet sand, skirt and petticoat up to her knees.

"I told you to look out," the sailor barked and lurched on.

A woman cried out then the earth and everything on it whirled out of control. Abby closed her eyes, and to her great relief, the spinning stopped. She sat there a second or two, eyes closed, listening to the shouts of the children and, close by, a whimpering baby. She took in deep breaths of sea air and something else—a heady mix of perspiration and musk and—*the stranger*. Her eyes snapped open. He was crouched by her side, his face tense. Clutching her baby, Goody Baxter peered over his shoulder. "Dear Lord, are you harmed, Abby?"

She shook her head, causing the spinning to start up again. "No, he jostled me, is all."

"Are you quite sure, Miss?" the stranger asked.

She sat without moving and stared up into his eyes. They were dark, lit with inner lights. Disarmed by his closeness and the impact of those eyes, a whispered "yes" was all she could manage.

"I'm thankful you're not harmed." The tension in his face eased. "I'd have my man apologize, but sorry to say, he wouldn't know how." He smiled, and she felt her body melt in response. "Will you accept my apology instead?"

She nodded.

He extended a hand. "May I help you up?" It was a strong hand, with long, tapering fingers and nails that were as clean as her own. For some reason she couldn't name, she didn't dare touch him after all. It would be like touching fire.

"Abby, act like a godly woman," Goody Baxter hissed. "Cover yourself."

What? Abby glanced down and gasped. *Her skirt.* Heat rose into her face, and ignoring the proffered hand, she scrambled to her feet unaided.

His lips twitched. She knew he wanted to laugh. He must think she had indulged in a childish prank. Even worse, a childish prank to gain his attention, whoever he was. Well, hadn't she? And made a fool of herself into the bargain.

With as much dignity as she could muster, she settled her skirt around her ankles and brushed off the sand clinging to it. "I accept your apology, sir, but if that sailor is your man, then you'd best teach him better manners. If you're able," she finished tartly.

A whoop of laughter greeted her retort as she stomped off, hoping to heaven she didn't have a wet spot on her rear. More curious than ever, she wended her way back to Emma. Who was this stranger? For all her embarrassment she hadn't learned very much. She should have asked his name or given him her own. Or told him how beautiful his ship was, even if such boldness wasn't seemly. If she had, no telling what might have happened. She whacked a clump of sea grass standing in her way, picked up her laden pail and said goodbye to a sputtering Emma.

As she trudged along the dusty path toward home, the salty breeze rustling the leaves did little to cool her way. She was hot and out of sorts, and with each step the bucket grew heavier.

"Abby," a voice called. "Over here."

Oh, no.

Sucking on a grass stem, Nate Harris lounged against the old elm that grew by the path. "I've been waiting for you." He stood upright and tossed the grass stem to the ground. "Saw you fall over on the sand with your skirts aflying. Shouldn't have happened. Wasn't seemly."

"Well, it did, and no harm done," she said, moving on.

"Mind if I walk with you?"

"Would that matter?"

He smiled, his eyes hiding in the folds of his broad cheeks. "No sense in fighting me, Abby," he said, falling into step beside her.

"No sense in not." She yanked the bucket away from his outstretched hand. "I can carry my own weight."

SQUINTING AGAINST THE SUN, Harry had watched the girl stomp off through the sea grass, a round damp spot on the back of her gown. The sight made him smile. Red hair and onyx eyes. An unusual combination. He'd seen red heads aplenty on his Irish estate, but none to compare to this one. He noticed her the minute he stepped off the skiff. How could he not? She had stared, her mouth half open, looking as if she wished to take a bite out of him. Well, he was accustomed to female attention and enjoyed it thoroughly. But this was a first. The girl had gazed at him as if he came from another world. In truth, perhaps he had, to a colonial lass.

He dried his brow with the back of his sleeve. This confounded sun burned a man to the bone. If there weren't so many villagers about, he'd strip and take a cooling swim. Later, perhaps, when the men finished the unloading and the villagers left for home.

That girl, she . . . He shook himself. He had a purpose for this voyage, and it didn't include women. Not even one whose hair rippled in the sun like a curtain of gold. His mission was to enrich the coffers of his investors and to discover what had happened to the father he never knew. He'd permit himself no distractions, for that long-awaited time had arrived at last.

CHAPTER THREE

A SHADOW FELL ACROSS THE OPEN DOORWAY. "Mistress O'Donnell?" The deep voice echoed through the keeping room.

Stunned, Abby whirled around nearly dropping the wooden trencher she'd been rinsing in the wash bucket. "*You*. The man from the landing."

His eyes flared wide for an instant and then, as it had yesterday, amusement hovered about his lips. For a certainty, he remembered her—flat on her rear in the sand. How humiliating. She rattled the trencher onto the sideboard with a thump.

Heat flared in her cheeks but at least, thank heaven, she had donned her new linen bodice and skirt this morning and bathed with the lavender soap. Her hands flew up to her hair. She'd not brushed it yet, and still tousled from sleep, it rioted, unkempt, to her shoulders. Worse, her feet were bare.

He stepped inside the doorway and bowed. And such a bow! One knee inclined, arms spread apart, the wide-brimmed hat in his hand nearly sweeping the puncheon floor.

"Lord Harry Rushmount at your service. I trust you are well after yesterday's unfortunate mishap."

"Yes, I am perfectly well," she replied, adding "thank you" but giving him no bow or curtsy in return. *The bow is a way of kneeling. In America, we kneel to no man.*

Yet his elegant gesture hadn't contained the slightest hint of subservience. How had he managed that?

For an instant, she wished she could dip to the floor in a long, velvet gown and have him come forward to take her hand and raise her up. But the wishful moment passed. She stood tall, keeping her back straight as a board.

He waited by the door as if expecting her to say something. Rooted to the floor, she stared at him without speaking, her heart pounding, her eyes taking in every detail of his long, lean form.

As the silence continued, his smile disappeared, and his expression grew thoughtful. "I've come to speak to Mistress Grace O'Donnell. I believe she lives here."

"Oh. Yes. She does."

"And you are?"

"Abby O'Donnell."

"Her daughter?"

She nodded, deflated. So he hadn't come to seek her out. She shouldn't have expected such a miracle. But what on earth could he want with Mam?

"Is she about? Your mother?"

"Oh. Yes. She's gone to bring my brother some fresh water." In a flood of confusion, her manners rushed back to her. "Will you enter?"

"Thank you, yes." With his hat tucked under an arm, he strode into the cabin and stood by the fireplace. She flushed at the sight of his shiny boots. Her shoes were under her bed somewhere, and it was too late to go searching for them. Of all the days in the year, why had she chosen this one to laze about after the sun shone?

"Do be seated, Lord Rushmount." She gestured at one of the three-legged stools by the table. Oh drat, a soiled apron covered the seat. She snatched it off and laid it on the tabletop. "I'll fetch my mother for you."

Abby fled the cabin without another word and raced out to the cornfield, her feet sinking into the soft soil between the green maize shoots. She'd soon be black to the ankles. No matter. She had to warn Mam that an elegant Englishman was searching for her. A lord he said, an aristocrat. For as long as she could remember, Mam had railed against the English gentry. How they starved her people and enslaved them, how they stole their land and called it their own. Then she'd say how happy she was to live in a new world that had no aristocrats with castles and thrones and power. Now to think a lord of the realm was calling on her. Abby picked up her pace. Whatever his reason for doing so might be, it smacked of trouble. Yes, she had to warn Mam and never let on, not even if it killed her to pretend otherwise, that she was mightily drawn to this one aristocrat.

Through the open door, he watched her run, fleet as a deer, her skirts hiked to her knees, her bright hair shining in the light.

So she was the O'Donnell woman's daughter? As he had surmised yesterday, a raw colonial with no social skills, without even the grace to respond to his bow. At least, the Boston settlers knew enough to do so.

His sister, Elizabeth, came to mind. Quiet, serene Elizabeth, in pale blue silk, every strand of hair in place, a necklace of matched pearls clasped at her throat. She was so different, so very, very different from this inarticulate hoyden with, yes, glorious red hair. And eyes like dark jewels. And bare feet. At midmorning.

He laughed and looked about the cabin she called home.

Though not much larger than the peasant dwellings of Ireland, it boasted a large fieldstone fireplace and a rough plank floor. Both notable improvements over most Irish cabins. Across the room, a closed door most likely led to a bed chamber. For the husband and wife, perhaps.

Against the far wall, clothes hung from a row of pegs. An old shag cloak such as he'd seen on the Irish natives, soiled and rubbed bare in places, clung to a peg next to a man's doublet in dark wool, and beside that a fringed green shawl. The color would become the girl.

A narrow chest took up most of the opposite wall, its top cluttered with a few pewter plates and mugs, a nest of wooden bowls and the trencher she had put down so abruptly. He smiled at the rumpled cot in the corner near the hearth. A pair of buckled shoes lay beneath it. The girl's, no doubt. The tabletop at his elbow appeared clean enough. He placed his hat on it and took a seat on a stool.

"Lord Rushmount?"

The icy voice brought him to his feet. Followed by the girl, a slender, fine-featured woman stepped into the cabin, her ankles as bare and dusty as her daughter's, her back as straight. Her hair, a paler version of the girl's, had been plaited and wrapped like a tiara around her head. Outlined against the dark wall, her profile had the purity of a cameo.

He bowed. "Mistress Grace O'Donnell?"

"Herself." She studied him openly without a smile or a hint of softness. No wonder the girl possessed so little charm. Her study complete, the woman said, "You resemble your father to great degree."

He inclined his head. "So I've been told. I wish I had known him to see the likeness for myself."

Her expression changed, but subtly, as if she intended to guard her face as carefully as he somehow knew she would guard her words.

"Do be seated, Lord Rushmount."

It was an order rather than an invitation, but, refusing to take offense, he said, "After you, Mistress O'Donnell."

She remained standing, her daughter next to her, and for a moment, looking at them, he forgot the purpose of his visit. Despite their coarse clothing and lack of ornament, or any evidence of careful grooming, they were the loveliest women he had ever seen. The mother, Grace, would be forty years old at least, but still she drew the eye and held it. This must be the Irish girl his mother had often mentioned. The one who had had the whole village of Ballybanree enthralled. And from his mother's tone of voice, his father as well. Easy to believe, he thought as he tried not to stare at her. If still so lovely this late in life, what had she been like twenty years earlier? *A woman worth dying for.*

And the girl, her cheeks pink from running, her eyes glowing, her hair entirely out of control, was breathtaking.

For a colonial.

How awkward for them all to be standing this way. Gesturing to the bench beside the table, he said, "Please be seated, ladies."

The girl went to move, but the mother stayed her with a light touch.

"'Tis my house you're in, Lord Rushmount. Within these walls, I do the inviting."

"Ah. Of course. I meant no offense." This was going to be more difficult than he had expected.

"Mam?" The girl sounded puzzled, even a tad angry. "His lordship was only being mannerly."

Grace turned to her, frowning. "Aye, you two have met."

"Not formally," he said smiling at his own jest. Would the woman know formality if it came up and bit her?

To his surprise, she waved a hand gracefully in the air and inclined her head. "Then sure and I have the honor of presenting my daughter, Absalom Grace O'Donnell."

"Absalom?" His astonishment at her name nearly overtook his irritation that *he*, a lord of the realm, had been presented to the girl. The woman was impossible. This country was impossible. But however true that might be, he had chosen to be here he reminded himself yet again, and for as long as he was, he'd tolerate its strange ways.

He bowed to the girl. "My pleasure, Absalom. You have a most unusual name."

"Aye, she's named for a dear friend of mine," Grace replied, "A Narragansett who was known by that same name. We call her Abby for short."

The girl sank onto the bench, her lips pressed together, her cheeks flushed. She looked angry and embarrassed. And why not? Absalom. What an outrageous name.

To the woman, he said, "I suspect you know why I'm here, ma'am."

She shook her head. "Sure and I have no idea."

"You were present when my father died?"

"I was that."

At least she didn't waste time with denials.

"I hoped you might tell me what happened that day. What you saw. His death is shrouded in mystery."

"In a manner of speaking, 'twas a duel. The nature of duels is to be mysterious. They're private quarrels, gentlemen's contests."

"Exactly. But in this *duel,* as you call it, my father didn't aim at a gentleman."

She sat, finally, on the bench next to Abby. "True enough. He aimed at me."

Chapter Four

"M**am?" Abby's shocked cry echoed throughout the cabin.** "You were nearly killed? You never told me so, I—"

Grace placed a hand on Abby's arm. "Shh. 'Twas a long time ago. There was no need for you to know."

Harry considered the woman carefully. That his father would aim at a woman with the intent of killing her was not to be believed. Not for an instant. Ross Rushmount had been a gentleman. He would never have harmed a woman. So why would she claim he had? As she stared at him with defiance in her eyes, he was certain she had no intention of telling him what she knew. Yet he'd wager she was hiding something and had been for years. But *what?*

Without warning, a heavy footstep struck the floor boards. A tall man, his upper body powerful, limped into the cabin. "Ah, my son was correct," he said. "We have a visitor. A fine one at that. Now you'd be . . ."

Harry bowed in greeting. So this silver-haired giant with the gaunt, sun-weathered face was the girl's father? How fortunate she favored her mother. "Lord Rushmount of London and more recently Ballybanree, Ireland."

"Lord Rushmount, is it? From Ballybanree? Sure and I know that sorry village well. Owen O'Donnell here, wondering what in God's name brings you to Providence."

The man had as much Irish in his voice as the woman, and like the woman, an antagonism Harry could slice with a sword. He had no quarrel with her or this crippled giant. Why did they have one with him?

"He's Ross Rushmount's son, Owen," Grace said. "He's after the circumstances of his father's death."

"Ah, is that so?" Owen rocked closer to Harry. With each step, the high wooden sole on his left shoe hit the rough floor with an ear-jarring thud. "Well, here they are, my fine young lord. The circumstances. Your father's dead and so is the innocent man he killed. That my wife and our daughter survived the day is one of God's own wonders."

The earlier, mocking tone had disappeared from Owen's voice. Swiveling away from Harry, he stomped across the room to Grace. Gently, he took her face in his hands and tilted her cheek toward the light.

"You see this?" He pointed to a fine crescent-shaped scar curved above her right eye. "This happened as we were leaving Ireland. Your father aimed at me. Grace paid the price."

"That never happened." Harry wanted, in that instant, to kill the man.

"Were you there to call me a liar?" Owen's quiet manner belied the glitter in his eyes. As his wife smiled up at him, he bent to brush the scar with his lips. "Unfortunately, on the day he shot Absalom, his lordship's aim had greatly improved."

Harry sucked in a breath. Who did this O'Donnell think he was to so insult the memory of his father? His hands fisted, but he kept them at his sides. This was the man's house. He would not lose control here, but neither would he ignore the insult.

"In Ireland, you'd be gaoled for saying that."

"Of a surety," Owen retorted, his voice soft, his eyes hard. "But we're no longer in Ireland. Now, as we have nothing more to add to our tale, I'll be asking you to leave my home."

With a snort of disdain, Harry picked up his hat. He bowed to his adversary, to the woman, and to the girl. The last thing he saw before exiting the cabin was the misery welling in her eyes.

ABBY SWIPED AT HER TEARS WITH THE BACK OF A HAND and ran to the open doorway. With his long-legged stride, Harry Rushmount was already half way across the meadow, about to disappear into the trees. She closed the door against the light and turned back to her parents.

"Why?"

"Why what, lass?" Owen asked.

"Don't pretend, Da. I'm not a child. I want you to tell me what you wouldn't tell him."

"'Tis none of your concern, Abby," Grace said. "What he's after knowing happened before you were born."

Puzzled, Abby glanced from Grace, still seated by the table, to Owen standing behind her, a hand on her shoulder, the need to be near her, to touch her, as unmistakable as always.

Abby's palms had gone damp. She wiped them on her skirt. "Why won't you tell me?" She glanced from one to the other, but they refused to meet her gaze. "You're hiding something, something I need to know . . . over the years I've heard hints of trouble long past, from Emma and others in the village . . . whispers that faded when I approached. Nothing more, and yet . . ." She looked to Owen. "You tell me, Da, that I'm as fair as Mam, that I'm nearly as good a cook. I can spin too and weave and keep a household in order. If all that is true, why is Nate Harris the only lad who's ever come courting?"

Owen's eyes locked with hers, but still he said nothing. She turned to go, to get away from this silence, a silence she realized now had gone on since her birth.

"Tell her, Owen," Grace said in a small, thin voice.

"No lass." He shook his head.

"Yes, my love, the time has come."

Her hand on the door latch, her heart in her throat, Abby waited.

Grace paused as if gathering strength to force out the words. "I killed young Rushmount's father."

Abby whirled around, her skirt tangling about her bare legs. "*You did what?*"

Grace nodded. "'Tis true."

"*Why?*"

"Rushmount's weapon was pointed at Owen's back. When I cried out, his musket swiveled toward me. Absalom leaped up and took the shot in my place." Grace looked away from Abby's wide-eyed stare. "He fell at my feet. I had to shoot."

"She was defending herself," Owen said, squeezing Grace's shoulder. "And you within her."

"So there was no duel?"

"No. But no one must know. What happened is a hanging offense. Promise me your silence in the matter."

Shocked to her very soul, Abby looked at her parents as if they were people she had never known. Her mother, her beautiful mother had *killed* a man. It was nigh impossible to believe, yet . . . "All those whispers over the years, I never dreamed they were about you."

Grace's green eyes pooled with tears. Abby knew she would say no more. Her da then. She turned to him. "Why was Lord Rushmount aiming at you, Da?"

Owen's face clouded, his anger as fresh as it had been twenty years earlier. "He was after your Mam. Followed her here from Ireland. I had no choice but to challenge him." Owen's jaw tightened. "To the death if necessary. When Grace approached and begged us to stop, I looked toward her and he raised his weapon. She shot at him to save me."

Abby sank onto a stool beside her mother and kissed her cheek. "Don't weep, Mam. You did what you had to do. You saved Da's life and mine. And I love you for that."

But what had she been saved for? To wed Nate Harris? *Never.* Yet nothing else awaited her. Nothing. If only she could leave and seek a life elsewhere, but the only one who might help her was walking away. She leaped up. "I'm going after him."

Grace shot to her feet. "*No.* That is madness. Let him have his questions, but that is all he can have. He cannot have answers."

"I'll give him none, but if I can heal the breach between us, maybe . . ."

Leaving her thought unsaid, Abby fled the cabin before they could stay her. If she hurried, she might catch up to him. Though he had a long stride, he hadn't been gone but a few minutes.

With her skirt hiked up, she raced through the cornfield, in her haste brushing the tall stalks aside, bending them, whipping them out of her way. As she ran, her bare feet didn't matter, nor the tumult of her hair, nor the fact that when she saw him she had no idea of what she'd say. Or do. All she knew was that he was striding out of her life with only a handful of words and a single, elegant bow between them and she couldn't let that happen.

Ignoring the stitch in her side, she picked up her pace. The path into the village would soon end. She had to reach him while there were no people about.

Ahead, around a bend, she spied him, his boot heels digging deep into the ruts, the hat in his hand swatting at the low-lying pine branches.

She stopped to catch her breath in a few shuddering gasps. "Lord Rushmount!"

He halted mid-stride, keeping his back to her as if he knew without seeing who had called to him. Then he slowly turned and scowled.

Dear God, he cared not to see her. He stood in the center of the path, striking his hat against his thigh and made no move to come closer. She took a few, tentative steps forward, her bare feet kicking up the dust. Though her breath had steadied, her heartbeat rioted in her chest as she came near enough to see the black lashes of his eyes, and the dark stubble on his chin, and his lips compressed into a single, frowning line.

Still, he didn't move.

When she came so close she could have touched his shirt with the tip of a finger, his lips relaxed into the hint of a smile.

Relief pulsed through her.

"You're following me," he said. "Why?"

"To ask you not to leave us in anger. My parents suffered much in the old world. Their memories are sometimes bitter."

He frowned, saying nothing, only striking his hat on his leg over and over, as if he needed to vent his ill feelings on something—anything—even himself. In the face of his sullen anger, she realized this had been a dreadful mistake. If he wouldn't speak to her in friendship, how could she voice her plea? "I'm sorry to have bothered you," she said, turning to leave.

"Are you, little peasant girl?"

She turned back. "What did you call me?"

He shrugged. "It makes no difference. I accept your apology." He closed the small distance between them. "You know what happened to my father. Tell me the truth of it."

Peasant, was she? *Bow to no man. Not even this one.*

She tossed her hair over her shoulders and raised her chin. "You want the truth? Well, hear it then. You're the spawn of a coward. You're not worthy to buckle my mother's shoes. Or mine."

No mistaking the smile on his face as he looked down at her feet. "What shoes?"

Standing straight as an arrow, she backed away from him, but before she could take another step, he reached out and caught her hand. "An insult received, an insult given. That makes us even."

"Equals, you mean."

"Equals?"

"Why not?" Head held high, wanting to slap the smile from his face, she waited.

He arched an eyebrow. "You actually want me to tell you?"

She nodded. "Try."

"If you insist." His maddening smile widened. "I'm named for the cousin of a king. You for a savage. There can never be an equation between us, a fact your lady mother understands perfectly well."

His tone was not to be borne. "I outrank you."

"*What?*" He dropped her hand as if it were aflame.

Ha. That had wiped off his smirk. She squared her shoulders and faced him, feet apart, arms akimbo. "I'm named for Absalom, the anointed son of Canonchet, sachem of all the Narragansetts. And for the O'Donnells. Kings, all of them, of County Mayo, and for a queen, a pirate queen, Granuaile O'Malley, who savaged the ships of your Elizabeth. Gave her such a run Elizabeth had to send a rat, Lord Bingham by name, to try and quell her."

Who did he think he was? Larger than God? She'd been a fool to believe for an instant that he would help her. But even now, furious at his condescension, she couldn't look away from the lure of him. From his dark eyes, his chiseled mouth, his broad shoulders hidden by that silky shirt. Her hot cheeks grew hotter still.

Dear heaven, what thoughts she was having for a man she hardly knew. "I've given my apology. I have nothing more to say to you. Good day."

She turned on her heel. Head high, spine stiff, she had moved no more than a pace away before he spun her around to face him.

"Your mother was there when my father was killed." His eyes explored her face. "She claims he aimed at her. Why? I need to know how he died. I need to know the truth."

She looked past him at a patch of sunshine in the distance. Only a robin's chirrup broke the hot, still air. "I can tell you nothing more," she said, Owen's warning echoing in her mind.

Did he believe her? She stole a glance at his face. No. He deserved to know his father's fate, and she longed to answer his questions, to tell him everything he asked, to take away the furrow creasing his brow. But so help her God, she could not.

"Let your father rest in peace. Nothing will change. Not the outcome. Not your life as his son."

"You have the boldness of a queen, all right."

She hated the disdain in his eyes. "So I'm a queen now, not a peasant?"

He tossed his hat to the side of the road and grasped her arms. "If it were your father, would you pursue the truth?"

She couldn't lie. Not with his breath warm on her cheek, his eyes staring into hers. "To my dying day."

"Ah, the truth at last. From the queen of Mayo." He bent down, his face mere inches away, his dark eyes near, so near. Her lashes fluttered to a close, blocking out the world and all of its sights and sounds. Then suddenly, without warning, he let her go. She stumbled back.

He retrieved his hat and bowing low, so low his brim skimmed the dust, he said. "Go home, little Irish queen. To your parents where you belong." Without another word, he clapped his hat on his head and strode on toward the village.

HE HAD TO WALK AWAY OR FLING HER TO THE GROUND and take her under the pine trees. Good Lord, what had possessed him just then? The queen of Mayo, indeed. He'd forgotten the old Irish boast that they were all descended from kings. He laughed out loud at her absurd claims and at his being here in this New World under its hot sun where everything possessed a heightened intensity—the tall trees, the expansive farmlands, the violent thunder, the pounding rain, the brashness of the people, the sudden plummet into night—no long, lingering gloaming, no gentle mists, no obsequiousness, no deference to his station. No ladies.

He laughed again, thinking of her. That glorious hair flowing over his hands as he held her crushed against him, her onyx eyes wide open when he bent down with a mind to kiss her, then fluttering to a close as if she wanted to block out the world. Perhaps those unknowing, closed eyes were why he hadn't kissed her after all. He'd swear she'd never been touched by anyone else, but that she would have given herself away without hesitation, he had little doubt. Yet she had refused to give him the one thing he asked for: the truth about his father's death.

ABBY WATCHED HIM STRIDE AWAY, STARING ALONG THE PATH until even the dust from his boots had settled back onto the earth. She heaved a heavy sigh and meandered through the meadow toward home. Mam would be needing help with the noon meal, though the thought of food made her ill. She would feast, instead, on the memory of a phantom kiss.

As she entered the keeping room, the odor of roasted guinea fowl caused her stomach to roll over in disgust. And there was Mam busily going about her duties as if nothing untoward had happened this day. As if in the single turn of an hourglass, Harry Rushmount hadn't swirled in and out of their lives.

Bent over the cooking fire, Mam glanced up at her, briefly. Without speaking, she moved from the spit to the chest against the wall and reached for a trencher. She took the largest one from the pile, deftly slipping the roasted fowl from its stake onto it and carrying the laden trencher to the table.

She's not meeting my eyes Abby thought. Whether feigned or not, Mam's serenity offended her. How could she be so mindless of what she had wrought? So unfeeling? Like an unleashed flood, Abby's grief burst forth, drowning the room's uneasy quiet.

"There'll never be another man like him, Mam. Not in this remote place."

"Remote is it?" Grace slammed the trencher onto the tabletop, spattering the boards with hot grease. "You don't know what you're saying, Abby. Life here is good. Better than good. And you've known no other way."

"In that you are right. I haven't." Abby rattled wooden trenchers and pewter spoons onto the table for the meal. She didn't set a place for her brother, Aiden. Since he'd built a wickiup on the edge of the fields, he seldom ate with them any more.

After wiping her hands on her apron, Grace cut up pieces of the browned meat to go with the wilted greens and corn bread she'd made earlier. The plates full, she said, "I'll call your father. The food's ready."

"None for me. I'm not hungry."

Grace spun around from the doorway, her calm gone, her eyes flashing fire.

"No, you never have been. You don't know the meaning of hunger. In Ballybanree under Lord Rushmount's thumb, you'd be well acquainted with it. That you've never known such a life, I say God bless this place and the land we live on."

Abby thumped down a crock of buttermilk. "You ask Him to bless the land you stole from the Indians?"

Grace stiffened and paused in the open door, the sun's rays flaming in her hair. "You're wrong. We bought our acres from Canonchet."

"He didn't know you meant to keep them forever. None of the Narragansetts did. Aiden told me so. They believe the land is loaned to you while you're alive. You don't *own* it. You just *use* it until you die."

Tears welled up in Grace's eyes. "Aye, perhaps that's the best way. But 'tis not our way. Yet we did not steal our land. No one in Providence colony did so."

Though Mam's tears tore her resolve into shreds, she would not give in so easily. "The Indians think you did. At least those still alive in the Great Swamp. Isn't that what the war, that King Philip's War, was about? Land?"

Grace nodded. "I fear so, but we bought our acres in all fairness. We had to have a place somewhere in the world to call our own."

Abby heard the tremor in her mother's voice, but the anger refused to release her. "You say you didn't steal the land, and I believe you." She moved forward a step, hands twisting in the folds of her skirt. "Say you didn't kill Harry's father, and I'll believe that, too."

The pleading note in her own voice shocked her. Never before had she begged anything of her parents, or of anyone. Her fingers working at the linen, she waited, sobs welling up in her throat.

Grace closed her eyes for a moment as if to block out Abby's anguish and the memory of a long remembered day of bloodshed. "Truly, I cannot deny what happened."

"Why, Mam, why? Was there no other way?"

Grace shook her head. "For that, I have no answer. Not even when I ask it of myself. And I ask it every day of my life." Her hand fell away from the door frame. She pulled herself erect. "Despite all, I'll never regret coming here. 'Twas a deliverance from what we endured in Ireland, God bless her beautiful, hapless soul . . . the food grows cold. I must find your father. He needs his meal."

Alone in the cabin, Abby paced the narrow space between table and wall, ignoring the damp summer air that had turned ferociously warm, heating her skin, making her clothes cling to her body, causing everything she touched to feel sticky as if even the household objects suffered in the heat. "'Tis good for the crops," Da would say. Always it was the crops.

She slumped onto a bench by the table and stared at her heaped plate, the drumstick crisped to a fare-thee-well, her mother's corn bread that would be light as feathers in a pillow. Without an appetite, she pushed the plate back, giving her elbows room to roost on the tabletop.

For years Mam had told stories of the old days in Ireland. How she went to bed hungry more often than not, how the O'Malley lands had been stolen from under her family, how the villagers worked from sun up to sun down with nothing to show for their labor, not even enough food to feed their children decently. It was an old, old story. So awful she'd begun to wonder if Mam exaggerated her tales. Or if her memories of Ballybanree took on fresh hardship each time she relived her days there.

She picked up a piece of corn bread and crumpled it between her fingers. Yet Da never corrected Mam's tales or interrupted them. Nor did he ever add to them. Each time, he just listened and at the end said the same thing. "That was then, lass, this is now." That "now" meant life was far better in the colonies, Abby had no doubt. In Providence, the land they labored on belonged to them, a marvel of a happening she'd always been told.

With a tip of one finger, she picked up the crumbs and popped them into her mouth. No, Mam wouldn't exaggerate. Her words were as straight as the arrows she shot from her beloved bow . . . the one she'd used to kill Harry's father.

An unaccustomed bitterness welled up in her heart as she heard her mother's voice outside the cabin and her father's deeper tones responding. It was surprising how much they found to talk of each day—it was as if the words were unimportant, the sound of each other's voice alone is what they sought. With a sudden, unexpected awareness, she realized they still loved each other very much. Amazing for two people so old. Why Mam must be near forty years and Da even older. Not everyone lived to such an age. Of those who did, how many sustained their love so long? Few, she reckoned. Lovely it was, and something she would never know, though she'd try not to hate them for that.

When Mam's arrow flew into Lord Rushmount's heart all those years ago, she had no way of knowing she was killing her child's happiness.

Chapter Five

From the top of the hill near where John Thayer had seen fit to perch his house, Harry had a clear view of the *Lady Anne* anchored in the harbor. He stood under the spreading oak enjoying the sight of the ship and the breeze that riffled his hair and cooled his skin. This New World heat continued fierce, unlike any he'd known in England or in the rainy, soft summers of Ireland.

On the beach below, he could see the men under the direction of the quartermaster, rolling barrels of fresh water along the shore into the skiffs. Fresh water and salt pork and beans. Beans kept well for months and, once boiled and mixed with molasses, made a dish the men favored. So beans it was and crates of last season's dried apples. In the tropical isles, they'd take lemons and limes aboard as well. It was said they helped against the scurvy. Who knew for certain? But if true, a good thing. He had no wish to become a toothless old man.

He tore his gaze from the activity on the beach to the rough-hewn stone by the oak tree that marked his father's grave. Moss obscured the name and the birth and death dates carved into the granite slab. It was a lonely grave, untended, unvisited, and the sight brought him as close to tears as a man could allow. He would never know how his father had died. Other than choking the truth out of the O'Donnell woman's throat, he had no choice but to let the mystery linger.

One last time, he ran his fingers over the mossy letters, stroking the stone, so damp and unfeeling under his hand. It was, he realized, his heart contracting with regret, the only caress he'd ever bestowed on his father.

It must be the heat that caused the damp in his eyes. He wiped at them with a shirt sleeve and clapped his hat back on his head. Just a few more days here and they'd be plowing through the deep heading to the Caribs and after that setting sail for home. The thought of spending one more night in John Thayer's stifling back room was suddenly too much to bear. He'd make an excuse, row out to the ship and sleep on board in the cool ocean air.

With a farewell salute to the headstone, he strode down the hill. Aye, less than a fortnight, and he'd be off in the *Lady Anne*. He couldn't wait. There was nothing to keep him here.

To Abby's relief, a late afternoon sea breeze cooled the shore, soothing her flushed skin. She needed to be alone for a while, away from the strain in the cabin. She and Mam hardly spoke; even worse, since Harry Rushmount's visit Da looked more worried every day, whether for Mam's safety or because of her own unhappiness, she couldn't tell . . . and Aiden off in the hut he'd fashioned Indian style.

She blew out a sigh as she paced along the beach. Shoes made walking on sand difficult. Her toes couldn't curl around the grains and feel their delicious wetness, and if the salt water reached the leather, it would be ruined for fair. She scanned the shore. *Deserted.* Only a few lads playing stick ball farther down the beach. Even the sailors who had been loading water casks into the skiffs had long since rowed out to the ship.

Well, then, why not? She dropped to the sand, unbuckled the shoes and pulled off her stockings. *There.* She wiggled her freed toes, cupped her eyes with a hand and peered out at the harbor, thrilled at the sight of the *Lady Anne*. She was like an elegant, tethered steed. Once freed of her anchors, the ship would run fast and furious, her sails filled to bursting and nothing between her and the Caribs. Wherever they might lie.

All along the beach, shadows thickened. She should return home, but why rush to a stuffy bed in a stuffy room? She picked up a handful of pebbles and plunked them at the water, watching as they sank from sight. Then tiring of the game, she rested her elbows on her tented knees and stared out to sea.

Like walls of stone, the future was closing in on her, offering no escape from the oily countenance of Nate Harris or another just like him. For soon she would be expected to marry. It was her destiny and that of every girl she knew. Trouble was, a married woman had no adventures. She led a staid, proper life. No walking alone on the shore without shoes and stockings, her skirts hiked up to her knees . . . only duties . . . some of which she couldn't bring herself to contemplate. And that fate was fast approaching, its very breath blowing on the back of her neck.

But not yet. There still was time. She'd do it. Go for a swim as she had years ago with Da. Why not? Who was to stay her? She looked left and right along the sandy strip. No one in sight anywhere. *Now.* She leaped to her feet and stripped off her skirt and waist. Standing in her shift and underdrawers, she made a bundle of her clothes, topping them with a rock for safe keeping.

The shift came to well below her knees, too long for swimming. Wrapped around her middle and tied tight with Mam's old green sash, it should keep out of her way. Many times over the years, before she was full grown, she'd gone swimming in the ocean with Da. It had been a while since then, but remembering the glory of it, she plunged into the surf without hesitation, reveling in the cold after days of sullen heat. Chest deep, she dove in head first and came up to the surface a moment later spouting and sputtering. She shook her wet hair out of her eyes and cut a path across the water. After a while, her limbs tiring, she flipped onto her back and floated until she'd caught her breath and eased her muscles. Then turning turtle, she dove under the water, resurfacing to the sight of the ship shining a few hundred yards away. One more dive and she'd return to the cove, none the worse for her little adventure.

She broke through to the surface and began stroking for shore. But no matter how hard she swam, she wasn't getting any nearer to land. If anything, the beach seemed farther away in the fading light, not closer. She increased her pace, striving with the waves until her arms and legs ached with effort. Fighting the panic rising into her throat, she floated for a few moments, resting atop the water.

A mistake. The brief respite had put her even farther from shore. Something fearsome was the matter. Could she be in the grip of one of the deadly tides Da had spoken of? So strong that once caught up in its power, no man could break free?

Dear God in heaven, if so, she would die. And then hope burst into her chest as she saw it—a few hundred yards away—the *Lady Anne*, its lanterns twinkling like stars in the growing dark.

Her energy renewed, she struck a path for the ship, not fighting the tide, letting it carry her straight out to sea. Out to a safe haven.

As she approached the ship, the soft music of the sea lapping against the hull and the creaking of shroud lines made the only sounds. Yet the ship couldn't be deserted. Ships were never left untended. The crew must be aboard her somewhere, but she heard no voices. Would they be asleep at this early hour? Or more likely below decks taking their evening meal? She nearly called out, but the shift clinging to her body gave her pause.

Small portholes set like eyes in the hull's sides were too high above the water line to peer into, but the aft light and a lantern or two shone from within somewhere. Abby clung to the thick anchor chain and gazed up at the towering masts. They looked like giant oak trunks. She sighed. She'd seen her fair share of trees.

Letting go of the anchor chain, she swam around the hull, passing under the lantern hung astern and over to the port beam. How did the sailors climb aboard? There had to be a way. She glanced up, searching for a clue, and found the answer so close she nearly laughed aloud. Suspended over her head, a rope ladder dangled within reach. By grasping the lower rung, she could pull herself hand over hand until she stood on deck. She treaded water, trying to decide. Did she dare? What if a sailor spied her like this? Wet as a drowned cat, her body exposed.

Her feet paddled furiously. It was go aboard or drown. She reached up, grasped the rope with one hand, and pressing her feet against the hull, lunged for the second rung. For a moment, she hung suspended between sea and sky, chilled of a sudden in her wet shift, before scrambling lightly up the ladder to the deck railing. The lantern that had winked her aboard swayed in front of her eyes. She peered forward, then aft. Nothing. Emboldened by the silence, she swung her legs aboard and dropped to the scrubbed deck.

Crouched low, she squeezed sea water from her hair and looked about. To her left, the pointed prow held the great wheel for steering the ship, to her right, the squared off stern. The stern's smaller second deck raised above the main deck held a cluster of barrels lashed together, the water supply the men had tumbled on shore earlier in the day. No matter. She'd seen barrels of water before.

From the square outcropping in the center of the deck, a light shone dimly. She crept closer and peered down. *Stairs.* Near by, at the bow, a cough, a deep rumbling male cough. *The watch.* She froze in place in her dripping shift. A long minute dragged by, but he made no move to come her way. So he hadn't spied her.

He coughed a second time and hawked over the railing. Now, while his back was turned, she scrambled down the steep stairs. A narrow corridor, wide enough for only one person to pass along at a time, ran from the prow to the stern. The wee cabins would be astern. That much she knew. That's where a voyaging lady would stay. If there were dry clothes anywhere, that is where they'd be.

From deeper in the hull, came the murmur of low-pitched voices and a quick, raucous laugh. She stood motionless, listening. The crew was aboard after all, in a lower deck, at their evening meal it sounded like. *Best be fast while they're occupied with their food.* Silently, she stole along the passageway. At the end, two closed doors faced her. The cabins, most likely. She grasped the latch of the paneled door to the left and raised it. The door opened a bit and she peeked through the crack into an empty room. Quick as lightning, she slipped in, latching the door behind her.

"WHERE IN HADES IS SHE, THE IMP?" Fear for Abby turned Aiden's blood cold one minute, then anger heated it to a boil in the next. After the evening meal, Mam had sent him looking for her. He scoured the farm and when she was nowhere to be seen, some instinct brought him to the shore. To his horror, he'd soon spotted her clothes hidden under a rock.

She must have gone for a swim. He knew how much she loved the water. But though he studied the pounding surf until his eyes ached, he saw no head of red hair, no white arms breaking through the waves. Only the English ship blocking the harbor like a huge toad. He'd be happy to see her and her ratty crew leave for good. *Ratty crew, aye. But it's not the crew that concerns you. It's that lord's son . . . Harry . . . he's the one you want gone. Him and the grudge he bears Grace.*

But for now Harry Rushmount wasn't the problem. Abby was. The undertow could be strong on this stretch of beach. It might have swept her out to sea. If she were out there somewhere struggling to stay afloat, he'd never find her, not through the fog that had rolled in with the dusk. Frantic, he paced the beach like a mad man, his moccasins digging into the sand, his eyes never leaving the water, hoping against hope she'd emerge like a vision out of the foaming surf.

For the merest instant, a breeze tore through the gathering mist, revealing the shimmer of the ship's lights. He stopped his wild pacing. Would she have dared?

WAS THAT THE DOOR? NO DOUBT THE CABIN BOY with his clean linen. Harry rolled over on his bunk and opened an eye. A white shift, a pair of bare legs, a pair of—

He bolted upright, banging his head against a low-lying deck beam. "You! What on earth are you doing here?"

Abby cried out, ready to flee, but he was too quick. He leapt off the bunk, grabbed her upper arm and slammed the door shut.

"Let me go!"

"How did you get on board? How did you know where I was?"

"I didn't, you arrogant fool." She squirmed to free herself.

Half dressed in breeches but no shirt, he pulled her to his bare chest. And in the next instant held her at arm's length. "You're all wet."

"Of a certainty. You would be, too."

Even in the cabin's half light, Abby could see his eyes widen. "You *swam* out here?"

"A brilliant deduction."

"True enough." He didn't even try to hide his grin. "My powers of deduction are also telling me you're nearly naked."

"So are you." She stared at him with an easy defiance she didn't feel.

"That's different. I'm decently covered—for a man." He glanced down, his gaze lingering on the linen stretched taut across her breasts. Her glance followed his. Under the wet fabric, her form was as clearly outlined as if the shift wasn't there at all.

She gasped and tried to wrestle out of his grip. But he held her fast, the grin still playing about his lips.

"Do you know you're trespassing?" he asked, the smile never leaving him. "That's a punishable offense."

"You'll have me hanged, then?"

"No, I think not. I'll inform your mam, instead."

"You wouldn't."

He laughed and ran his hands up and down her arms as if testing them for smoothness. Trapped, she tossed her head, flinging her hair away from her eyes so the wetness would drip down her back and not be trickling along her face, making her look as if she were shedding tears.

"Little girl . . . little wild colonial girl," his voice purred each word, "You have no idea of the danger you're in."

Somehow, she did know and welcomed it, even the spurt of fear shivering along her spine. But he was not to realize that. "If you think I'm afraid, think again."

"Think?" he drawled, a frown replacing the amusement on his face. "You're the one who needs to think. Something you weren't doing when you decided to swim out here. You could have drowned and no one the wiser."

"I had no intention of drowning."

"What was your intent? Coming onto a ship full of men with no clothes on your body. Are you that innocent? Or that stupid?"

His words, and even more, the contempt in his tone, shamed her. "You don't understand," she said, determined not to let her voice quiver, or her chin for that matter.

"Enlighten me."

"I've never been anywhere. Or seen anything. Only trees and grass and cattle. I've never been aboard a ship," she said softly, not meeting the storm cloud in his eyes. "The *Lady Anne* is very beautiful. I wondered what she would be like. She seemed so quiet in the dusk, I thought no one would—"

"Thought? So you did think after all, but not rightly." He let go of her shoulders. "You're fortunate I'm a gentleman or else—"

"Abby? Abby? Where are you?"

"Oh my God," Abby whispered. "That's Aiden."

"Who's Aiden?"

"My brother. He mustn't find me." She glanced down at herself. "Not like this. Not in here."

Harry yanked a shirt off a chair back. She recognized it as the very silk one he had worn the first day she laid eyes on him. "Cover yourself with this." He unlatched the door. "Stay here. I'll go speak to your brother."

"Abby!" Aiden's voice echoed throughout the ship.

"Keep hidden. I'll be back."

"Abby!"

Listen to the man. Brother Aiden has quite a set of lungs on him. Harry ran down the companion to the sound of feet tramping up from below. No need for the whole crew to learn of this. "Avast," he called down the stair well. "I'll handle the matter."

Where was the watch? Two trespassers and no alarms given. He'd have the man's hide.

"She has to be aboard. I want the ship searched."

His head and shoulders halfway through the bulkhead, he saw the watch, alert at last, with a knife to a man's throat. Aiden, no doubt, and a riveting sight in a motley mix of clothes that was neither fish nor fowl—a fringed leather shirt paired with canvas breeches, his hair clubbed back like an Englishman's, his feet shod in beaded moccasins. "Get that knife away from me throat, you ass," he snarled. "It's me sister I'm after."

In no way could this man be kin to the girl. A full-blooded Indian from the look of him, he glared at the wizened little tar as if ready to snatch the blade out of his hand and toss him overboard.

Harry emerged through the open hatch. "Back to your post, man," he said to the watch. The captain will deal with you later when he returns from town. As for you," he swiveled his attention to the Indian. "You can stop shouting. The girl's below deck."

"Why you—"

Aiden lunged for him. Anticipating his thrust, Harry sidestepped neatly and whirled around, fists up.

But Aiden made no further move. Still as a deer stalker, he eyed Harry narrowly. "Is she harmed?"

A smile lifted Harry's lips. "Not at all. If anything, the swim invigorated her."

"She swam out here? She came aboard uninvited? You didn't—"

"I did not."

"Ah." Aiden let out a pent up breath whether of relief or vexation or both, Harry couldn't be certain. Without bowing as a gentleman should, the man stood arrow straight and extended his hand. Suppressing a sigh, Harry accepted the peace offering and tried not to wince when his fingers were seized in an iron grip.

"I'm grateful, you've kept her safe," Aiden said. "I've been deeply concerned."

"I understand. She took an enormous risk."

"True, but she meant no harm. 'Tis the longing for something new, I fear, that drew her here."

Harry nodded, quite sure he understood what that something might be. He liked this Indian Aiden who spoke so sensibly with a hint of the O'Donnells' Irish lilt in his voice. And he liked his concern for the little hoyden below. How they came to be called brother and sister would make a tale worth listening to.

"Where is she?" Aiden asked.

"In my cabin. I'll fetch her."

"Let me. We need to speak before I take her home."

Harry shrugged. This was not the evening's end he would have preferred, but common sense told him it was the best one. He waved an arm toward the open bulkhead. "Be my guest, Master Aiden. My cabin lies aft."

A brief nod and Aiden disappeared down the stairs.

Harry leaned on the railing and waited. Obviously the girl needed discipline, to be taught a lady's way of behaving, to be made aware of certain obvious dangers for a beauty with onyx eyes in a slim, pale face and a tumble of red curls. Did they reach all the way to her bottom? He'd have to check for that the next—

"Injuns! Injuns! We're being attacked. Help. Help!"

An unholy scream tore him from the railing and sent him racing for the stairs.

The galley. Cookie was screaming his head off. Their visitor must have lost his bearings in the dim companionway. Harry dashed below deck in time to see Cookie pointing a trembling finger at Aiden. "Don't come any closer. I'll have no truck with savages."

"But sir, I assure you—"

"Sir, is it? You mockin' me? Bloody savage." Rum bottle in hand, Cookie lurched toward the fire.

God Lord, he's drunk again. Harry had hardly formed the thought when Cookie bent over the brick-lined fire pit and reached for the bubbling pot to use as a weapon. Before he could fling its boiling contents at Aiden, he tripped over his own feet and fell to the floor. The bottle slipped from his grasp, flew through the air and crashed into the fire.

Whoosh. Fueled by old cooking grease and soot from a thousand fires, the flames shot out of the pit and following the trail of spilled rum, roared up the galley wall, lapping at the dried deck timbers overhead.

Without a care for the flesh on his palms, Aiden grabbed the boiling pot by the handle and flung its contents into the pit. The fire lowered, sputtered, and burst forth again. He picked up a bucket of cooking water standing nearby and tossed that over the flames. Far from defeated, the fire rallied and flared up anew.

Where were those deckhands now that he needed them? Harry, turning to run for help, stumbled over Cookie passed out on the slimy floor. *Damn the man.* "Cookie's in the way," he yelled. "Let's get him out of here."

In one step, Aiden was beside him. Together they heaved the cook, still asleep, to the rear of the companion and dropped him in a corpulent heap.

"Fire," Harry shouted down the stair well. "Fire!" Pounding feet rushed up the stairs. A second later, the startled face of First Mate

Johnson hove into view. "Mister Johnson, the galley's afire. Align your men for a bucket brigade. Hurry."

Never had Harry been so frightened. His life, his estate, his future, was disappearing in front of his eyes as flames, drawn by the air filtering through the open ceiling grid, ate at the galley timbers. Left unchecked, the fire would spread throughout the ship, virulent as plague in a crowded city.

Seconds as long as hours crawled by. "Where's the damned water, Johnson?" Harry roared. The words were hardly out of his mouth when the crew in smallclothes and breeches and little else formed a line from the upper deck along the stairs and into the galley, passing buckets of sea water hand over hand. They worked with haste, sweating and grunting, but their efforts, Harry saw, were as effective as cups of water pitched into hell.

"Harry. Aiden." In a man's white shirt that fell below her knees, her hair as bright as the flames, Abby appeared in the galley opening.

"Get out of here, Abby," Aiden shouted. "Go up on deck."

"*Immediately,*" Harry thundered.

Abby grabbed Aiden's arm. "Listen to me, use the . . ." Coarse black smoke, thicker than fog, caught in her throat. She struggled for a breath then choked out, "The barrels on the aft deck. They're full of water. Empty them down the ceiling grid. They'll douse the fire."

The two men looked at each other for an instant, weighing her idea. "She's right," Aiden said.

"Aye. Let's go." Harry seized Abby's arm, pulling her toward the stairs.

"Let me be," she gasped as the cloud of smoke engulfed them. "I can walk by myself."

"Don't be a little fool," Harry muttered, half carrying, half dragging her along. "You want to die down here?"

On the main deck, Harry released Abby so fast she stumbled against the railing. "Mister Johnson," he shouted. "The barrels stowed aft? Roll them to the ventilation grid over the galley and smash them open. Be quick, man."

The mate needed no further orders. With two of his men, he raced for the barrels and slashed the rope binding that held them together. Working in unison with a speed Harry admired, two of the hands laid planks on the short flight of steps and rolled the kegs down them. Above the galley, billows of black smoke rose into the evening fog.

"Faster," Harry urged as a bright tongue of flame shot to the upper deck. "Faster. It's getting ahead of us."

"Aye, aye. Put her atop the grate, boys," Johnson ordered. The men hurried to obey. One quick chop of his hatchet on the side of the barrel, and without a drop wasted, the water poured down the opening. "Another one." The men rushed the second barrel into position. Again Johnson wielded his hatchet, again, and again, until nothing rose from the galley hatch but the foul, acrid odor of burnt wood. At last, covered with soot, sagging with fatigue, he said, "I believe she's out."

Harry nodded. "Aye." *And a good part of my profits as well.*

Holding a lantern aloft, they went below to view the damage—smoking, charred timbers, and a wasted, blackened galley.

The water pouring out to the companion had finally reached Cookie. He awoke with a little cry of distress, raised his head a few inches then fell back with a sigh, muttering, "I'm all over wet, I am."

Mate Johnson toed him in the gut with the tip of his boot. "I heard tell it's you and your rum caused the fire."

"Me rum? Where's me rum?" Cook felt around for his flask. "Oh, aye." He fell back onto the planking. "She smashed into smithereens, she did."

"You've been warned enough," Johnson said. "This time it's the brig."

"Yes," Harry agreed. "And send a boat to shore for the captain."

Their faces grim, Aiden and Abby followed Harry about the lower deck in silence. The men were already working in the companion with mops and buckets swabbing up the mess. There'll be no meals cooked in here, Harry thought, eyeing the smoldering galley. He glanced up at the supporting timbers. At the first light of day, the ship's carpenter could assess the full extent of the damage.

Though Abby was adequately covered by his shirt, as they walked about the ship, Harry could feel the men's eyes follow her. Their muffled snickers swiftly died when he glared their way, annoyed both at them and at Abby for exposing herself so.

"This is all my fault," Aiden said, studying the damage.

"No." Harry laid a hand on his shoulder. "Cookie's the one. Sober he wouldn't have reacted as he did."

A wry smile lifted Aiden's lips. "Drunk or sober, men fear what they don't understand." He let out a breath. "But I agree the rum didn't help."

Abby looked about, her eyes dull. "The guilt is mine, Aiden. Not yours. You came to help me. I just came here . . ." she shrugged, "adventuring." She clutched Harry's shirt tight to her throat. "I have never been so ashamed." She lifted her soot-stained face to his, willing herself to meet his gaze no matter what she found there. "I must repay you somehow. Until I do, can you forgive me?"

A forlorn sight, she is, Harry thought. As well she should be. He bowed slightly, acknowledging her remorse. "You weren't the one to set the *Lady* ablaze, however much you may have set the wheels in motion. But I can't speak for monetary forgiveness. That will depend on the owners. All hard-headed men of commerce."

"I see." She lowered her gaze from Harry's stony countenance and stared down at the soiled silk of his shirt, pock-mocked with scorch holes from flying sparks. Her eyes still downcast, she murmured, "I pray you find it in your heart to forgive me, for I can't forgive myself."

Not waiting for an answer, she walked out of the galley with as much dignity as she could muster in a dirty silk shirt and bare, blackened feet

Chapter Six

"**M**OTHER IN HEAVEN, WE'LL LOSE OUR LAND," Grace said, her face white and drawn.

"Now, Mam, don't leap to such fearsome conclusions," Aiden chided gently, his face under its stubble as strained as her own. "Tell them everything, Abby," he ordered. "From the beginning."

Look at him, standing in the middle of the keeping room like a judge and jury, ready to pronounce her guilty. And rightly so.

Abby sighed and sank onto a stool by the table. She darted a glance at her parents. Even in the light of the single candle, they looked grimmer than she'd ever seen them. From their worried expressions alone she knew she deserved whatever punishment would be meted out to her, for what she'd done this night was terribly wrong. With her heart like a stone in her chest, she began in a trembling voice.

Half way through her tale, before the candle guttered into a puddle of wax, Grace interrupted. "How could you do anything so shameless? Swimming out to the ship in your smallclothes for all to see."

"It was near dark, Mam."

Da smiled and seized Grace's hand, squeezing it in his own. "Lest you forget, love."

Grace flushed and pulled her hand free. "That was different," she declared, not giving in to his smile as she always did.

"Aye. You wore no shift that day."

Ah, so Mam had gone aswimming like—

"I was trying to wash the filth from an ocean crossing off me. Never would I have gone out to meet a ship."

"No, love. You can't swim."

They looked in each other's eyes and something passed between them, something that caused Grace's face to ease as if into a cherished memory. An instant later, she frowned at Abby and said, "Go on."

After that, no more smiles swept across either of their faces. Abby finished her tale and sat still in the thick silence, waiting for them to say something, to make dire predictions for her future, to tell her she had shamed them beyond repair, to remind her of the heavy cost they must pay to correct her disaster. Nothing.

The silence continued until finally Owen asked, "Is that all that happened? Have you anything else to tell us?"

She shook her head.

"That's it then," he said, clapping his palms on his thighs, plainly relieved by her denial. "I'm a blacksmith by trade and a decent carpenter as well. I'll offer my services in payment for the damage."

"As will I," Aiden said quickly.

"We've trees aplenty to retimber the decks if need be. And two strong backs to put to the task."

Abby darted a glance at Aiden. The strain in his face broke her heart.

"What say I row out to the ship tomorrow and speak to the captain?" he asked. "'Twould be nonsensical to waste time."

"Aye," Owen agreed, his tea forgotten and cold at his elbow.

Dear God, Abby thought, with a single, willful swim, she'd brought strife and unhappiness to her entire family. The future that a day ago had merely seemed dull now loomed ahead like an eternity in hell.

"I HAVE NO CHOICE BUT TO ACCEPT YOUR OFFER," Captain Tamworth told Aiden the next morning, his English tones clipped and curt, his small, tidy body bristling with resentment. "We need all the aid we can get. Tell your father his indebtedness, however, is not solely mine to resolve. There are investors who must be satisfied. We'll waste precious time on the repairs. And time, Mister . . . ah . . . O'Donnell, is money. Do you understand me?"

"Your intent is perfectly clear," Aiden said. Feeling his own anger rise, he fought to keep his voice low and controlled. "My family is willing to make reparation. But I'm after reminding you, with all due respect, that a man in your employ set the ship ablaze."

Captain Tamworth drew himself erect. "And what impelled him to do so, pray tell?"

"The rum, sir. The demon rum."

"And fear. Mortal fear at the surprise he was given." With insulting slowness, the captain's gaze swept over him. "The woman you call your sister was the root cause of the entire disaster. I tell you with all seriousness, she needs to be taken in hand."

About Abby, Aiden didn't trust himself to speak. To keep from harming the man, he jammed his hands into his breeches pockets. "My father and I will be here at first light to take instruction from your master carpenter."

"Fine. He'll await you."

Aiden paddled his canoe back to shore telling himself he couldn't blame the man for his anger, but for the insolent sweep of his eyes, he could kill him. It didn't help that he'd been correct about Abby. She did need to be taken in hand, but he feared it was too late. Da had never been able to deny her a thing, and Mam, well Abby and Mam were as alike as one spirit in two bodies—a formidable spirit. He doubted anyone would ever tame Abby.

At the shore, he wove his way through the breakers into a sheltered cove where he beached his canoe. He upended it out of the water's reach and headed for the farm. Owen would want to know more about the task that faced them, the easier one, repairing the *Lady Anne*. The more daunting one, controlling Mistress Absolom O'Donnell, he'd leave to another man.

WOULD THE SOUND NEVER STOP? ON and on, Abby could hear the axe chop into the trunk, the bite of the blade ripping through the meadow reminding her of her sin. Da sat at the bench by the table eating his morning eggs. "As soon as Aiden has the oak felled, I'll help him trim off the branches. That sea captain is in a tear to be off. But 'twill take time. Oak is a damnably hard wood."

Mam sent a flashing glance her way. Abby had said she was sorry so many times she couldn't bear to repeat the words. They did no good. They only gave Mam another chance to glare at her. That her mother's worry about her father was fueling her anger, Abby understood full well. Da was not a young man any longer. The added work would be a heavy burden for him. She rose from her stool and began a listless washing of the soiled trenchers.

"Notching the trunk to fit under the ceiling grid as a deck support shouldn't be difficult," Da was saying. "We've taken careful measurements. Luckily the entire decking doesn't need replacing. Only the section above the galley." He sipped his tea and smiled at Abby. "Your quick thinking saved the ship. Without those barrels of water, the damage would have been much worse."

"No one but you sees it that way," Abby said, a bitter edge to her voice.

"'Twill all work out. Never fear,"

A shadow fell across the open doorway.

Him.

"Lord Rushmount, is it?" Grace said, her voice colder, if anything, than the day they first met.

Owen took her hand as if in silent warning. "Come in," he said.

What did he want? Abby took a seat by the table. At least she was decently dressed, with her hair neatly combed and shoes on her feet. But like the last time he'd walked into the cabin unannounced, her heart beat so wildly she was sure he could see it throbbing through her clothes.

Harry swept his hat off his head and presented Mam with one of those exquisite bows. Abby was certain no other man in the world had mastered that gesture with the same grace.

"Mistress O'Donnell. Miss Abby." He smiled, not at her in particular, she noted, but at the room, at them all, at the absurdity of the situation. Aye, that must be it, at the absurd state he found himself in . . . in this *village.*

She stared at him, unable to pull her gaze away. He wore a linen shirt. One without scorch marks. As soon as she finished mending the silk one, she'd launder it and give it back to him. Because of the heat, no doubt, he'd not worn his doublet, and to her surprise, he'd replaced his English breeches with a pair made of canvas such as Aiden and Da wore.

"How is the timber progressing?"

"As you hear," Owen said. "My son's at it full tilt."

"I wonder if I could be of assistance? Captain Tamworth and I are eager to resume our journey. Perhaps my aid would speed the repairs."

So he had come prepared to work. Abby remembered the day he first arrived and how he had let the men empty the dinghies without even a glance in their direction. He must be very anxious, then, to depart this place. She understood completely. She'd escape it in a heartbeat, if she could.

"Have you an axe?" Owen asked, apparently not as astounded as she was that a lord of the realm would succumb to physical labor.

"By the door."

"Then follow your ears. Sure and Aiden will welcome your assistance."

With a farewell bow, but not so much as a glance at her eyes, he left taking all the light and air with him.

"Well," Grace said, blowing out a breath. "'Tis amazed, I am."

Owen laughed. "A good thing, that. You haven't been for a long stretch of time."

One of those looks Abby had come to recognize passed between them. At the sight of it, she fled the cabin and ran across the meadow away from their love and away from the sound of the axe. But there was no way she could run from the yearning in her soul.

GRACE STOOD IN THE OPEN DOORWAY and watched Abby flee across the meadow. "I'm worried for her."

"Don't be, love. She came home from the ship unharmed. That's what matters."

"Unharmed in body, but her spirit's wounded. She's not been the same since young Harry came to Providence." Grace swiveled away from the open doorway. "Damn the Rushmounts. They're still tormenting us. I pray to all the saints that he goes soon and leaves Abby at peace. She's like one possessed. Like I was by you."

Owen laughed and rose up to hold her tight against his chest. "Possessed, were you?" he murmured into her hair. "Such power I had and never knew."

But she couldn't be cajoled from her black humor. "Power, aye. I fear that's what he has over her. Where will it end, Owen? Where will it end?"

HARRY HAD REMOVED HIS SHIRT and, like Aiden, worked bare-chested, lopping branches off the felled oak trunk.

"There's wood aplenty," John Thayer had assured him. "Lumber in the raw," he'd added with a sly grin. "First, you'll have to fell your trees, taking care to do so on the common ground. Don't strip any colonist's holding or there'll be the very hell to pay."

True enough, there were trees everywhere. Of every type and description: oak, birch, maple, pine, fruit woods. Yet hardly a damn board at the ready for a man to lay hands on. To make the matter worse, Harry fumed, the ship's carpenter insisted on oak to replace the charred deck beams, and the wood was hard as stone.

"We'll shape the trunk here as much as possible," Aiden said, "then borrow a team of oxen from our neighbor Martin Harris to drag it to shore."

"Then what?"

"We'll be needing a day with no wind whipping at the surf. When the sea runs calm, we'll lash the trunk between two dinghies and float it out to the ship. As for the cross braces, they're short enough to fit in a canoe. Another fortnight at the most and you should be ready to sail."

"A fortnight? That long?"

"Aye. Working oak takes time. And 'tis not the deck bracing alone that needs mending, but the water casks as well. The lathes for them must be shaped and caulked against leakage."

"A fortnight's too long. We must work with greater speed."

A worried frown creased Aiden's forehead. "I might start felling the second oak your carpenter selected. 'Tis hard labor for my father. I'd like to spare him."

Harry swiped an arm along his damp forehead. "Go on. I'll stay and finish here." The work was hard, very hard, and made worse by the gnats attracted to the sweat rolling down his back and under his arms. A glance at Aiden's gleaming torso showed him to be well muscled, toughened, no doubt, by years at such labor. His own lanky frame was no match, but a fortnight of such striving and it well might be.

"I'll leave you to the trimming, then, and start on the other trunk," Aiden said.

Panting with effort, Harry just nodded as Aiden slipped away through the trees. As the day wore on, an errant breeze occasionally cooled his heated skin, but not enough to keep him from sweating like a common laborer. How the sight would shock his mother were she here to see. No matter, he was nearly finished for the day. It would be dark soon and time for a cool swim in the ocean water, another activity she would undoubtedly frown upon. Nevertheless, he needed the cool touch of the ocean on his body. Yet the weather alone wasn't the only reason he'd been overheated of late. The girl, so subdued this morning in the presence of her parents, had remained a hot coal in his mind since that night aboard the *Lady Anne*. . . imagine her swimming through the fog, so willful, so eager for life, and so damn near naked. What other woman would have dared do so? A foolish question that— no other in the world.

He lopped off the last branch, slung the axe over his shoulder and headed toward the meadow and the path that led from it to the shore.

A FEATHER BRUSHED AGAINST HER CHEEK threatening to draw her from the dream. Eyes closed, she reached up to wave it away. The beautiful dream couldn't end. Not so soon. Not while she was floating free in an emerald sea with Harry swimming by her side.

Again, the feather tickled her nose.

Achoo!

The force of the sneeze awakened her to a pair of amused brown eyes inches from her own, and smiling lips and a hand holding a blade of grass.

"I knew it was you," she said at the figure crouched in front of her.

"How?" he whispered.

"No one else enters my dreams. Only you."

"This isn't a dream, though you were asleep and looking so lovely I had to stop and tell you so."

"You surprise me, Lord Rushmount. This morning in the cabin you didn't meet my eyes."

"We were not alone."

"Must we be alone to look into each other's eyes?"

"Yes, we must, for what flares between them is not for anyone else to see."

No need to ask what that meant. She remembered well the lingering look her parents had shared this very day. A heated, secret glance belonging only to the two of them. Could it be that she and Harry could share such a moment? The possibility enthralled her. She lay her hands on his shoulders for a moment feeling the hardness of him, then sent her fingers curling up and around to twine in the hair at his nape. Fingers locked together, she drew him near, increasing the pressure until he bent to her. In another instant, she'd know his lips again as she had that one golden time.

He knelt, pulling her closer to him, away from the tree trunk and into his arms. Yes, just as she remembered, his lips were warm and yielding. The pressure of his mouth increased until her own lips opened, and as she remembered, his tongue darted between them.

"Am I truly awake?" she murmured when his mouth left hers to begin a nuzzling at her throat.

"Yes, this is no dream."

"No. I know that now." Awake she might be, but the need to lie down overwhelmed her. She moved from his embrace, stretched out on the grass and held up her arms. "Come."

At her invitation, he reared back a little. "You don't know what you're saying."

She couldn't let him slip away, not now. Her pulse thudding in her temples, she grasped his arm, staying him. "I never will if I'm kept in ignorance. Teach me," she pleaded.

"Then what? *Marry* you?" He pulled free and stood towering over her. "You're a vixen, you know that?"

"Vixen, is it? You came to me this time. Why?"

He had the decency to look abashed. "You want the truth, Mistress O'Donnell? You looked so sad sitting there alone, I sought to make amends. But you took matters into your own hands." A muscle clenched along his jaw. "As usual."

She scrambled to her feet. "You're a bloody liar."

"How dare you—"

"Insult his great lordship?" She stepped in so close she could have kissed the perfect mole by his upper lip. Or slapped it. "You woke me because you couldn't help yourself. Now good day, sir."

She stalked off, once more walking away from the only thing on earth she wanted more than life itself. When she put enough trees between them, she stopped and leaned against a trunk to sort out her thinking and quiet her heartbeat.

But the path her thinking took gave her no peace. If she wanted him more than life, why hadn't she begged for his favor, his forgiveness? She exhaled a sigh so deep she could hear the sound of it in her own ears. Ah no, begging wasn't the way to win him. It would have been a humiliation without reward. Far better to keep her pride and take satisfaction in that. She had descended from kings and queens. From pirates. Such people didn't beg for what they wanted in life; they seized it. Or did without.

She stood up straight and continued along the trail for home. She would be as strong as her forebears had been, as Mam was to this day. And she would strive to be as content with her lot in life as her mother had always been. But then a thought struck her with the force of a hammer blow. The man Mam loved had married her and tied his life to hers forever.

Her father had never looked at her mother with contempt in his eyes and uttered, "Then what? *Marry* you?" as if that would be the worst fate he could imagine. Clearly, she wasn't worthy of Harry Rushmount. She was a peasant in truth, a trouble maker. That was all. Not a woman to be cherished for a lifetime.

A good thing she had clung to her pride. But oh, God, how hollow the victory.

CHAPTER SEVEN

LIKE A SNEAK THIEF, THE STORM GAVE NO WARNING before it struck. From a pink sky at dawn and a harmless cresting of white caps in the harbor, the day quickly descended into madness.

At noon, the surf pounded the beach, flinging spray onto the houses closest to shore. By two of the clock, water flooded low-lying Main Street and the wind tormented the trees.

Harry had never known the like, not even on the ocean crossing, and certainly never at home in England or Ireland. Where had all the violence come from? Trees were crashing to the ground—the biggest, strongest of all—while saplings bent and swayed but remained rooted. Broken branches, fire wood, wagon wheels, empty buckets—any objects not secured—tore through the torrential, rain-soaked air like lethal cannon fire.

With its shutters closed and locked and the fire extinguished for safety's sake, John Thayer's keeping room was damp and dark. At one howling gust, half-grown Sarah, cowered in his arms. "The roof, Poppa. What if it comes off?"

"Don't be frightened, poppet. Take heart from your mother there going about her duties as if the day were balmy. You're not feared, are you, Margaret?" he asked his wife.

The woman, a stout, phlegmatic sort, was slicing cheese and bread for a cold meal. She looked up briefly, said, "Nay," and went on with her task.

"See," John said lifting Sarah's chin with a finger. "Your mother and I lived through a storm like this long ago, before you were born, and we're here to tell of it. After this powerful blast, there'll be the peace of the gods for a few minutes, then another onslaught of wind and rain and then, poof—it'll be over. Now, be a good lass and bring us our ale. There's a dear."

Half willing but obedient, Sarah tapped the ironstone demijohn, returning to her father and their guest with two brimming tankards. Harry took his with a distracted smile. He couldn't drink, or eat, or sit or lie down. The *Lady Anne* contained all his hopes and dreaming. If her anchors didn't hold, or she capsized or ran aground, his future would be grim. The thought of the debt he'd incur had him half crazed . . . the investors like rabid dogs at his heels demanding payment he had no means to honor . . . except for his estate in Ballybanree. Yes, they'd seize that, everything his father had left him heir to . . . a sorry pile of stone right now, but soon, very soon, a manor house worthy of the name Rushmount. *If the ship survives.*

He paced the floor, frantic with worry, until finally, for politeness's sake, he gave in to John's urging to eat a bite of food. He sat and nibbled a piece of cheese and sipped his ale, trying to calm himself. Nearly an hour passed before a silence like death settled over the house. John cocked an ear to the shuttered window.

"Ah, the first half of the storm has passed us by. A few minutes now and she'll begin again. But not for overly long. Sarah! Refill the tankards!"

Harry had reversed the hourglass three times since being locked in with the Thayers. As soon as the calm began, he flipped the glass again and watched the sand slowly trickle into the empty half, willing the grains to hurry through the narrow opening. For if John were right, until the calm passed and the howling began anew, the storm would not truly be over, and until it was, he had no way of judging his fate. The sand had nearly all poured through when the violence started up anew. After another hour of battering, the calm returned just as John had predicted. Within minutes, the sounds of the storm faded as if they had never been; only the lingering rain dripping off the roof broke the silence. Though eager to go outside, Harry feared what he might see. What if—

"Shall we have a look at what God has wrought?" John rose unsteadily from his seat and shuffled to the door. He shot the bolt and peered outside.

"Ah, that loud crack we heard?" he called over his shoulder, "As I suspected, Margaret, the oak's down across the way."

Harry hardly saw it. He stepped outside, easing around the Thayers clustered in the open doorway and raced to the summit of the hill, scrambling over fallen trees and branches and all manner of debris. His heart was pounding with fear of what he might see. One more step.

There she was. His beauty of a ship riding the water like a sea creature, graceful, elegant. And intact. He blew out a pent up breath, ready to sink to the ground so great was the enormity of his relief.

"There's a fine ship for you," John said, a few moments later, out of breath and puffing by his side. "Rode out that storm like a mermaid, she did."

"What sort of storm *was* that? I've never seen the like of it."

"No, I expect not. Hurricane is what the Caribs call them. They blow up from tropical waters. Why? No one knows. I've only endured one other in all my years in the colonies . . . they're rare enough, but vicious. One thing for certain, young Lord Rushmount, if you'd been out to sea during her you'd likely be at the bottom of the ocean now." He gave Harry a hearty clap on the back. "Keeping you in port the way she did, that O'Donnell girl likely saved your ship. And your life."

Abby.

Christ, in the thick of the hurricane, he'd given little thought to her or her family, or to anyone or anything except his fortune. His bloody fortune.

When John Thayer trudged back to the house to seek another tankard of ale, Harry sank onto the summit of the hill, not caring whether the rain-soaked earth dampened the seat of his breeches.

Shame overwhelmed him. Though he'd never met his father, Harry was sure he would say a man's actions under pressure were a test of his character. And he had failed the test miserably. Oh, no doubt, thrifty colonists like the Thayers would understand his self-interest. But he'd thought himself better than that. He hadn't been raised as a rustic but as a lord of the realm. His forebears, his privileges, his background . . . his very name . . . demanded a code of behavior that had fled his mind at the first sign of danger to the ship.

Yes, he was grateful she hadn't plummeted to the bottom of the harbor. Why add hypocrisy to his other failings? But money grubbing wasn't all of life, nor the sole measure of a man. Harry smashed a fist into his open palm. What his father hadn't lived to teach him, the storm had. While it raged, he had acted like a merchant, crass, without honor, worried only for his profits.

He looked down the hill at the disheveled village then lifted his eyes to stare out to sea once more and saw, not the ship, but a pair of shining onyx eyes. He had to see her, to know she was well. He rose, swiped a hand across his chilled rear and headed down the storm-tossed slope for the O'Donnell farm.

Aiden stood with Grace and Owen in the open field fronting their cabin, surveying the broken branches and leaves littering the ground. "The wickiup's gone," he said, "blown away like a leaf in the wind. And the old oak nearby it crashed and uprooted some of the pines as it fell." He gave Grace and Owen a rueful smile. "If the storm had come earlier, I'd have saved myself a bit of chopping."

"Thanks be to God you weren't harmed when the wickiup flew away," Grace said, scrutinizing him with a mother's careful eye.

"Aye," Owen agreed. "That none of us was hurt is a blessing from God. The crops have weathered the storm well, too. Except for some of the corn. And we've just a few shingles missing from the roof."

"Have you forgotten that our single pane of window glass was smashed to smithereens?" Grace said.

Owen patted her hand. "We'll buy another, lass. Perhaps young Rushmount has some for sale aboard his ship."

"I do, indeed," said a voice from the edge of the clearing.

Grace spun around to face him. "So you're back again, are you?"

"Yes. To see if you're all well after the hurricane."

"We are that," she replied without willing him a smile.

"How did the Thayers fare?" Owen asked.

"They're fine. Little damage to their property."

"Or to you and yours. Owen tells me your ship is still floating in the harbor. 'Tis as fit as if there had never been a storm." Grace glared at him, her mouth set in a rigid, challenging line.

The woman would never warm to him, nor, he told himself, did that matter. It was her daughter's opinion he cared about, realizing of a sudden he cared about it very much. He glanced around with anxious eyes. "Miss Abby?"

"She's out exploring," Aiden said. "Had to see the storm's destruction for herself."

Harry felt his tension ease. "I would have a word with her if I may. Where might I find her?"

Grace looked past his shoulder without answering.

"She's fond of the meadow with the tall maple at its edge," Aiden told him. "She feared it might have gone down."

"I know the tree. I'll search for her there." With a farewell bow to Grace, he left glad to be gone from the woman's icy stare.

He stepped over soggy ground, the water seeping into his boot soles, his silk shirt clinging to his chest. Heated by the late day sun, the air was humid and warm, redolent of earth and leaves and a salt-laden sea. The change in the weather, from hellish to glorious, was typical of everything in the colonies. Everything in extremes. No moderation anywhere.

In the back meadow, the maple still stood though shorn of most of its leaves, its bare branches reaching for the sun like gnarled fingers seeking warmth. His breath catching in his throat, he saw her standing beneath the tree's limbs, a hand resting on the trunk as if she were caressing it. In the afternoon light, her unplaited hair shone like molten gold, cascading down her back all the way to—yes—her bottom. So it was that long. He suppressed a smile and called to her.

At the sound of his voice, she whirled around.

She knows me.

"Ah, so you're back again are you?" she said.

Good God, she's the mother all over. Just as difficult. Just as beautiful. Her face framed in that cloud of curls, her eyes shining . . . her jaw tight with irritation.

He was close enough to see an unladylike dusting of freckles along the low bridge of her nose. She must spend too much time in the sun. His sister Elizabeth would be distraught to have a single freckle mar her ivory complexion. He doubted Abby even knew she had a freckle. Or how delightful they were scattered carelessly across—

"Why are you here?" she asked in a voice cold as winter. "I thought never to see you again."

He gulped a deep breath of the sea-laden air, though he could hardly inhale it, his throat was that dry. "I'm here to humbly beg your pardon."

Her eyes rounded into dark pools. "You *are*? Whatever for? Oh." She flushed and glanced away. "Because I asked you to lie with me. I was wrong to ask. Very wrong."

"You honored me, and I was too much the fool to know it."

To his relief she nodded, considering what he said. "Aye, you destroyed the moment, but in so doing you saved me. Yourself, too," she added with an impish smile. "Since now I know you aren't the marrying kind, we've both avoided a great deal of trouble."

"Then you forgive me?"

"Of course. It's the Christian thing to do." Her chin came up, tight and defiant. "But I'll not offer you a moment like that again."

Ah, so he was to be punished, after all. It was no more than he deserved. He bowed to her, acknowledging his own stupidity and the rightness of what she said. She'd offered him a feast and he'd refused it. He deserved to starve. Though his hands itched to hold her and watch her eyes close and her lips open, to feel her pressed against his chest, he kept a distance between them, one she made no move to close and never would again, the stubborn little minx.

He uttered a sigh. Let her interpret it as she would. "There's more I would say to you."

She had half turned to walk away. "Oh?"

"Yes." This apology business was difficult. To keep his hands occupied, he twirled his hat brim between his fingers. "My ship . . ."

"Go on," she said, her mouth set in the exact same line as her mother's. God, they were both relentless.

"Elder Thayer pointed out a truth to me."

She waited, quietly staring into his eyes as if she guessed what he might say. He had no choice but to plunge ahead. "He told me you undoubtedly saved the *Lady Anne*. And my life and that of every man aboard her."

"*I did?*" Clearly astonished, she stared at him with her mouth agape.

So she hadn't guessed. "According to John Thayer, had we sailed from Providence on schedule, we would have gone down in the storm. The delay you . . . inadvertently . . . caused saved us from that fate." Another bow. "I am deeply in your debt."

"I love it that you are," she said, the honesty of her response reinforced by a smile. "For every debt there must be a payment, is that not true?"

"Absolutely." His pulse quickened. He knew the payment she would extract. Another kiss. Another moment clasped in her slender arms, pressed to her breast. "Demand away. I'll repay whatever you ask."

"Excellent." She grinned then caught her lower lip in her white teeth. She was contemplating his fate—he knew it for a certainty. Any moment now she'd fling her arms around him and draw him close. He could hardly wait. How well he remembered her soft, full—

Her teeth let go of her lower lip, readying herself, no doubt for the first kiss. "When you sail from Providence," she said, "I want you to take me with you."

He leaned in closer, his thoughts tangled in the sweet scent of her hair. Then it hit him.

"*What?* I'll do no such thing. God, you're impossible."

Her happy grin fled. "And you're not a man of your word. Not a gentleman at all."

"You know I cannot take you aboard."

"You said you'd pay whatever I asked." Her hot eyes seared him like a flame. "You lied."

The damned hat filled his hands. He jammed it on his head and pointed a finger directly at a freckle on her nose. "I thought you wanted a kiss. Not a voyage."

"Why would I ever, ever want to kiss you? I told you that moment would never come again." Hands on hips, elbows akimbo, she added, "And I don't lie."

With hands balled into little fists, her spine rigid, she stalked off. He stared at her retreating back. Every time they were together, their meetings turned into disputes. Clearly, she was a vixen, a woman to stay clear of. He should be grateful for her anger. It rid him of her.

He huffed out a breath. To think just a few minutes earlier he couldn't wait for the touch of her lips. They turned up at the corners at the slightest provocation and . . . well, no matter. He'd put her out of mind. Tomorrow he'd see how the new water casks were coming along and work on the ship alongside Aiden and the carpenter. Anything to hurry the repairs so he could sail away from her and the colonies and leave them behind. Strange, though, how the thought didn't make him as happy as it should.

On his way up the hill to John Thayer's house, he passed along the shore, surprised to see the ship's small, flat-bottomed skiff pulling onto the sand. Johnson, the mate, leapt out nimbly enough for a man in his fourth decade.

"Lord Rushmount, avast! I was about to come searching for you," he said, haste making his gravely Cornwall accent more pronounced than ever. "The captain sent me. We're in need of a ship's carpenter."

"Another one? Why so? Doesn't your man suit?"

Johnson shook his head. "He's gone."

"Deserted?"

A shrug lifted the mate's shoulders. "In a manner of speaking. He up and died. That beast of a storm did him in, it did. Frightened him to death. Don't know why. We've ridden out many a nor'easter together. But he'd been poorly of late."

"A shame," Harry said. "He was a good man."

"Aye."

Though past middle age, corpulent and big bellied, the carpenter had been a capable craftsman. Sorry to lose him, Harry determined to send the man's share of the profits to his widow. He had performed his duties well, ably overseeing the repairs. Under his direction, the main supporting timbers had been reinstalled, and the work was now more than half finished. No doubt they could complete the task and get underway in a timely fashion, but what of the rest of the voyage? No telling what emergencies might arise. To go on without a skilled carpenter aboard would be foolhardy. So what did the captain have in mind? "Who are you seeking as a replacement?" he asked the mate.

"That injun who calls himself O'Donnell."

Abby's brother. What would she think when she learned of their choice? He pushed the troubling thought aside and nodded. "Excellent. I'll show you the way."

Injun. Since the night of the ship's fire, Cookie's words and his wild reaction to the sight of him echoed in Aiden's head, though he knew he was foolish to dwell on it. He *was* an Indian. A Narragansett, the son of Comise. The adopted son of Owen. A white man. With Abby as much his sister as if they were kin. She had saved his life when they were children. Abandoned and ill after the Great Swamp fight, he would have died in the woods if she hadn't stumbled on him. From that day, a tie strong as blood bound them together.

Still, the drunken cook had forced home a problem he'd been pondering for the last year or more. The time had come to make his way in the world. But in which world? An Indian raised as a white, where did he belong?

He'd been considering leaving, striking out for the west. He'd wondered if the stories about a vast continent were true or the exaggerated lies of a few trappers and scouts . . . he picked up a stone, took aim and watched it plink into the heart of a stump. He had the skills to survive. He could hunt, fish, build a wickiup, read the Bible, speak English, work a farm like a white man . . . but now this offer to ship out on the *Lady Anne* had him intrigued.

The problem was that meant leaving soon, before harvest. He couldn't, in his heart, bear to abandon Owen just before the busiest season of the year. A strong man still, nonetheless, Owen needed his help, and he owed him so much. He owed him his life.

No, he plinked another stone at the stump. He'd stay where he was needed. The trout skewered over his campfire had cooked through, its aroma causing his mouth to water. He pulled the skewer out of the ground and set the fish aside to cool.

"Aiden?"

He sent a startled glance over his shoulder. "Owen! You caught me unaware. Like a white man."

"Like a white man." A wry smile lifted Owen's lips. He eased himself onto a fallen tree trunk. "I've searched the farm for you. You've kept yourself scarce lately."

"The weather's good. I prefer the outdoors."

"No other reason?" Before Aiden could reply, Owen held up a palm. "No need to answer. You're a man grown. Your reasons are your own." He shifted his position as if seeking a more comfortable spot. "Lord Rushmount stopped by the cabin. He told us of his offer to you."

"Aye, he offered, but I haven't accepted."

"'Tis a chance to see the world. Seize it, Aiden."

Aiden nodded, his eyes never leaving Owen's face. "The farm . . . you'll need help with the harvest. The work's too much for one man alone."

"Don't worry your head on that account, lad. True, no one will ever match you in my estimation, but young Nate Harris has a strong back and will work with me for a share of the crops." Owen rubbed his injured leg, an all too familiar gesture.

"I don't know," Aiden said uncertainly.

"Nate's already offered his help." Owen stretched out his leg with a grunt and sat up straight. "He made his offer the day he asked permission to court Abby."

Aiden smiled for the first time that day. "She'll not have him."

"You think not? He's a steady lad."

"He's a clod. He's no match for Abby."

Owen sighed, nodding a reluctant agreement. "I fear you're right. There may never be a man to match her. I thought I had no worries for Abby, she's so beautiful. Like her mother, and in God's truth as willful. But of late she's been . . . sure and I can't voice it. Unhappy is as good a word as any."

Aiden didn't answer. Didn't dare. How could he tell Owen what he suspected? That when Harry Rushmount sailed away, he would be taking all joy from Abby's life. By sailing off with Harry while she stayed behind, he would be compounding her disappointment.

Yet the temptation to see the sights of the great world was so over-whelming, he didn't, in truth, want to refuse. Not now that he had Owen's blessing. First, though, he'd make certain of Nate. Once he had his firm promise to work the O'Donnell fields, he would be truly free. But he'd leave for a single voyage only. After it ended, he'd be back, a year older, and no doubt wiser about the ways of the world.

Three more days the mate had said and they'd be off. An exultation swept through him at the thought of the adventurous year ahead. But despite his excitement, a piece of his heart was heavy. He well knew how Abby longed for the same chance to see the world. Grace would ac-cept his decision as something a man must do. But Abby? She would be heartbroken. And angry.

As twilight fell, he made his way home with his burden of news, but Abby surprised him. Studying him gravely, her dark eyes deep and prob-ing, she said, "You must go. It's your duty to do so."

"My duty?" This was not the reaction he had expected. Tears, aye, anger, even hot words, but not this strange, resigned acceptance.

"When life presents wondrous gifts, refusing them is the same as cursing them. It's an affront to the gods."

"The gods?"

"Have you nothing new to say for yourself? Or are you just going to repeat my words?"

To his relief, the dull resignation had disappeared from her eyes. They snapped at him, sparking with passion. This was the Abby he knew so well, the vexatious little sister who had saved his life so long ago. For his sake she was concealing bitter disappointment at being left behind, and he loved her for it.

"I'll bring you back a special gift," he told her, anxious to make her happy, though he was aware her happiness or unhappiness did not rest in his hands. "So tell me. What would you like from the Old World?"

"The sights. The sounds. The smells. Can you put those in a bottle and carry them home to me?"

"Oh Abby, if life were different, I'd bring you with me. You know I would but—"

"No need to say more. I understand." She shrugged, her narrow shoulders rising and falling in a sad, defeated little gesture. "Harry re-fused me also."

"Harry refused you?"

"There you go again, Sir Echo."

He blew out a breath. So she'd offered herself to the man and he'd rejected her. No wonder she'd looked so hang-dog of late. "It's only for a year. I'll be back, I promise." He tried to smile. "I'll be bearing gifts. All will be well here while I'm gone, you'll see. Nate Harris has promised to work the farm with Quinn." Was she aware of Nate's motive for doing so? He needed to know. "Quinn tells me Nate wants to court you."

"*Court* me?"

"Now who's the echo?"

"Never. I'll die an old maid first."

Aiden grinned from ear to ear. Her fire was returning. "Ah, an old maid is it?"

"There you go again, aping everything I say."

"Chances are you'll be married before I return." He doubted that would be true, but he wanted one more peppery retort from her lips to prove she'd not lapsed back into sorrow. But she merely shook her head, and with her face still and thoughtful, gave him a quick, distracted kiss on the cheek. He eyed her warily, for he'd seen that look before. It usually meant she was conjuring up some sort of mischief.

CHAPTER EIGHT

OVERNIGHT, A FROST SETTLED ON PROVIDENCE, painting the leaves that still clung to the trees with vivid color. A few more cool nights and the scarlets, rusts and yellows would intensify, though not as riotously, Abby knew, as in storm-free years.

Next leaf-falling season when she returned a woman who had seen the world, she'd find the countryside in its full glory, for hurricanes were rare and another might not strike again in her lifetime. Wild storms at sea were not rare, though. Mam had told her of a fearsome night on her crossing from England, the time she'd lost the babe from her womb. Abby remembered, too, Mam's stories of the hateful food. The weevils, the salt meat.

Well, so be it. She wasn't afraid of hardship. But what of her parents? She would be causing them sorrow, a poor repayment for all their loving kindness. For all their sacrifice and work.

Tortured by her thoughts and the guilt they brought, she escaped the cabin to roam the meadow, settling finally beneath her favorite maple, its few remaining brilliant red leaves floating around her with each puff of errant breeze. She sniffed the air. The rich, fecund scent of decaying vegetation rose to fill her nostrils. She inhaled deeply, drawing in an aroma she might not experience for weeks, even months to come. Not if she left as she ached to do. The salt smell of the sea would replace it . . . along with the noxious odors Mam had said invaded every ship.

A dutiful daughter would stay at home, not dream the dream that filled her mind. A dutiful daughter would make corn bread each morning and knit woolen stockings each evening. A dutiful daughter would marry a man like Nate Harris and sleep in his bed. A dutiful daughter . . .

Dear God. She folded her arms on her tented knees and lowered her head to them, letting the tears flow, letting the sobs rack her shoulders. How could she deny the power of her own longing? Yet how could she *not* deny it? And put her own needs first? Before her mother. Before her father.

Truly, she was despicable. But still, she longed to go to sea with every beat of her heart. Longed to feel the ship stir beneath her feet like a live creature, fearlessly meeting the ocean swells, its prow headed for the far horizon and all of its mysteries. Over the years, hadn't Mam told her the blood of Granuaile O'Malley, the pirate queen, flowed in her veins? And that she should take pride in the knowledge.

Granuaile had gone to sea as a girl, as a young woman, as a wife, as a mother. She had fought battles, seized booty, commanded ships of men.

Had that fierce blood thinned so much she should weaken and give herself up to Nate Harris of the thick, sweaty hands? Should she give up the most secret dream of all and watch Harry Rushmount sail away from her forever?

No. Such a fate was not to be borne. She leapt to her feet. She had much to do in the next few hours.

"Psst. Psst." The pebble clunked against the side of the steep-roofed loft where Emma slept with her little sisters. Abby weighed the fistful of pebbles she held in her palm. She'd already thrown three, yet Emma slept on like one of the dead. Did she dare risk another toss?

One more. The stone struck the closed shutter. *Plink.* There. Emma must have heard that. A moment later, the shutter parted, and Emma, her head covered with a white nightcap, peeked out. "Who's there?"

"It's me. Abby. Come down."

"Abby? Whatever for?"

All this chatter would waken the whole house. "Shhhh. Just come."

The shutter closed with a soft click. Abby waited out of sight in the shadow of the barn listening to an owl hoot, the sound eerily like a warning. The cottage door opened on silent hinges and Emma, in bare feet, a shawl flung over her nightdress, stepped out into the chilly air.

"Over here," Abby called softly.

"What on earth . . ." Emma walked closer then stopped in her tracks, fear rushing into her face as Abby stepped out into the light of the full moon. "Who are you?"

"For heaven's sake. It's me. Abby."

"You don't look like her. You must be a ghost," Emma's voice faded to a frightened whimper.

"Don't be silly." Abby reached out and took her hand. It was ice cold whether with the night chill or fright, she couldn't be certain. "I'm wearing boys' clothes. Aiden's old things."

"What happened to your hair?" Emma whispered.

"I've plaited it under his cap. I had a mind to cut it off, but I couldn't bring myself to do so."

Emma let go of her hand. "Abby O'Donnell, either you tell me what this is about, or I swear I'll go right back inside."

"I'm leaving. On the *Lady Anne*."

Emma gasped, shocked surprise flooding her round, moonlit features.

"I need your help," Abby said quickly.

"How can I—"

"Go to my Mam and Da. Tell them I've gone off with Aiden. Tell them I'll be safe with him and not to worry. We'll both return together next year. And . . . and . . . tell them I love them," she added, feeling guilty even as she spoke the words.

"They'll stop you." Emma shivered and drawing her shawl tightly around her shoulders, she clutched it to her chest. "As they should," she said primly. "The very idea."

"They won't stop me, not if you wait until the ship leaves the harbor."

Emma's chin quivered. "They'll blame me for not warning them in time."

"No, they won't. They know me too well to do so." Had Emma always been so fearful? Abby wondered. Telling her was the weak link in her plan, but she couldn't leave without a word for her parents. She might have searched the cabin for a scrap of parchment and left a letter—she had been well taught in the dame school—but where would she have left it and been certain it wouldn't be found too early or, worse, never? No, confiding in Emma was better.

She seized her hand again. "Do this for me, and I'll bring you a gift when I return. Something wonderful," she bribed. "Stockings of silk may be."

A tear slid along Emma's check. "I promise," she murmured. "May God watch over you, Abby O'Donnell. You're a wild girl."

Abby sighed and nodded. "True." She gave Emma's fingers a final squeeze. "One other thing. Don't breathe a word of this to Nate. Not until after you tell my parents."

"But—"

"Not a word." She kissed Emma's damp cheek, and bending down, picked up her bundle and fled into the darkness.

ON THE DESERTED, MOONLIT BEACH, Abby reached into her breeches pocket and fingered the ha'penny she'd been saving for new ribbons. Would the lure of it pull young Josh Carter from his warm bed, after all? For the coin, he'd promised to paddle her out to the ship two hours before dawn. She strode the beach, her heart pounding furiously, her stomach rumbling. Where was he?

The night wore on as still as death. No owls, no scampering nocturnal creatures made a sound. All she could detect was the lapping of the incoming tide and the odor of seaweed it carried. When Aiden bade them farewell earlier in the day, trying mightily to tamp down his excitement, he'd said the ship would sail at high tide with the first light. She glanced skyward. Oh God, had the heavens lightened already?

No, except for the moon, the night remained black as ebony wood. She forced herself to stop pacing the sand. She could be early. The breeches had freed her stride to a remarkable degree. Without a skirt and petticoats to tangle around her legs, she might have reached the shore far earlier than the agreed time. Aye, her heartbeat calmed; that must be why Josh wasn't here yet.

Something stirred. She looked toward the sound. Silhouetted against the moon, Josh came scuffing along the sand, sleepy and slow as if the night would last forever. She ran to him.

"Hurry."

"My ha'penny?"

"It's in my pocket. It'll be yours as soon as we reach the ship."

"You look different," he said, eying her up and down.

"Good. I'm supposed to." She picked up her bundle. "Where's the canoe?"

"Around the bend." He took off his hat to scratch at his head. "I could be in trouble for this."

She resisted an urge to agree. "Then say nothing to anyone. Can you do that?"

He nodded, uncertain, but hurried along beside her.

"I'll help you slide the canoe into the water."

"I can do it," he said, a bit sullenly. "You'd best get in. Up front." She did as he directed. Not quite full grown, but strong of arm and back, he'd have no difficulty paddling out to the bay and returning to safety.

He shoved off, leapt aboard and soon had the paddle in his hands, stirring them to the hulking shadow in the middle of Providence harbor.

As they approached the ship, she whispered over her shoulder, "Go full around the hull." His paddle dipping and lifting noiselessly, he circled the ship. Abby prayed as she'd never prayed before. If the rope ladder had been pulled up on deck, how would she climb aboard?

They completed their silent circle, but her prayers had been consigned to hell. The ladder was nowhere in sight. It must have been drawn up on deck in preparation for the morning's departure. She slumped in the bottom of the canoe, the ship's slick sides hovering above her like a mountain slope.

"What are you going to do now?" Josh hissed.

"Go round again," she whispered, "toward the stern."

"Why? There's no ladder."

"Sssh. Do as I say."

"Go on," she urged, as Josh sat unmoving. "Go on."

He heaved a sigh but did as she asked. Suspended from the port beam, the anchor chain as thick around as a man's arm, swung down to the water line and disappeared below the ocean's surface.

"Can you get in closer to the chain?" she asked.

"I don't think so."

"Here's your penny, Josh."

He stopped paddling long enough to put the coin in his pocket then moved in until the side of the canoe bumped against the ship's hull. Abby reached out and grasped the chain with both hands. The links were large enough to slip her fingers into the spaces, giving her a bit of a purchase. Wasting not a moment, she lofted herself from the canoe and hung suspended between sea and sky, her weight full on her arms, straining them to the utmost. For an awful instant, she feared she'd fall back into the ocean, but her feet came together, and the heels of her shoes clamped the chain, easing the strain on her arms.

Holding tight with her left hand, she let go with her right and reached above her head for a higher link. Her left hand followed suit, and with her feet clamped onto the chain, her knees flexed, she propelled herself upward a few inches, then again, and again.

Halfway along the chain, she heard a soft "Abby" over the lapping of the waves. She glanced down. In the glow of the moon, Josh held up her bundle. "You forgot this."

Drat. "Give it to Emma Harris," she whispered over her shoulder. "She'll know what to do with it."

Only a few more feet to the deck. "Go now," she urged Josh. "Go."

Like the last time she'd stolen aboard, silence reigned on the *Lady Anne.* Fortunate for her, the watch was a lax guardian.

Its taper low, the lantern at the hatch winked feebly. It would fail before long, but no matter, the first faint fingers of light would soon probe the night sky. Abby crouched motionless beside the railing, her eyes searching out a possible hiding place. She wouldn't go below where the crew would be sure to come upon her. Hide in plain sight she told herself. But where? Where?

Keeping low, she inched farther aft and crept up the few steps to the small raised deck. Most of the precious water casks were gone, no doubt stowed below for safe keeping. A few remained, for easy access most likely. They were arranged in a tidy square, a tarpaulin tossed over them and strapped down with a length of rope. Where the tarp rounded the barrels, she could see the swell of a bit of extra canvas. If she lifted the end of the tarp and huddled underneath, it might suffice to hide her for a while. Once they hoisted sail, a single turn of the hour glass is all the time she'd need. She'd make herself small, hug her legs close to her body, wrap her arms around them, and rest her head on her knees. Busy getting under way, the crew wouldn't be expecting a stowaway.

She released a sigh then quickly glanced around to see if anyone had heard. No, all was quiet. She was alone and the moon had faded to a pale wafer.

She'd hardly formed the thought when a bell shattered the stillness. Eight gongs in all, and soon heavy feet pounded up the stairs. She ducked under the canvas, tucking her feet beneath her, making certain the toes of her shoes were concealed. Hugging her knees and bringing her head to her chest she prayed the old prayer Mam had taught, the one not said in Roger William's church, but the one she loved the most. "Hail Mary, full of grace . . ." It was Mam's favorite and hers for that reason, though she hardly dared think of Mam right now or her resolve would disappear.

Over and over she repeated the prayer, silently mouthing the ancient words while heavy footsteps fell around her as the men hurried to carry out shouted orders. The capstan creaked when the heavy anchor chain was wound around it and then thumped aboard. With a flap loud as a musket shot, the sails sprang free from their restraints, once, twice, three times, and the ship leapt forward like a stallion eager to race. Even lacking sight to guide her, she understood these sounds and motions as clearly as if she'd been born on the waves, and her prayer to Mother Mary encompassed Granuaile now, a woman fate had led to the sea, a woman she hoped would guide her on this voyage.

"Mister Johnson, hold course."

Her heart soared at the shouted command. It could mean only one thing. They were heading out of Providence harbor into the open water. Not long now and she would step out of her hiding place and meet her destiny head on.

CHAPTER NINE

Breathing in the crisp, morning air, Harry stood on the aft deck and stretched, glad to be underway for the Caribs at last. Any regret he might feel at leaving the colonies . . . and Abby . . . he'd tamp down. He had voyaged to the New World to trade, and that was still his goal. His only goal.

As he glanced toward the prow, something strange near the covered barrels caught his eye. It looked like a shoe, but with the ship rocking under his feet and the light reflecting off the water, he couldn't be certain. He strode to the barrels and peered closer. Yes, that *was* a shoe jutting out from under the tarpaulin, and an ankle, by God, in a gray woolen stocking. A malingerer.

A quick yank on the edge of the canvas revealed a lad crouched into a ball and far gone in sleep. Had Captain Tamworth hired a cabin boy? He hadn't said so. None too gently, Harry prodded the sleeping figure with a toe of his boot. No response.

He prodded him again, harder this time. The boy yawned and straightened his legs before raising dark, sleep-fogged eyes to his own. Then with a gasp, he scrambled to his feet. "Why did you kick me like that?"

"I'll ask the questions. You'll give the answers."

To his astonishment, the lad ignored him and stood on tip toes to glance astern at the thin slice of shoreline still visible in the distance. The insolence of the freckle-faced pup looking past him as if he were a shadow.

Harry grabbed the shoulder of his doublet and gave him a shake. "What are you doing here?"

At least the lad had the grace to lower his gaze to his shoes. As he did so, his lashes fanned his smooth cheeks. "I'm a stowaway," he muttered.

Not a cabin boy, then, and young, with a voice like a girl's. "Your name?"

"Absalom O'Donnell."

"What!" No wonder the eyes had looked familiar. And the freckles dotting her nose. "You rigged yourself out like a boy and stole aboard like a thief—"

"I've stolen nothing."

"—against my direct orders."

Her eyes snapped up. "I remember no such orders."

"That day in the meadow, I said you couldn't travel aboard this ship."

Abby lifted her head higher, sure of herself. "That was a refusal. Not an order."

"They are one and the same." He wanted to shout, but kept his voice low and glanced about. Luckily, the men were busy and hadn't noticed her yet. He took off his hat and slapped it on his thigh. "I represent the owners of this vessel, and as such I have the right to say who's welcome aboard and who isn't. And you are not." To his satisfaction, or dismay, he couldn't be certain which, tears filmed her eyes.

"I mean no harm," she said.

"But you've caused it, nevertheless. Do you have any idea what being the only woman on board ship means? How much trouble it causes? The danger for you?"

A tear slid down her cheek, then another.

A crazed impulse to wipe them away assailed him, but this was not a time to weaken. "Of course, you don't. Or you wouldn't be here."

"This was the only way."

A gust of wind burst into the sails. Bracing himself against the ship's sudden lurching, he planted his legs wide apart, locking her in next to the barrels. "The only way? Explain yourself."

"I don't expect you to understand."

"Try me," he said, determined to remain implacable in voice, in posture, in the set of his jaw. Let her realize this was no light matter.

"I've seen nothing of the world except my village, and trees and the strip of sand edging the ocean," she said in a low voice. "All of my life, I've looked out over the water and wondered what lay beyond the horizon. The thought of growing old without seeing anything more of God's great creation," her arms stretched out to encompass the horizon on either side, "caused me to—"

"Stowaway."

She nodded.

He forced himself to frown. "So your thirst for adventure set you off on this hair-brained scheme?" The salt breeze billowing in the sails had dried the remnants of her tears. No more escaped from under her lids.

"It's not the only reason. There are others."

"I can't wait to hear them," he said, his voice layered with sarcasm. "Go on."

She straightened and looked him square in the eye. "As I recalling telling you, I have the blood of a pirate woman in my veins. Granuaile was her name. She drew me here."

"That's ridiculous." She couldn't mean it. But one look at her determined expression, and he knew she did. The imp.

A pirate woman, indeed. He fought the urge to laugh, but the situation was too serious to give in to levity, much as he might wish to. Look at her, tear streaks on her face, her chin firm as a rock, togged out in boys' clothing that hid all her female attributes. His glance slid over her. Well, perhaps not.

"What happened to your hair?"

"I chopped it off," she said with a grin.

He gasped. Not her hair, that beautiful curtain of gold. He reached out and snatched the cap off her head. Her tresses were plaited and tightly wound around her head, secured in place with pins. He gave her back her cap. "Put it on," he said, annoyed at the relief he felt.

His sister Elizabeth popped into his head. In his wildest dreams, he couldn't imagine her as a stowaway in breeches, sleeping on the deck of a ship. He'd fear for her safety, like he feared for this little hellion standing in front of him. She had the courage of ten men; he'd give her that, and the cool nerve of a hundred, stealing aboard a ship this way, penniless and alone.

Alone? "Your brother, Aiden. Does he know you're aboard?"

She shook her head. "No. He wouldn't have allowed it."

"Well, there's a measure of sanity in your family after all." How they had come to be kin, he'd have to find out some day soon.

The ship plowed steadily forward, the parting waves sending cold spume flying over the deck. Abby shivered. He had to get her to a safe haven below decks, but first Tamworth must be informed that they had a stowaway.

"Come, the men are staring. I'll take you to the captain."

A glimmer of fear crossed her face. "He'll be angry, I know. What do you think he'll do with me?"

It was on the tip of his tongue to say, "Throw you overboard." But that tiny glimmer stayed him. "He'll put you to work. To earn your keep." He regarded her carefully. Her disguise would fool anyone into believing she was a slim, beardless lad. As cabin boy, she'd run errands for the captain and the mate, aid Cookie in the galley, serve meals to the men . . . sling a hammock in the lower deck and sleep alongside the crew . . . not good.

On the other hand, if the men knew a woman was aboard, a stowaway with no resources, no husband to protect her, even her Indian brother might not be able to keep her from harm. Not good, either. He blew out a breath, the sound mingling in the air with the cawing of the gulls. The first day he'd clapped eyes on her, he'd known she was trouble.

The buffeting breeze tugged tendrils of her fair hair into curls about her forehead. His hands itched to finger them, to wind them around. "When we get to the captain," he said, deciding in a trice what to do, "you'll not tell him you're a girl. Nor will you tell anyone else. You'll be safer that way."

"What of Aiden?" she asked, a crease furrowing her brow.

"No need to inform him straightaway. He has enough worry getting used to life aboard ship without the shock of you. Wait a few days till he gets his sea legs. In the meanwhile, you'll sleep with me. In my cabin."

"I'll do no such thing," she said, her eyes flashing black fire.

"Oh yes, you will. It's me or the entire crew. Do you understand?"

She stared at the scuffed toes of her shoes. "Aye," she said, suddenly subdued.

Not exactly flattering, he thought. Even worse, the men would think he'd brought a catamite aboard for his personal pleasure.

Christ. Well, let them think what they would. If being his private property meant she'd be left alone, then so be it. As they walked toward the wheelhouse, it occurred to him that marriage to her would solve the problem as well. Captain Tamworth could perform the task handily. And legally. He cast a sidelong glance at Abby. In her faded breeches and doublet, she walked by his side ready to face her punishment like a man. A surge of pride in her swept through him.

Little though she might be, what a formidable woman she was in truth. He suppressed a grin. Thank God she couldn't read his mind.

"A stowaway?" Captain Tamworth roared. "Who had the bloody nerve?"

After uttering a terse "keep her steady" to the helmsman, he whirled away from the wheel to confront the culprit.

Determined not to show fear, Abby threw back her shoulders and faced him without flinching.

"Ah, a lad is it?" Tamworth said, eying her balefully. "How did you get aboard?"

"I climbed the anchor chain, sir," she said, keeping her voice low pitched.

"Humph," he said, obviously surprised. "Cheeky of you, to say the least. Your parents? They're Providence colonists?"

"Yes sir."

"They knew your intent?"

"No, sir."

"They'll think we snatched you off the street, or worse, they'll think you dead."

Abby shook her head. "I left word for them."

"You did, did you? Mister, ah . . ."

"Guy, sir. They call me Guy. Delighted to be aboard, sir."

To her amazement, the merest hint of a smile played about the captain's thin lips. "You're not the first boy who ran away to sea, nor the last, I imagine." He looked Abby up and down as if weighing her usefulness. "I could throw you to the fishes." He paused to let his threat sink in. "But I prefer to put you to work. You're small enough, you won't eat much. And you'll earn every mouthful you do eat. Cookie will see to that." The smile he'd been holding in check broke free. "The galley's a fine place to be cured of the sea."

Harry cleared his throat. "He's an innocent country lad, sir. With your permission, he'll be safer billeted in my cabin."

The captain's smile disappeared, but he shrugged. "As you wish, Lord Rushmount." He turned to the helmsman. "I'll take the wheel. Find the first mate. I want the night watch clapped in irons for the next forty-eight hours."

He inclined his head at Abby. "Now get to work, or it'll be the fishes for you, after all."

An idle threat, Abby knew, as she hurried along the companion to the galley. Under his bluster, the captain hadn't been so very angry. Besides, Harry wouldn't have let her come to harm even though he'd looked like a thunder storm about to flare into lightning. She wondered if he'd ever smile at her again then put the wishful thought aside. She was at sea, and that is what she'd longed for.

As she hurried along, the ship swayed gently, riding the waves with ease. Abby sent up a prayer of thanksgiving. The Narragansetts prayed to the Great Mother Earth who nurtured and sustained them. She'd always prayed to Mother Mary in heaven, and to the spirit of Granuaile, but this day her prayer was to Great Mother Ocean whose billows were buoying them up and carrying them to new and exciting places.

"Lordy, I've got me a visitor, I 'ave," Cookie said when she walked into the galley. "And 'oo might you be?"

"I'm Guy, the new cabin boy. I've come to aid you. Captain's orders."

Clearly astonished, Cookie lowered the jug he was hefting without taking a swig. "'igh time I got me a galley slave," he chortled then had himself a long swallow.

Abby looked around. The galley's brick-lined walls were permanently blackened by the fire. Overhead, the new raw beams gleamed palely in the light filtering from above. The grid was still missing, but she could hear the distant pounding of a striking hammer. Aiden, perhaps, finishing the repairs. A goodly fire glowed in the pit, and over it a caldron bubbled, sending an occasional froth sizzling onto the flames.

"Them's beans," Cookie said, pointing to the giant kettle. "They're needin' a stir. Step lively now."

An iron spoon hung suspended from an overhead rack. She poked at the beans with it, turning them over, distributing the heat, peering into the kettle as she did so. Mam had been wrong. No weevils in there. A wonderful aroma, though, and grease aplenty from the luscious chunks of salt pork floating among the beans. Her stomach rumbled. She'd been too excited, or too fearful, to eat last evening's meal. It wouldn't do to faint from hunger and be discovered for what she truly was, but the beans would be ready soon and surely she'd be allowed a taste. For now, she'd keep on stirring and ignore Cookie's grumbling.

"The crew'll be eatin' sea biscuits with them beans, but the captain and his lordship gets fresh cornbread and that chicken on the skewer. It's about done." His narrow eyes scrutinized her as she worked at the kettle. "Faster with that spoon. Scrape the bottom good." He reached into a barrel under his work table, lifted out a scoop of corn meal and dropped it into a wooden bowl.

"Watch me close," he said. "Tomorrow you'll be doin' this."

Though she knew the steps to making cornbread by heart, Abby observed him attentively. From the careless way he was measuring, his version would be heavy and doughy. Tomorrow, the captain and his lordship would be in for a treat when she followed the receipt Mam had taught her. She smiled for the first time in two days. Being cabin boy might not be so bad after all.

Cookie swigged from his jug, and without letting it go, leaned perilously close to the bubbling kettle to sniff the air. "Them beans is done. Here, clamp a lid on them and carry them to the wardroom. The men'll be wantin' their food."

Abby swallowed. "Sir . . . Cookie . . . I don't believe I can lift that kettle. It's too heavy for me."

"Ah, you're a useless scut," he said, putting down his jug and cuffing her out of the way.

"Sorry."

Cookie yanked at the rag tucked into his belt, grabbed the pot handle off the hook and with a mighty grunt lifted the laden vessel from the fire. A little of its contents slopped over onto his bare feet.

"Yow!" Hopping from one foot to another, he rested his burden on the work shelf.

Abby darted a glance at his feet. They were dirty, with horned nails and covered with scars. She resolved never to work in the galley without wearing shoes.

"Put the cornbread over the fire," he ordered, "and fill that basket with biscuits from the barrel over there. Then follow me."

She placed the iron spider over the flames, filled the basket, and keeping a safe distance between them, walked behind Cookie to the wardroom. With a groan of relief, he set the kettle on the scarred tabletop. "Put the basket down," he said. "Ye'll ladle out the food. One scoop for each. Biscuit on top. The lads from the first dog watch'll be in as soon as I sound the bell. Then the lads from the second watch'll be pantin' for their grub. See that ye save enough beans for them. If need be, go and get more biscuits. When the second shift's through, clear up in here and wash them bowls."

"There are no utensils. What do the men eat with?"

Cookie's lips curled in disgust. "Never shipped out before, have ye?"

"No."

"They carry their own spoons. Knives, too. We can't be providin' everything, ye know. Bowls is enough."

"Oh, I see." Phew, she had a lot to learn about life at sea.

"Now I'm off for the cornbread, and then I'll be deliverin' their meal to the captain and his lordship. When ye're finished dishin' out food to the crew, go to the captain's stateroom to see what needs doin'." Halfway out the door, he warned, "I'll be waitin' for ye in the galley."

He lurched off and left her alone with the steaming caldron.

Somewhere overhead, a bell sounded, and soon the men streamed in, boisterous, sharp tongued, foul smelling. Amidst their raucous calls at the sight of this new Cookie, she ladled the beans quietly, doling out seconds when asked, speaking as little as possible. One seaman with mean, hot eyes, glared at her as he ate. She stared him down and, finally, he gave up and concentrated on his bowl.

The men served, she helped herself to a spoonful of beans and a biscuit. As she chewed, she dared take a quick peek at Aiden. He sat calmly, in the middle of a rowdy knot of men, listening to their banter, saying little. When he happened to glance up at her, a puzzled expression crossed his face. Her heart beat faster and her palms got sweaty, but he shook his head and looked away. He knew her, she was sure of it. A spark of recognition had lit his face for an instant, but he refused to credit his own senses. The idea that the cabin boy might be his sister was too outrageous to believe. She pulled her cap brim further down on her forehead and lowered her eyes to her food.

On his way out of the wardroom, the mean-eyed hand dropped his empty bowl by her elbow where it rattled against the kettle. "It's all yours, boyo," he said with a sneer. "Black Jack'll have somethin' more for ye when he gets freed of the irons."

A sliver of fear rode her spine as he stalked off. It wasn't easy being a cabin boy, after all. Maybe Mam had some of it right. Stowing away had been foolhardy, though it was a little late to worry about that now. At least, thanks to Harry, she wouldn't be sleeping below deck with the men. Still, Emma had judged her correctly. She *was* a wild girl, and her own impulsive actions had placed her in harm's way.

As soon as the last man left, she piled the discarded bowls in the empty caldron and headed down the companion to the captain's stateroom. To her relief, it was empty, the table littered with soiled pewter plates, chicken bones, and a half-filled flagon of wine.

She wiped the table with Cookie's rag, put the stopper on the wine, added the plates to the caldron, and hurried back to the galley. She had to get the bowls washed and ready for the next meal.

"High time ye got here," Cookie announced when she staggered in under her heavy burden. "Use sea water for the washin' up. No wastin' drinkin' water for that lot." He shoved a wooden pail attached to a length of sodden hemp at her. "Here's the bucket. Drop it over the side and step lively. Now that he's got himself a slavey, Cookie's goin' to have a nap, he is." With a happy chuckle, he snugged the jug under his arm and took a stumbling step out of the galley. A burly deck hand, busy fingering his jaw, banged into him nearly sending him sprawling.

"Watch where yer walkin', Toby me lad," Cookie ordered, hugging his jug tight to his chest. "I nearly dropped me mother 'ere."

His hand on his jaw, Toby looked at Abby in surprise. "Where'd you come from?" he snarled.

"I stowed away," she mumbled.

"More power to ye, boyo." He turned to Cookie. "I've a powerful pain in me tooth. Look." He opened his mouth so Cookie could take a look see at his collection of blackened stumps. Abby glanced away with a shudder.

"Ah, nothin' for it but pullin'." Cookie said. "That tooth's rotted clear through. I don't envy ye, mate. Ye'll go through the agonies of hell gettin' that out. Unless," he added slyly, "ye can convince the captain to give ye a swig of that there laudanum he keeps in his sea chest. One taste and you'll be out like a light. Then I can get me tweezers and yank at the roots, and you'll never feel a thing. But gettin' the captain to part with the poison is the trick o' the thing."

Cookie cackled, his grip loosening on his jug. Before he could stop him, Toby snatched the bottle and took a hefty swig.

Abby ducked out of the way as Cookie snatched at his prize. "Hey. Give 'er over, Toby. Give 'er over."

"Here. To hell with you and your tweezers." He shoved the jug at Cookie and stomped off.

Abby grabbed the bucket and headed for the upper deck. She'd never had so much washing up to do at one time in her entire life.

So far, being at sea wasn't much different from being at home in Mam's cabin. Only now she was cleaning up after a ship full of men, not just two. But what manner of men? She thought of the mean-eyed sailor and the way he'd sneered at her. Less than a day into her voyage and she'd already been threatened.

Abby straightened her shoulders and took a deep breath. The key was to not let the men see she was frightened. What they didn't know was that Absalom O'Donnell came from sturdy stock. As she watched the bucket sink into the ocean water, she silently thanked Granuaile for giving her the spirit to endure whatever life had to offer. Even Black Jack, whoever he might be, wouldn't best her.

Chapter Ten

S HE COULDN'T WAIT ANY LONGER. Her bladder was about to burst. It
didn't help to see one of the crew at the rail, his member in his hand,
sending an arcing stream cascading into the ocean.

She quickly averted her gaze and returned to the galley, but too late.
He had reminded her of her own pressing necessity. Mam hadn't mentioned how women relieved themselves aboard ship. There had to be a
way and a place, but how and where? She had no one to ask except . . . oh
no . . . not Harry. She'd rather die.

Tears filled her eyes, clouding her vision of the tidied galley, the
bowls neatly dried and stacked, the caldron scoured clean with beach
sand and rinsed for the morrow, the floor swabbed of at least its top
layer of spilled cooking.

Every muscle in her arms and shoulders ached from hauling in buckets of sea water, but she hardly felt the aching; the pressure below was far
worse. In another minute, she'd be bawling like a babe, blubbering for
her mam. Or flooding the galley floor.

She crossed her ankles, clutching her thighs tightly together. What
choice did she have but to go to Harry and admit her human frailty? The
problem was, he'd been out of sight for hours, ever since he took her to
the wheelhouse. She'd have to go searching for him and fast. Her decision made, she yanked Cookie's dirty rag out of her belt, flung it on his
work shelf and headed down the companion. A minute or two, no more,
is all she had.

She found Harry in the captain's stateroom sitting at his ease, reading a book. "Thank God, you're here," she said. "I've no time left."

"What's wrong?" He dropped the book and jumped up, knocking the chair over in his haste. "You're as white as a ghost. Has anyone—?"

"I have to . . . I have to . . . She felt her cheeks grow warm.

"For God's sake, *what?*"

"Make water."

He looked blank for a moment, then comprehending her meaning, threw back his head and laughed, the peals bouncing off the low ceiling. "*Now.*"

"Come." He took her by the hand and led her to a little opening in the stern, over the rudder. It had a wooden slab for a seat and when she glanced down the opening, she could see the ocean water boiling below.

"I'll leave you," he said, his eyes twinkling.

She was beyond caring. The instant he was gone, she tugged down her breeches and sat, the relief so great, her whole body sagged with pleasure, the cold breeze from beneath caressing her bare bottom. It felt good simply to sit, and she was tempted to stay where she was for the rest of the day, out of reach of Cookie and his tasks.

But with a final sigh of relief, she stood and adjusted her clothes, dreading having to face Harry. No doubt there would be a smirk on his lips and disgust in his eyes.

As Mam would no doubt say, no lady ever let a gentleman direct her to the jakes. But why should that disturb her? She was no lady. Harry had told her so to her face. She gave her breeches a final hitch and walked back inside.

He stood waiting for her near the captain's cabin.

"You're still here," she said, her cheeks flaming hot. She kept her gaze lowered, not wanting to see what would be painted all over his face.

"I stayed to tell you to use this convenience when you must. Should you see the men at the railing, ignore them. They would be more circumspect if they knew you were a girl."

She risked looking up but saw no sign of a smirk or disgust on his face. His expression held something else entirely. Sympathy, perhaps?

"Are you feeling sorry for me?"

He shook his head. "Not at all. I'm merely trying to be of help. Under the circumstances," he added. This time he did smile.

So he *was* amused. "How good of you," she said tart as a crisp apple. "But please don't worry for me, Lord Rushmount. I'm where I want to be."

She headed along the companion to the galley, wondering if her words were true. All she'd seen of her beloved ocean this day were the buckets of water she'd pulled up on deck and brief glimpses of the vast green expanse that led to the horizon, exactly as it had from the beach at Providence. So far, the only difference was the roil of the *Lady Anne* under her feet, the snap of her shroud lines and the scents of the sea: salt air and salt pork—and unwashed male bodies.

In the galley, Cookie awaited her, revived by his nap. "We won't be makin' any fire the rest o' the day," he said. "The coals is banked for mornin'. Tomorrow it's oatmeal gruel early on, and cheese with apples for the evenin' meal. Might as well eat 'em before they goes and rots." He chuckled at his own jest. "They're in that barrel in the corner. First thing in the mornin', fill the bucket with fresh water and set it to boil.

Freeing a key from the ring hanging on his belt, he unlocked a storage closet and took down a round of cheese covered with black wax. He held it to his nose and sniffed it. "You colonists make a tasty good cheese, I'll give ye that," he said lobbing off a chunk and biting into it without offering her any. "Tomorrow, we'll need them bowls in the mornin' but not afterwards. This ain't the governor's palace."

Hmph, she sniffed. No need to tell her that.

THE SUN, AN ENORMOUS ORANGE BALL, SANK INTO THE SEA, and a darkness such as Abby had never known fell over the vast ocean—until she looked up at God's heaven and found it winking at her. Like friends she'd known all her life, the same, familiar stars shone down. Some she could name. To the north, Little Dipper and to its right, Big Dipper, and above them, the North Star. Pharis, Da had called it. He'd learned of the stars from the sailors when he and Mam crossed the Atlantic years ago. At this very moment, they might be looking at these diamonds in the sky thinking of her . . . wondering . . . she hoped they didn't hate her for leaving them . . . for longing . . .

"I've been looking for you." Harry's deep voice came out of the dark. "You've had me worried."

Startled, she looked up from where she sat huddled by the railing, though all she could see was his dim shadow.

"It's late. The men are all abed," he said. "Except for the watch. Come, you must be ready for rest." He paused. "After the day you've had."

Was she again a source of amusement to him? She couldn't be sure. His voice was noncommittal enough, but there was no reading his face.

"If I had a covering, I could stay the night here," she said.

"No, you will not. I won't allow it."

"You have nothing to say about the matter."

She felt rather than saw him crouch beside her on the deck.

"Now you listen to me, you little hot head. You'll get up from there and follow me to my cabin, or I'll take you there by the scruff of your neck."

"How dare you?"

"How dare *you*? Hasn't anyone ever made you obey?"

"Obey?"

"Quiet," he hissed in her ear. "You'll have the watch on us." His hand shot out and, like a ring of steel, circled her arm. He pulled her to her feet. "Come along. Be a good girl."

His patronizing voice infuriated her, and she tried to yank free, but the clamp of his fingers held her imprisoned in a lock-step beside him. The thought of spending the night in his cabin had her uncertain, and she shivered.

"You see," he said. "It's too cold to sleep on deck."

Did he think her so stupid as to believe that rubbish about the cold? She kept up with his pace, not wanting to let on she was afraid. And she was, she realized. She was terrified.

In the meadow, she had pressed herself to him, wanting him, wanting life, with every pulse of her heart. The memory of her eager blood that day caused her face to burn in the gloom as he hurried her along the companionway. To slow him, she dragged her heels. This was not the meadow. That day they'd been in the open air, in the sunshine, with her mam and da within calling distance and herself willing and ready. Not like this . . . forced to his room in the dead of night.

No, this was not the same, not the same at all. She was a fool, a hot-headed, impetuous, stupid fool. And now it was too late. He had her in his grip, and from the pressure of his fingers on her arm, no intention of releasing her until he had his way.

On either side, the unlit companion loomed ominously. The cabin door was only steps away. With her free hand, she tried to pry his fingers off her arm. "Let me go. I'm not sleeping in there."

"Quiet. You'll do as you're told. For once."

From below, she heard the coughs and snoring of the sleeping men. She could scream and rouse them, and twist and fight. It was said a kick to a man's parts rendered him useless. Then what? She was on the high seas with a rowdy crew that thought she was a boy. Let them keep thinking so. Aiden, too. If he found her like this, being forced to a man's bed, he'd place himself in jeopardy for certain—the last thing in the world she wanted. Screaming would do no good. She had to rely on her wits.

Without letting go of her hand, Harry flung the cabin door wide and shoved her inside. When the door snapped shut behind them, he released her, and she spun around to face him, panting, ready to kick him anywhere. Then her gaze fell on a strange contraption strung across the small room.

"What's that?" she asked.

He leaned against the door, holding it closed. "You've never seen one before?"

She stared at it, her mouth agape. "It's a hammock for—"

"Sleeping," he finished. "And that," he pointed to a bucket on the floor and next to it a china bowl cleverly set into a hole carved into a chest top, "is fresh water for bathing. That," he went on, pointing to the neatly made bunk, "is your bed. The nightshirt is for you as well." He gave her a slight, graceful bow. "Now if you'll excuse me, I'll go up on deck for a while until you get settled."

"Wait," she said, taking a tentative step toward him. "You're sleeping in the hammock."

"I am."

"Thank you. It's not what I expected."

"What did you expect?"

That humor again in his mouth and eyes. He was taunting her. He knew full well what she'd had in mind. Why pretend? Her chin came up with a defiance she didn't really feel. "I thought you'd have your way with me."

He didn't even try to hide his smile. "I'm afraid you have a highly inflated sense of your own charms . . . ah . . . Guy. This is my way. You're in the bunk. I'm in the hammock. Perfecto. Now make haste with your ablutions. The night, as they say, grows old. "

With that and a laugh, he walked out.

Chapter Eleven

A S THEY SAILED SOUTH PAST THE FLORIDA STRAITS and beyond the turbulent Gulf Stream, the days and the nights became as warm as summertime.

Each evening, after darkness descended over the water, Harry climbed into his hammock, rocking in it, making the ropes squeal as he tried to find comfort and ease in his strange, swaying bed. On most nights, exhausted by Cookie's demands, Abby fell asleep first, and in the dim light of the lantern swinging from a deck beam, he lay awake gazing at her bright hair flaming across her pillow.

It was then he needed all his resolve to keep to his hammock. It was then he longed to leap out and spend the night beside her, stroking that glorious fall, that slim, straight body, telling her the truth of his heart, telling her he had lied; she could never, ever, overestimate her charms. They had him ensnared, permanently he feared.

For in no manner was she the mate his family name demanded. Her forebears had been serfs on Rushmount land, her ancestors pirates and worse. Hadn't her grandfather been hanged for his crimes? Her namesake was an Indian, for God's sake. She had no knowledge of proper behavior, of her place in society, no elegance, no grace. . .

He rolled onto his side in the hammock, always a risky business that threatened to pitch him onto the floor boards. But it was well worth the risk to lie facing her as she slept, a hand under her chin, her lips slightly parted, her breathing soft and sweet.

At morning's light those eyes would snap open, that firm chin would come up and her soft breath would give way to unveiled words totally lacking in feminine diplomacy. He smiled, watching her. She made every other woman in the world fade into nothing.

A shame she was impossible. He owed it to his father's memory to marry a peer, someone whose lustrous name and background would match his own or, better, outshine it. Such an alliance would guarantee his future children's place in society, a gift he had the power to bestow on his offspring. If he stayed in the damned hammock.

On one such night, tormented by his thoughts, he climbed out of his swinging bed and stole up on deck. The sea was calm, and even so late into the night, the air held a cloying, languorous warmth. In another day or two, if the prevailing winds continued to buoy them onward, they'd reach Jamaica Island and complete the trading. Then, with the hull well stocked with furs and timber, rum and sugar cane, they'd sail for home. A brief stop in London to sell his cargo and divide the profits, a short visit with his mother and Elizabeth, and after that Ireland and Rushmount Manor.

His jaw tightened. That still meant weeks of sharing his cabin with Abby. With his resolve already at the breaking point, he wasn't sure he could manage it. Damn. The little vixen, sleeping right now like an angel from heaven without the slightest realization of the turmoil she caused within him. On the other hand—though not in a smiling mood, he found himself smiling—she well might realize everything. He remembered her grin the day he snatched the cap from her head thinking she'd cut off her hair.

Eight bells. The night watch had ended. Any possibility of sleep long gone, he remained leaning on the rail feeling the pulse of the ocean's heartbeat reverberate through the *Lady Anne*, inhaling the freshening breeze as dawn, redolent with moisture, slowly emerged from the shadows.

Shattering the peace, the early watch clambered about the ship in rhythm to mate Johnson's shouted orders. Close hauled during the night, the sails soon snapped their canvas as they unfurled, moving the ship through the water with greater speed.

Surely Abby couldn't be sleeping through all this noisy activity. She must be plaiting her hair and pinning it under the cap readying herself for the day's tasks. He hated seeing her work from sunup to sundown, but under the circumstances, the disguise provided her the most safety. His fingers drummed on the railing, and he found himself frowning. It might be wiser to put her ashore on the island and pay for her passage back to Providence on the next available ship. He'd be free from her disturbing presence and better able to focus on the task he'd set himself. Yes, maybe leaving her in Jamaica was the best solution for him and the safest place for her.

"Sail off the larboard bow! Heading our way!"

The shout from the crow's nest brought Captain Tamworth hurrying out of the foc'scle onto the bow. He peered through the half dark at the straining sails in the distance. "The glass," he barked to the mate who thrust it into his outstretched hand.

The spyglass telescoped and up to his eye, he watched with an intensity that caught Harry's attention. Then with a loud "Christ," he collapsed the glass and shoved it back at the mate. "Sound the alarm. Trouble ahead. Change course, ten degrees to port. All sails to the wind." The ship lurched into the swift change, the half-filled sails surging wide, the flogging canvas loud with effort. "Mister Johnson, cannon in firing position."

A sea battle? Harry peered out at the fast-approaching vessel. A single-masted sloop with a fore-and-aft rig, she was smaller than the *Lady Anne* and narrower hulled. She rode high in the water, cutting through the waves like a knife through flesh. After squinting at the flag flying from her mainmast, he rushed to Tamworth's side. "That flag. It's a red petticoat. Does that mean what I think?"

"Aye. She's an undeclared vessel," Tamworth said, his face grim. "They're brigands. Out of Tortuga most likely."

"You mean pirates?"

"I do."

Harry felt all warmth drain from his face. Should they be overtaken, that spelled the end of everything, of all his hopes and dreams. Worse, the danger this meant for Abby made his blood run cold. While the captain barked orders to the mate, and the men scurried to carry them out, he went in search of her. She should be warned. After that, he'd seek out Aiden. The man needed to know his sister was aboard; his help might well be needed to keep her out of danger. As if anything could protect her from the evil that, in his bones, he knew was coming. Still, they must try with every ounce of strength they possessed.

He took the stairs two at a time and raced along the companion to his cabin. Given any luck, he'd find her still there dressing for the day. Without knocking, he yanked open the door. At the sudden sound, she gasped and whirled around to face him while he froze in the open doorway stupefied. Slowly, his eyes never leaving the sight that filled them, he closed the door and leaned against it. Unmoving, he stared at her as she stood revealed to him in every way. Without hurry, his gaze stroked her, loving every inch and surprised, so surprised, that her body wasn't straight and slim like a boy's at all, but curved and gloriously rounded, her breasts full, her waist tiny, her hips in perfect harmony with every other part.

A little smile lifted her lips. She faced him straight and unafraid making no attempt to cover herself. Most women would have, he realized, the thought like all thoughts, disappearing as she took a step closer to him.

"I've dreamed of you looking at me exactly as you're doing," she murmured. "Thank you. It's a memory I'll take to my grave."

With a single stride, he covered the distance between them and seized her in his arms, his mouth descending to capture hers, bruising it with kisses. Once, if only this once, he had to kiss her breasts, and he did hurriedly. Frenzied by her moans, he wanted to caress her forever, but this single, stolen moment was all they might ever have. A loud thump sounded overhead. He forced his mouth and hands away. "You must hurry and dress. I'm here to warn you. A pirate ship approaches."

She paled but calmly turned away, delighting him with a view of her softly sculpted rear. Her breasts swaying, she bent down and plucked a band of white cloth off the bunk. To his astonishment, she wound the cloth over her breasts pressing them against her chest. No wonder she had appeared so boyish in her disguise. She pulled on her linen shirt and breeches and slid her bare feet into shoes.

"Now for my hair. You have a knife?"

"Of course," he said warily, afraid he knew her intent.

"Cut off my hair. Hurry. If they're almost on us, we don't have much time."

He shook his head. "No, not that. I can't do it."

"It's the only way."

"No."

"Harry, the crew here is rowdy but not vicious, but what of these others? Should one snatch off my cap, I'll be doomed. Would you have me raped? Get out your knife. Cut off my plaits."

"No."

"Yes. Unless the pirates are sodomites, I'll be safe. It's the only way."

"What do you know of sodomites? No decent woman should know such things."

"Mam told me much about life. I'm glad she did. Be quick."

He didn't move.

"Step lively, man."

The 'step lively' coming from Abby's slim throat spurred Harry into action. Though he doubted cutting her hair would be enough to keep her safe, not to do so would court disaster. He slid his knife out of the sheath suspended from his belt His hand trembling, he hacked at her hair unevenly, cutting off her plaits at her chin. The red-gold coils fell to the floor, taking a piece of his heart with them.

Without checking herself in the looking glass, Abby ran a hand through the shorn locks, tumbling them into a halo of curls. "I don't see my cap." Harry found it on top of a sea chest and handed it to her. "You look like a thunder cloud," she said. No need. My tresses will grow back."

He nodded, unhappy, he knew, over a trifle when death, or worse, awaited them.

She gave him a quick kiss on the cheek. "I must get to Cookie in the galley. No matter what, he'll be expecting me." She paused in the doorway. "Will you toss my hair overboard when you go up on deck? We can't have the brigands guess at the truth."

Before he could respond, she was gone, running to fulfill her tasks, not cowering in her bunk as most women would. He shook his head, stuffed the severed plaits in his pockets, and ran for the stairs. He must stop comparing Abby to other women. He was fast learning she was incomparable.

In the few minutes he'd been below, the rogue ship had gained on them. There was no time to waste; he had to locate Aiden. He strode the upper deck and spied him working the shrouds with another hand, too busy to approach. Later then. Harry heaved a sigh and made his way to the wheelhouse where, sweat beading his forehead, Captain Tamworth stood giving orders through clenched teeth to the beefy helmsman.

Why hadn't he ordered the men at the cannons to fire? Shoot holes in the sloop, send her to the bottom of the Atlantic? And then, heart sinking, Harry saw why. Forced to sail close to the wind in a desperate effort to outmaneuver the rogue and get her cannon into firing position, the *Lady Anne* had lost momentum, her canvas half-full, she was slowing dangerously.

Coming at them full speed ahead, the bow of the marauder offered a slim, moving target. She had maneuvered herself abeam of them. The entire length of their hull lay exposed to the cannon thrusting out of her breach holes.

"Point her to windward, Master Johnson," the captain ordered. "Hold our speed. She's bearing down."

Harry watched silently, admiring Tamworth's tenacity and quiet resolve, but he knew they were no match for their pursuer. Square rigged, broad of beam, their hull crowded with cargo, they could never outrun the smaller, fleeter sloop. Their only hope was to catch her broadside and empty their cannon into her, but as they tacked out of the wind trying to come about, their sails sagged, and they floundered, helpless as a beached fish.

"Ten degrees to port," Tamworth ordered, in a voice frayed with strain.

Too late. Harry saw a brief fire flash and a warning shot careened across their bow.

Clearly visible now, the red petticoat waved jauntily from the yardarm.

"Fire!" Tamworth shouted.

Chapter Twelve

The balls flew high then fell harmlessly into the sea, sending fountains of spume washing over the sloop. Raucous cries rose from the rogue ship's decks, and as she drew nigh, Harry saw she was a scurvy bitch, filthy and ill kept. Her name had been filed off the hull, the wound in the wood left raw to the salt spray. Buckets and ropes and odd bits of canvas littered her deck. Up close, the red petticoat flag bore stains and, like the straining sails, showed signs of hard wear.

Above the water line, a menacing row of cannon aimed their snouts at the *Lady Anne*. Behind each gun, a man crouched ready to fire. The rest of her crew, armed with knives and clubs and lengths of chain lined the deck, or hung on the rigging, jeering at them across the fast-narrowing strip of water.

Harry prayed Abby's disguise would hold and that, God willing, they would both live to tell this tale to their grandchildren.

"Ahoy there!" came a shout over the water. "Slayton here, comin' to pay you a call . . . me and me mates and me cannon."

At the jibe, his men howled, slapping at each other, laughing boisterously. They're enjoying this, Harry thought. They can't wait to come aboard and kill us all.

"State your business, Slayton," Captain Tamworth barked. If he knew fear, he gave no hint of it.

"Me business? You're me business," Slayton shouted back. "You and your cargo."

His unruly crew leaped and whooped like monkeys in a tree. He turned on them savage with sudden anger. "Shut your mugs."

At his command, they quieted immediately. The creaking sails and the lapping of the waves against the ships' hulls made the only sounds in the morning air.

Harry knew the brigands would do nothing to harm the *Lady Anne* and her valuable cargo; the ship's crew, however, they'd slaughter without a second thought. He moved closer to Captain Tamworth and whispered in his ear. After flashing him a startled glance, the captain nodded. "It's worth a chance," he said in a low voice.

His hands gripping the rail the only sign of his tension, Tamworth called out, "I like the way you talk, Slayton. Come aboard."

HIDING JUST BENEATH THE OPEN HATCH, Abby crouched on the stairs listening to the shouted exchange. *The captain wasn't putting up a fight.*

"You be a wise man," Slayton yelled. "Trim your sails. We'll board you now."

"Not so fast."

Abby peeked over the edge of the open hatch. The pirate ship was frighteningly close. With grappling hooks in their fists, Slayton's men crouched by their sloop's starboard railing, ready to leap across the gap and secure their prize. He waved them back with a jerk of his wrist. "Me men grow impatient, captain. Say your piece."

"Board my ship. Take what you want, but harm no one on board. No one."

"Ha, you bargain with me?" Slayton threw back his head, his guffaw mingling with the creaking canvas and the slap of water on the hulls. Then his head snapped upright. "Enough chatter. Move, mates!"

With lightning speed, the rogue ship's grappling hooks clawed at the *Lady Anne's* rigging, drawing her into a tight embrace. As Abby watched, terrified, she saw Harry whisper again to the captain.

"Wait up, I say," Tamworth shouted over the din. "Kill us and you kill your chance to be rich as a king."

"You lie," Slayton snarled. "Go men. Step lively." Wild as animals, screaming invective, his men leapt across onto their prey. Almost as an afterthought, Slayton bellowed, "Harm no one on board. No one. Wait for me order."

Heart pounding, Abby slid down the stairs and huddled in a corner of the galley watching the roaches scurry about on the floor boards, not knowing whether to feel disgust or hope. Was Captain Tamworth a gutless coward, or did he have a plan?

A burly brigand with greasy hair to his shoulders burst through the open doorway. "You. On deck with the others." He prodded Abby's shirt with the tip of his knife, slicing a hole in the fabric. Would her knees hold her? Terrified, using her shaking hands as props, she got to her feet and crept along the companion wall keeping as much space as possible between herself and his stinking bulk. Enraged at her slowness, he grabbed her shirt, yanked her up the stairs, and flung her through the hatch. She landed on her stomach at Harry's feet. At his sudden in-take of breath, she looked up, but with a warning glance, he motioned her to silence.

Slayton, in command on the poop, glared down at his prisoners. "Who's the Cookie on this scow?"

Cookie stumbled forward.

"Get to your fire. Feed me men. They grow hungry, and they thirst. For now mates," he said swinging his attention back to his crew, "food and water only."

A howl of protest filled the air.

"You heard me. You'll get what you're pantin' for, but not now."

One of the brigands, sweat rolling from his forehead into his unkempt beard, took knife in hand and stepped closer to Slayton. "I say that ain't the way o' things, cap'n, and you know it."

Slayton yanked his cutlass from his belt. "And I say no grog. Our prisoners need guardin'. Get back with your mates." He glared at the man, pointing his weapon at him until he gave way with a muttered oath. "Boyo," Slayton shouted, sliding his blade back into his belt. With a start, Abby realized he meant her. "Roll out a barrel of fresh water."

She ran to the galley. Where was the water stored? She hoped to God Cookie would be there to tell her. To her relief, he awaited at the galley doorway, sober, his flask nowhere in sight. "I heard 'em," he said. "Ye'll need help with the barrel. It's heavy as a fat whore."

Together, grunting and straining, they lifted a cask up the stairs then rolled it onto the deck. One of Slayton's crew, axe in hand, split open the barrelhead, and his men dipped in with tin cups or their bare hands.

Still in command on the poop, Slayton said, "Captain Tamworth, address your crew. Tell them it's me orders they obey now, not yours. Any man who heeds this warnin' will be spared. Any who does not will be killed."

Captain Tamworth stepped forward, his hands bound behind him with a leather thong. His coat had been stripped away and searched, the pockets of his breeches turned inside out. The indignities hadn't diminished his calm, Abby noticed, surprised and glad that this was so.

"You heard," he said to his men. "Obey and you'll live. Later, some of you will go aboard the . . . ah . . ." he dared to turn and smile at Slayton, "the *Petticoat*." The rest will remain here. Go about your duties as if your orders came from me."

Slayton grasped the captain by his bound arms and shoved him away. "Now mates, when the grub's ready, eat your fill. After we feast, we haul supplies to our own ship. Leach is in command of her."

Abby heard muttering start up among the brigands. "No grumblin,'" Slayton shouted. "That's me order. Next we head north for Captiva. Once we make the island, we break out the grog."

A thunderous roar went up from his men. They howled with glee, clasping each other about the back and shoulders. Two danced an impromptu jig.

"What is this Captiva they seem to love?" Abby whispered to Cookie.

"An island off the west coast of Florida. It's rumored there's where they keep their women."

COOKIE WRUNG THE NECKS OF MOST OF THE CHICKENS in the holding cages next to the galley. He gutted them and dropped them, feathers and all, into boiling water. When they were barely cooked through, he fished them out of the cook pot, and Abby carried them and buckets of steaming brown rice onto the deck. Pushing and shoving, Slayton's men fell on the food, devoured it and demanded more.

Abby's arms and shoulders ached from carrying the heavy buckets of food about the ship. She grew so wearied, she feared her legs and feet would slip out from beneath her and land her on the decking spread-eagled and beslopped. That must not happen. A beating would be sure to follow. She willed herself to carry out orders with head down, eyes averted, legs scurrying fast. At least the work kept her knees from knocking and strengthened her resolve to avoid scrutiny from the pirates.

In the captain's stateroom, the rich cloth and gleaming china she remembered had been flung into a corner. On the table's once polished surface, she placed trays of boiled chicken and rice

Hoisting a crystal decanter of Madeira in his fist, Slayton gulped so fast, the wine leaked from the corners of his mouth and ran, unheeded, along his neck to his belly. After an endless swallow left him gasping for air, he thumped the decanter on the table and tore at a chicken leg. "Boyo," he called, as Abby was about to slip away to the fragile safety of the galley. "Take me knife and cut your captain loose. I don't want him starvin' before he tells me his tale of riches." He guffawed and reached for the wine.

Abby approached the table and picked up the knife resting by Slayton's wrist. It had been honed razor sharp. The thought of turning it on him didn't last long; she'd never be able to overpower him. But the captain might. She hoped, as she cut his wrists free, he'd grasp the weapon and spring at the pig's throat.

But Captain Tamworth merely rubbed his wrists, first one then the other, and said into her eyes, "Put the captain's blade back where you found it, lad."

"Aye, sir."

"You're no fool," Slayton said, and drawing a second knife from the open neck of his shirt, he laid it on the table.

"Nor are you, captain," Tamworth replied calmly.

The pirate shoved one of the knives in his belt next to his cutlass and dropped the other in his boot. "Now that we understand each other, eat. Then you'll tell me your tale." He swigged the dregs from the decanter then flung it against the wall where it crashed into splinters. His chin jerked up at Abby. "Boyo, fetch more wine."

"The lad has no keys for the closet," Tamworth said.

"Where be they?"

"You took them from my breeches belt."

"Oh, aye." Slayton grunted, reached into his coat and tossed the ring at Abby. She missed the catch, and the keys clattered to the floor. She looked up in alarm. Would he strike her for that? And where was the wine stored?

Captain Tamworth bowed slightly from the waist. "With your permission, I'll aid the lad." Another grunt from Slayton. Tamworth left his place and retrieved the ring. He walked to a paneled closet in the cabin's rear wall, unlocked it, removed two bottles of Madeira and carried them to the table. "We have no need of decanters, I warrant."

"You said right." Slayton twisted the cork off a bottle with his knife tip and took a swallow before placing the knife on the table by his elbow. He nodded at the second bottle. "Help yourself. It'll loosen your tongue with what I'm waitin' to hear."

Captain Tamworth settled into his seat and laid the key ring on the table. He ignored both the knife and the untouched bottle. "What I know was told to me by the young merchant who travels with us. His cartel owns this ship and all that's on it."

"No longer," Slayton growled.

"True," Tamworth replied, a dry smile hovering about his thin lips. "Nevertheless, Harry Rushmount is the man to tell you the tale."

Picking at his teeth with the point of his knife blade, Slayton eyed him narrowly. "You better not be lyin'. Boyo," he shouted, his voice so loud Abby jumped. "Fetch this Rushmount. Step lively. I grow impatient."

She ran to the deck. Under the watchful eyes of the renegade crew, the men of the *Lady Anne*, bound hand and foot, sat sweating in the tropical sun.

"Your captain wants Harry Rushmount brought to him," she told a grinning thug with a cutlass in his hand.

"Who's 'e?"

"I am," Harry said.

"Then yer in luck. It's the captain's table for ye," he said with a laugh, bending down to cut the rope at Harry's ankles.

"My arms?" Harry asked as he got to his feet.

"What about 'em?"

"Would you free them as well?"

Quick as a snake, the man's fist darted out and struck Harry in the jaw, knocking him to the deck. "How's about I free some teeth fer ye? Now get below." Then, "Avast," he yelled as Abby followed Harry to the hatch. "Where ye think yer goin'?"

"To your captain, sir, he needs me for serving." She swallowed hard, hoping her voice hadn't quavered.

"Be gone, then," he said waving her off.

By some miracle, the companion was empty, and seizing the moment, Harry said. "Wait up, Abby. I need to know if you've been harmed."

"Not at all, but there's something I must warn you of. Slayton thinks you'll tell him of a king's treasure."

"I know."

"You *do?*"

He grinned at her astonishment. "We're buying time is all. I spoke to Aiden. He knows you're aboard. He's not happy at the news."

"I know he must be angry. He has every right to be."

"There's something else." Harry straightened his shoulders, gazing at her in her boy's cap, her hair sticking out at odd angles, her jaw quivering slightly, but her eyes flashing. "There may not be another time to say the words."

She eyed him. "Yes?"

"Stop a moment and put your arms around me." She looked both ways to make certain no one watched, then did as he asked, kissing the swelling on his jaw, trying to ignore the shouts and thumps from overhead.

His breath came fast, and he hurried his words. "This is not something a man wants to say with his hands tied behind his back."

"What, Harry? What?" Her heart pounding, she moved a step away. Any second now Slayton could come roaring down the companion ready to kill them for their lack of haste.

"I love you."

Too shocked to speak, all she could do was stare at him.

"Your mouth is hanging open," he said with a smile. "You might like to close it."

Weak kneed and dizzy, she wanted to slide down the wall and sit crumpled on the planking, hugging his words to her heart. Or leap into the air and shout "alleluia!" at the sky. Instead, she stood limp and gape mouthed, her hair shorn, her boys' clothing soiled, her eyes filling with tears.

"I can't be hearing aright," she murmured.

The one man in the world whose voice and hands and smile thrilled her each time he spoke to her, or looked at her, or touched her face—this man *loved* her?

It was unbelievable.

"When you lie breathing in the night, the sound makes me happy," she whispered. "But the sound of this . . . what you just said . . . is more than—"

"You listen to me sleep?"

She nodded, shy at the admission. "Yes, always."

"Oh my love, if only I could hold you. I love you so."

She raised her eyes to his. "It's not possible. I'm so . . . you're so . . ."

He dropped a quick kiss on her open mouth. "If we live through this, I'll repeat those words to you every day for the rest of our lives. Now let's make haste. I have a yarn to spin."

Together, taking comfort in one another's closeness. they walked along the companion to the wardroom door. When they entered, Slayton acknowledged Harry with a growled, "You took your time gettin' here. I'm waitin' on your tale."

"May I sit to tell it?" Harry asked.

Slayton jerked his chin at a chair by the table. Harry sat awkwardly, his bound arms forcing him forward in his seat.

"Begin," Slayton ordered.

Harry eyed the pirate levelly. "If I do, what's in it for me and my crew?"

Slayton pounded the table, sending an overturned goblet crashing to the deck. "*Your* crew?" He leaned forward, his features twisted into a snarl. "Start talkin', or I'll tell you what's in it for Slayton's crew." He pointed a long, dirty finger at Abby. "For starters, I'll toss 'em this here Nancy Boy."

Harry darted a glance at Abby frozen in horror against the wardroom wall. He shrugged nonchalantly. "The lad's an innocent. You leave me little choice, captain."

"You're right there. So begin." Grasping the neck of a Maderia bottle, Slayton leaned back to listen.

"The treasure belonged to the Spanish king. At least it did after he stole it from the Indians," Harry added, a wry smile flitting across his bruised face. "Silver and gold. Tons of it, shaped into bouillon. His troops hauled it through Panama on mule back from Mexico. They were on their way to Cordoba aboard the *Montezuma*. Unfortunately, she was overloaded and sank in a hurricane off the Florida coast."

Slayton leaped to his feet sending his heavy chair crashing against the cabin wall. "This is your treasure? At the bottom of the Atlantic? Hell, man, I'll send you after it." He snatched up his knife ready to slash Harry's throat.

"Will that be all, captain?" Abby asked.

Both captains swiveled around in their seats, Tamworth white about the lips, Slayton with an oath, the knife in his hand now pointed at her. "Cheese," he said, "and bread. And send Leach in here."

She nodded, hurrying off without acknowledging the smile on Harry's face. How *could* he be amused? Out in the companionway, she crept back to the partially opened door to listen.

"There's more to my tale," Harry said.

"Aye, there better be."

"Before the *Montezuma* went down, she was, you could say . . . relieved . . . of part of her cargo."

"How much of it?"

"The stones. All of them."

"Stones? Speak plain, mate."

"Emeralds from the mines in Mexico. A sea chest full of them."

"Emeralds? They're better than gold. A chest full, you say?"

Harry nodded. "They're not cut, but once they are . . . the value goes beyond my knowledge to—"

"But not mine. Where are they hid?"

"Ah," for the first time, Abby sensed a hesitation in Harry's voice. A second passed before he answered. "Their whereabouts is known only to me."

What a clever liar Harry is. Buried treasure, indeed. What a ridiculous idea. She didn't dare wait to hear more. Bread and cheese Slayton said. But first find Leach. Her feet flew up the stairs. Then a thought gripped her heart, nearly stopping its beat.

Had Harry also lied when he said he loved her?

Chapter Thirteen

"**P**SST. GUY. GUY."

She had found the man named Leach and informed him Slayton awaited. Harried nearly beyond endurance, she didn't respond to the unfamiliar name.

"Abby." A mere whisper, but she heard and whirled toward the voice. "Aiden."

He looked dreadful. The brigands had ripped open his shirtfront. Searching for a weapon? Or coin? His lip was bruised and swollen. Blood dripped from a gash on his chin. He must have resisted. Aiden would, she knew. Worst of all, a manacle around his right ankle chained him to the main mast. A fireball from hell, the sun blazed down on his uncovered head. Like the rest of their crew huddled together on the deck, he was the picture of misery.

"We need water, Guy," Aiden said through parched lips.

She wanted to reach out and brush his hair back from his brow and kiss his bruised cheek, but she didn't dare. "First, I must get food to Slayton then I'll be back."

She risked a squeeze to his shoulder. He looked up at her with so much love in his face she wanted to cry but didn't. No time for that. She had to obey Slayton's command. The bastard, she'd rather kill him. As she raced across the deck slippery now with spilled food, she gasped out loud at her own evil thought.

Kill a man? Without regret. Without hesitation. How quickly she had lost her moral compass. Yet Slayton had had her in his clutches for only a few hours . . . she was no better than a pirate, no different. Though the idea didn't slow her running feet, it shocked her.

Should it? What of her own mam? Hadn't Grace killed a man? For good reason, she'd said, but he was no less dead for that. Would Harry love her still when he learned how his father had died? No, it was too much to expect. She'd have to keep the truth from him and make up for it by loving him without stint for their entire lives. She sighed as she raced along. Slayton waited. Their entire lives might last only another hour or two.

In the galley, Cookie tossed two loaves of flat bread and a great wedge of cheese into a rough-hewn basket. He didn't bother to hack off the green mold furring the rind. She hoped Slayton wouldn't object and backhand her for it. But she had no time to worry about that. She grabbed the basket and sped to the wardroom.

The men were deep in talk when she entered. In their eagerness to hear what Harry was saying, Slayton and Leach ignored her as if she were an insect. Slowly, she piled the food on the tabletop and listened.

"Where is this isle you're speakin' of?" Leach asked. "I never heard of her, and I've been roamin' these waters me whole life."

"If I could draw a map, you'd see the very place," Harry said.

"Boyo," Slayton shouted, as if noticing her for the first time. "Bring paper and quill."

"Where—"

"In my cabin, Guy, in the desk under the portholes," Captain Tamworth said.

"Aye, sir." Again, she scurried to carry out an order. Poor Aiden, he'd have to wait a while longer.

Despite her frantic haste and worry, she closed the door to Captain Tamworth's quiet compartment behind her with a sigh of relief. Everything was as it should be—the bunk unrumpled, the pillow and blanket folded in place, his clothes neatly hung from pegs along the wall. Even the sea chest containing the ship's store of medicines remained untouched, firmly locked. So the cabin hadn't been searched. The marauders had left it intact for their leader's use.

On the desk, she spied a quill and a small pot of ink anchored in its tiny well. The paper would be in the center drawer. She pulled it open and gasped. Paper in good supply and a dirk. A small shiny tool for slitting open documents. What a piece of good fortune. She picked up the knife and dropped it down the front of her shirt hoping to heaven she wouldn't slice herself accidentally.

Moving quickly, she pulled out a sheaf of papers, picked up the quill and lifted the ink pot out of its protective well. Careful not to spill it, she slowed her pace a bit, but not too much. To rouse Slayton's ire would be a mistake. Then for the second time in a few minutes, another thought seized her that was powerful enough to make her blood run cold. Once Harry had drawn the location of his treasure, would the pirates kill him?

As she came into the wardroom, Slayton eyed her hotly, his glance flicking over her for a long moment. "You were slow this time, me boy," he snarled. "It must be them mincin' steps you take, swayin' your hips, like." The wine had flushed his features and slurred his speech, but she was certain if he knew she were a woman, he would seize her.

"Leach," he said to his foul-smelling mate. "Cut his ties."

Harry's thongs fell away. He rubbed at his wrists, flexing the feeling back into his hands. Abby put the quill and the ink pot on the table by his elbow. When he reached for the quill, his fingers touched hers, a brief contact she found as comforting as a kiss.

"Get to it," Leach ordered.

Poised to escape the room, she had a hand on the door latch when Slayton barked, "Not so fast, boyo. Hustle your ass back to the captain here's cabin." He thrust a thumb in Tamworth's direction. "Me and the man have much the same heft, and I've a mind to buy meself some new rags." He laughed at his own humor, banging the tabletop with a closed fist. "Breeches I'm wantin' and a shirt. And smallclothes for a change, if they be not fouled." He glanced over at his crony. "What about you, mate? You fancy new rags?"

Leach guffawed. "Ye be the fop, not me."

Slayton grunted, his glance roaming over Abby once more. She prayed that wasn't suspicion about her true nature glinting in his eyes. There had been no chance to slip the weapon to Harry. And now another errand to run while Aiden perished from thirst. His suffering must be terrible. She had to get water to him and the others and fast.

The water. Of course.

Her blood quickened of a sudden, banishing the fearful chill from around her heart.

Dear God, why hadn't she thought of it earlier? But her elation lasted only a second before sinking to her shoe tops. Without Captain Tamworth's keys to the lock box, her idea meant nothing. And she didn't have a prayer of getting her hands on them.

Or did she?

Keeping her voice as noncommittal as she could, she said, "The captain's best clothes are locked in his trunk. I'll need the key." She stared at Captain Tamworth hoping to God he'd recognize her ploy and not blurt out that he kept his clothes hanging from pegs on his cabin walls.

A startled glance flashed over his face, but quick witted, he said. "I know the key. Shall I give it to the lad?"

"Aye." Slayton tossed him the key ring. The captain removed one and handed it to her. "Be quick this time," Slayton ordered.

"Aye, sir." *The pig.*

In the cabin, she grasped a white shirt, tucked, ruffled and starched to stiffness, and a pair of dark blue breeches of fine worsted wool off their pegs and dropped them on the bunk. Then, her pulses drumming in her ears, she bent down to insert the key into the lock box. One twist and it opened. Clean hose and smallclothes were kept there under a row of tightly corked bottles each one nestled in a felt-covered cubby for safe keeping. She removed the underclothes, tossed them on the bunk atop the shirt and breeches and picked up the vials. She tried to read two or three labels, but the words meant nothing to her.

Would she recognize the word laudanum? Was it spelled the way it sounded? Yes! The label on one vial read l-a-u-d-a-n-u-m in a fine, spidery hand. Only a tiny amount had been taken from it. Next to it she found a larger, fuller vial. She tucked them both in her breeches pockets then grabbed the pile of clothes. Without wasting another minute, she hurried back to the stateroom.

"Ah, finery fit for the gentry," Slayton roared when she came in with loaded arms. He lurched to his feet, laid his cutlass on the edge of the table top and stabbed both knives into the wood beside it where they quivered before coming to an upright stop. Disregarding the fastenings, he tore off his shirt and flung it away. He reached for the new one and struggled into it. Then he pushed his breeches down to his shanks before slumping his naked buttocks back onto the chair.

Abby gasped at the sight of his male organ but, with relief, saw it hung flaccid and useless.

Slayton chuckled at her quick, in-drawn breath. "Never saw one so huge, did you, boyo? Now for me boots. Off with them."

She knelt in front of him and grasped his right boot. One firm pull sent her sprawling on her back, the boot in her hands, a filthy, stinking foot in her face.

"The other," he demanded. She grasped his left boot and tugged hard with the same result. "Now, for me smallclothes and me hose."

Holding her breath from the powerful stench coming off his body, Abby helped him don his pilfered clothing. Good that she was familiar with a man's way of dressing, or ignorance might have given her away.

Leach grinned at the sight of Slayton in his finery, treating them all to a view of his mouth full of blackened teeth. Abby shuddered

"Throw me old rags overboard," Slayton ordered. "I want them be-gone." He turned his attention to his second in command. "Half of our men will stay here with me. You take what you need from the crew of this scow and make sail for Captiva. I'll meet up with you there. We leave as soon as me new map maker here tells me all he knows."

Then what? Would he kill him? Her stomach heaving, Abby bent to pick up Slayton's discarded garments. As she leaned over, she risked a quick peek at Harry. A smile, broad as ever, wreathed his face. Not to worry, he was saying, all would be well. Perhaps he was right. If she could get to a cask of water in time.

As she left with the reeking clothing held at arm's length, she heard Slayton say, "Tell of it once more, mate. How far along the shore is that cypress stand?"

Humph, Abby sniffed as she maneuvered the stairs, if Harry tells him a thousand times, the state he's in, he'll most likely forget. A good thing. It would buy them a little more time. Aft of the stateroom, she tossed the louse-infested rags overboard and watched them sink beneath the turquoise water. She hoped to God her plan would work. If not, she, too, might soon be sinking beneath the waves like a bundle of dirty clothes.

She wasted no time hurrying back to the galley. When the guard went up on deck to relieve himself, she whispered, "Cookie, you have salt pork on board?"

"Aye."

"Feed that to the brigands for the next meal."

Cookie yanked up his low-slung breeches with his elbows. "I decides the eats . . . me and the captain."

"The captain's no longer in charge. None of us is. Not even you."

"Sez you. What's a cabin boy know? I'm the 'ead cook 'ere, and don't you forget it."

"If you want to keep alive, you'll do as I say," she urged. "Make them drink deep." She held up the vials. "I'm poisoning the water."

Cookie's eyes bulged, and he scratched his bald scalp with the tip of his boning knife. "About that, I dunno."

"Lord Rushmount's drawing Slayton a map. When he gets his hands on it, he'll likely kill us all."

"But poison—"

"It's laudanum. A sleep potion only. Once Slayton's men are overcome, we can tie them up."

"I dunno."

"Cook your salt meat. Make them thirst." She put the vials back in her pockets and hurried to a small cask stowed in a corner. "This one's half empty. That'll make the potion strong. Help me open it. Hurry, before the guard returns."

Moaning and complaining all the while, he did as she asked, flipping the cork from the cask with the tip of his knife. She twisted off the top of a vial and poured its contents into the small opening. There was no way to tell how much would be needed for a sleep potion. She'd use it all. It was their only chance. The contents of the second vial followed the first into the cask. If the potion wasn't powerful enough to cause sleep, it might daze the rogues, making them easy to overcome. All except Slayton and Leach. They wouldn't touch the water, not while they had a ship's store of Madeira to themselves. But alone and drunk, they wouldn't be the same menace even with their weapons.

The dirk pressed hard against the flesh of her belly. She had to get it to Aiden and warn their crew not to touch the water.

"After the brigands eat the salt pork and beans, bring out this cask. And don't add any more water to it," she said, leaving before Cookie could protest further. She climbed the stairs to the deck quickly and efficiently like the boy they thought she was, blessing the breeches and low shoes that made movement so fluid. How could she ever go back to skirts and petticoats and laces? If she lived, it wouldn't be easy. But the word "if" loomed larger with every passing minute.

By the railing, Cookie's guard, a toothless old tar with matted, gray hair to his shoulders, came toward her buttoning his flies. He'd been pissing out of the wind, but she pretended not to notice. Her one ladylike act the whole day, she realized with a start. Civilization was only skin deep when the stakes were life and death.

She trudged the deck slowly, head down, avoiding the eye of anyone who might try to waylay her with a barked order. The ploy worked. She drew near to where Aiden sat still chained to the mast, but she blew out a sigh of disappointment. Two louts from the sloop had sprawled on the deck beside him, their knees tented, their guffaws soiling the air. "Captiva," she heard and "the Spanish whore." They were talking filth of the women on the island hardly able to contain themselves at what lay ahead.

Anxious, eyes darting, she fingered the knife hidden in her shirt. She needed to be careful. They'd be in worse danger than ever if the pirates suspected a plot.

Too close to Aiden to risk cutting his hands free, she slouched down next to a nearly unconscious young hand she had seen scampering up and down the shrouds earlier as if born to the task. Was that only this morning? She didn't know his name. No matter. "Are you awake?" she whispered. He didn't answer. She bumped her shoulder against him. "Are you awake, man?"

His eyelids flickered and closed again. "Aye."

Abby scratched at her mouth as she spoke so no one else could hear. "I have a knife. I'm going to cut your bonds and leave it with you. Free the man closest to you." His lids opened wide. "Pass the word. Don't drink. The water's poisoned."

He stared at her, his disbelieving eyes a pure, sky blue. "All of it?"

"No, the small cask Cookie will bring up soon."

She slipped the dirk from under her shirt. With one fast slice, she severed the thong holding his wrists together. "Take it," she whispered, thrusting the blade into his hands.

Inching along on her bottom, she put some distance between them before she stood and stared over at Aiden. She had no water for him. Did she dare approach him and tell him why?

"What're ye staring at?" the lout crouched nearest to him growled. "Tell Cookie to bring on the grub. The cap'n's not the only one with a belly."

"Aye," his companion snickered. "Get a move on, or I'll backhand ye on yer way."

She'd do what they asked, but first she'd risk a word in Aiden's ear. He had to know of the poisoned water. She stepped in close to him and bent down.

The fist shot out of nowhere. She never saw it coming, and before Aiden could give her warning, the blow sent her sailing across the deck and into the ship's railing.

In the bright daylight, stars exploded in her head. From a far distance, she heard Aiden cry out. Clear as a bell came his anguished voice, "No. Don't!"

Then the stars disappeared.

CHAPTER FOURTEEN

Someone had propped her up against the railing. Crouched in front of her, he was busily chaffing her hands. Who *was* that? She snatched her fingers free, slit her eyes open for an instant then quickly snapped them shut against the glare.

"Harry?"

"Yes, it's me," he said, his voice strangely excited. "Look around you, Abby. See what you've done."

What *had* she done? Cupping her forehead with a hand, she forced her lids apart.

The deck was strewn with sleeping men. Everywhere she looked, they lay sprawled about, groaning or snoring, arms and legs slumped on top of each other. The *Lady Anne's* crew was moving around the sleepers with lengths of rope.

"Step lively. Bind them all hand and foot." Captain Tamworth's raised voice reverberated around the ship. She couldn't remember ever hearing him shout so before. If only he wouldn't; the noise pounded through her head.

"Are all the brigands asleep?" she asked, her vision clouded with pain.

"Not all. Their skeleton crew on the sloop didn't drink from the cask. But they were no match for our lads."

"Slayton?"

"Bound. And gagged." Harry had a grin tugging at his lips. "I drew my map slowly while he drank himself into a stupor. And not from the water."

"No." The wardroom planking must be littered with smashed Madeira bottles.

Her head throbbed so much she was sure its pulse showed through her scalp. She sat up with care, fingering for the lump certain to be there.

"Ouch." Her forehead was swollen and tender to the touch.

Concern leapt into Harry's eyes. He leaned over and lightly stroked her hair back from her injury. She stiffened, glancing about. What if the men saw?

"No need to worry about keeping up your disguise, Abby. Our crew knows the truth about you. I told them everything . . . how you saved the ship and every man aboard her." He pulled her into his arms. "When I saw you lying there, I thought . . . I thought—"

"I was dead," she finished tartly.

He nodded. "That was my first thought."

"And your second?"

"I wanted to die, too."

"No." She shook her head, the slight motion instantly setting the whole world rocking. She closed her eyes. "You don't mean that."

"I've never meant anything more."

"But you wouldn't have. Died, I mean."

Stretching out his long legs, he leaned against the rail beside her and gathered her in his arms, easing her injured head onto his chest. "Suicide is a coward's act. I would have lived, but without a heart in my body, without joy, without purpose." His grip on her shoulders tightened. "Without you." He bent down to brush a kiss on her hair. "How can I tell you what I felt when I saw you lying here pale and unmoving . . . lifeless . . . will you open your eyes again, Abby?"

She risked raising her lids. The sunlight sparkling on the water turned each wavelet into a cascade of color that pierced her eyes with fire. She closed them with a sigh. "It's too bright," she murmured.

"When I thought I'd lost you, all that light turned gray. And so it would have remained for however long I lived." She could feel his breath warm on her cheek. "Do you understand?"

She nestled her face into his shirt front. It smelled of sweat and salt and something more—his very essence. "You must love me."

"More than I ever believed it was possible to love." He hesitated, a tremor coming into his voice. "I love you the way my father loved your mother."

"What?" Her eyes flashed open and her neck snapped back, sending shards of pain shooting through her head.

"I've no proof, but I've long suspected so. There was an Irish girl who once had the whole of Ballybanree enchanted. And my father as well, or so my mother surmised. Who else could that girl have been but the legendary Grace O'Malley?"

And she killed him.

Cradled in Harry's arms, hearing him whisper his love, the temptation to tell him what she knew of his father's death overwhelmed her. Yet she feared doing so. This love was too new, too precious to risk losing to old hatreds. But if she didn't tell him, she would have to live with the secret day after day and carry it to her grave. She clenched her jaw to kill the sob rising in her throat. It might be better by far to confess all in this instant. To strip away every barrier between them, to let nothing keep their souls apart, to let nothing fester.

Perhaps Mam and Da were wrong. Perhaps Harry could be trusted with the truth. Yes, better to tell him and waste no time in doing so. While the men hurried about the ship, setting the sails, racing to fill Captain Tamworth's shouted commands, in the midst of this chaos, she'd reveal everything . . . Aiden would help her. He knew about the deaths of his uncle Absalom and Lord Rushmount. And he knew why Chief Canonchet and Roger Williams had demanded public silence in the matter, a silence that had never been broken.

"Can you call Aiden to us, Harry? I would speak to him."

He held her tighter. "I can take you to him, but he can't speak to you."

"He's busy about the ship?"

"No. It isn't that, lass."

Lass? Coming from his lips, the word sounded tender, a cushion, somehow, for a blow to come. She drew away a little to peer up at his face. His expression was grave. "We can't wake him, Abby. He drank deep of the water. The warning never reached him."

Before Harry could stop her, she flung herself from his arms and stood, the ship reeling crazily at her sudden movement. She grasped the railing to steady herself.

"Where is he?" she demanded.

"Abby, wait." Harry scrambled to his feet and took her arm. "You can't help him. All we can do is wait and see."

A puzzled frown creased her forehead. "Wait for what? Tell me, for God's sake."

A terrible realization assailed her. "He won't . . . he hasn't . . .?" The image of Slayton's dirty clothes sinking beneath the waves flooded her mind, drowning every other thought.

Eyes brimming with tenderness, Harry shook his head. "He's still alive, but that's all I can tell you, Abby. We fear he may never waken."

"Where is he?" she repeated.

"In my cabin. We laid him on the bunk."

"I must go to him." She took a step and would have fallen but for Harry tightening his hold on her arm and pulling her to his side. "Help me below," she pleaded.

"Yes. Come."

Like an aged crone, she leaned on him as they wove past the busy deck hands, his body bracing them against the ship's sudden roll when a passing breeze caught the sails. She walked through brilliant sunlight without noting its glare or the relief offered by a few dark patches of shade, her mind only on Aiden.

Harry helped her slowly down the stairs. Outside the cabin door, he paused to take her in his arms. He tangled his fingers in her shorn curls, gently raising her face until her eyes met his. "What you'll see inside wasn't your fault, Abby." She tried to free herself from his grasp, but he held her fast. "Hear me through. If Slayton hadn't killed us all, he would have sold us."

"*Sold* us?"

"Exactly. Ship captains are always in need of extra hands. Many don't care how they get them." His eyes bore into hers. They were dark, penetrating, filled with tension. "There's something else. How long do you think you could have kept Slayton and the others from learning the truth about you?" He shook her shoulders a little. "Then what?"

Hardly feeling the jarring, she reached for the door latch without answering. He was trying to comfort her, but she'd have none of it. Aiden alive would be her comfort. "Let me get to him." She paused. "I would see him alone, please."

He released her with a sigh and stepped aside.

In the dim light from the small portholes, Aiden lay, as Harry had said, on the bunk stretched out on his back. Someone had folded his hands over his chest. She approached the bunk softly as if her footfalls might awaken him.

As peaceful as stone, and as unknowing, he didn't stir when she drew near. He didn't raise his head or smile at her in the quick, welcoming way he always had for the little sister who trailed him around the cabin and the yard and the fields and the woods . . . watching out for her, protecting her, guarding her from danger . . . she had come to resent his loving concern, his presence, his hovering about, always there hampering her movements.

Oh, Aiden. How wrong she had been. Her pulses throbbing at her temples, she bent over him and whispered his name. When he heard her voice, his eyes would flare open. The familiar white smile would wreath his face, and he'd stretch his arms, banging them on the low deck beam. Then he'd leap from the bunk, wondering what time of day it might be and why he had slept so long. But his dark skin was pale now, his lids closed. "Aiden?"

He hadn't heard. Louder, then.

"Aiden."

Nothing.

She grasped his folded hands and squeezed them. There. He had to feel that.

No?

His cheeks. First, she patted the left side, then the right. Again. Again. That failing, she shook him by the shoulders. He didn't move. She ran her hands over his body, pressing on him, jostling him, willing him awake. But he slept on.

One of his hands had fallen to his side. She picked it up and kissed each finger. He was cold. She reached for the blanket at the foot of the bed, raised it over him, and bent down to lay her head on his chest, listening for his heartbeat which she knew would be as steady as the rhythm of the tides. Earlier, when she had lain against Harry's chest, she had heard the pulse of life throbbing into her ear. Young and strong, Aiden's heart would sound alike.

Still on her knees, she eagerly sought the same music, but Aiden had no sound to give her. She must be listening in the wrong place. His heart must be more to the left.

No? Then to the right.

Higher?

Lower? *There.* Her face pressed to his chest, she listened eagerly, but the faint sound, like the beat of a distant drum, had disappeared. She fell to her knees by the bunk. He wouldn't waken for her. Why should he? She had poisoned him. If he died, it would be she who killed him.

If only she hadn't been so willful. If only she had stayed where she belonged, at home with Mam and Da, then Aiden would be awake and smiling, warming her life with his presence . . . better still, he'd have a life of his own to unfold and follow down through the years. If she had cheated him of that, how could she ever forgive herself? Guilt stronger than sorrow swept through her, the despair leaking from her eyes, running drop by drop down her cheeks.

"Abby."

In the room's quiet, the deep voice startled her. She drew in a breath and glanced over her shoulder. "Harry."

"Yes."

She pretended not to recognize the pity in his face. He rested a hand on her shoulder. "Come away now. You can do no more for him."

"Aye," she said bitterly. "I've done enough, haven't I? I can't rouse him."

"You did more than any man on this ship. When your story is told, and it will be, you'll be a fabled woman."

She reached for his hand. It was warm and alive, not like the cold fingers she had just kissed. "I must do something more, Harry."

He crouched next to her. "What do you want to do? I'll help you whatever it is."

"I want to stay with him tonight. I can't leave him here in the dark."

His eyes were luminous with love in the fast-fading light. "I'll keep the vigil with you."

"No, please. It's something I must do alone."

"But—"

"It will be for the last time. I'll never have the chance to be near him again."

"As you wish," he said, making no effort to touch her. "Till morning, then. Should you need me, I'll be outside the cabin."

From the tone of his voice, she feared her rejection had hurt him, but in that moment, unable to speak, she turned back to Aiden without answering.

HARRY HATED LEAVING HER ALONE WITH AIDEN'S BODY. She was so little, so vulnerable, so saddened. He wanted nothing more than to stay with her, cradle her in his arms, comfort her. But if he did, she would believe he thought her weak. He smiled at the idea. Weak? She was the strongest person he had ever known, and when she looked at him with those dark, liquid eyes, he knew passion ran deep within her.

Outside the cabin, in the companion, he sank to the decking. What was she going through in that room behind him? Agonizing over losing Aiden? Caressing his face, murmuring to him, trying in every way she could to express her love? His thoughts raced ahead, over the highway of the years to the time of his own death . . . Abby beside him speaking of her love, refusing to leave him . . . God, he was getting maudlin, but the kernel of truth in the dark path his thoughts had taken wouldn't fade. She would be steadfast for a lifetime, loyal and devoted, always giving the full measure of herself. Holding nothing back. In return, she deserved undying devotion. His devotion.

He glanced at the cabin door, hoping to hear a voice, but the silence remained unbroken. He heaved a sigh and leaned against the wall. This woman, this wonderful, giving woman, he would keep close for a lifetime. He wanted her. He needed her. And whether she knew it or not, the little hellion needed him.

Chapter Fifteen

From a long distance away, through fog and murky air, she heard her name spoken. Strange.

"Abby, wake up."

She tried to move, but her legs, stiff and cumbersome as lumber were useless, and a vicious pain danced in her head, kicking at her skull, her eyes, her temples.

"Abby."

The voice refused to go away and leave her in peace.

Eyes focusing, she gasped. *Aiden?* Her hand flew up to her mouth.

"Aiden?" she whispered, frightened, wanting to be sure he was real, not a ghost.

"Aye." Still lying on his back, he grasped her arm, a look of confusion on his face. "Where am I? What's happened?"

"You've been asleep here in Harry Rushmount's cabin."

From where he lay on the bunk, Aiden's gaze swept the dimly lit cabin—the pegs holding Harry's clothes, the desk by the porthole, the hammock piled in a corner.

"We overcame the brigands and seized their ship," Abby said.

The grip on her arm tightened. "How?"

"I poisoned the water." A sob caught in her throat. "I thought I'd killed you. But you're alive."

"Of a certainty, I am. Though when you wake in a private cabin you wonder." He laughed, rising a little on his elbows.

"You're positive all's well with you?" she asked, her voice riddled with concern though a quick glimpse at his eyes told her they were clear and focused.

"I've never felt better. Sure and I've had the sleep of my life." With one fluid motion, he flung off the blanket, stood and stretched. In the early dawn light, she could see the outline of his body arching, taut as a bow string before it relaxed, muscle by muscle. Then supple as a cat, he stooped and raised her to her feet.

The room reeled beneath her for a moment then steadied. "My head isn't right," she said, slumping onto the edge of the bunk.

"I would agree with that," he said, his bantering tone disappearing. "It hasn't been right for some time. Otherwise you wouldn't be a stowaway on a ship full of men." He yanked the desk chair across the room and sat facing her. "Now Mistress O'Donnell, explain. What in the name of all the Christs are you doing here?"

In spite of her pounding head, she half flew off the bunk. "Who do you think you are, speaking to me like that?"

He leaned forward and with a hand on each shoulder pressed her back, pinning her down. "I'm your brother in responsibility if not in blood, and I want a damned answer."

"I've been weeping for you all night," she said hotly. "Is this all you can say to me?"

He leaned even closer. "Oh no, I have more to say. Much more. But first, I want to get a good look at you. Where's the tinder? Don't move," he warned as he got up from his seat.

A few minutes of fumbling before a spark struck and flared. The lantern swinging abeam cast a soft golden glow in the shadowed room.

"Better," he said, resuming his seat, his eyes studying her in the lantern light. "Look at you? Are those my old breeches and shirt? And what happened to your hair?"

"It'll grow back," she said glumly, running her hands over her short curls.

His glance swept over her from head to foot. "This is what you wanted? To become a dirty-faced boy?" Anger flashed in his hooded, hawk eyes. "In your eagerness to become Guy and go adventuring, did you give a thought to Mam and Da? A single, God-damned thought?"

She flinched and looked away. "Yes, I sent Emma Harris to say I'd be with you. That I'd be safe."

"Ha, *safe*. They know life aboard ship. They must be frantic with worry. How could you have left them like that?"

Her gaze swung back to meet his own. "How could you leave your own blood parents to go hiding in the woods?"

He reared back as though she had struck him. It was a moment before he spoke. "I went in search of my father." His voice scratched. "My mother was dead when I left."

She sagged against the wall behind the bunk. "Oh, Aiden, I didn't know. You never said." Her eyes filled with tears.

"Some things are best left unsaid." He sighed and stood. "Enough talk of the past. It's now that matters. I worry for you. You've been my little sister since the day you found me dying in those woods. You saved me then, and from what you've just told me, you've saved us all this day as well. But at what cost to you?" His arms rose wide in an arc that encompassed all of her: her soot-stained face, her cropped hair, her soiled clothes, her dirty feet. "You've turned yourself into an unrecognizable hoyden. What now? What's to become of you?"

"Perhaps I can answer that."

Startled, they both whirled around. Harry stepped into the room, closing the door behind him. Relief shining in his eyes, he walked up to Aiden and clapped him on the back. "You've awakened, I see."

"Aye, no need to throw me overboard."

"Oh," Abby cried. "Like Slayton's clothes."

"What?" Aiden asked.

She shook her head. "Just a nasty memory not worth repeating."

Harry brushed her hair back from her face, kissed her cheek, and turning to Aiden, extended him an elegant bow. "We'll explain everything, but before we do, in the midst of so much happiness," he sent an arch glance winging over to Abby, "and in the unfortunate absence of your father . . . may I have the great honor, Master O'Donnell, of your sister's hand in marriage?"

"What?" Aiden's voice, usually so deep and resonant, rose an octave. "You want to *marry* her?"

"Very much."

Aiden's mouth fell open. "You're asking my permission?"

"Yes."

"Well you have it. Absolutely." Aiden gave Harry a resounding clap on the back. "Marriage. What a marvelous idea."

"My sentiment exactly." Harry beamed a smile at Aiden. "I'll have Captain Tamworth marry us. It'll be perfectly legal. Though after the ceremony, I'll ask you to vacate this cabin."

"You've no need to ask." Aiden's grin matched Harry's. "Besides, the lads must be missing my company below decks." He held out his hand in the direct, colonial way of greeting and Harry shook it, pumping it for all he was worth.

"'Tis a brother-in-law I'll be having. What do you know about that? I couldn't be more pleased with any turn of events." Aiden said, a deeper touch of the Irish returning to his voice as it always did, Abby knew, when he was moved.

Harry's grin grew broader. "Nor I."

"Well, I'm not." Staring up at two tall men while seated was a distinct disadvantage. Head reeling, Abby stood as quickly as she dared, and arms akimbo frowned first at one then the other. "You're both rattling on like two old matchmakers. Have either of you considered what my wish may be?"

Harry's jaw went slack. "But you showed every sign. . . I was certain . . . I . . . I thought you'd be pleased," he finished lamely, the smile leaving him.

"Aye." Aiden's glower of a few minutes ago returned in full force. "Don't create a problem, Abby, where none exists."

Sudden heat flooded her cheeks. A trouble maker is what she was in truth, always causing problems for those around her. She deserved Aiden's warning and almost decided not to speak. But her temper got the better of her. Chin up, she looked straight into Harry's eyes. The very next time they disagreed, she'd keep her peace she promised herself, but not this time. Harry Rushmount had best know the manner of woman he would take to wife. "I have never told you that I love you," she said.

He stared at her, baffled. "But you've given me every indication."

"Don't you want to hear the words before we marry?"

He glanced over at Aiden.

"I'll leave you," Aiden said, making for the door.

"No need," Abby replied. "I'm proud to say the words in front of my brother." She turned to Harry. "I love you, Harry Rushmount with all my heart, my soul and the body God gave me."

His face suffusing with pleasure, he took a step toward her.

She held up a palm. "But there are words I need to hear from you."

"I've already spoken of my love," Harry said, looking like he would never smile again. "You should have no doubt of it. None at all."

"I must go," Aiden said.

"No. Stay." Harry and Abby said in one voice.

Aiden inched toward the door. "The man's asked you to marry him, Abby. I'll go fetch the captain."

She shook her head. "That's the problem. I haven't been asked." She looked down at her begrimed fingernails. "Isn't it customary for the bride to also give her consent?"

"Egad, you're impossible," Harry exclaimed, picking her up and whirling her around in his arms. When, finally, he put her down, she would have fallen from dizziness, but he held her tight and kissed her, his mouth as full and warm and demanding as any woman could desire.

"I'm leaving," Aiden said.

"No," Harry fairly shouted. "Witness my proposal." He swept Abby a bow. "Mistress Absalom Grace O'Donnell, will you marry me and make me the happiest man on earth?"

"Yes and no," she said as primly as if the question had been posed by Old Granny Chase in the dame school.

"Abby." Aiden groaned and rolled his eyes.

"Harry, my love, my dearest, dearest love, there is nothing on earth or on the seas that I would rather do than marry you."

"Well then?" he growled.

"But not like this." She held her arms out by her sides inviting them to examine her. She glanced at Aiden, and though she wasn't in a smiling mood, the expression on his face made her want to smile. "You've already told me how dreadful I look, Aiden. You were right."

"You're beautiful to me in all your guises," Harry said. "Your clothes don't matter."

"They do to me. I'm not a boy. A dirty boy," she added ruefully. "I'm a woman, and above all, I want to come to you as one. I can't do so like this," she added, her voice breaking into a muffled sob.

She sank onto the bunk again, her head still pounding, her face, her feet, her clothes, her hair, all, all dirty. "There are no women's clothes on the *Lady Anne*, and even if there were, I have no money to purchase any."

"As far as there being no female attire on board the ship, you're correct," Harry said, looking for all the world like he wanted to laugh. "But as for not having the money to purchase them, you're mistaken. You're an heiress, Abby. *An heiress.*"

Chapter Sixteen

"T**hat's impossible**," A**bby protested.**

"No. It is not." Harry's eyes sparkled with humor. "Not when you have faith."

"You're jesting with me."

He wagged a finger before her eyes. "Would I do such a thing?"

"Yes."

He stretched a hand toward the door. "I invite you both to go up on deck and speak to the captain. Hear what he told me while the two of you were . . . ah . . . asleep."

Abby looked at Aiden who shrugged. "I know nothing of this." He darted a keen glance at Harry, "but I believe I'm following his drift. Go with the man, Abby. As for me, I'd best get back to my mates. The lads must be thinking I'll never wake up."

Puzzled by Harry's catlike grin, she stood unmoving.

"Aren't you the least bit curious?" he asked.

She nodded, the dizziness gone from her head, a mounting excitement taking its place. "I am. I'm fairly burning up with it."

"I thought you might be. And there's something else. I told the captain the truth about you."

"Good. I'm glad he knows." Her days as Guy were over forever, or they would be as soon as she could find some proper clothes. Though she would miss the freedom of breeches, it was time she looked like a woman again.

On the main deck, the buccaneers, bound hand and foot, sat muttering in the sun, staring as she and Harry made their way to the wheelhouse.

Astern, hard by their port side, was the rogue ship, her sails billowing nicely in the morning breeze.

"Who's manning her?" Abby asked.

"Master Johnson, with a few of our men as crew. Both ships are short handed, but Jamaica's less than a day's sail away." He squinted at the flawless blue sky. "If this weather holds, we'll be in Port Royal by early tomorrow." He grasped her hand and hurried her along the deck. "Now let's hear what the captain has to tell you."

"You're being very mysterious."

"I don't want to spoil the surprise. I love seeing you with your mouth agape."

"What a thing to say."

"I know. Wait up," he said, stopping mid-stride. "Our men need help, so I'll leave you with the captain. But hear me first. If it were solely up to me, the instant he had a free moment, I'd marry you. Boy's clothes or no boy's clothes." Before she could shake her head, he added, "But since you wish it, we'll wait until we make landfall. Either way, you're mine, little Guy. You're mine."

She eyed him, hardly able to believe that he looked at her, a dirty-faced boy to all appearances, with such love. "I've been yours since I first saw you on the Providence shore. The day you didn't lift a finger to help unload the skiff."

His expression clouded. "I didn't, did I? But I should have."

"I thought so at the time," she said, her mouth twitching with amusement.

"See how I've changed since meeting you? And we're not even wed yet. Once we are, I'll be unrecognizable."

"Oh Lord, I hope not. I love your faults," she taunted, letting the hint of a smile take the sting from her words.

"Faults?" he replied, miming an anger she knew he didn't feel. "I thought I was perfect in your eyes."

"How dull that would be."

"Indeed. So it's best you're not perfect, either."

She laughed out loud, loving the banter, loving the way the humor sparked in his eyes and lifted his mouth, a mouth that now dropped to hers, kissing her in sight of all.

A snicker rose up from the bound men.

"Look at that will ye? Two sodomites."

"Filthy buggers."

Harry kissed Abby again, so thoroughly she lost her breath for a moment.

The buzz rose higher.

"She's a girl, you swabbies. A girl!" Harry shouted, the triumph in his voice a trumpet call of sheer, exuberant joy. "And she put you where you are today. Snicker at that when you're in prison."

At the binnacle, the captain was busy charting their course, a burly young sailor at the wheel carrying out his quiet instructions. He'd put the pockets back inside his breeches, she noted, but hadn't resumed wearing his jacket. Maybe Slayton had donned it, or Leach. She shuddered. He'd hardly want it returned now.

"Captain Tamworth," she said softly.

He looked up, frowning at the interruption, but at the sight of her, the frown melted away. "Ah, Guy. Or should I say Mistress Abby O'Donnell?"

She nodded, flushing, as his stern gaze flashed over her.

He extended a palm. "As long as you're dressed as you are, let us shake hands man to man." She took his hand; it was the first time anyone had greeted her this way, and she liked the straightforward directness of it. To her surprise, though, he didn't let go of her fingers but clung to them, sandwiching her hand between both of his own.

"Every man aboard this ship owes you his life, Mistress O'Donnell. Are you aware of that?"

She shook her head. "You owe me nothing. I'm a stowaway."

"Aye. True. But your tale doesn't end there." He released her and pointed at their prisoners slumped together on the decking. "Once we reached this Captiva Island of theirs, God knows what would have become of us. Death or worse. There's no denying we're all in your debt." He cleared his throat. "As are the ship's owners. Along with our lives, Slayton would have claimed the *Lady* and her cargo. We were a rich prize, Mistress O'Donnell. A rich prize."

He studied the compass for a moment. "Two points east."

"Aye, sir." The seaman, his hands firm on the wheel, darted a quick glance at Abby. She warmed at the approval shining in his eyes.

"Thank, you captain, but if Lord Rushmount hadn't distracted Slayton with his map, I couldn't have moved about the ship as I did. Without that, I don't think—"

"Guy. Ah, Mistress—"

"Abby, please."

"Abby. Lord Rushmount's ruse of buried treasure kept Slayton from slaughtering us the moment his crew leapt aboard. Except, of course, for the few he would have kept alive to help sail the ship to Captiva. Either way, we were doomed. Harry bought us time, and you used it to the best of all possible advantages." For an instant only, his attention left her as his eyes sought the compass. "So all's well that ends well as the poets tell us, eh?"

"Yes, sir." She had known Captain Tamworth to be a man chary of words and those dry and to the point. Today, he was positively chatty. Why? Where was all this talk leading?

Feet apart, hands clasped behind his back, he said, "Are you also aware, Mistress O'Donnell, that aboard ship the captain is king?"

"I've heard such mentioned, sir, but I care not for kings."

"Ah, dangerous talk, but spoken like a true colonial. Well, be that as it may, on the open water my word is king. Will you accept that?"

"Certainly, sir."

"Good. So look astern. Go on, go on." He waved a hand. "Turn about."

To please him, she looked aft.

"What do you see?" he asked.

"I see our wake following us like a white path, and portside I see the rogue ship close by our stern."

"A pretty sight, is she not?"

"No sir, she's filthy and ill kept."

"True. True. But dirt can be washed away." He sent his gaze wandering over her attire.

Oh God, she was filthy and ill kept herself. She needed a tub full of fresh, warm water and a bit of lavender-scented soap. Given that, she'd soap herself everywhere and not come out of the tub until she was wrinkled all over like a prune.

"The dirt on her can be washed away, Abby," the captain said. "Her decks scrubbed till they're white . . . cats set loose to kill the rats . . . her hull scraped and painted, her sails mended. Do you see what I'm getting at?"

She shook her head. "Not really, sir."

"That sloop is a beauty in disguise . . . rather like yourself, if you take my meaning."

If only he'd get to the point he was laboriously trying to make. What did her dirty face and clothes have to do with a run-down pirate ship?

"This is a complex tale you're weaving, Captain. I'm afraid I don't understand."

He drew himself erect as befitted the bestowing of an honor. "As captain of this vessel, it is my determination to gift you in a way that recognizes your heroic action." He pointed a bony finger astern. "Because of you, that sloop is our prize, not the reverse. And from this day forward, it belongs to you."

As Harry had predicted, her mouth fell open. "But, but," she sputtered.

A rare smile warmed the captain's lips. "I'm sure the *Lady Anne's* owners will agree, though if necessary, I will convince them of that opinion. Without you, there would be no *Lady Anne*. You saved us, not once, Abby, but twice. You've earned your prize."

She blushed remembering the galley fire and the turmoil it caused. She wasn't worthy of such an honor. "Words fail me," she murmured. "I'm speechless."

"Once again, you demonstrate a rare female quality. My congratulations to you."

He swept her a bow, not nearly as elegant as Harry's, but filled, she recognized, with the same admiration she saw shining in the young seaman's eyes. It was a magnificent compliment, one well worth cutting off her hair for.

"Now that you have your ship, there's the matter of her name," Captain Tamworth said, obviously enjoying her stunned delight. "Petticoat really won't do,"

"No." She looked astern once more, watching the red taffeta flag wave from atop the sloop's main mast. "Once she's cleaned and made presentable again, there's only one name that would suit. Granuaile. I'll call her Granuaile."

His forehead puckered. "A strange name, I must say. Why that?"

"For my ancestress, sir." She hesitated. Should she tell him or not? Aye, she decided. No need to hide the truth. "She was an Irish pirate."

"Indeed?" A trace of disbelief lifted the captain's upper lip.

"Aye, sir. She robbed English ships to help her people."

"Good lord." The captain clapped his hands behind his back and frowned.

"She seized Spanish ships as well. When they invaded Irish waters."

"Spanish, you say?"

Abby nodded. Perhaps now he'd take back his gift. If he did, then so be it. Granuaile had been an extraordinary woman. She could never deny her kinship.

"Ah, well if this Granuaile, as you call her, went after Spanish booty, that's different. My offer still stands, Mistress O'Donnell." To her amazement, a twinkle lit up his eyes. "In fact, it's entirely fitting that the descendant of a pirate should own a pirate ship. Furthermore, in attacking the Spanish, your ancestress proved herself a patriot."

"My mother would agree, sir. Granuaile was a patriot, indeed." *For Ireland.*

Chapter Seventeen

Abby's feet fairly flew as she left the wheelhouse. When Mam heard a ship had been named for an O'Malley woman, she'd likely seize Da and dance a jig around the cabin. Never, not even in her fondest dreams, would Mam have expected to see the legendary Granuaile riding the seas once more. Mayhap this would help make up for all the heartache she had endured.

Abby hurried past the bound prisoners, ignoring their glares, but not the hot, parched look of them. Pirates or not, they sat in the fierce sun and would need water soon. Untainted this time. She'd fill a pail and give them swallows from a tin cup, though she should have asked the captain for his permission to do so. Truly, she should have asked him a score of questions, beginning with what she was going to do with a ship. Other than small personal belongings, she'd never owned anything. And now to think she owned a ship—a whole ship. The magnitude of the captain's gift would have her tingling for days.

"Abby, up here!"

She glanced up at the rigging, her heart leaping into her mouth. Harry was scrambling overhead on the ratlines as if born to the task. He could fall to his death. Aiden, too, grinned down at her from high on the main topgallant.

The sight of the two of them in harm's way unhinged her. That the men she loved were independent and took on dangerous tasks was one reason she loved them, but she didn't have to watch. She'd go below where she couldn't see their peril and find a bucket and some water. Later, she'd talk with Harry and Aiden about the ship. But for now, she'd do best to keep busy. One thing she'd learned about life at sea, the chores never ended.

In the galley, a sober Cookie was tending his fire efficiently, a boiling a caldron of beans and another of brown rice at the ready. She helped him carry the steaming kettles onto the deck where the crew could help themselves whenever they had a free moment to scoop up a handful of food.

"What about the prisoners?" Abby asked Cookie.

"What about 'em?"

"No food for them?"

Cookie grunted. "Eatin's a hard task with yer hands tied behind yer back, missy."

"Water then? Or they'll die in the sun."

Cookie shrugged. "That's no skin off me nose. Them's killers."

"Well, we're not," she replied, wishing she wore a skirt so she could twitch it in irritation as she walked off. She stomped down to the galley and after a little banging around of pots and pans, found a tin mug and a water bucket. Once she received permission, she'd slake the men's thirst. Why be afraid of them? Bound as they were, they couldn't harm her. Using the mug as a dipper, she had nearly filled the bucket when a shout came from atop the rigging.

"Land ho!"

That sounded like Aiden. Abby seized the bucket by the handle, dropped in the mug and headed for the stairs, water spilling onto her ankles as she ran. Could they be at Jamaica Island so soon? Early next morning is what Harry had said, but this day had not yet ended.

On deck, she risked a quick look up at the rigging. Aiden, hands cupped around his eyes, stared out over the water. Harry blew her a kiss from the yardarm above the mainsail, letting go of the shrouds with one hand to do so. She shuddered and shook her head, fear for him clogging her throat.

The sky, blazing with color—purple shot through with orange and turquoise—made a glory out of the late afternoon. The pirates, in their misery, their weatherworn faces darker than ever, sat listlessly, not seeming to have heard or taken note of the cry from the rigging, or of the beauty of the day.

At the portside railing, Abby put down the bucket and peered out to sea. Nothing but ocean to the far horizon. She crossed the deck, but even from starboard saw nothing but a scrap of sandy beach in the distance, little more than a low, treeless outcropping in the watery vastness. Surely this was not Jamaica. It was hardly worth calling attention to. She'd see about giving the brigands a drink, but before she could ask permission, a shout from the fo'c'sle stopped her where she stood.

"Mister Johnson, bring the prisoners out of the bilge."

The first mate hurried to carry out Captain Tamworth's order and within minutes, chains shackled to their ankles, hands bound behind their backs, Slayton and Leach were hauled on deck, beslopped with stinking bilge water and blinking in the light. At the sight of them, a mutinous murmur rose up from the other prisoners.

"Quiet there!" Captain Tamworth roared. "Bring them forward, Mister Johnson."

Prodded with cudgels, they staggered past their men, eyeing Tamworth warily.

"Avast," Johnson said at the foot of the fo'c'sle stairs.

Above them, disgust clear on his face, Captain Tamworth stared down at the sorry pair glaring up at him. "You're in luck today, Captain Slayton."

"So you say," Slayton snarled. Hampered by his shackles, he half turned toward his crew. "Do I look like a lucky bloke?"

Hoots and catcalls met his jibe.

"One more outburst, Slayton, and I'll have you gagged." Captain Tamworth let his eyes wander over the prisoners. "Now hear this, all of you. I'm within my rights to hang your captain and his mate from the yardarm. Every man of you knows it. But I choose not to do so." He shifted his gaze downward to the two shackled men. "You hear me, Slayton? I'll not hang you."

The pirate chieftain raised sullen eyes to Tamworth. "Aye. You be a saint."

A guffaw from the bound men.

"Laugh at this, then," Captain Tamworth said, his tight jaw alone revealing his anger. "I'm freeing your captain and his mate."

A roar of approval met his words.

"If any of you lads care to join them, speak up. Freedom is yours."

Other than quiet mutterings and the creaking of the sails, the ship fell silent at the hidden menace in his offer.

"No one? I thought not." An icy satisfaction chilled Tamworth's voice. "Captain Slayton, you see that spit of land lying off our starboard beam?"

Stiffness in his neck and reluctance in his every move, Slayton glanced over his shoulder then back at the captain, a sudden realization dawning on his face.

"Aye, you're going to swim for it. You, too, Mister Leach."

"There's sharks in that water," a prisoner called out.

"Aye, I spied fins a while ago."

"I thought you was a saint," Slayton said, rattling his chains in a show of defiance. "Now you're feedin' us to the bloody sharks."

"Swim fast," Tamworth said, his eyes stone cold, one side of his mouth lifting in a half smile. He sent Mate Johnson a curt nod. "Release them. One at a time."

Johnson pointed to Slayton. "Unchain his legs," he said to a crewman who hastened to do his bidding. "Now cut his hands loose." Musket cocked, Johnson marched the pirate chieftain to the rail.

"Captain Slayton," Tamworth called. The pirate turned to him, a spurt of hope leaping into his eyes. "My doublet, if you please."

Clutching the empty tin cup, Abby wasn't sure she heard him aright. The garment would be crawling with fleas by now. Why would he want it?

"You'll swim far better without it hampering your movements," Tamworth said lightly. "If your good luck holds, Captain Slayton, a passing ship will find you in a few days, or a few weeks, or a few months. Keep a weather eye out for one."

He's enjoying himself, Abby realized. Calm, bloodless, correct at all times, the captain was playing with men's lives and loving every move of the game. The spit of land lay a good distance from the ship. Reaching it would be a challenge even for a strong swimmer. Wine soaked as they were, she wondered if the two rogues had a chance of succeeding and knew the captain and crew of the *Lady Anne* cared not a whit.

"The coat," Captain Tamworth said.

Mate Johnson prodded Slayton with the musket barrel.

"Good riddance to your rag," Slayton shouted. He shrugged out of the garment, swung it in a wide circle overhead and flung it into the sea.

A loud burst of laughter rose up from his men.

"Send him after it, Mister Johnson." Tamworth's voice was calm.

Two of the crew seized Slayton who struck out kicking and howling. "I can't swim. I can't swim."

Without a word, the sailors lifted him and threw him overboard where he fell with a splash and a shrill scream.

The mate looked toward the fo'c'sle. Captain Tamworth merely nodded. Leach was quickly relieved of his bonds and pitched into the sea, kicking and howling as loud as his master.

Bent far over the railing, Abby watched the two men sink below the waves like the dirty bundle of clothes she had cast overboard that morning. Her heart in her mouth, she gripped the edge of the rail. In a moment, sputtering and gasping for air, one dark head emerged from the depths and then, and then, *yes*, another.

They struck out, the two of them, for the spit of land in the distance. Shielding her eyes from the lowering sun, she watched them slice through the waves. So Slayton had lied; he could swim after all. But whether he and Leach would reach the islet safely, she might never know. Nor whether they would find water on that barren stretch or shelter from the sun.

She glanced up at Harry and Aiden still hanging onto the rigging. From so high, they must be able to see the swimmers clearly. She caught Harry's eye. He shook his head. One, or both, wasn't going to make it to safety.

And then she saw why not. A fin sharp as a razor was cutting through the water toward the struggling men. *Oh no.*

"Watch out, Slayton! Shark in the water," a crewman shouted. "Shark comin'. Shark in the water!"

With a splash and a scream, in a shower of spume, a dark head disappeared beneath the surface. Cupping her hands against the glare, Abby peered out over the waves, but which of the two had been struck, she couldn't tell, only that now just one dark head remained above the water, its owner paddling furiously toward the scrap of sand.

At the prow, his expression unreadable, Captain Tamworth followed the struggle of the remaining swimmer. She knew the captain to be a kindly man, yet he had sent the two pirates to almost certain death without, apparently, a single qualm. Life was difficult everywhere on earth, but she was beginning to believe it was more difficult at sea than anywhere else. Maybe even worse than the Ballybanree Mam had told her of.

With a heavy heart, Abby picked up the bucket of water and moved among the parched men, not asking for the right to do so. Captain Tamworth's benevolence had been exhausted. She'd do what she could without asking. Let him stop her if he would. But he did not, and she kept on, holding the cup to the men's lips as if they were babes. A few thanked her, a few muttered curses, but not one questioned whether the water be tainted or not. Perhaps they wished it were, so they could sleep away their misery.

She'd filled and emptied the pail three times, her back aching with the effort of lifting and stooping, when a hand fell on her arm. She swiveled her gaze up to its owner.

"Harry, thanks be to God, you're off the rigging."

"I am," he replied, his smile whiter than ever in his bronzed face. "You're sunburned," he said.

"And you. But why, Harry, why?"

"Why the sunburn? Or why something else?"

"Please don't jest, love. Why were the brigands thrown overboard? Most likely they've drowned. Why were they not brought to justice in Jamaica? You said we'd reach the island by daybreak."

Harry tugged on her sleeve. "Come with me where we can be alone for a bit." Their eyes met, and hand in hand they hurried to his cabin.

With the door bolted behind them, he took her in his arms and kissed her. They were urgent, hungry kisses, and her lips opened, ripening under the heat of his mouth.

Finally, to slow the wild beating of her heart, she put her hands on his shirt. "I would speak seriously to you."

Keeping her tight inside the circle of his arms, he brushed her earlobe with his lips. "Slayton's fate troubles you?"

"Yes."

He shrugged. "Slayton and Leach were given a chance. That was more than they would have given us."

She loosened herself in his embrace. "That doesn't answer why? Why were they not brought to Jamaica?"

"Because rogues use the island as a home base. They mostly go after French and Spanish ships, but still, the justice meted out there cannot be entirely trusted."

"Then why are we going there? I don't understand."

"Can you sit by me?" he asked, drawing her to the bunk. As she nestled beside him, he said "We're going to Jamaica to trade for rum. Port Royal is under English rule. We're an English ship, so chances are strong the rogues won't bother us and risk losing their safe haven. We won't linger long in any case. Just long enough to complete our business." His arm stole around her waist. "All of it." She leaned into him and stroked his arm. "All of it," he repeated.

"You'll not know me in girl's attire."

"You're wrong, little Guy. I'll know you in any guise, in any land, in any clime."

As she would know him. "But if Jamaica is held by England why wouldn't—"

"Slayton be brought to justice there?"

"Exactly."

"The governor of Jamaica licenses privateers like Slayton to assail enemy ships. He shares in the profits."

Abby stiffened. "We're not an enemy ship. You and Captain Tamworth . . . the entire crew . . . why, as you've just said, you're all English."

"True, but what if Slayton were to lie, tell the governor he intended all along to divide the spoils with him? Would the governor be disposed to hang him then turn the *Petticoat* over to—"

"The *Granuaile*."

"What?"

She shook her head. "I'll explain later. Please go on."

"If Slayton had reached Captiva, it's highly doubtful the governor would ever have learned of our capture and profited from it. But if we brought Slayton in, you can be assured he would have lied to the governor's face. Told him he never intended to cheat him, didn't know we were an English vessel . . . anything . . . to get his way." Harry kicked off his shoes, stretching out on the bunk with a sigh of content. "On the other hand, since we bear an English license, the governor may have had no choice except to rule against him. Nevertheless, Captain Tamworth sought his own brand of justice. He didn't want to risk having the man set free and his ship returned to him."

Her shoulders sagging in fatigue, Abby slumped forward on the bunk. "So what man can be trusted?"

Harry rose on an elbow. With a finger under her chin, he turned her face to his. "I can be. You can trust me with your very life. That's what husbands are for." He dropped back on the pillow, a sudden grin lighting his face. "And for more, of course. Far more." He patted the bunk beside him. "Lie with me for a while. I have middle watch tonight, from midnight to four in the morning. I must be alert for that."

She wanted to. They had never lain together side by side, feeling the length of each other's bodies hip to hip, thigh to thigh. It would be wonderful, yet she hesitated. They had waited thus far. A few more hours and they'd be on land and would promise each other a lifetime of love. That moment shouldn't be rushed. It was too precious.

Still she hesitated and sat unmoving except for her eyes that swept over him, over his long, rangy legs, his narrow hips and concave belly, over the powerful sun-browned arms folded on his chest, over the full lips she knew to be warm and soft, over the perfectly placed mole above them . . . over the luxuriant lashes sweeping his bronzed cheeks. They were beautiful, long and lustrous.

She blinked. Ah, no, he couldn't be. To be certain, she leaned in closer, her breath fanning his cheeks, fluttering his lashes. True enough, he was sound asleep, unaware of her presence, resting as peacefully as a babe in his mother's arms.

For a long while, she sat quietly beside him loving him with her eyes until with a sigh, whether of relief or disappointment, she couldn't be sure, she got up and covered him with a light blanket. Then without making a sound, she slung the hammock across the cabin from its wall hooks. Now to climb into the tippy pouch, hoping she didn't flip out the other side and land on her rump with a loud bang.

Even if she could manage to stay in the confounded contraption, she knew sleep was impossible for her tonight. Tomorrow, she'd have her first sight of a tropical island, an adventure few people in the world got to experience. There would be so much to tell Mam and Da when she returned to Providence some day.

Her heart slowed its beating for an instant.

Some day might never come.

CHAPTER EIGHTEEN

Emeralds, Abby had heard, were of a brilliant green hue. Were they as beautiful, she wondered, as Jamaica Island lying in the ocean before them like a vivid green jewel? The early morning light revealed the island to be hilly, much like Providence, though with the coming of winter, the hills of home would be barren now. Here all was sunshine and warmth and soft, perfumed air.

"A lovely place, this Jamaica," she said to Harry who stood by her side at the railing. As the capstan lowered the anchor, its creaking vied with the cawing of gulls and the splash of waves on the shore. She pointed toward the land. "Oh, look, the houses are nestled on the hills, much like at home. Yet so different, somehow." She clapped a hand to her mouth. "They have no walls."

"Aye, they do," a seaman said, coming up to them. "They're shutters. They open and close as the weather dictates."

"Shutters from ceiling to floor?" Abby asked. "How amazing. Like moveable walls."

He nodded. "They're seldom needed. Except when the rains come."

"You don't even need walls here. Why it's a paradise," Abby said.

"With all due respect, mistress, I doubt you'll find it so, but it has its compensations." He winked at Harry, adding, "The captain would have a word with both of you."

"I know what he meant by compensations," Abby said with a sniff when the man walked off.

"You do, do you?"

"Yes. So you can wipe that smirk off your face, Harry Rushmount."

"No Jamaica compensations for me then, little wife-to-be?"

She smiled into his eyes. "Many, my love. Many. But I hope not those the crewman hinted at."

"They're not the ones I'm panting for." He took her arm. "Come, the captain awaits."

They found him by the bow, his attention focused on the *Granuaile*. First Mate Johnson, about to berth her alongside the *Lady Anne*, was busily directing his short-handed crew in furling the tattered sails and lowering the anchor. Up close, the ship looked as dreadful as when the rogue captain had commanded her. Her paint peeling, her fittings dull, her deck littered with trash. The vermin about such a vessel must be fearsome. Abby shuddered as she studied her prize.

"Ah, young Rushmount and Mistress Abby. Good. Good." Captain Tamworth, looking pleased to see them, pointed a finger at the sloop. "Your ship has arrived safely. Mate Johnson's a reliable man."

"Yes, sir," Abby said, "but I lay awake a good part of the night, wondering what on earth I'll do with a ship. Not that I'm not grateful to you. I am, very, very grateful, but—" She raised her arms then let them fall to her sides.

"May I intervene?" Harry quietly asked, a trace of amusement in his tone.

"Of course," Tamworth and Abby answered in unison.

"It's clear the sloop needs refurbishing. Not only to bring out the beauty of her sleek lines," he darted a humor-filled glance at Abby, "but to make her sea worthy. Judging from the sorry state of what we see, I can only imagine the condition of what lies below the water line."

"You echo my own thoughts," Tamworth said.

"Then you agree she should be careened and thoroughly overhauled?"

"I do, indeed. It's the most sensible course to take."

Harry nodded. "Once that's done, I think Abby will find a very good use for her prize."

"Excellent." Captain Tamworth cleared his throat. "But as to the cost of this refurbishing . . ."

"That will come from my share of the *Lady Anne's* profits," Harry said.

"But—" Abby began.

"It's the only way," Harry said. "And a fine investment. For I'll expect to be repaid. In full."

Heat rose into Abby's face. She knew the payment he had in mind wouldn't be made in coin.

"You will be paid, my lord. In full," she replied gravely, her cheeks on fire, for truth be told, she could hardly wait to begin settling her debt.

Captain Tamworth cleared his throat a tad louder than necessary. "There's also the matter of a crew. You might have trouble securing enough men to sail her. That lot," he pointed his chin at the prisoners still tied in place, "aren't used to working for a seaman's wages. They're buccaneers. They'll expect a share of the spoils."

"Spoils?" Abby asked.

"A mere figure of speech, my dear," Captain Tamworth replied. "The profits, I meant to say."

"Then why not give them a share?" Abby's words tumbled out as the idea seized her. "When I walked among them yesterday and again this morning with cups of water, some of them thanked me kindly. Is it possible that given a chance to be honest seamen they would be?"

"Could they be trusted?"

"I don't know," Abby replied. "But as you pointed out, captain, the *Granuaile* can't sail herself."

"My soon-to-be wife is fast becoming a merchant princess," Harry said.

Abby looked up quickly. Though amused, his tone suggested something else as well. Dismay, perhaps. The women in his family never immersed themselves in talk of ships and trade as she was doing . . . mayhap dismay *was* what she heard in his voice. For despite his obvious pride in her, she had violated a code of behavior he had been raised to admire. A sigh of frustration escaped her. She hadn't been born an aristocrat but the daughter of a colonist who worked for his bread. Yet what was trading if not work? And what was Harry himself if not a trader? The thought pleased her. If they were both traders, would they not be equals in fact if not in station? For that possibility alone, she would treasure the *Granuaile* forever.

"Before we do anything about the sloop, however," Harry said, "we have an urgent request."

"Yes, urgent," Abby echoed.

Harry reached for her hand and placed it over his arm. "Mistress O'Donnell needs to revert to her true identity. She requires a lady's dressing room and a change of clothing."

"And a bath," she interjected.

"For me as well," Harry said, all signs of troubling thoughts gone from his face as if they had never been. "In short, captain, we need lodgings. And later in the day, at sunset, perhaps, will you perform our wedding service?"

Captain Tamworth bowed from the waist. "I'll be honored to do so. And I have just the place for you to lodge. The governor's palace."

As the captain walked away to order the lowering of the skiff, Abby dug her fingers into Harry's arm. "I can't go to the governor's palace. I'm too ashamed."

"Oh?" Pretending offense, he gazed at her along his straight, aristocratic nose. "You are my betrothed. As such, you can go anywhere with aplomb."

She shook her head. "No."

"Yes. You saved a ship, its cargo, and the lives of scores of men. What do your torn clothes matter?" His eyes swept over her, a grin threatening to surface and mar his haughty expression. "Or your dirty face? Or your short, very short hair? Or your—"

She put her hands over her ears. "Stop."

"Besides," his said, his grin breaking free, "you're not too ashamed to meet the governor in your . . ." he held up his hands, palms out as if words failed him, ". . . current state. You're too proud to do so."

"Shame and pride are two sides of the same coin."

"Marvelous. I must write that down when I'm back at my desk. In the meanwhile, I have a gift for you. Something from Aiden. It might make you feel better." Reaching into his doublet pocket, he withdrew two shining coils of plaited red hair.

A gasp caught in her throat. "My hair! But I thought you tossed it into the sea."

"I was about to, but Aiden knew how much I hated to part with it, so he hid it. If the plaits were found, he planned to say he'd scalped a colonial woman."

"Aiden? He wouldn't hurt a flea."

"You're wrong there, my love. Men do what they must. Surely this voyage has taught you that for a fact."

She nodded, took the plaits without a protest, and dropped them into her breeches pockets. What he said was true. Had the laudanum the power to do so, she would have killed every man who drank of the tainted water. Nor would she have suffered a pang of conscience. But not for gain. Not for greed . . . still, in acting as she did, she had placed her own life and the lives of those she loved above all others. That had to be a violation of God's law, but what means did she—

A sailor came hurrying along the deck. "Lord Rushmount, the skiff's ready."

Harry extended an elbow. "Shall we see what enticements Port Royal has to offer?"

"You're sure?" she asked, glancing down at her soiled boy's clothing.

His bantering stopped abruptly. "I would proudly take you anywhere in the world, Abby."

"In that case, yes," she said, her spirits buoying. She had seen no place but Providence her whole life. What would Port Royal be like? Brimming with excitement, she could hardly keep her shoes from tapping the deck planking. "What of Aiden?" she asked. "Can he join us?"

"He's needed aboard ship, but he'll be with us at sunset."

"In time for our marriage?"

"Yes. His exact words were, 'Sure and I wouldn't have it any other way.'"

Nor I, thought Abby, joy filling her heart at the future spread before them like a wondrous, God-given feast.

WITH TWO SEAMEN AT THE OARS, THEY RODE TO SHORE in the skiff with Captain Tamworth, pulling up to a wooden wharf in front of the largest building Abby had ever seen. Made entirely of red brick, it presented a windowless wall to the shore, the opposite of the airy structures on the hillsides.

The men secured the boat to a piling. Gripping Harry's hand, she stepped onto the wharf, the solid, unmoving surface a strange sensation under foot after days on the rolling sea. They walked around the enormous building and saw that the side facing the town boasted double oak doors wide enough to drive a horse-drawn wagon through them. Two armed men stood by the doors, as alert as soldiers, muskets at the ready.

"What manner of building is this?" Abby asked.

"The rum warehouse," Captain Tamworth said. "Liquid gold it's called and guarded day and night." He looked about, frowning as he searched for a familiar face. Seeing none, he said, "The governor apparently knows nothing of our arrival. Ah well, we'll excuse him. It's still early in the day. Come, follow me. We'll inform him of our presence and have him remove Slayton's men from the *Lady Anne*. Her decks are overdue for a scrubbing."

"And those men are overdue for a meal," Abby said.

Tamworth stopped mid-stride. "No need to pamper them. Men like that respect only one thing, a firm hand. Nothing else keeps them in line."

She met his irritated stare without flinching. "What of kindness?" she asked softly.

"Bah, they'd see that as weakness."

For the first time since the voyage began, she doubted the captain's wisdom, but this was not the time for sparring, not when she was on fire with excitement at the wondrous sights she'd soon behold.

The odor is what she noticed first. In the heat of the tropical morning, piss and rotten fruit and the scent of exotic flowers mingled in the air, strong enough to take her breath away. And the noise assailing her ears was fearsome. No wonder. On the upper balconies of the stone houses lining Port Royal's narrow main street, people sat eating and drinking and calling down to passersby. They spoke in English and a cacophony of languages she'd never heard before. And everyone was talking at once—the people crowding the balconies, the passersby, the merchants hawking goods from overflowing baskets, even to her amazement, a brilliant bird, feathered in red and green with a great yellow beak. Perched on one merchant's shoulder, it screeched, "More rum, matey. More rum."

How strange. In Providence, the wooden houses stood apart from their neighbors, each on its own bit of land, their doors and windows nearly always closed, the people circumspect, going about their business quietly.

At a corner, a barmaid, her white bosom swelling over the top of her bodice, sold rum by the cupful. She was doing a lively business. Coins rattled noisily onto the barrel top she used as a store. As she bent to pour a mug of rum, a customer dropped a coin down the hollow between her breasts, pawing her as he did so.

Abby drew in a sharp breath. Wouldn't Emma Harris be taken aback at the sight? And Mam? Why, she'd be outraged.

"One of the compensations, no doubt," Harry said wryly.

"No doubt," Abby replied, hoping her prim response gave no indication of how she longed to have Harry's long, lean fingers touch her in much the same way.

She shivered in the heat, glancing away from the barmaid to a girl selling exotic produce heaped high in wicker baskets. Abby recognized the oranges. Once or twice, she'd been given an orange at Christmas time, but never the long yellow fruits that looked like fingers, or the hairy brown globes the shape of a man's skull and just as hard.

"They're nuts," Captain Tamworth told her. "Coconuts. Their fluid sweeter than a mother's milk."

"Ah, that's—" Abby began.

Without warning, he said, "Step aside. Be quick."

Harry yanked her into a doorway as a group of men came marching down the center of the street toward the wharf, not caring who scurried out of their path, or what goods they toppled from the baskets and stalls. As they passed by, Abby gasped, shocked wide eyed. Guards in front and behind were force marching a half dozen of the blackest men she had ever seen. Chains suspended from leather collars around the prisoners' necks tethered them together. More chains on their ankles forced them into an awkward shuffle. One of the black men slipped on the uneven paving stones. A vicious yank on his neck chain pulled him upright. For an instant, hatred flared in his face and then like the others, he struggled on, head down, the life force gone from his eyes.

What breed of men had such dark skin, Abby wondered, and what terrible crimes had they committed to be chained together so? She had no chance to ask, for Captain Tamworth stopped suddenly in front of a large stone house at the end of the crowded main street.

"The governor's manse," he said, rapping on the door with the heel of his hand, "where I trust we'll be as welcome as flowers in springtime."

Abby's heart pounded as they waited for the door to open. After all of Mam's warnings, she would soon be the guest of a nobleman. What would Mam say if she knew? Worse, what would she say if she knew she was about to marry one? With a silent sigh, Abby dismissed the question from her mind. She already knew the answer.

Chapter Nineteen

THE MAN WHO CAME TO THE DOOR had glistening ebony skin and, at
the sight of Captain Tamworth, a grin that split his face in two.

"Captain Tamworth, sir. The governor will be pleased to see you."

"Thank you, Caspar, but I'm not alone. Two guests accompany me."

"Yes, sir." Caspar held the door wide open but came close to shutting
it in Abby's face as she stepped forward, dirty and unkempt in her boy's
guise.

"It's all right, Caspar," the captain said. "If you will inform your master, I'll explain all to him."

Dignified in a white shirt that flowed about his wrists, dark breeches
and soft-soled shoes, the butler relented enough to usher them into a
front parlor. His sense of propriety obviously offended, he gave Abby
a cool appraisal before leaving, stiff-backed, to inform the governor of
their arrival.

"I do look terrible," Abby said painfully aware, in this lovely room
with its soft cushioned seats and polished mahogany tables, of her broken nails and shorn hair.

She ran her fingers through her curls and straightened her spine. At
the moment, nothing could be done about her appearance, so she'd just
face the governor with a smile, pretending she wasn't embarrassed.

"Sit next to me, Abby," Harry said, sending her a wink. He patted the
sofa cushion with maddening good cheer. "It's more than wide enough
for a grown man and a small lad."

"Please, don't. I'm not ready for jesting."

"You soon will be. You'll see."

Fearing her dirty clothes would soil the elaborate silk, she sat gingerly on the edge of the seat beside him.

"Ah, Tamworth," a smooth voice murmured, "so pleased to see you once more."

He was a resplendent sight, in a brocade frock coat of a lustrous green fabric Abby couldn't name, pale breeches and stockings, and shoes with unbelievably high heels. A white wig topped his head, the curls cascading in tight rows to his shoulders.

He has more hair than I do, she thought, appalled, as the men rose to greet him. The captain said, "Governor Hender Molesworth, may I present my colleagues in my current endeavor? Lord Harry Rushmount and Mistress Abby O'Donnell."

"My Lord, I'm honored." Governor Molesworth inclined his head in a token bow. Harry stood and returned the gesture.

"Mistress O'Donnell, a great pleasure." With a quick, barely observable flicker of his eyes at her appearance, the governor took her grubby hand and bent over it as if greeting a queen.

She wanted to die.

After lightly brushing the back of her hand with his lips, he straightened, looking her full in the face with questions in his eyes.

"You find me in a sorry state, sir," she managed to say.

"I know the hazards of the sea and the stories it inspires. Your . . . ah . . . costume suggests a fascinating tale," he said. "I look forward to hearing it, but first, please tell me, how may I serve you?"

Abby, thunder struck, knew her jaw had fallen open. He was greeting her with total acceptance, the last thing she'd expected. Mam, she was certain, would never believe it. She wanted to leap up and kiss him but was unable to move a muscle or say a single word.

"Mistress O'Donnell has come through an ordeal with great bravery, governor," Harry said, sitting back beside her, putting an arm about her waist. "I'm sure she'll be happy to tell you of it, but first, on her behalf, may I ask that a bath be readied for her? Also she does require women's clothing. Hopefully, it's attainable."

"My dear," the governor took both her hands in his, "it will be my pleasure to grant your requests."

Abby sent a startled glance at Harry whose face was wreathed with an I-told-you-so-grin. Heels clicking on the hardwood floor, the governor stepped to the mahogany door and opened it. Outside, in the central hallway, Caspar stood waiting, his bearing as alert as if he were guarding the warehouse.

"Send Mattie to me," the governor said.

Caspar slipped away on silent feet. A few moments later, a young woman with skin the color of light Jamaican rum, in a neat housewife's frock of gray, a white turban covering her hair, appeared in the doorway.

"Ah, Mattie. This is Mistress Abby O'Donnell."

To her credit, Mattie's expression didn't change a whit.

"Mistress O'Donnell requires a bath and clothing. Show her to the blue bed chamber and see to her needs whatever they may be."

"Yes, suh." Mattie said, her voice, like her complexion, mellow and rich.

IT HAD TO BE THE MOST BEAUTIFUL BED CHAMBER EVER CREATED. As soon as Mattie left to prepare her bath, Abby explored every inch. Floor to ceiling shutters opened onto a balcony overlooking a quiet garden lush with fragrant, tropical foliage. To her delight, the walls between the white shutters were painted a pretty sky blue. There were few painted walls in Providence. Paint, she knew, was fiercely expensive.

She moved about, examining one lovely object after another—the chest of drawers with intricate brass pulls and a glass mirror above it, the pale-hued rug, so luxuriant underfoot, the pair of easy chairs with rose-colored cushions and a round tea table between them. And the bedstead. Easily wide enough for two, its feather mattress piled high with lace-edged pillows, its mahogany posts reaching to the very ceiling.

The image of Harry lying here beside her through the long night to come, touching her everywhere and revealing the secrets of his own body flamed in her imagination like a fevered dream. With a hand on one of the posts, she studied the bed until she had memorized the wood's sheen, the carved headboard, the curved moldings. She wanted to remember every detail of this, her wedding bed, to carry down through the years.

Satisfied at last, she looked to a cunning screen standing in a corner, its four panels painted with a magical scene of mountains and clouds and flowing rivers. As she peered closer, she saw images of people whose eyes were set aslant in their heads and who were strangely garbed in loose-fitting breeches and jackets. She wondered why the artist had depicted them so.

A discreet tap on the door. "Come in," she said.

Mattie entered with an armful of towels and a basket containing bottles and unguents and creams and a myriad of mysterious grooming supplies. Behind her, Caspar and another dark-skinned man followed carrying a copper tub filled with steaming water. They set the tub in the center of the room then left. Mattie pulled the painted screen next to the tub, shielding it from the door. Drawing a stool up close, she rested her basket on it, selected a bottle and poured its perfumed oil into the water.

"What a heavenly scent," Abby exclaimed.

"Nothing smell better than gardenias."

"If gardenias look as glorious as they smell, they must be wondrous blossoms."

"Yes, mistress." Mattie's voice was noncommittal. With a long-handled brush, she swirled the oil through the bath water, testing its temperature with a single finger. "It be just right," she said. "I'll help you undress, mistress."

Strip naked in front of this formidable woman? "I don't think so."

"You be shy, mistress?"

"My name is Abby. And yes, I am."

Mattie cackled like a barnyard hen, but somehow the sound gave no offense. "I seen what you have many times over. Many, many times. I care for the governor's wife before she pass."

"Oh, I'm sorry."

"Me be sorry, too."

"She was your friend?"

Mattie's eyes widened as if such a possibility had never occurred to her. "Ah, no. She be my mistress."

"But you're sorry to have lost her."

After a furtive glance at the closed door, Mattie whispered, "My life be easier then."

"How so?"

The woman's expression closed like a fist. "Mattie say too much. I'm not here for talk. I help you bathe."

"I prefer to do so alone."

"The governor, he be angry with me if I not help you."

"Why should he be? I'm perfectly capable of washing my own body."

"He give me orders. I must obey."

"Obey? Really?" Abby looked at the steaming bath longingly. At that moment, she wanted nothing more than to be left alone to sink into the scented water and stay submerged for hours, but one glance at Mattie's troubled face told her that wouldn't be possible. "Are you a bondwoman, Mattie?"

"I be a slave."

"He *owns* you?"

"Yes, mistress."

How awful, Abby thought, to be owned as if you were a cow or a dog. It was hard to believe this dignified woman gliding about the room with the bearing of a queen was a man's possession like the . . . the tub or the screen or the mirror on the wall . . . or worse, like the chained men who had passed by in the street. She had known bondmen in Providence. Emma Harris's father employed one, but the man had knowingly incurred his debt, and once he repaid the cost of his passage from England, he'd be free again, his temporary indenture what Harry would call a business transaction.

Mattie must have been enslaved against her will. Of course, she had been. No need to pose the question.

"Where is your home?" Abby asked.

"Africa. A long way."

"Yes." Where Africa lay, exactly, Abby didn't know, but the far voyage from there must have been hideous, with only enslavement waiting at the end. As she had already learned, all voyages were not necessarily glorious adventures; Mattie must have endured great suffering during her passage to this far-flung island.

"The water grow cold, mistress."

"I know. That won't do, will it?" She couldn't change Mattie's plight, but at least she could make this day's task easier for her. Abby took off her cap and tossed it on the bed. "What do you think of my hair?"

A swift intake of breath told her what Mattie didn't dare say.

"There's more." Abby reached into her breeches and pulled out her plaits. "I keep them in my pockets."

Mattie rewarded her with a look of stunned disbelief. "No gal I know keep her hair in her pockets."

"Or wears boys' clothes, either, I wager."

"True, mistress. You be the only one."

Abby could see Mattie wanted to laugh but didn't dare. "Well, underneath I'm the same as every other woman." She had waited long enough. Not wasting another second, she stripped off her clothes with such haste all Mattie could do was stand aside until she stood naked in front of her. "See?" Abby said, twirling around. "The same. I told you so." Without further ado, she stepped into the copper tub, sinking into the warm water with a sigh of content. "At last. Honestly, Mattie, I thought I'd never see a tub of hot water again. This is heaven."

"Heaven? If you say so," Mattie replied as she picked up the discarded garments. "These clothes. You like them washed?"

"I never want to see them again."

"A boy I know could use new clothes."

"Give them to him, please." They were little more than rags. She feared it would be a sorry kind of boy who would welcome them.

Mattie folded the garments under her arm. "I leave you for now. In a while I bring tea?"

"That would be grand," Abby said, her eyes closed. A soft click of the door latch told her she was alone.

SHE MUST HAVE DOZED OFF FOR A WHILE. At a knock on the door, she awaked with a start. She still sat in the tub, but the water had chilled and the tips of her fingers were wrinkled.

Mattie came in carrying a jug of warm water followed by a young, brown-skinned housemaid balancing a covered tray of food. The girl placed the tray on the round table between the cushioned chairs, curtsied and left without a word. Mattie put the jug on the floor next to the tub and from the basket of supplies selected a green glass bottle.

"For the hair," she said. "Make it shine."

Abby nodded and Mattie poured a little of the scented fluid on her hands and massaged it into Abby's hair. Her fingers, strong and soothing, moved rhythmically over Abby's scalp. "Now I wash the soap away," she said, pouring warm water from the jug. A brisk rub with a linen cloth and, "You be finish," she declared, dropping the damp cloth into the basket then holding up a linen towel the size of a bed sheet. Abby stepped out of the tub, letting Mattie envelope her from breast to toes in the dry toweling.

Mattie pointed to Abby's hair. "We trim. Make even."

"It needs a proper cutting, I know. It was just hacked off."

Mattie lifted the basket off the bath stool. "Here, mistress, for you."

Abby sat on the stool while Mattie fished in her apron pocket for a pair of shears. She draped the smaller damp towel over Abby's shoulders and with a series of efficient snips, trimmed the wet, jagged ends of her hair.

"Now all grow the same." She walked around the stool to gauge the effect of her handiwork then stood in front of Abby frowning.

"I know. It looks dreadful," Abby said. "But nothing can be done until it grows."

"There is something."

"What?"

Mattie pointed to her white turban. "How you say? The forehead. If we cut the hair short there, little curls be freed while the hair in back grows long again. Mistress very pretty. Even prettier with curls on the forehead." She fluttered her fingers to demonstrate.

"Cut off more? I don't know . . ."

"Trust Mattie." She paused, a hint of pride in her voice. "The governor's wife, she trust."

"I see," Abby said.

"The plaits. We use them, too."

"How?"

"I be a lady's maid. I know how. Soon, you see, I fix your hair and your nails, but now the tea grow cold. You be hungry, mistress?"

"Starving." She couldn't remember the last time she'd eaten, except for a crust of sea biscuit at first light. Under the linen napkin, the tray held a small pot of hot tea, juice pressed from oranges, buttered scones and dainty cakes drizzled with honey. After the ship's coarse food, she tucked into the repast with gusto. Holding the towel tight to her body with her upper arms, she reached for a honey cake and bit into it. Ambrosia.

"This is delicious, Mattie. More than I can finish. Have something. Try a honey cake. They're divine."

"This not for me."

"You'll regret it. Come, have one."

Mattie shook her head. "No. Mistress and slave, they no eat together."

Abby put a half-eaten cake back onto the tray. The Harris's bondman ate every meal with the family. True, he slept in the barn on all but the bitterest nights, but that was because the snug farmhouse had so little room. "You're not allowed to eat in here?" she asked.

"No, mistress."

"Then I won't eat, either."

"You said you be hungry."

Abby nodded. "Where I come from, there are rules, too. No one eats in front of someone without offering to share. It's considered rude to do so." She clutched the towel tight to her body. "This is my room, is it not?"

Mattie nodded, solemn faced.

"Then I can make the rules here." Trying to duplicate the governor's smooth manner of speaking, she added, "It would give me great pleasure to have you join me. Providing, of course, that it would please you."

Mattie eyed the food, her glance lingering on the buttered scones.

"Come." Abby patted one of the two rose-cushioned chairs. "We'll have a tea party. Just the two of us. No one need know."

A cautious glimmer flitted across Mattie's face.

Encouraged, Abby said, "While we sup, I'll tell you a story. About pirates. A true one."

A spark of interest leapt in Mattie's dark eye. "Pirates? They be like slavers?"

"Much the same, I fear. They're why I cut off my hair. It used to be very long. All the way down to . . ." She reached back to demonstrate, lost her grip on the towel, and it slipped to the floor. ". . . here."

As Abby scrambled to wrap the linen around herself again, Mattie covered her mouth with a hand. She tried to choke back a giggle, but the sound of it leaked out between her fingers.

Abby laughed, too, tucked the towel around her torso, and picked up the dish of scones. "For you, if you please, Mistress Mattie."

"SHERRY, YOUR LORDSHIP?"

Harry accepted the crystal glass Caspar offered. How pleasant to be formally served from a silver tray. He had to admit he'd missed the amenities of a gentleman's life. The servants' attention, the civility, the deference to his station. In the colonies, he had begun to forget the essential difference between men with breeding and men without. The governor's urbane company, his tasteful possessions, his news from London, all brought his own position in life surging back. This was the atmosphere he'd enjoyed until recently, the atmosphere he'd like to return to. But what of Abby?

Earlier, when the slavers had marched the Negroes through the town, she had visibly paled. Not from fear. He could be certain of that. The chained men had been a brutal introduction to the reality of slavery. He agreed with her totally; slavery was a bad business. He twirled the cut glass between his fingers, admiring the way its etched facets caught the light. No doubt about it, civilities such as he was enjoying at the moment—that raised daily life to a kinder, gentler plane—were made possible by the enforced labor of those less fortunate. A fact Abby would surely bring up at the first opportunity.

"More sherry, sir?" Caspar asked.

A second round so soon? He must have been daydreaming. Harry extended his glass, forcing himself to concentrate on the talk swirling about him. It was difficult to concentrate, he admitted dryly, with his mind on the night to come.

Burned into his brain was the sight of Abby the time she'd stood so white and softly curved before him, clothed only in her long, glorious hair. He winced, remembering how he'd hacked off her tresses. But her hair would grow again. In a few months, it would be as long and luxuriant as ever. Yet he cared not if it never grew an inch. What mattered most was her essence—her stubbornness, her integrity, her wit—and the passion he longed to ignite in her slim body.

With a muffled groan, he sipped at his sherry, forcing himself to listen to what Governor Molesworth was saying.

"In truth, I'm glad to be rid of Slayton. Oh, he served his purpose, but he was a sly devil, totally untrustworthy." The governor flicked his wrist lace. "In seizing your vessel, he violated our agreement. English ships were not to be harmed. So you're correct, captain, in your interpretation of the law. Their sloop is yours to dispose of as you see fit, just as the fate of the brigands is in my hands. Incarcerating so many will strain the resources of our local jail, but I'll see that extra men are put on watch until they can be dealt with."

Captain Tamworth leaned back in his chair, sipping his sherry, relieved, Harry could tell, to have the governor's approval. "The sloop has to be careened and made seaworthy before we sail her to England."

"That shouldn't be a problem. Kingston across the bay has a sheltered cove with a shallow beach. It will serve your needs nicely," the governor said.

"Excellent. My men can do the bulk of the work, but they'll be hard pressed to do so in a timely fashion. Can you help us find extra hands?"

Lips pursed in thought, the governor studied the dregs in his glass. "As to that, I'm not sure. Most able-bodied men on the island have ships of their own to outfit, or they're slaves. However, the planting season has ended . . . perhaps you could prevail on one of the plantation owners to hire out his slaves."

"No, gentlemen." Harry said.

"No?" The governor looked up, surprised. "Then I'm afraid I can't be of assistance."

"Pardon me, governor," Captain Tamworth interrupted. "Harry, we need to complete our business and be on our way. The winter gales will be starting soon. We don't want to be caught in them mid-ocean."

"True enough. But I know Abby won't hire slaves to refurbish the ship."

"*Abby* won't allow?"

Harry shrugged. "I'm afraid not. As you know, the decision is hers. You gave her possession of the ship."

"But . . . but . . . this is outrageous," Tamworth sputtered.

Harry rested his glass on the table by his chair. "It is also a problem for tomorrow." He stood and picked up a canvas carry-all he'd brought from the *Lady Anne*. He held it high. "In here are bills of lading listing the goods we have for trade, governor. And my wedding clothes. Shall we plan to discuss our business in the morning? For now, with your kind indulgence, I, too, earnestly desire a bath."

Chapter Twenty

Harry surveyed his freshly barbered appearance in the room's pier glass. Nearly ready. He picked up the pair of brushes from the dresser top and ran them through his hair, clubbing it at the nape with a short length of black ribbon. Governor Molesworth favored formal wigs, but as for himself, he doubted he'd ever suffer through wearing one again. On that subject, he completely agreed with the colonials.

Caspar had done an admirable job of refreshing his clothing and polishing his shoes. His black broad cloth doublet had been pressed, his white shirt laundered and, from the crisp state of the stock, lightly starched as well. With his fawn colored breeches and white stockings, he was sure he looked as a man should on the single most important day—and night—of his life.

To the calm image in the mirror he posed a question, though he had no intention of allowing it to mar his joy or weaken his certainty. Still, he wondered. What would his lady mother say about his forthcoming nuptials? He scowled, knowing the answer full well, and knowing no one and nothing on earth could keep him from making Abby his wife.

A light tap sounded at the door.

"Come in."

"The flowers you asked for, sir."

"Ah, yes." Harry turned from the image in the glass.

In his large hand, Caspar clutched a dainty nosegay of white blossoms caught together with a pale blue streamer.

"Very nice," Harry said, "though I don't recognize the flowers."

"Orchids, sir. Mattie said only the blue ribbon would do."

"Pretty, indeed."

"For you, sir. For your coat." Caspar held up a single bloom.

Harry shrugged. Someone had gone to the trouble of providing it for him. He wouldn't refuse. He took the blossom and tucked it into a buttonhole in his doublet.

"You look fine, sir, mighty fine."

"Thank you, Caspar. It's not every day a man marries."

"Praise the Lord for that."

Harry laughed. "I agree marriage isn't for everyone." *But I'm so eager for it I'm practically panting.*

The lowering sunlight cast purple shadows into the room. Candle-lighting time at last. "Are the arrangements complete?"

"Yes, sir."

"The front parlor where we sat this morning?"

"The same, sir. Captain Tamworth awaits there with the governor and a young man." Caspar frowned. "An Indian, by the look of him."

"Ah, yes. Good. So all that's lacking is the bride?"

The butler nodded.

"In the blue bed chamber, is she?"

"Across the hall. Shall I fetch her for you?"

"No, no thank you. I'll do the honors. And while we're occupied downstairs, will you have my things moved into Mistress Abby's room?" *The sort of room that in a few minutes, after a few spoken words, would be opened to him always.*

"Very good, sir." Caspar left, and Harry picked up the nosegay. With pulses pounding, he tapped on Abby's door.

Mattie opened it, approval of his appearance glowing in her face. "Mistress be ready," she said.

Harry tried to peer around her, but a Chinese screen blocked his view. Fleetingly, he noted the screen was beautifully rendered before dismissing it from mind. Tonight he had only one objective.

Abby stepped out from behind the screen, and his heart stood still.

"Oh, my love," he said, too stunned to move.

Her eyes sparkling with mischief, she pointed to the bouquet. "The flowers are lovely with your broadcloth. Will you carry them during our wedding"

"Oh." He laughed. "For you." But rooted to the spot, he stood where he was, enthralled with her transformation. "You've gone from urchin to goddess," he murmured.

She was gowned in white silk embroidered with tiny bluebells, her narrow waist encircled with a wide blue sash the exact shade of the streamers cascading from the nosegay. Even the tips of her shoes peeping out from below the gown were the same blue.

Released from their boyish binding, her breasts swelled over the top of the low cut bodice. His glance lingered there. Back in Providence, dressed in her own girls' clothing, she hadn't revealed such a generous display . . . surely he would have remembered.

"You like the frock," she said. It wasn't a question.

Dry mouthed, he nodded. "Very much."

"It belonged to the governor's wife's." Her hand stroked the silk. "I've never seen such a frock, much less worn one."

"You are utterly beautiful."

She blushed under his continuing stare. "If I am, I owe everything to Mattie's skill."

Mattie shook her head, beaming.

Harry raised his hands to his temples. "Your hair? It . . . it's . . . much like it used to be." Tiny tendrils curled at her forehead, and entwined with narrow blue ribbon, the plaits Aiden had saved coiled around her head, looking for all the world like a golden crown. "Do I dare kiss such a vision?"

"Of course." She came toward him, radiant and smiling.

"You won't disappear like a figment of my imagination?"

"Absolutely not. I'm real. Feel me," she said, holding out an arm.

"That's exactly what I intend to do," he said with a grin. "But first, your flowers." He handed them to her with a flourish. "And next, your vows." He took her arm and folding it over his own, asked, "Shall we?"

"Oh, yes."

SURE, SHE'S GONE AND DONE IT, THE LITTLE SCAMP," Aiden thought. And look at Harry, his wedding vows freshly spoken, standing tight by Abby's side, his arm around her waist as if he never wanted to let her go. And she gazing up at him as if he were the very moon and all the stars. If only Mam and Da could see her this day, looking like a rose, gowned in silk and better still, in her own happiness. He strode across the parlor to her. "A kiss from the bride?"

"Aiden." She didn't wait for him to reach for her, but flung her arms around him, spilling a bit of wine from her glass down the back of his borrowed doublet and kissing him heartily.

"Harry is a lucky man," he said, happy for her and ashamed, suddenly, of a sharp stab of envy. Abby had achieved his own deepest, secret desire: she had found a place where she truly belonged.

Perceptive as always, she regarded him thoughtfully. "I know you're happy for me, Aiden. I wish the same happiness for you one day." She studied what remained of the rich, red wine in her glass. "If only Mam and Da could be here."

"They'd be happy for you, too."

"Da perhaps . . . Mam, I fear, not so . . ." Her voice trailed off, then, "You have no wine."

"Sure and the dark man's been walking rings around me."

"Ah, that won't do. Caspar," she said softly as he passed by with a tray of wine glasses. "A Madeira for my brother, please."

His expression leaden, Caspar paused long enough for Aiden to pluck a glass from the tray. He raised it in a silent toast before taking a tentative sip. This was his first taste of wine, and he was aware of how quickly its warming jolt reached his belly. As he sipped appreciatively—this was a far different quaff from the home-brewed beers he'd known—his thoughts shifted to his parents. Abby was correct; Da would be delighted for her, but Mam's hatred of the Rushmounts ran so deep that if she were here, her lips would be compressed into a thin line of cold, white fury.

And what of Harry's mother, LadyAnne, an elegant descendant, so he had heard, of Norman rulers? What would her reaction be to her son's taking an obscure colonial bride with no ties at all to the kings of England?

An unease roiled in his gut. Perhaps Abby hadn't found her true place after all.

Chapter Twenty-One

Like a large, white island in the midst of a blue sea, the bed dominated the room. Everything else—the screen, the chest of drawers, the chairs, the tea table—faded into the shadows. Only the bed, lit by candles in sheltering hurricane lamps, captured Abby's attention. Uncanny how it drew the eye. Someone had folded the blanket neatly at the foot and removed the coverlet to a wooden stand in a corner. Just the lace-edged sheet lay smoothed atop the mattress. Enough covering for a tropical night with warm, perfumed breezes.

Harry shrugged out of his doublet, tossed it on a chair and bolted the bed chamber door. The click of the metal rod shooting home startled Abby, and she whirled toward the sound.

"Anxious, love, at being locked in with me?" Harry asked hurrying across the room to hold her.

She lifted her face to his, kissing the mole by his upper lip, something she'd been longing to do for hours. "I don't feel anxious, my love, just . . . untutored."

"A good thing I made a study of the topic," he said in her ear, pulling her tight as he spoke. She rewarded him with an indignant gasp and tried to wrench free. "Actually, I've had a few lessons only," he said holding her even tighter.

She sighed and kissed him again. "One of us has to know what to do. As for me, I don't even know how to take off this gown. It's like nothing I've ever worn before. Mattie did up all the ties and laces."

"Disrobing was lesson one in my course of study." His eyes glinted in the candle light. "Let me help. Turn, please."

She did as he asked, speaking to him over her shoulder. "The gown came from France, Mattie said. I wonder why they do that?"

"Do what?"

"Put the laces in back where you can't get at them."

"Well, for one thing, it leaves the front unencumbered, which," he leaned over her shoulder to nuzzle her neck, "makes great good sense to me. And second, anyone who can afford a French gown has a lady's maid to help her undress."

She spun around to face him, whipping the loosened laces from his fingers. "Or a husband."

"Exactly. A husband. Funny, I love how the word sounds. Or maybe I love hearing you say it with that faint trace of Irish in your voice." Ignoring the partially untied bodice still dangling between them, he wrapped his arms around her waist. "Above all, I love you."

In the first, full kiss of her married life, Abby opened her lips and from them sent Harry all the passion in her heart.

"Did you feel that?" she asked, when they parted, gasping for air.

"It took my breath away."

"Aye, I passed my soul to you."

"The rush, I felt? Is that what it was?"

"Yes." She reached up and, placing her hands on his cheeks, whispered, "We're one and the same now. I'm yours body and soul."

He grinned. "Not quite. Let's rid ourselves of all this cloth."

She turned around again. His fingers trembling, he finished untying the laces and the bodice fell to the floor. Without stooping to pick it up, he fumbled for the ribbon at her waist, and her skirt slipped to her ankles. "Now the petticoat. God, this is maddening."

In a moment, she stood clothed only in her shift, the pretty blue shoes and the white silk stockings. She kicked off the shoes, slid down the blue silk garters and stripped off the stockings. "The shift," she said shyly, "is pretty, too."

"I can see that," he said, impatient with his shirt and its fastenings. Freed from it at last, he flung it over a chair, kicked off his shoes and began unbuttoning his breeches.

Her eyes, dark jewels in her pale face, followed his fingers. He paused. This was not the time to frighten her.

In his stocking feet, he padded to the candles still gleaming within their hurricane lamps and blew them out. Only then did he remove the rest of his clothes until he stood naked beside the bed. "Come to me, darling."

A soft rustle. The shift sliding to the floor?

A moment later, he knew the answer as she moved, noiseless, into the circle of his arms and pressed her softness against him. In the dark, he heard her whisper, "I've waited for this moment all my life."

"As you waited, love, did you dream it would be wonderful?"

"Yes. Always it was. In my dream."

"Then I must make it so," he said, his voice hoarse. He began to kiss her. "I'll start here," he murmured, his lips brushing the curls at her forehead, "and here," her eyelids, "and here." His mouth lingered long at her lips. "Here." He paused at her throat. "Now here." He bent to her breast.

"Don't talk," she begged.

The urgency in her voice thrilled him. This is what he wanted above all else—to fill her with desire. He would go on as she urged without speaking, using his mouth and his hands to caress her, rousing her to a pitch he knew she had never reached before now. And then he would be the instrument of her release.

God, why was he *thinking*?

Like an idol to be worshipped, she stood beside the bed while he knelt before her, kissing the satin flesh of her belly. As he bent lower, he heard a shocked, inhaled breath, and her hands flashed down to twist in his hair. It was time. He stood and pressed himself against her thigh.

"I want to feel you," she whispered. "All of you." Her fingers reached down, tentative at first, exploring, then understanding, she grasped him. A growl erupted from his throat.

As if one, they moved onto the bed, onto the crisp white sheet luminous in the moonlight. He hovered over her, his knees flexed on either side of her slim hips.

"I love you," she said.

"And I love you. My whole lifetime won't be long enough to show you how much." As he lowered himself, she rose up to meet him, knowing this was what he wanted and what she wanted, too.

"So," he said the next morning, rising on one elbow to gaze at her as she lay beside him, "how are you this day, Lady Rushmount?"

Lady Rushmount? The words echoed somewhere deep in her brain, but she didn't answer. Languorous, half asleep, half awake, all she wanted was to lie unthinking, cushioned in the bliss of the remembered night. For now, let the world and everything in it keep far, far away.

"Well?"

A kiss feathered on her cheek. Another, then another.

She opened her eyes to a sun-bronzed face and a brilliant, white smile.

"I asked, how are you this day?"

She stretched, extending every muscle in her body and breathed out a long sigh of sheer content. "I'm feeling wonderful today," she said. Looking up at his happy face, she laughed. "As you very well know."

"Then shall we call for food? Or would you rather . . ."

"I'd rather," she said reaching up to slide her arms around his neck and pull him down to her.

LATER, MUCH LATER, WHEN THE SUN HAD PASSED ITS ZENITH, they heard a gentle knocking on the door. Abby covered herself with the sheet. Harry grabbed his breeches off the floor, scrambled into them and unbolted the door.

Mattie stood in the passageway, amusement simmering beneath her dutiful expression.

"Yes, Mattie?"

"Caspar sent me, sir. He be wondering if you and the missus would like some food."

"Excellent idea, Mattie. Lots of it. And if it's possible, my lady wife and I would prefer to dine in here. Perhaps on the balcony."

"Yes, sir. I'll see to it. Right away, sir."

He winked at her before she hurried off, and her hidden grin broke free.

Harry chuckled, closed the door and walked back to the bed. "Up, wife. Food's on the way."

Abby had rolled over and lay on her side facing the windows, her rump clearly outlined under the sheet. He gave it a playful tap. "Up, Lady Rushmount, up I say."

She sat, tenting her knees. "I must obey my husband," she said sleepily.

"Exactly. In all things."

"Correct. Especially when I want to," she replied.

"Ah, already there's dissention in the ranks." He bent over the bed to kiss her.

"No, not dissention," she said, falling back onto the welter of pillows. "But I do have a request."

"Anything. How can I deny you a solitary thing while you lie there naked under that thin, very thin, covering?"

"In that case," she said, playing with the lace trim, avoiding his eyes. "I ask that you call me Mistress Rushmount, not Lady."

He stared at her, disbelieving, the bantering expression gone from his face. "But you're my wife. I am Lord Rushmount. Ergo, you are Lady Rushmount."

"No I'm a colonial woman. I can't be called lady. My mother—"

"Isn't overly fond of me, I know but—"

"The past torments her. We must give her time. When she gets to know you, she'll love you as I do."

He arched an eyebrow. "How will she get to know me well enough to, as you say, love me?"

Pulling the tousled sheet off the bed, she wrapped herself in it, bewildered for an instant by his irony, then, in the next moment, fearing she understood it all too well. "When our voyage is over and your trading finished, we'll return to Providence, will we not?"

He shook his head. "No, my intent is to restore my estate in Ballybanree. Ireland will be our home."

Ireland. With the sheet enveloping her like a shroud, she sank into a chair by the tea table. Eyes unfocused, she looked past him toward the garden and, beyond, to her future. Through all that had occurred in the last fevered days, only one thought had filled her mind: to be with Harry forever. In her eagerness to be his wife, she'd not asked how and where they would live. She'd stolen from home hoping to see something of the wonders of the world but hadn't planned on never going back, on never seeing Da and Mam again.

The sky darkened. A tropical storm threatened, its breeze riffling the sheet covering her. She shivered, her skin erupting into gooseflesh.

"Ireland is beautiful," Harry was saying. "Very green from all the rains. My dream is to restore my manor house to its former glory. We'll do so together, love." She didn't answer but clutched the sheet tighter. "You're cold," he said. A dressing gown they hadn't noticed last evening lay across a chair. He held it up. "Come, you'll be more comfortable in this."

Mattie must have left it out for her. She dropped the sheet and slid into the robe.

"You'll love Ireland," Harry said standing behind her, wrapping his arms around her.

She feared she wouldn't. But she would live there, nonetheless. "You must go where your heart lies," she said, turning to embrace him.

A knock sounded. "Food," he said, kissing her cheek quickly and hurrying to the door. Laden with covered trays, Caspar and a young lad stood in the doorway. A delicious aroma of hot coffee, ham and fresh baked bread rose in the air.

"Come in, Caspar, come in. I'll move the tea table by the window. Lady Rushmount and I will dine there and look at the rain fall. Something I think we'll be doing a good deal in the years to come."

More rain in Ireland than sunshine. Abby pulled the robe close about her throat. All her life she'd heard harsh tales of Ireland. Of the people's misery. Of how Mam and Da had been forced to flee or be jailed or worse. They had always said for common men such as her people, such as herself, the colonies offered a far better way of life. But Harry was not a common man; he was an aristocrat. An aristocrat who possessed land the English king had stolen from Mam's family. She stifled the sigh welling up in her throat. She was a married woman now, not a child to be crying for her parents.

As she looked on, Caspar and the boy settled the trays on the tea table. Harry placed a chair beside it for her. He was her husband, a man she would follow to the ends of the earth if need be. Keeping the robe wrapped snugly about her, she sat beside the table. "Caspar, we won't need you any longer," she said. "I'll serve my husband."

Brave words, she thought, as Caspar and his helper, with nods of utmost courtesy, left the chamber, quietly closing the door behind them. Only wed a few hours and already the challenges of married life were upon her, nor would she have it any other way.

"A scone, Harry, or a honey cake?"

"Both. I've the appetite of ten men. And you, my love, have given it to me." He raised her hand to his lips, kissing each finger tip, then her open palm. No, she would not have it any other way, no matter what the cost.

Chapter Twenty-Two

"I've examined the *Granuaile* from top to bottom, Abby. She's basically sound," Aiden said. "More in need of a thorough cleaning and some paint and polish than anything else. For an ocean voyage, though, she should be careened and the keel scraped clear of barnacles and caulked."

I agree," Captain Tamworth said. "To do less would be foolhardy. What of her sails? They're in need of repair from what I could see."

Aiden nodded. "Two of our crew are already busy patching and reinforcing them." He laughed. "Rats have been gnawing on the canvas. We could do with a few cats. Some good ratters."

Tamworth pointed out the parlor window. "You should be able to purchase whatever you want out there."

"Excellent," Aiden replied. "I'll try later."

He looks happier than I've ever seen him, Abby thought. He's enjoying the challenge of refitting the *Granuaile*. For that reason alone, she'd be forever grateful for the captain's generosity.

She nestled next to Harry on the cushioned settle, holding his left hand in her right, feeling very much a married woman in her day frock of green and white striped cotton, a small lace fichu tucked into the neckline. Earlier that morning, she had refused Mattie's offer to arrange the plaits around her cropped hair. She hadn't the woman's skill at hair dressing, and when they left Jamaica, she'd not be able to achieve the same effect. Instead, she'd pinned a green bow at the nape to help cover her short locks. Her hair would grow long soon enough, and besides, Harry had said the ribbon looked fetching.

"We'll soon have the sloop in good repair," Aiden said. "I've no doubt of that at all."

"How long do you think it will take?" Harry asked.

"Ten days, or thereabouts."

Harry nodded, content with Aiden's answer. The *Lady Anne's* condition was good, Abby knew. She needed minimal outfitting for the Atlantic crossing—her stores and water barrels refilled, her seams recaulked and the rum supply Harry had come for stowed aboard. The time would fly by, and they'd soon be on their way. She felt excitement in the squeeze of Harry's hand, the pressure telling her he could hardly wait to be home once more.

Captain Tamworth's voice, sounding troubled, pulled her back into the conversation. "Our major problem isn't the outfitting."

"What is?" Abby asked.

"Assembling a crew. After we overcame the brigands, we managed a day's sail short-handed on each vessel. But we can't head into an ocean passage short-handed, and from what you say, governor, able seamen are hard to come by in Port Royal."

The governor, sitting quietly up to now, said, "The trick is finding men who know their way around a ship and can be trusted not to slice your throat in the middle of the night. Or in broad daylight for that matter." He crossed his legs in their white silk stockings and drew on his pipe, sending a smoky tendril into the air.

A curious man, Abby thought, the soul of hospitality; her wedding gown, her nuptial dinner, the very clothes she was wearing this day, were gifts from him, but she sensed Mattie feared him. Her face clouded when she spoke his name, each time averting her gaze as if she were hiding something.

"Without a crew, we can't sail," Harry said, letting go of her hand to stand and pace the colorful Persian carpet. "Landlocked, the sloop's of little value to you, Abby."

At the obvious truth in Harry's words, the excitement of a few minutes ago died in Aiden's eyes. The sight made Abby want to weep. There had to be a solution. There had to be. And there was.

"I know of a possible crew," Abby said, her words a lightning bolt that startled even herself.

"You do?" The governor snorted.

"Abby?" Harry asked, perplexed.

"The pirates we captured."

"You're jesting. They're thieves and killers," the governor said.

"Sailors, too, I warrant," Abby replied, a touch of brisk assurance in her voice.

"Really, Abby," Harry began.

"Let her speak, please," Aiden said.

"As I went among them with cups of water, some of them thanked me kindly. True, most did not. Some were surly, and some were mere lads, perhaps forced by Slayton into serving him. Maybe they would be grateful to be released from jail, with the governor's approval, of course, and have a chance to return to England."

"They already know the ship," Harry said, catching fire from Abby's idea, "and her idiosyncrasies. That would be invaluable in a storm."

The governor tamped the ashes from his clay pipe into an ironstone dish. "The chance of foul play is too great. I don't advise it."

As was ever his way, Aiden said nothing, letting the talk swirl around him, yet one quick look told Abby hope had returned to his eyes. Sailing aboard the *Granuaile* must mean a great deal to him, but only the governor could make it possible.

Sitting ramrod straight, she turned to him smiling sweetly, though she wasn't in the mood for smiling. "Governor Molesworth, if the ship's owner paid you a bounty for each brigand released to him . . . ah, her . . . what would you say?"

"A bounty?"

She had no money to pay bounties, but two days ago, she didn't have a ship, either. With Harry's help surely she'd find the money somehow.

The governor refilled his pipe from a leather pouch, holding it by the bowl until Caspar could return with a lighted taper. He looked over at Abby, grudging respect mingling with the admiration he had shown her since her wedding day when she'd appeared in female attire. "Say I agree. That doesn't solve the problem. You'd have a ship full of cut throats."

"There might be a way to deal with that." With their attention riveted on her, she plunged ahead, inventing as she went. "Suppose we divide the crews? Half of the *Lady Anne's* men go aboard the *Granuaile*, and vice versa?"

"Then both ships would be in jeopardy," the governor scoffed.

"Our men could watch over the newcomers. Have them work in pairs. One of our men responsible for one of Slayton's. A watch dog effect. Such a plan would keep Slayton's men from plotting against us. If they even be of such a mind," she added hastily.

"That still won't—"

"What if we promise they'll go free once we reach England?"

"You may never get that far," the governor said as Caspar entered with a burning taper and touched it to the tobacco. The governor sucked on the pipe stem until another aromatic tendril rose in the air.

She was not to be deterred, not now, with Aiden hanging on her every word. "Supposing we give each man a percentage of our profits?"

"Ha. Now you've joined the ranks of the buccaneers," the governor retorted puffing away furiously. "That's what Slayton and his ilk do. Share the booty. It's how they keep their men loyal. That and putting the fear of death into them."

"I'd leave out the death threats, but as for the rest . . ." Abby shrugged.

Harry strode over to her and kissed her cheek. "God, you're a wonder of a woman," he said in her ear. Straightening, he turned to the others. "Abby's plan might work. I'm willing to take the chance. What of you, Aiden?"

"Sure and you know the answer to that already," he said with a grin.

"Governor?"

"It's your skin, not mine. Pay a bounty, one we agree upon, and the men are yours. In God's truth, I'll be glad to rid my jail of them."

"Consider it done, sir, and my thanks to you, but another issue remains," Harry said. "I have trade goods to barter for the rum and coin I'm hoping will suffice for the bounty my lovely wife suggested." He turned to her. "But I don't have the wherewithal to fill the hulls of both ships. So if you have no goods to trade, where will your profits come from, my dear?"

Abby slumped against the settle back, not wanting to see the defeat sure to be painted all over Aiden's face. Where would she find the money to buy rum and sugar cane and molasses? All she owned in the world was the *Granuaile*.

Of course. She sat up straight once more. "What of the ship herself? Suppose I sign a paper turning her over to the rum merchants until I deliver the goods they entrust to me? Would it be possible to do that?"

One glance at Harry's amused expression and she knew he had been testing her, waiting to see if she would come to the same conclusion he had. Playing with her he was, and she loved it knowing in that moment that theirs would be a marriage of equals, no matter what title they each bore.

The governor blew a ring of smoke into the room. "Lady Rushmount, you look like a woman but you think like a man." He sent a heated glance her way. "Most unusual. Most intriguing."

"I couldn't agree more," Harry said, clapping a smiling Aiden on the back. "And now, lady wife, shall we pay a visit to the jail?"

Chapter Twenty-Three

Dark, lit by one small, barred window near the rafters, the Port Royal jail stank of unwashed bodies and feces and rotted food. Abby tried not to inhale as she stepped inside and glanced about. It was obvious the jail was ill equipped to imprison a ship's entire crew. Crowded together, immobile and miserable, the erstwhile buccaneers lay chained to the walls or shackled to the cell bars.

Governor Molesworth strode in, his ebony-handled cane striking the floor stones with a resounding ring. A few dull eyes looked up as he entered. A single guffaw broke the silence, followed by a smattering of raucous insults.

"Look at the 'eels on 'is shoes. Red they be, by gar."

"Fancy that, will ye? Is it a growed man or a doxy I'm lookin' at?"

"Over 'ere gov'nor, over 'ere. Lemme stroke yer curls for ye."

Most of the men hardly raised their heads to look up until they spied Abby standing near the doorway, her hand on Harry's arm. The sight of her caused a stirring and a loud rattling of chains.

"Ah, that's more like it now."

"Wake up, lads, we've got a beauty callin' on us."

"Quiet!" the governor commanded. "I could hang the lot of you. And I may yet." He held a lawn handkerchief to his sizeable nose in a futile attempt to screen out the feral air.

The men look wretched, Abby thought. No wonder they acted like animals; that's how they were treated, and most of them had never known anything better. She knew now that life at sea was harsh, harsher than she had imagined from the safety of home. Mam had been right about that. Had she had been right, too, in saying that life in the colonies was good, better than good, that they had land and freedom and food aplenty, none of which was easily obtained elsewhere?

One thing for certain, Abby had never seen misery such as this. She glanced at Aiden to judge his reaction. His expression was grim. Was he worried that their attempt to collect a crew might not succeed, or was he thinking of his people isolated in the Great Swamp, imprisoned by its boundaries?

The strange, disturbing thought fled her mind as Harry said, "I fear for your safety, Abby, sailing with this rough lot. It's not too late to try elsewhere."

She shook her head. "There is nowhere else." She glanced up at him and saw his jaw tighten into stone. Her heart sank. As her husband, he had the right to insist she give up her ship. To sell her for what they could raise. But for Aiden's sake, she couldn't let that happen.

She was grateful the governor pounded his cane on the stone floor, distracting them. "Attention, rogues," he said, his voice ringing with authority. His handkerchief back at his nose, he paused until the muttering ceased and the listless ones opened their eyes. "I have good news." He paused again for the mumbling and chain rattling to die away. "You'll be freed this day, but there are conditions to that freedom. Violate them and you'll die."

"We're all dyin' men, gov'nor. You too."

Loud guffaws burst out of a score of mouths. The men were awake and alert, energized, Abby realized, by the merest wisp of freedom in the offing.

"A bounty will be paid on each of your heads," the governor said, speaking slowly, letting his words sink in, "providing you agree to ship out with the captain here." He pointed his walking stick at Tamworth. "You'll be split between two ships. No need to name them. You know the ones." He glared into the cells. "So help me God and king if any ill comes to them you'll be hunted down like dogs. Drawn and quartered. I'll see to it personally, I'll . . ."

"He's being brutal," Abby murmured to Harry. "That's not the way I would speak to them."

"The *Granuaile* belongs to you, love. Show him the way. Go ahead." He glanced over at the prisoners, held at bay like beasts in cages. "They can't harm you here."

She eyed him uncertainly. Yes, the ship had been gifted to her, but as a married woman, she well knew everything she possessed was under the control of her husband. An unjust law if ever she had heard of one. Thank God Harry was a reasonable man. But if he were not, what would her fate be then? Truly, life became more unfathomable the more one experienced it.

"Well, love?" Harry whispered. From his expression, she knew he wanted her to speak out though instinctively she knew the women in his family never did. She had taken a rare man for husband. Some time soon they would have to discuss the nature of laws and why they came into being. For now, skirts rustling about her ankles, she stepped up to the governor and laid a hand on his arm. Startled by her touch, he fluttered his handkerchief before his face causing a burst of merriment from the prisoners.

"She too close for comfort, gov'nor?"

"Send 'er to me. I can 'andle 'er."

"No. Over 'ere. Over 'ere."

She stood poised, waiting for the tumult to die down before saying, "My name is

Abby . . . ah . . . Rushmount," stumbling for an instant over her unfamiliar new name. "You knew me aboard the *Lady Anne* as Guy, the cabin boy."

A flurry of whispers. Like the governor had done, she waited, letting her words sink in. "According to the law of the sea, Captain Tamworth here . . ." she nodded courteously at him

". . . took possession of Slayton's vessel." A low growl started up, but this time she didn't pause. "He kindly turned her ownership over to me."

"To you? A slip of a girl. We can guess why, aye, lads?"

A few of the ruffians chortled, but not all.

She looked directly at the man who spoke. Toothless and ragged, clutching his bars, he leered at her.

She squared her shoulders. "Speculate all you wish on the reasons why. It will make for interesting conversation during our journey."

"Ha, she got you good with that one, 'awkins," one of the men shouted. Coarse laughter erupted from the cells. Hawkins snarled in the direction of the shout then turned back to Abby. "Me mate is right, Miss, you got me fair and square. Now tell us what's yer meanin'?"

"If you agree to sail with us to London, the governor will give me a blanket pardon for all of you. Once we dock safely, you may choose to remain in my service or to leave. As you see fit."

A buzz spread from cell to cell.

Abby let it continue for a while before saying, "There's more." To her immense satisfaction, they fell silent. "Each man will be paid from my ship's profits. One half share at least, more if her cargo fetches a good price. You have my word on that."

"You're doing very well," Harry said under his breath.

She looked at him beneath her lashes. "Thank you, but I'm not through yet."

"There's more? God, you're a force to be reckoned with."

"I'm about finished," Abby replied. "This last bit is very important."

"I'm all ears," he said, grinning, as she raised her voice over the increasing din.

"One final thing. Before you're released, your heads will be shaved, and you'll be required to bathe. Your clothes," she added, "will be boiled. The *Lady Anne* and the one known now as the *Granuaile* are no scurvy ships."

A unified wail of protest greeted her words.

"That's awful. Yer a killer of a woman," came from a cell.

She ignored the comment. "You'll have fresh bread, fruit and ale with your next meal. Now I'll leave you gentlemen to think over my offer," and with a swish of her skirts, she walked out of the jailhouse.

HARRY FOUND HER OUTSIDE, LEANING AGAINST THE WALL, drawing in gulps of fresh air.

"You belong on stage, Abby," he said, kissing her cheek. "That was as fine a performance as I've seen on Drury Lane."

"Whatever that is," she said, basking in his approval.

"It's a theater we'll frequent once we reach London. Have you ever seen a play?"

"No, I've never seen much of anything." She sighed. "That's why I'm here. And now, I fear, I may have seen more than I wanted to."

He laughed. "Aye, that's not a pretty sight in there, I grant you. The order to bathe nearly lost you a crew." He took her hand and placed it on his arm. "No, not true, I watched their faces as you spoke. There is some risk in sailing with them, but not as much as I thought earlier. You've given them hope, Abby, and they'll cling to it."

Arm in arm, contented with each other, they strolled along Port Royal's cobblestoned thoroughfare. As usual, the street vendors were out in force hawking their wares on every corner. She stopped in front of a girl with baskets piled high with exotic produce.

"I'd love one of those fruits," she said. "One of those that looks like a man's head."

"It's a nut, love. One of those coconuts. And you shall have one."

She'd never seen a coconut in Providence. Nor a jail full of filthy men, either. The wonders of the world, she'd learned, seesawed crazily between good and evil.

"EATING OUT OF YOUR HAND THEY WERE, Abby, and asking for more," Aiden exulted later that day. "They're a savage lot, if you'll pardon my saying so," he said, smiling at his own jest. "But after you left this morning, they were full of questions about you and talked of how you worried for their welfare aboard ship. They even asked how they all came to fall asleep at once. I told them what you did with the laudanum, and they roared with laughter. They loved the way you outfoxed them all. I truly believe Harry need have no worry for you on their account. On the contrary, I think they would fight to keep you safe."

Harry arched an eyebrow at her. She blushed under his amused glance. "Aiden's correct. You bound them to you today, Abby. You'll have a ship full of knights. In not-so-shining armor. But knights all the same."

"'Tis true," Aiden said. "Absolutely true." He strode restlessly about the parlor, his soft-soled moccasins making no sound on the hardwood floor. "It's been agreed that Mate Johnson will captain the sloop, and I'll sail with him. I've much to learn about seamanship, especially navigation. He'll be a fine teacher."

"And this time I'll not be an idle passenger as I was when we headed for New England," Harry said. "I've much to learn as well, and without Johnson aboard, the captain will need my help."

"And Cookie will need mine," Abby said.

Aiden nodded. "We'll all be busy then. Tomorrow I'm planning to careen the *Granuaile*. The keel is long overdue for a thorough scraping and caulking. I can see the seaweed hanging from her planking. I'll beach her at Kingston bay, that sheltered cove the governor mentioned. Slayton's crew have agreed to help with the work."

"How do they fare this night?" Abby asked.

"They'll sleep in the jail house until we sail. Their cells are unlocked, and they've been released from their chains, each man washed pink and white as a new-born babe. I had them sweep out the old flea-ridden straw and replace it with fresh strewing. They grumbled but did so willingly enough."

"Heads shaved as well?" Harry asked with a laugh.

Aiden nodded. "Sure and didn't the governor send his men to carry out Abby's instructions? In no time, they had kettles boiling in the prison yard. All the rogues scrubbed themselves raw then tossed their clothes into the stew pots. For a good part of the afternoon, they stood about naked as the day they were born eating the food Abby ordered, but their garments dried quickly enough in the sun."

"You look troubled, Aiden," Abby said. "Was I wrong to have them cleansed of the lice and filth?"

"Ach, not at all. 'Tis something else entirely that's bothering me. "

"What?"

"The men the governor sent. They were slaves." His frown increased. "A bad business, slavery."

"The worst," Harry agreed. "Here in Jamaica, the practice flourishes, but until parliament bans the practice, little can be done to stamp it out. And as long as slavery makes men rich, parliament won't act. On our own land, Abby, all will be different."

"Yes." She squeezed his hand. Mam had been right about some things, but about Harry not being a suitable mate for her daughter, she had been completely wrong. They were perfect for each other.

The day had been long, and their bed awaited. Though not in the least fatigued, she stood, smoothing her skirt with her hands, pretending to yawn for Aiden's sake.

"I believe I'm ready to retire," she said, keeping her voice as demure as she could manage.

A spark flared in Harry's eyes. "I'll join you in a few minutes, love, as soon as Aiden and I finish our ales."

She bade them good night and hurried up to the blue room. For as long as their stay on the island lasted, it was their patch of heaven on earth, and she ascended the stairs fairly dancing on her toes. She lifted their door latch and strolled in humming a tune. It died in her throat.

"Mattie, what's wrong?"

With a startled gasp at Abby's sudden appearance, Mattie averted her face as she bent to turn down the coverlet on the four poster bed. Abby ran over to her and took her arm. "You're crying. Why? Please look at me."

Slowly, unwillingly, Mattie straightened and turned to face Abby. Her eyes were red and swollen, her mouth bruised. "It be nothing, Mistress."

"Did someone hurt you?"

Mattie turned back to her task. "I be a slave, Mistress."

"That's no answer," Abby said. "Come." Despite Mattie's protests, she took her by the hand, drawing her across the room to one of the chairs by the tea table. Finally, yielding to the pressure of Abby's hands on her shoulders, Mattie slumped into the seat.

"This be wrong, Mistress."

"Let me worry about that." Abby pulled up the other chair and sat on its edge. "Now tell me what happened."

"Nothing, Mistress."

"Nothing? You're crying. Your lip is purple like someone struck you. That's not nothing." She leaned forward, soothing Mattie's damp, twisting hands with her own. "I'm your friend. You can tell me the truth."

"No, Mistress."

"Say 'Yes,'" Abby said softly. "Don't be afraid. Say yes." What can happen if you do? Tell me."

"Death. Death can happen."

ROCKED BACK IN HER SEAT BY MATTIE'S TERROR, Abby stared at her in disbelief. Someone had frightened the woman into fearing for her life. Her bruised lips trembled, her rich, golden skin had turned an ashy gray.

"Who hurt you, Mattie? Who?"

Mattie shook her head and hid her red-rimmed eyes with the palms of her hands.

If one of the household men was abusing her, surely she would complain, Abby thought. The governor wouldn't want his property damaged. Or worse, killed . . . of course . . . the governor. Who else held the power of life and death over his slaves? Who else could terrorize Mattie like this?

"It's him, isn't it? The governor?"

With a shocked, in-drawn breath, Mattie dropped her hands from her tear-soaked lids and stared straight ahead.

"He struck you, didn't he?"

Lips compressed into a tight line, Mattie didn't speak.

"You don't have to say a word. You're already given me the answer. Has he . . . has he harmed you in other ways?" Abby asked, fearing she already knew the answer to that as well.

Mattie hung her head and sat staring at her hands.

Abby stood. "He has."

Her fingers quivering like leaves in a storm, Mattie managed to grasp the hem of Abby's skirt. "No one must know, Mistress. No one. Not your man, even. If the governor find out he—"

"Don't be afraid. I won't tell anyone," Abby said. "Not a soul. Not even my husband, I promise. This is between you and me. Between two women only."

It was best that way, Abby thought, for instinct told her no man, not even Harry, one of the best in the world, could completely understand how Mattie must feel. The violation. The stripping away of all dignity.

"Is there nothing to be done?" Abby asked, as much of herself as of Mattie.

"Nothing, Mistress. Nothing can be done."

Abby dropped to her knees in front of the trembling woman. "No. Don't say that, Mattie. He's enslaved your body. Not your mind. Within yourself you're still free to think and feel as you wish. He can't stop that."

"No, Mistress." Mattie's voice was dull as an overused blade,

"This has happened before, hasn't it?"

After a furtive glance around the bed chamber, Mattie gave her a timid nod.

"But tonight he was brutal," Abby persisted. "Why?"

"Someone say something today. Call him a name. He say he show me he be a man. *A man.*" Mattie broke down in sobs.

The jail. The men had jeered at him.

Abby leapt up. "We'll buy your freedom." Somehow, somewhere she'd find the money. The same rum merchants Harry would see in the morning, perhaps they could help.

Mattie shook her head. "It's no good, Mistress. A planter want to buy me for his self. Caspar hear him. The governor say he no sell me. Never. I be his favorite slave." She shuddered.

"There's only one solution then," Abby said, tugging the bodice out of her skirt waistband. Harry would be joining her soon, and she wanted to be ready for him. Mattie rose to help her. "No need to get up, Mattie, rest for a while. I'm getting used to undressing myself in clothes like this." Her fingers busy at the laces, she asked, "Do you still have the boy's garments I wore here?"

Mattie nodded. "They be washed. I fetch them for you?"

"I have no need of them. They're yours to keep." She had nearly freed the bodice lacings. "Tell me something, is your hair long under that turban?"

Mattie's forlorn face cracked into a smile, and she raised her hands to her head. "Like the governor's wife? No, Mistress. My hair not be like that."

"May I see it?" Abby shrugged out of the bodice and untied her skirt, letting it slide to the floor.

A puzzled expression replaced Mattie's smile, but she complied and with shaky fingers unwound the white cloth from around her head.

"Oh, I see," Abby said. "It's in tiny curls. Have you just cut it?"

Half laughing, half crying, Mattie shook her head. No need, Mistress." She shrugged. "Only once in a while."

Abby had never seen hair quite like it, and fascinated, she stepped in closer. "May I touch it?"

"Yes, Mistress." With a humble bowing of her head that made Abby want to cry, Mattie leaned forward to let her hair be stroked.

"Why, it's like gossamer," Abby exclaimed. "As wispy as a butterfly's wings. And short. That's what I needed to know. Short is important." With one fluid motion, she whipped off her shift, picked up the fine lawn nightgown lying on the bed and dropped it over her head. "I have a story to tell you, but not now. Lord Rushmount will soon be joining me. In the morning, come help me dress for the day. And keep those boy's clothes for a while yet, Mattie. At least until you hear my tale."

Chapter Twenty Four

"Meow."

Aiden looked down at his feet. The tomcat rubbed against his ankles, mewling for attention, for a scratch behind the ears, for a touch of affection. He picked up the tabby, its coat, partly black, partly white, patched with golden brown.

"Are we alike, boy?" he asked, stroking the fur. "A little of this, a little of that, not one of any single thing. 'Tis a fine job, you're doing," he said into one arched ear. "You and your brother there, lazing in the sun. A fearsome number of rats you've caught so far, and no doubt more are hiding away from you." His hand moved to stroke the soft underbelly. "You ready for a sail?"

"Meow."

He put down the cat and strode the deck taking pleasure in the sight of her brass fittings gleaming in the sun, her scrubbed decks, the name *Granuaile* pricked out in gilt on both sides of the hull, as Abby had requested. Best of all, under Captain Johnson's instruction, the fore and aft sails had been enlarged, increasing their maneuverability for the challenge of the crossing. And due to Harry's astute bargaining, the hull had been filled to capacity with molasses, sugar and rum, a cargo that should fetch a fine price in England.

Abby had overseen the galley's food stores, insisting they include those odd looking coconuts that took an axe to break open, and a barrel of limes and another of lemons, and a huge branch of a strange island fruit shaped like fingers that the natives called bananas. A deep green color, they would ripen into yellow and last for many days. Abby had also ordered barrels of salt meat and sea biscuit and flour. When he reminded her they had no cook to turn the flour into bread, she'd just shrugged and said, "You'll find a way." Rather than argue the point, he agreed, and a barrel of white flour stood taking up room in the tiny galley space, along with a few chickens in cages. "For their eggs," Abby had said.

So all was in readiness. Including Aiden O'Donnell, he thought with a wry spurt of amusement at his own eagerness. The days he'd spent at sea traveling from Providence to the tropics had been all too brief. During them, he'd been at home on board ship in a way he'd never been on land, and he was keen to experience that same sense of belonging once again. He was fearful, though, that the release he'd known in those few brief days wouldn't return. If it didn't, he wouldn't know . . .

"Aiden, Aiden, over here!" Abby called from her seat in a fast-approaching skiff.

Ah, there they were, the newlyweds, looking happy. Looking fulfilled. Looking like nights of love hadn't tired them a bit. There were, he conceded ruefully, things more miraculous than sleep. He waved, watching as their dinghy cut through the surf, the men plying the oars aiming for the *Lady Anne* anchored nearby.

At first light of dawn, with high tide and the stirring of an off shore breeze, both ships would lift their anchors and pulse to life, their sails snapping, their prows heading north toward the Florida Straits, then north-northeast across the deep Atlantic.

Several nights ago, he had begun studying the stars with Carl Johnson as his guide. All his life, he'd used the stars to find his way through the woodlands after dark, but at sea their importance increased beyond measure. With no other markers in the watery vastness, the ability to read them could mean the difference between life and death. He had listened carefully to Johnson's instructions on how to employ the sexton and the compass, and there would be many more lessons, all of which he looked forward to. Somewhat to his embarrassment, Abby had insisted he assume the first mate's position; Carl Johnson had agreed saying he was a quick study. He intended to make himself worthy of their confidence in as short a time as possible.

As he looked toward the island, he spied a second small boat coming toward him, a rickety, water-logged bit of wood, hardly safe for man or beast. It drew closer, and curious, he leaned on the rail to watch its progress. A pair of thick-armed black men pulled at the oars; a slim black lad with a cap pulled low on his forehead crouched between them.

Strange.

They came abeam and stowed their oars. One of the men grasped the ship's rope ladder, snugging the makeshift skiff close to the hull. Aiden leaned over the railing. "You have business with us?"

The men remained silent. Only the boy spoke. "I have a message. It be for First Mate Aiden O'Donnell." He raised a hand. A piece of paper in his fingers rustled in the breeze.

Ye gads, who would be writing to him? Last minute orders from the governor, perhaps.

"Very well. Bring it on board."

To his surprise, the lad stuffed the paper into his breeches pocket and reached for a bundle lying in the bottom of the boat. He slung its strap over his shoulder and with one of the oarsmen steadying their leaky craft, he grasped the ladder and nimbly enough climbed up toward the deck. As his head and shoulders cleared the rail, Aiden grabbed his arm and swung him aboard. The lad dropped the bundle to the planking, reached into his pocket and held out the crumpled letter then stood unmoving his eyes cast down.

Stranger and stranger.

Aiden slid a fingertip under the red wax seal, unfolded the page and began to read:

> *My dearest Aiden,*
> *The bearer of this letter wishes to sail aboard the Granuaile*
> *as cabin boy. When he knows you better and can trust you,*
> *he will tell you his real name. For now, call him Matt. He*
> *can cook and will be very helpful to you during the voyage.*
> *It is my wish that he be kept from the crew at night and*
> *that you allow him to share your cabin.*
> *Until we meet again in London, may God keep you safe.*
> *Your loving sister,*
> *Abby R.*

Aiden crushed the paper in his fist and shoved it in a pocket. My loving sister and legal owner of this vessel, he thought, vexed at her request. He stared at Matt who still hadn't moved a muscle. "You're staying, then?" he asked the lad.

A slight nod was his only reply.

Aiden leaned over the railing. "You can go back. He'll remain aboard."

Without a word of farewell, the two men pushed off. Sighing with irritation, Aiden surveyed his newest crew member. He stood straight, not flinching under Aiden's gaze. Though slim, he had a hint of roundness to his form that spoke of good food or, in the way of boys, a weight gain presaging a sudden growth spurt. His skin had the polished sheen of silk, and the teeth caught between his full lower lip were white and clean. The lad appeared healthy and fit; he might be helpful after all.

In any event, since he couldn't change the situation, he'd make the best of it. Abby was given to impulsive doings, as he very well knew, but somehow he felt her involvement with this lad was more than mere caprice. Well, whatever her reason, he'd find out in due time.

"Follow me below. I'll show you where to stow your gear. Quarters are tight. You and I will room together. You get a hammock. I get the bunk. Are we clear on that?"

Another nod.

"Then I'll take you to what passes for a galley. Mistress Rushmount says you can cook, so you might as well get started."

"Yes, Master."

"What?" Half turned to lead the way toward the hatch, Aiden swiveled back. "What did you call me?"

Matt recoiled against the railing as if Aiden had struck him. The bundle slid from his hand to the deck and he glanced fearfully around, his large brown eyes flashing left and right at the sailors going about their tasks.

Aiden stepped in closer to him. "You need have no fear, lad. They're paying you no attention."

The boy began to tremble. A leaf in a storm, he met Aiden's eyes, helpless to control his body's shaking, helpless to control his fate. There could be only one reason for such fright.

"You're a runaway slave, are you not?"

Again the fearful darting of brown eyes. "Yes, I be a slave."

"Mistress Rushmount knows that?"

Matt nodded.

"She aided you," Aiden said. "Why?"

"She be the only one to know, Master."

Aiden's hand darted out to seize the boy's wrist. "Never call me that again. Do you hear me? Never again."

To his horror, tears pooled in Matt's eyes, ready to leak along his cheeks. "Enough of that. We're men on board ship, and we act as such." He let go of his wrist. "Keep your secrets, Matt. They're of no use to me. You understand?"

"Yes."

"Call me Aiden," he said. "Come along now. Dry your tears and follow me." He was about to enter the open hatch when it hit him. "Just a wee minute," he exclaimed. Turning to the boy, he ordered, "Go ahead of me. Go on." He urged him forward with a wave of his hand. "Down that open stairway there. Go on. Go on."

His eyes huge, his expression tense, Matt did as he was told and started down the stairs. At the bottom, he turned aft—how did he know that's where the cabin lay?—his hips gently swaying.

History, Aiden thought grimly, was about to repeat itself. In that moment, he didn't know whether to burst out laughing or to wring Abby's neck.

They entered his cabin, and he closed the door behind them. At the click of the latch, a film of fear broke out on Matt's gleaming face. Aiden leaned against the door jamb. "How did you come to know Mistress Rushmount?"

"I tend to her needs, sir."

"In the governor's house?"

After a second's hesitation, Matt nodded.

"Running errands? Carrying trays? That sort of thing?"

Wary, the boy nodded again, and kept inching away, putting as much space as possible in the small room between himself and Aiden. Finally, the back of his legs hit the bunk, he lost his balance and fell onto the pallet. As if he'd landed on a sheet of flame, he leapt up and stood trembling by its edge.

"Did you put fresh flowers in her bed chamber?" Aiden asked, lowering his voice, making it soft.

"Yes, Mas. . . . sir."

"And carry in pitchers of water for bathing?"

"I do that, too."

"And help her dress?"

"Yes, sir." Matt's eyes, huge in his face, widened at his mistake.

Aiden drew in a deep breath and let it out again. "Sure and you're a woman."

Mattie's head dropped to her chest. "That's what I be," she admitted, her voice no more than a whisper.

"Mistress Rushmount must have put you up to this. I know her well. She's my sister."

Mattie's head snapped up, her big brown eyes widening until they nearly filled her face.

"'Tis a long story," Aiden said drily, "one for another day. For now, it's your story that needs the telling."

He folded his arms, leaning on the door as if he had all the time in the world. Though truth to tell, from the sounds of activity overhead, he knew he should be up on deck. "Be quick," he said. "I have work to do."

"I be a lady's maid." Mattie began, her voice quivering.

"Go on."

"The governor . . . the governor . . . he . . ."

What was she trying to tell him?

"He . . . he . . . force me. Many times."

"Oh." The old, old story. "Abby knew?"

"She know. And she know I kill myself." The quiver in Mattie's voice had disappeared, and her silken jaw firmed into iron.

"So it was escape or die. That it?"

"Yes, sir."

"So now you're my problem." He eyed her carefully. Half a head taller than Abby and bigger boned, she filled out the boy's clothes nearly to bursting, making her disguise fragile at best. No wonder Abby wanted her away from the crew of nights. He sighed again. She was, indeed, going to be a problem. Even without a woman on board, the motley crew was problematical at best. And sharing this tiny space, little more than a closet, with a female would be disturbing, to say the least. Well, it wasn't too late. He could have her put ashore.

"What's your name?" he asked.

"I be called Mattie."

"If you return now, Mattie, the governor need never know you left."

Her lip curled up at one corner. "He be knowing. I drown myself before I reach shore."

She stood facing him, all trace of uncertainty gone. That she had made up her mind, Aiden hadn't the slightest doubt. Abby must have sensed the depth of the girl's desperation. She wouldn't have violated the governor's hospitality otherwise—or virtually stolen his property.

He gritted his teeth. By God, he should swim over to the *Lady Anne* and confront Abby with this latest complication. It would serve her right, presenting him with a problem like this. Then a thought struck him: Had she told Harry she'd engineered Mattie's escape? He breathed yet another sigh. Probably not, or she would have taken the girl with her. Thinking to keep Mattie's flight as secret as possible, she'd told no one, not even her husband. To press the issue now on the eve of an ocean crossing meant creating trouble at the worst possible time. The wisest course was to wait until they reached their destination and confront Abby then. And confront her, he would.

His decision made, he looked at Mattie and sighed. She stood alert, quivering before him like a forest creature whose fate lay in his hands. Though he had no intention of harming her, the knowledge humbled him.

He eyed her carefully. "For that disguise to work, you need larger clothes, especially on top." He'd stowed his spare garments in his sea chest. He opened it, fumbling through its contents until he found an old buckskin shirt. He handed it to her. "Here, put this on. 'Tis clean. The fringe will help to conceal your . . . ah . . . you."

Obedient, she turned away and pulled off the boy's shirt. How could he help but notice the exquisite way her back tapered into a hand-span of a waist? With a gesture as graceful as flowing water, she slid his old shirt over her head, and the image disappeared. He cleared his throat.

"You can have the bunk, I'll take the hammock."

"No, mas . . . sir. I take the hammock. Every night, I take the hammock."

CHAPTER TWENTY-FIVE

STAYING TRUE TO THE COURSE CARL JOHNSON HAD SET, Aiden gripped the wheel, the sea breeze pouring over him salt heavy and warm as a breath. He had never known such peace. With patched sails overhead and a few score yards of oak planking under foot, he was home at last. A home he never wanted to leave.

For an instant, he took his gaze from the horizon and glanced aft. Silhouetted against the blue sky, he could see the billowing sails of the *Lady Anne.* Like the sloop, she rode low in the water. Wider abeam, she was less maneuverable, but coming on steadily nonetheless, keeping to the same northerly course.

For five days they had been cutting through the smooth, glass green water of the tropics. So far, all had been well. Not a hint of trouble had rippled through the blended crew, though with the weather so flawless, keeping the ship on course required minimal effort from the men. The rough Atlantic would put them all to the test Carl had warned, and that testing time was approaching fast, for they would soon veer to the northeast. At least, Aiden thought, watching the men go about in pairs, the bald, shaven heads of the former brigands made them easy to spot. He had Abby to thank for that.

And for so much else. She had saved him when he was no more than a sprout freezing in the woods and now again as he rode this wondrous sea horse of hers. Some day, he vowed, he'd have a ship of his own and that was the name he'd give her—*Sea Horse.* Aye, he owed Abby much. His baby sister grown to adulthood, a married woman now, sharing

Harry's bunk . . . that thought the only worm in his peace . . . for his own bunk was empty and would remain so, though the woman Mattie lay disturbingly close in her hammock. And as far away as the stars. She was his ward to be delivered safe unto Abby's hands. What Harry would think when he saw her disembark, he could only surmise, but playing with the possibilities caused a smile to flit across his face.

"Enjoying yourself?" Carl Johnson asked suddenly, startling Aiden into jerking the wheel. "Steady there. Steady."

"Sure and my mind drifted off for a moment," Aiden admitted.

"It happens to a man when he stares out to sea." Carl looked into the binnacle. "Another hour, if the wind holds, we'll change course. Expect rougher weather. In the meantime, I'll get me some grub."

He walked away, no doubt heading toward the tantalizing odor vying with the salt air for Aiden's attention. He risked a quick glimpse over his shoulder, seeking the source of the aroma. Someone had set a kettle on the deck amidships. Next to it, in the fringed shirt, snug boy's breeches and bare feet, Mattie was doling out food. But what kind of food? Whatever it was, the men were crowding around the kettle, holding out their bowls, emptying them and asking for more.

On a ship too small for a wardroom, all meals were taken on deck, weather permitting, and when not, the men ate wherever they could find a place to sit—their hammocks, the lower hold, the companion. Where didn't matter; the sea air gave one a powerful appetite. By the time his watch ended, the food would be gone. Oh, well. Biscuit and cheese would keep him going.

"You be hungry?" a quiet voice asked.

Mattie stood at his side with a wooden bowl in her hands, the steam wafting from it making his mouth water. "What is that?" he asked.

She shrugged. "My mama, she make it in our village."

White, bite-sized morsels topped with a trickle of molasses filled the bowl.

"What did you put in it?"

"Eggs to make light. Salt. Lemon. Most of it be flour."

Ah, the flour.

"There be no oven to bake bread for so many."

"So this is the next best thing?"

She nodded, uncertain.

"It smells delicious, but I can't eat now."

"I save for you," she said, "by the cook fire."

He turned back to the sea, a small smile hovering about his lips. At least some of his needs were being attended to.

Carl Johnson hadn't lied. Within hours, the sea roughened, the glassy calmness of the last several days giving over to sporadic gusts of turbulence.

"It will get worse," Carl said. "A week from now this chop will seem like a rocking cradle." As if to prove his words, within days the ship began a constant battle with a furious sea. Over and over, she plunged into deep troughs then heaved up to meet the next wall of water sweeping over her decks. With a relentless energy, the sea raged and the wind howled as they bobbed like a toy in the vast, endless expanse, and always the patched sails billowed, straining and bucking against the shrouds. About to begin the second dog watch, Aiden eyed the sails in the fading light. Would the canvas hold? Or shred to pieces, leaving them adrift?

"We're making good time," Carl said coming up to the fo'c'sle to check on their progress. "Though the sea's a mite wild today."

A mite? Was the man jesting?

Aye, a cat's grin split Carl's face. "Are you worried, lad?" he asked.

"That I am. She's an old girl and heavily laden. 'Tis the pounding has me worried."

"Don't be. She'll hold. She was meant for this." He clapped a hand on Aiden's shoulder. "The pounding's not what bothers me. It's the cold." Carl pulled his wool stocking cap over his ears and hugged himself with both arms. "That's a devil of a wind out of a frigid hell." He glanced at the binnacle then peered over at Aiden. "You've hours left on your watch. All's well with you?"

"Aye, I'm fine." Assured that the sloop could stand up to the weather, what did it matter if his fingers froze to the wheel? This was a wind worthy of the name, every inhaled breath ambrosia. "But how are the men faring? Slayton's crew has little warm clothing against these winds. I've been thinking Tamworth's men might be persuaded to share their garments. I doubt they'd refuse. They all need each other."

Carl eyed him, serious faced. "You'll make a good captain some day. One the men will respect." Another clap on the shoulder. "I'll go below and give the order."

Though warmed by Carl's compliment, Aiden knew that until he was well versed in calculating longitude and latitude, he would be no captain. But for now this was enough. Gripping the wheel with renewed

energy, he inhaled, exhilarated by the air and the cold and the sough-
ing of the sea.

EIGHT BELLS. HIS WATCH HAD ENDED.

"From the look of ye, yer ready fer yer bunk." His replacement, young
Josh Smith, one of Tamworth's original crew, had arrived for his stint at
the helm, looking none too happy about it.

With a weariness he'd seldom experienced, Aiden gave over the
wheel, staggered amidships and, opening the hatch, made his way stiff-
legged with cold down the stairs. By God, his bunk would be welcome
this night.

HE COULDN'T BELIEVE THE SOFTNESS. AND THE WARMTH. Through the
chill that had reached his bones, heat began radiating from his shoulders
along his back to his buttocks, touching on his thighs, even cupping his
feet. An arm stole around his waist, bringing the softness closer.

She was in the bunk with him. He lay there unmoving, luxuriating in
the totally new sensation. The chill that had gripped him vanquished, his
shaking stopped. His eyes snapped open in the dark and stared unseeing
at the paneled wall.

For a long while, she lay still, pressed against him. He didn't move.
Should this be a dream, he wanted it to linger on and on. Forever, if possible. But it was no dream. She rose up on an elbow and leaning over
him, whispered in his ear, "You be warm now?"

He rolled over and gripped her shoulders. The flesh of them like satin
. . . all of her like satin . . . how could he have lived so long without realizing this is how a woman felt in a man's arms?

"Why?" he asked. "Why are you here?"

"You be cold. So cold I hear you shiver."

"That's no answer." His grip tightened, the need to keep her with him
too strong to loosen his hands on her flesh. "Give me a true reason."

"You want to make talk?" she asked. "Or something else?"

The tips of her breasts grazed his chest. His hands fell away from her.

"I never have," he said. At the admission, his face grew hot.

"I have," she said. "I teach."

It was as if he had never been chilled, never been cold, never stood
shivering for hours at the helm. Pulling the blanket with her to cover
them both, she straddled him and, to his utter amazement, bent to cover
his lips with hers, her breasts teasing at his chest.

He reached for them as she reached for him. He gasped. Was this truly happening? No one had ever held him so. Had he known . . .

"You be ready," she said, stroking him, then letting go. He wanted to groan aloud with disappointment, but in the same instant, she opened herself to him, and with a thrust as natural as breathing, he entered her silken place.

She had been right. No need for talk at all. He knew exactly what to do.

Chapter Twenty-Six

AT NOON ON A FOUL, DARK DAY, THE OFF DUTY CREW sat resting in a circle in the companion, staying close to the galley, soaking up the heat of the fire, and hoping to snag seconds.

His mouth half full of apple dumpling, Josh Smith said, "I swear that lad's the best Cookie I ever sailed with."

One of Slayton's crew, a hand by the name of Maggot, a loud-mouthed oaf with narrow, pink eyes and skin white as a corpse, looked up from his empty bowl. "What lad ye talkin' about?"

Josh jerked a thumb toward the galley. "Matt. That lad. The same one who's been cooking for us since Jamaica. Who else?"

"I'm not faultin' 'is cookin', mind ye, but that ain't no lad."

Josh swallowed his last bite and stood up, ready to seek more. "If he's not a lad, what is he?"

"A woman, ye fool. A full-blooded woman, by God."

"No." Josh's mouth fell open.

Maggot jeered and the others joined in, chortling, slapping the thighs and shoulders of whoever sat beside them.

"Surprised are ye? Well, me and me mates weren't fooled, not fer a minute." Maggot pointed a dirty finger at the galley. "Bringin' a woman aboard ship's a 'angin' offense." He eyeballed the group, zeroing in on those from Slayton's bristle-headed band. "'At's why we've said nuffin' so far. But the time's come. Aye, mates?"

"Aye!" they shouted, the sound bouncing off the walls, echoing in the air.

Stunned, Josh stood rooted in place, his empty bowl forgotten in his hand. "You want to hang somebody?"

"Nah, nuffin' like that. We just wants us a piece."

"Aye," piped up Monkey, a skinny hand who climbed the shrouds with the agility of a jungle creature. "A piece of what a woman's for. Ain't that so, swabies?"

"Wait up," Josh said. "You don't know for sure if he's . . . if she's . . ."

"Oh, we knows, all right," Maggot retorted. "And that first mate, as they calls him, the Injun she's bunkin' with, he knows, too."

"Well, I don't," Josh said, "and we have no right to—"

"No right? Who's to take it from us?" Maggot scrambled to his feet. "Only one way to find out what's what."

Cheered on by the others, he strode toward the galley, the men crowding behind him.

Engrossed in her work, Mattie paid no attention to the noise. Like overgrown children, the men jeered and guffawed together whenever they had a leisure moment. Let them enjoy, she thought, their lives were harsh. Quietly, to herself, she hummed a half-forgotten tune from her childhood. For the first time since she could remember, life was once again worth living. This man, this Aiden, he was good to her.

She dropped the last batch of dough balls in the boiling water, glancing up as a shadow fell across the galley's open wall. One of the men. She lowered her eyes, a habit she'd learned early in her capture. It deflected trouble, helped her to pass unnoticed under a bully's gaze.

The shadow loomed larger, bringing with it the odor of heated sweat. She looked up again. The strange looking white man stepped in closer, his pale pink eyes filled with lust. She well knew that look. This time she would not take her eyes away. This time, she would stare evil in the face.

"What's yer name, gal? he asked, his lashless lids arching suggestively. "You can tell ole Maggot. He means no harm."

A murmur of agreement from the men pressing in closer.

Gal. They knew.

Trapped on three sides by walls and by men jamming the only opening, she huddled in a corner.

"Don't be scared, gal. Maggot just wants a look see. At first, that is."

A howl of glee rose up. "Go, on Mag. We all wants us a look see. Go on. Do it."

Her eyes dilated, sweeping left, right . . . left, right . . . seeking escape. He was nearly on her, his breath hot on her face. Frantic, she moaned aloud. Like a viper, Maggot's long, dirty paw darted out and seized the front of her fringed shirt. He gave it a vicious yank, splitting it open from neck to waist.

"Ha, what did I tell ye?" he asked, half turning to his audience.

Triumphant, he took one of Mattie's exposed breasts into his hand, kneading it between his thumb and forefinger. As he pleasured himself, she eyed the knife gleaming on its hook by the stove.

"That's the way, Mag. But don't be a pig. We all wants a turn."

"Not so fast, not so fast." Maggot let go of Mattie to reach down and unfasten his breeches.

The instant he released her, she stretched forward. Her hand, like a lightning flash, grabbed the butcher knife from the hook. Holding it tight in both hands, she rushed at him.

"Watch out, Mag, she's comin' at ye!"

Before he could straighten up, she plunged the blade deep into his side.

"Aaaarrrrggh." Shock and disbelief mingling in his face, Maggot dropped to his knees then slumped, like a collapsed sail, to the galley floor, the knife hilt jutting out from between his ribs.

The men fell back. Her breasts breaking free from the torn shirt, Mattie walked toward them, not bothering to cover herself.

"You want something from me?" she challenged them in turn. "You want? And you?" She jabbed a finger at Monkey. "You?"

With his open mouth displaying a row of blackened teeth, he scurried away, seeking refuge behind a burly hand.

Mattie stood tall, her shoulders back. "I be a woman, as you see. You want do bad to me? Hmmm? You? What say you? You want do bad?"

Her wrath, like that of a demon woman, stopped them where they stood. She had won, she thought, staring into their shocked faces. For the first time in her life, she had won.

Then Maggot moaned.

"He's alive." A man close to him knelt by his side. "He's still breathin'."

"She tried to kill 'im," someone shouted. "Are we goin' let her get away with that?"

"No!" A roar went up.

The man by Maggot leapt to his feet. "The Mag meant no 'arm. Just bein' a man is all."

"Seize 'er! She's a killer, she is."

The men surged forward, crowding into the galley, shouting invective.

In the frenzy, a careless foot kicked the fallen Maggot in the ribs. He let out a scream that rose, soaring like a high note, over their noise.

At the helm, Aiden and Carl Johnson cast startled glances at each other. "Trouble," Aiden said.

"You, take the wheel," Carl shouted at an astounded deck hand. Together, he and Aiden raced below.

Alone, in a corner, cowering like a trapped animal, Mattie faced the mob. At the sight of her, frightened for her life, her breasts exposed, Aiden knew in a flash what had happened. The strength of ten rippling through him, he waded into the crowd, seizing arms, ripping shirt sleeves, shoving men out of his way to get to her.

"Fall back," Carl shouted. "This is your captain. Fall back, I say."

Gradually, mumbling curses, they followed orders and gave way. Aiden had reached Mattie. He closed the shirt to cover her and held her in his arms. "All's well. All's well. They won't hurt you."

Carl pointed to a now unconscious Maggot.

"Who did this?"

"She did," Monkey said to a muttered ripple of agreement.

"A woman attacked a ruffian like Maggot? Why?"

A silence fell over the galley. Carl studied the prone figure on the galley floor. "His flies are unfastened." He looked up, letting his glance rest on the men, one by one. He took his time. No one spoke. "So that was the way of it," he said. No one answered him.

He pointed to Maggot. "Lift him onto the shelf so we can tend to him."

Four hands stepped forward. Hauling Maggot by the arms and legs, they laid him with a thud on the galley work shelf. His feet dangled over the edge.

Carl seized the butcher knife by the hilt and pulled it free. Instantly, a bloody spurt bloomed on Maggot's canvas shirt and spread to his breeches, pooling on the shelf underneath him.

"Get the sail maker here to stitch him afore he bleeds to bloody death," Carl shouted. He gave Maggot a disgusted look. "Not that it will help him, I'm thinking." He looked around. No one had moved. "Well?" he thundered.

"I'm going, cap'n." Josh Smith said, hurrying out of the galley.

Carl nodded at two men in front. "You both stay here with him. The rest get back to your duties. You two," he upped his chin at Aiden and Mattie, "See me in my cabin. Be quick about it."

IN HIS CABIN, CARL STOOD WITH HIS HANDS behind his back glaring at them.

"You're directly responsible for what happened," he said to Aiden, his voice as cold as the wind howling around the ship. "You brought an unattached woman on board knowing what that does to men at sea, deprived for months."

At his harsh tone, Mattie gripped Aiden's arm.

"She was sent to me as a cabin boy, Carl."

"But you knew what she was."

"After she was aboard, yes. Not before. By then, there was little could be done about it." Not entirely true, but he would never regret having Mattie aboard, no matter what happened. Not even Maggot's certain death. He had acted like an animal and been slaughtered like one. An act of justice, if ever there was one.

"I want to believe you." Carl said. "I like you, and you've the makings of a fine sailor, but—"

"There be a letter that tells," Mattie said soft as velvet.

Carl arched an eyebrow at her. "A letter?"

She nodded. "I give it to Aiden from Mistress Rushmount."

"If such a letter exists, I'd like to read it."

"I discarded it," Aiden said.

"I save," Mattie said. She released Aiden's arm and hurried from the cabin, returning in a few moments holding a crumpled sheet of paper.

Carl took it from her outstretched hand and perused its contents. He raised his sea blue eyes to hers. "Can you read?"

"No, sir."

"So you have no idea of its contents?"

Mattie shook her head. "Only what Mistress tell me she write."

He glanced over at Aiden, frowning. "So Abby's a party to this?"

"She meant well, Carl. She was trying to protect Mattie."

Carl raised a hand, palm out. "Let her tell it. Go on," he said to Mattie.

"Mistress know about the governor."

"The governor? What does he have to . . . are you his slave?"

Mattie hung her head.

"Answer me, girl."

She looked up, her brown eyes luminous, her chin defiant. "He call me slave. But I be no slave."

"The man paid money for you?"

She jerked her head up and down, once.

"Then you belong to him," Carl said flatly.

"She's free of him now," Aiden said.

"Not under English law, and this is an English ship. God knows, I don't hold with slaving, but the woman's legally Molesworth's property. Worse, she's probably killed a man. I doubt Maggot will survive that wound."

"She acted in self defense."

"Aye, she did." Carl sighed in exasperation. "Let's hope an English jury will agree as well." He held up the crumpled paper. "In the meantime, I'll keep this document. I may need it when we get to London."

IN THEIR OWN CABIN, AIDEN STRUCK A SPARK from the tinder box and lit the lantern swinging from an overhead beam. It cast a warm glow in the center of the room, leaving the edges in shadow.

Mattie sank onto the bunk, her head in her hands. "Look at me," Aiden said, sitting beside her, prying her fingers away from her face.

She raised huge eyes to his. Tears slid along her cheeks. Aiden thumbed them away, gently, each touch to her skin a caress.

"Why are you crying?" he asked.

She didn't answer but raised her hands to her face again, sobbing silently, the wetness leaking out between her fingers, dropping onto the torn shirt she had tied together.

He asked no more questions but cradled her in his arms, rocking her, murmuring her name over and over until her grief shuddered into a final sob, and she sat up straight, wiping her eyes with the back of a hand, giving him a lopsided attempt at a smile.

"Ah, that's better," he said. "No more tears, all right?"

She nodded and shyly kissed his check,

"Now will you tell me why you're crying?"

"The captain," she began, "he speak of London. I heard of London. The governor, he be from there. A big place, he say."

"Yes, I've never seen it myself. It should be wondrous."

"Not for me. For me, punishment is there."

"I refuse to believe that." He got up from the bunk to pour two mugs of port wine from a carafe on his desk. He handed one to her. "Here. It will make you feel better."

She took the mug and sipped, grateful for the wine's warmth, though it didn't ease the chill in her heart. For Aiden was wrong. She knew in her bones she would suffer for what she had wrought this day. To undo what had happened was impossible. Yet even if she were given the power to change the outcome, she would refuse to do so. She had been violated for the last time. It would never happen again. She squared her shoulders and finished her wine.

"More?" Aiden asked.

"That be good."

He laughed. "I agree. One of the great pleasures of life." He poured more for them both then returned to sit by her side. "In London, the three of us, I mean Abby and Harry and I, will join forces to keep you safe. There will be no trial, you'll see."

"Trial?"

"Yes." He took her hand in his. "The jury Carl spoke of. A group of people, usually twelve in number, determine a person's guilt or innocence."

"I be not innocent."

"You were defending yourself. No man on earth could blame you for that."

Oh, you be wrong, she thought, sipping her wine, keeping her eyes on its ruby red color. Like blood, it was . . . so much blood came from that evil one.

"Harry won't want my sister's role in this revealed," Aiden was saying. "For that reason alone, there'll be no trial. He'll find a way to prevent it."

"The governor, he'll want me back."

"Together we'll raise the money somehow and buy you from him."

"He no sell me. I know."

"That's ridiculous. We'll offer a price he can't refuse."

"He refuse. He no want money, he want something else."

As her meaning dawned on him, Aiden pulled her close, holding her as if he never wanted to let her go.

He was so earnest, so sincere, so worried, she had to comfort him. She put down her empty mug and flung her arms around his neck, drawing his face to her own. Even if she escaped what he called a trial, she still belonged to the governor. The captain knew so, and he was correct. The governor would not take money for her; he had refused it before, he would refuse it again. She would be sent back to him, and he would be vicious.

No more.

She knew what to do.

Lifting her face, she looked straight into Aiden's eyes. "Kiss me," she murmured. "Please kiss me."

Afterward, his steady breathing told her he slept. A deep sleep, the rise and fall of his chest calm and steady. He had been well loved. Every part of him knew it and was at peace. How she had gloried in doing that for him.

As silent as when she stalked birds in the forests of home, she stole from the bunk. Her bare feet made no sound on the floor boards nor her fingers on the door latch. Out in the companion, she eased the cabin door closed and crept along the dark stairs to the upper deck. The raging wind of earlier had calmed; still the air blew cold on her naked skin, and coming from her warm bed, she shivered. Soon she would be warm again. And soon, warm or cold, she wouldn't care. She stood unmoving by the hatch. No hint of dawn light fingered the sky. Good. She wanted no one to see and later tell Aiden what she had looked like.

Close by, a man coughed. The helmsman? She stood still as a hunted creature, ears alert, eyes nearly useless in the gloom. Low voices near the wheelhouse. How many men were on watch in the night? She had never ventured up on deck so late . . . no matter, it was but a few steps to the railing.

Now. As naked as when she had been created, she vaulted the rail with ease and plunged into the water.

"Hey," Josh said from the helm, "did you hear something just then?"

"Nah, nuffin," Monkey replied. "Yer imaginin' things. The cold does that to a body."

Somehow, as she had known it would be, the water was warm. And then there was no warmth, or cold, at all.

Chapter Twenty-Seven

"**M**attie," Aiden whispered as the first dawn light filtered into the portholes, waking him. He reached out a hand, but he was alone in the bunk. She must have risen early and gone to the galley.

Thoughtful as always, she had been careful not to wake him. He stretched and flung his arms overhead. What a night she had given him. Each time they lay together, he discovered something new, a deeper awareness, a keener pleasure. An amazing woman, she held nothing back. Nothing. He grew heated remembering how she had clung to him. Too bad she left so early, just the thought of her aroused him. Those liquid eyes when they looked at him, ready to obey any wish, any command, and her tenderness, stroking him and murmuring his name: Aiden. The very way she pronounced it made it sound like a love word: Aiden.

Yet despite their nights of loving, they hadn't spoken of love. The next time, he vowed. This coming night. Aye.

Four bells. Two more hours before his watch. He had the forenoon watch today, from eight of the clock to noon.

He tossed off the covers and leapt out of the bunk. For some reason, he had a fierce appetite this morning. Before he took the wheel, he'd see what was cooking and chat a while with Mattie.

In the galley, the shelf where Maggot had lain was washed clean, all trace of blood gone, but the fire pit was cold, only a few banked coals winking under the ashes. He wondered how Maggot fared, but where Mattie might be interested him more. He was about to leave and go in search of her when two of the off duty men came in.

Monkey's face fell at the sight of the cold fire pit. "No porridge for us this mornin'? And us up most of the night. Where's the gal?"

Josh looked around the small space as if she might be hiding somewhere. "She must've quit the job, Monkey. Can you blame her? Well, I know where she keeps the cheese. We can have some of that."

The rest of the crew would soon be looking for their morning meal. Serve them right, Aiden thought, if Mattie refused to cook for the rest of the voyage. The louts. What better way to let them know the depth of her offense? Carl had said they'd be at sea a fortnight longer, maybe less. Well, sea biscuit and cheese and what was left of the apples would keep them going if need be.

He strode the upper deck searching for her but didn't see her anywhere. He decided to look below and came upon Carl on the narrow stairs. In response to his "good day," the captain favored him with a curt nod.

"Maggot's dead," he said. "As soon as his shroud's ready, we'll bury him. Let the men know."

Regretful, but not a source of sorrow. He must find Mattie and tell her before anyone else did. He raced down the rest of the stairs. The cabin was empty. Strange. And then he saw them, her boy's clothes, neatly folded over the back of his desk chair, her shoes placed side-by-side beneath them. She must have dressed in her woman's clothes, the ones she'd brought aboard in her bundle. But the bundle lay unopened where she'd placed it weeks ago.

His heart racing faster than his feet, he took the stairs to the upper deck two at a time. He had to get to Carl and fast. If the men had harmed her, retaliating for Maggot's death, he'd kill every one with his bare hands.

No, don't take that tack, he admonished himself. Slow down. She needs you to be calm. Besides, she might have hidden herself away, wanting to be alone and private for a while. But the demon of truth refused to let him find solace in that thought. She would never do anything to stress him so. Not Mattie. Not his love.

He found Carl staring aloft, watching the men on the rigging unfurl the sails full into the wind.

As Aiden approached, he sent him another curt nod. "We should make good time today. There's a head wind blowing. May even shave a day or two off our voyage." Carl cupped his eyes with a hand and peered astern. "The *Lady Anne's* coming along smartly. Very good."

"Mattie's missing," Aiden said.

Carl dropped his hand from his eye to turn and stare at Aiden. "You're sure?"

Was the man daft? He was horribly sure. "I'm sure."

Carl didn't hesitate. "We'll divide into two parties," he said immediately. "You take a man with you. Search the bilge and the hold. I'll take the lower deck." "Here, you two, he called to two hands who were swabbing the boards with salt water. "Let that go for now. Come below." To Aiden he said, "Search every cubby."

"Don't worry," Aiden said, fear for her mounting like a fever within him.

"Report to me when you're finished." Carl said.

Already halfway through the hatch, with a young sailor at his heels, Aiden nodded. "Bring a lantern," he said to the man, "The cook's gone missing."

It took a long time to search the hull. The cargo boxes and barrels had been closely stacked and lashed into place, leaving little space for hiding. But someone determined not to be seen, someone lithe and nimble, could curl up in a small chink between the boxes.

She could be anywhere. But she was nowhere.

Holding the flickering lantern on high, Aiden trudged up the stairs, the young sailor close behind him. From the look on Carl's face when they reached the main deck, he knew he'd had no luck, either.

"We've covered every inch, but she's nowhere to be seen," Carl said, worry creasing his forehead. "There's only one answer. She must have gone overboard."

"No, God not that."

The men working on deck looked at each other then looked away. By now news of Mattie's disappearance had sped throughout the ship. A bad business. An ill omen.

The lantern forgotten in Aiden's hand burned in the clear morning light. Carl took it from him, blew it out and hung it from a hook over the hatch. One glance at Aiden's stricken face and he said, "Get a grip on yourself, man."

"If she's in the water, someone did it to her. Christ, half the crew are rogues and thieves and killers."

"Don't be so quick with that. She was a troubled girl. For a fact, she feared being returned to her owner."

Aiden fell silent. Aye, her first night aboard she had threatened to drown herself if he sent her back to Jamaica. She must have believed no force on earth could save her. Last night, they spoke of reaching London soon. Of what might happen there. Dear God, had he not been as—

"When did you see her last?" Carl asked. "Aiden, did you hear me?"

With an effort, he pulled himself out of his musing. "I heard, Carl. The last I remember, four bells rang, then a single toll. After that I fell asleep."

"After two in the morning." Carl eyed him. "You were awake late."

Aiden flushed. "Aye, but I arose early. At dawn. She was gone then."

"So she disappeared sometime after two and before six." Carl turned to a deck hand. "Bring me the men who were on last night's middle watch. Make haste."

"Aye, sir."

The man hustled below, returning in a few minutes with Josh and Monkey dressed against the cold and half asleep.

"The girl Mattie can't be found," Carl told them. "We think something happened to her a while before dawn. Probably on your watch. Did either of you see anything unusual last night?"

Monkey shook his head. "'Twas as dark as a witch's—beggin' yer pardon, sir—ye couldn't see a hand in front of yer face. Not a star in the sky. And the cold, brrrrr."

"Spare me the histrionics, Monkey. You?" Carl upped his chin at Josh.

"No, sir. I saw nothing untoward. But I did hear something toward the end of my watch."

"Going on four of the morning?"

"Aye, after the bells rang marking half past three."

"What kind of sound?"

"Now that I think on it, it was a splash, like a shark or a marlin makes when it leaps up."

"Did you hear it, too?" Carl asked Monkey.

"I 'eard nuffin', sir, me ears were froze beyond 'earin'. So when Josh asked me if I 'eard somethin', I told him no."

"Thank you. Go back to your hammocks, men."

"A fine thing, breakin' into a man's sleep like that, and us up half the night."

As Monkey's grousing faded away, Carl clapped a hand on Aiden's shoulder. "That's the closest we'll ever come to the whole truth, and I'm sorry for it, Aiden. She was a star-crossed girl." From inside his doublet pocket, he removed a crumpled sheet of paper. "Here, you might want this. I'd destroy it if I were you. When we reach London, I'll report her as a stowaway lost at sea, identity unknown. And that will be the end of the matter."

His fingers gripped Aiden's shoulder one last time before he turned and walked away. Aiden followed him with his eyes until he disappeared behind the fo'c'sle, then he looked out to sea. The wind-tossed water swelled, buffeting the *Granuaile* as she sliced on eastward. Strange how the winter sky shed a high summer light on all below, gilding the ocean's surface, making it gleam as if polished by a gigantic hand.

As Aiden strode to the wheelhouse, he inhaled the salt air, pulling it into his lungs in great, shuddering gulps. This beautiful place was Mattie's home now, and it would always be his. He had lost one love, but by God, he had one left. She was a jealous bitch, but he would never leave her.

Chapter Twenty-Eight

London at last. A city worthy of the name. Abby stood at the prow of the *Lady Anne* bundled against the cold in one of Harry's doublets, drinking in the sights as they sailed up the Thames. Ships of all sizes and shapes clogged the banks, sea-going tall masters, coastal traders and small skiffs that darted around the larger vessels like little, harrowing dogs. Built to the very edge of the river, buildings grander than any she had ever seen stretched on as far as the eye could reach. People were everywhere, plying crafts, barking orders, rolling barrels onto horse-drawn carts, talking, singing, shouting. Ahead, she spied the stern of the *Granuaile* moving along in the river's central channel. She squeezed Harry's arm. He smiled, telling her he shared her excitement.

"The sights that make London spectacular can't be spied from the river," he said.

"There's more? Oh, I can't wait. I want to see everything!" She flung her arms wide, taking in the whole panorama spread before them.

"And so you shall." He bent to kiss her cheek. "I'll love showing you around. And showing you off."

"Oh, Harry. Bless you for saying that. But I'm a sorry sight, I fear. My hair's still too short to dress properly, and my clothes from Jamaica are soiled. Your doublet is wonderfully warm, but it looks so dreadful on me."

"We'll find a seamstress. In a few days, she'll have new clothes ready for you. And your hair is longer. I can see little tendrils escaping below your nape."

He stretched out a finger to twirl a curl around it.

"Warm clothes would be lovely."

"My mother will know just where to take you."

His mother. Lady Anne Rushmount. The thought of meeting her looking like a bedraggled frump in a thin cotton gown topped with a man's doublet quieted Abby's excitement. Worse, they had married without his mother's presence or permission. Worse still, the woman Harry had married was not of his own social class. Lady Anne would view her as a wild colonial, ignorant of proper mannerisms, her speech blunt and to the point. A woman with no feminine charms, no breeding . . . no hair.

She sighed with the weight of it all, but not even these worries could quell her excitement for long. She sniffed the air. "I smell smoke." She gazed up at the clouds. "Look, the sky's full of it. The city's on fire."

"What you're sniffing is thousands of chimneys burning at once. Get used to it, love. It's a price of city life."

That and the filthy water, she thought, looking over the side into the murky river. So different from the clean, blue breakers rolling in on the Providence shore. A dead rat floated by, or was it a dog? No matter, there was more to London than a dirty river, and besides, she'd soon be seeing Aiden again. Mattie, too. Surely by now, after sharing a tiny cabin for weeks, Aiden had learned Mattie's true identity. She hoped he had learned to care for her. Mattie had had little affection in her life. Once thing for certain, she'd never have to return to Jamaica. She was free now.

"I don't suppose you'd like to come below and get out of this chill wind?" Harry asked.

"No, there's too much to see."

He laughed. "From the shine in your eyes, I thought not. I'm trying to see everything as you do, as if I'd never seen it all before. Though it has been a while, I'll admit. Nearly a year. My mother will be very happy that I've, that we've, arrived safely. You'll meet each other soon."

Soon. Abby shivered and gripped Harry's arm. "I can't do it," she said. "I can't meet her."

"I'm shocked," he said, clutching his chest. "There's actually something you can't do?"

"I'm not jesting, Harry. I can't meet your mother. I'm too frightened."

"After taking on a ship full of pirates? I don't believe it."

"It's God's honest truth."

"My lady mother is lovely, the soul of tact. She'll love you on sight." He lifted her hand from his arm and stepped back, letting his glance roam over her. "On second thought, maybe not," he drawled.

"Oh, Harry. Don't. I can't bear it."

"When she gets to know you as I do . . ." a lazy smile drifted across his face ". . . well, perhaps not quite as I do. Nevertheless, she'll adore you. As I do," he said planting a kiss on the tip of her nose.

"You're impossible," she said.

"You stole that saying from me."

"Yes, I did. It's one of my favorites."

He laughed. He did so frequently when they conversed, she noted with satisfaction, loving the sound of his joy.

"Look. Over there." He pointed to a flight of stone steps on the left bank and a high, windowless stone building behind the stairs. "That's our warehouse. We're here."

Bustling with renewed energy, the crew moved about the shrouds, lowering the sails, slowing their steady progress. Up ahead, the *Granuaile* had come to a full stop, the anchor chain already snaking over her hull into the gray Thames.

Once the ships were unloaded and the cargo stored in the warehouse overnight, the men who wished to go ashore would be given a few coppers for a lodging or, more likely, a night's debauchery. They would receive their full share in a day or two, as soon as the cargo was sold.

No wonder they were hopping about the ship like frogs in a meadow. The dinghy was lowered over the side. "We disembark here," Harry said. "Let's go below now and gather our things."

She had precious little to gather, a few ribbons, a hair brush she had limited use for at the moment, and a second set of light clothes suitable for the tropics but inadequate against London's penetrating damp. Still, as she bundled her things together, her heart lifted. Though she wished she could postpone forever the meeting with Lady Rushmount, she could hardly wait to see Aiden and Mattie.

SOMETHING WAS WRONG. SHE KNEW IT THE INSTANT she saw Aiden moving slowly toward her along the stone quay, dragging his steps as if he never wanted to reach her with his evil tidings. What could it be? The ship had arrived intact, he looked as strong and stalwart as ever . . . Mattie. Where was Mattie?

She ran over the last few yards of rough cobbles separating them and flung herself into his arms. "Aiden, I'm so happy to see you again."

"And I you." He hugged her close before bending down to kiss her cheek. "But—"

"Something's wrong," she said.

"Aye. Something is." He looked past her into the horizon.

Why wouldn't he meet her gaze? What could be the reason? *Oh, no.* Her hand flew up to her mouth to smother a scream. "It's Mattie, isn't it?"

He nodded, his eyes bleak. "She's gone."

"Gone? What do you mean, gone?"

The noisy tumult of the dock, the sharp odor of decay rising from the river, the chill breeze rippling her skirts, all disappeared as she waited for him to explain.

"It's simple enough," he said. "She didn't want to live anymore."

"Oh, my God."

Harry came up to clasp Aiden's hand. From his expression, she knew he had heard.

"Why?" he asked, puzzled.

"What happened is my fault, Harry," Abby said, plunging in before Aiden could reply. "I gave her the boy's clothes. I told her to steal away. I even bribed the oarsmen who brought her out to the *Granuaile*. I shouldn't have done it."

"You helped her escape?" Harry sounded incredulous.

Abby hung her head, not wanting to see the accusation sure to be on his face. "Yes. It's all my fault she died."

"No." Harry shook his head. "Mattie was a desperate woman. You told me in Jamaica she had thoughts of death. Nothing you did caused that. Her life was in her own hands." A spurt of anger flashed in his eye. He took a step away from her. She wished he hadn't; the breeze had turned bitter cold. "But you shouldn't have concealed this from me. You didn't trust me with the truth. That's unfortunate. Any marriage worthy of the name is based on trust."

She glanced from Harry to Aiden but found no comfort there. He looked stricken, as if he had lost the love of his life. Could that be?

"We need lodging for the night, Aiden," Harry said, anger simmering in his voice. "There's a snug inn not far from here. Once Abby's settled, I'll return, and we can oversee the unloading."

"Harry?" Abby asked. He looked at her without a smile. "I want to stay here while the *Granuaile* is unloaded. She's my ship and . . ." She stopped.

Everything she owned legally belonged to her husband, a husband who was frowning at her, a husband not in the mood to grant requests.

His frown deepened. "In London, no lady consorts on a public dock with stevedores."

"I went to the dock with you in Jamaica. Even into a prison."

"That was different. The islands play by different rules."

"This is an island."

"That's enough, Abby. I'm escorting you to our lodgings, and that's the end of it. Will you come with us, Aiden?"

"No need, Harry. I'll sleep on board ship."

"Very well. I'll be back within a turn of the glass."

Abby kissed Aiden good-bye. She could argue further, but common sense told her not to as with fingers of steel, Harry took her elbow and led her away, taking care, she noticed, not to let his arm or any other part of him touch her.

HARRY HURRIED ALONG THE BUSY STREETS too fast for her to enjoy the excitement and the smells and the sounds of so many people, so many buildings. As she struggled to keep up, she risked a peek at his stony profile. Still angry. Hurt, too, she suspected though he would never admit to that.

She should have told him about Mattie but had been uncertain of how he would react. She hadn't, in truth, trusted him. Once again, she had taken matters into her own hands and flirted with danger as well as with the law. She had been wrong to do so though all she'd wanted was Mattie's happiness. Poor Mattie. The thought that she might have hastened her death sent a chill colder than the frigid breeze racing along Abby's spine. She quickened her pace, wanting to ask Harry to slow down a bit, but a single peek at his face convinced her otherwise.

Never discourteous, always concerned for her welfare, he must be aware of her puffing away at his side. It was as if the glorious nights aboard ship had never happened. The love words, the tenderness, the caresses, all gone. A vicious eddy of raw air swept up under her skirt. Dejected, shivering in her thin frock, she trudged beside him without speaking. Nor did he say a word. Just as well. His words right now would not be fit to hear.

He came to a halt in front of a half-timbered house, the sign above its red door squeaking on rusty hinges: The Ram's Horn.

"Shall we?" he asked, steering her toward the entrance, no softening smile lifting his mouth.

"As you wish." She had made a grave error, true, but did he have to be so unforgiving, acting as if she were mere baggage he had brought along? Aye, maybe that's all she was. Baggage. Shabby and shorn and alone. She stifled the urge to cry.

In the inn's public room, a fire leapt high in the cavernous stone fireplace. She ran to it, stretching out her hands over the flames, basking in the warmth. The smell of baking bread mingled in the air with the mouth-watering aroma rising from a joint of mutton browning to a fare-thee-well on the fire spit.

She looked over her shoulder to see Harry in conversation with the innkeeper, a fat man of middle age, a stained leather apron tied over his paunch. She caught a little of their talk, but was too upset, too cold, too distracted by a sudden ravenous hunger to follow what they were saying. She turned back to the comfort of the fire.

"Abby." She looked into Harry's unyielding face. "I've made arrangements for a room. And a bath for you. The innkeeper will see to everything, and he'll bring you some food. Stay in our room until I return. Do you hear me? In our room."

She nodded. "It was good of you to arrange for a bath."

"You'll be meeting my mother. I thought you'd want one."

"Oh. Yes." His mother.

"I'll bathe when I return from the dock."

"When will that be?"

"When my work is finished." His voice carried the same chill as the wind off the river. "Remember, stay in our room. You'll be safer there."

He wanted her safe, but he didn't want her kiss. Turning on his heel, he left her alone with the innkeeper who stood staring at her, wringing his hands, no doubt in glee at the coin Harry had paid him.

"My lady." The innkeeper paused as if not quite believing this grubby girl could be a member of the gentry. Aye, she thought, a dirty frock and a man's doublet will do that every time. "My wife will soon have your room made ready. Will you take a seat by the fire? And what say you to a hot toddy?"

"That would be wonderful," she said. God knows, she needed something to help her cope with the cold.

IN THE DARK, SHE HEARD WATER splashing. Was she back on the ship? Shaking off sleep, she half rose on her elbows. Where was she? Oh, yes, in bed in The Ram's Horn. She fell back against the pillows, but the splashing continued. She sat up and peered over the footboard.

"Harry, is that you?"

"Yes. I'm bathing. Go back to sleep."

He didn't want to talk to her, but she needed some answers. "You've been gone nearly two days. Where have you been?"

"You know where I've been. On the docks."

"I didn't think you were coming back," she said, hating the quiver that crept into her voice.

"You actually thought I'd abandon my wife, Lady Rushmount, in a public house?"

"I didn't know what to think. I've been here alone. Bored to death and worried sick." *With London outside her window like a feast she was forbidden to taste.* "If you hadn't returned by daylight, I was going to go looking for you." *Either that or go mad.*

"You don't have enough faith in me," he said.

She fell back onto the pillows without replying. True, she hadn't told him about Mattie, and she was still concealing the truth about his father's death. Some day he would insist on being told, and when that day arrived, her life would fall apart.

She rolled onto her side facing the wall, her back rigid under the fine linen nightgown Mattie had laundered for her before they left Port Royal. It had once belonged to the governor's wife, a marvel of tiny stitches and tucks and small, embroidered flowers. Though one of the loveliest garments she'd ever seen, she'd had no use for it until now. In the face of Harry's coldness, she hadn't wanted to lie in bed naked, inviting his touch.

A final splash followed by silence. *He must be drying himself with the toweling cloth.*

A moment later, he slipped into bed beside her. She had a million questions for him: Had he sold the cargo? Had he paid the crew their share? Did he have enough left to refurbish his estate? Had any of the men agreed to another voyage?

And when would he forgive her?

Yet she asked nothing, waiting in the dark for him to reach for her, to tell her he loved her despite all her faults, but he lay beside her like a stranger. No words, no touching, nothing . . . and was soon asleep, his breathing deep and steady.

Throughout the long, dark hours, she lay awake, watching the fire in the grate descend into ash.

AT DAWN, HARRY STRETCHED AND LEAPT OUT OF BED. He drew on his breeches and poked at the fire, uncovering a few red coals.

"Ah, not out yet," he said, settling a few sticks from the basket by the hearth over the live coals. "That should help."

He came back to stand by the bed.

"Abby, wake up."

Wanting to scream, "I am awake. I've been awake all night," she rolled toward him, opening her eyes, pretending she had to be coaxed from sleep.

She sat up against the pillows and stared at him. He was so handsome, his shoulders tapering down to a narrow waist, his flat stomach, his—she raised her eyes to his face, half expecting to see amusement at where her gaze had rested. She sighed. He stared at her, his expression as stern as she remembered. No relenting, then.

He pointed a finger. "What are you wearing? I've never seen that gown before."

She fought an insane urge to laugh. She could match him stern face for stern face. "No, you haven't."

He ran a hand through his thick, dark hair. "Anyway, I've ordered breakfast for an hour after dawn. It should be here shortly."

"Then what?"

"Then we go to see my lady mother."

"We have to talk before I go anywhere with you," Abby said.

Leaning over the hearth to add more kindling to the fire, Harry reared up as if she had struck him. "You'll go where I say."

"No, I won't." Ignoring the bed pillows, she sat straight as a ramrod. "By talk, I don't mean little frozen words you spit out like pieces of ice. I know it was wrong not to tell you what I did, but I've been well punished. You've seen to that for sure, leaving me alone in here for two days and two nights." She sniffed and looking away from him, studied a stain on the plaster wall. "Not knowing where you were or what you were doing."

"I was occupied. You knew that." Using the poker like a sword, Harry jabbed at the burning wood.

"You could have sent word. I've been frantic with worry."

"The cargo of two ships had to be disposed of. That isn't done in the turning of an hour glass."

"I could have been by your side. I could have helped."

"No, you could not. What do you know about bills of lading, merchants' demands, margin of profit?"

"Nothing. And at this rate, I never will."

"Which is as it should be."

Her chin came up. "Ignorance is never admirable. I could learn. If you trusted *me*, you'd teach me."

Harry flung the poker against the hearth and strode over to the bed. "This is not a matter of trust. It's doing what's seemly. What's correct. I will not have you working at the docks alongside of God knows who, like a common doxy."

"Oh, really?" she drawled. "Aboard ship, Black Jack, Stayton and all the rest were hardly lords of the realm."

"That was different." His eyes smoldered with rage. "And unavoidable. For a stowaway."

"If you had agreed to take me with you, I wouldn't have been forced to steal aboard."

"You weren't forced to. You chose to."

"Stop shouting. The landlord will hear every word."

"Who gives a damn what the man hears. Or what he thinks?"

"I do."

"That is because you have no experience with the lower orders." He came in closer, his hands clenched at his sides. "They do not matter. Not what they hear. Nor what they think."

"You, sir, are a snob, a bloody English snob."

"I, Madam, am your husband."

"Then act like one."

"Oh, so that's what you want? Well, Madam, your wish is about to be granted."

With lightening speed, he slipped off his breeches, kicked them into a corner and stood before her, furious, unclothed, and erect.

"That's not what I meant at all." Throwing the covers aside, Abby scrambled to the bottom of the bed about to leap over the footboard into the tub of cold, scummy bath water.

Too fast for her, he seized an ankle and yanked her back onto the pillows.

"Let go!"

He thrust her onto her back. Before she could leap up, he straddled her, pinning her in place. He grasped her head in both hands and kissed her, a bruising, punishing kiss that forced her lips apart. His tongue darted into her mouth. She'd bite it if she could, but he held her jaw so tight between his fingers, she could do nothing but pant and wait for release.

His right hand left her face. He reached for the hem of her gown, found it, and yanked it up to her waist. She gasped, bucking under him, desperate to scratch at his face with her nails, but she couldn't move her arms.

She filled her lungs ready to scream, ready to bring the landlord racing into the room, but then, as suddenly as he had begun, Harry let her go. He rolled to the side of the bed, flung an arm over his face and lay still as stone.

She sucked in deep, ragged gulps of air, calming her breathing until her pulse no longer thundered in her ears. She glanced over at Harry lying beside her. He hadn't moved a muscle nor lowered his arm from his face.

The few inches of space between them might as well have been a continent. This was no way to live with the one you loved, snarling at each other like feral creatures. And love him she did. In her heart, she knew he would never have harmed her. Now, not knowing if he would rebuff her, she stretched out a hand. It found his thigh, hard and warm, living marble. She stroked it from knee to hip, gently letting the tips of her fingers say the words for her. Gradually, as if reluctant to do so, he lowered his arm. She was shocked to see his face wet with tears.

"Harry, my love. Please don't."

He swept her into his arms, burying his face in her hair. "I came so close. I nearly harmed you."

"But you didn't." She took his damp face between her hands and kissed him, a soft, sweet kiss that lasted until once again she nearly lost her breath, but this time she closed her eyes, luxuriating in the feel of his eager mouth against hers.

"I love you, Abby," he murmured in her ear. "I'll spend my life loving you."

Her eyes snapped open. She grinned. "You will? Well then, what are you waiting for?"

With a shout of joy, he pulled her tight and began.

CHAPTER TWENTY-NINE

ABBY PEERED OUT OF THE CARRIAGE WINDOW, drinking in the sights. A few kilometers back, they had left the teeming London streets for quiet country lanes. How lovely it all was, the clear winter air, the evergreens, the bare oaks, the grass beside the road rimed with hoarfrost that glistened whenever a ray of sun penetrated the clouds. A wave of longing overcame her for an instant. London was an alien world, but this rolling countryside reminded her of home.

Harry lifted off his seat to rap on the carriage roof. A few hundred yards down the road, the horses clomped to the right, along a broad, gravel drive lined on either side with towering fir trees. At the end of the long, shaded lane, the vista widened and as if a door had been flung open, a giant house suddenly loomed ahead. It sat in the center of a meadow, dwarfing everything in sight, storied, upright, windows gleaming, chimney turrets reaching for the sky. The house was as large and imposing as the public buildings she'd glimpsed during their ride through the London streets. Unbelievable that only one family lived here.

She glanced over at Harry sitting beside her. He didn't seem in awe of the place, and why should he? He'd grown up here. His uncle's estate, he'd told her, his mother's brother, the Earl Ducharme. Refusing to remarry after his wife died, he had made it home for Lady Anne and Elizabeth, Harry's sister. As a result of her uncle's influence, Elizabeth had made a brilliant marriage.

Abby was relieved she'd had the presence of mind to ask Aiden to accompany them. At her request, Harry had hesitated, though only for an instant. She glanced across at Aiden. Deep in his thoughts, he was silent, not looking about, not curious as to what was unfolding before them. Handsome Aiden. For the occasion, he'd donned his best fringed buckskin shirt and breeches and his most intricately beaded moccasins. She was glad he'd changed. The shirt he'd worn when they met on the docks had been ripped down the front and clumsily mended. That wouldn't do for meeting Harry's mother who had probably never before met a Narragansett Indian in tribal regalia

That morning, at the inn, she had taken great pains with her own appearance. Her hair was long enough now to brush back from her temples and tie at her crown with a length of green ribbon. The rest of her lengthening curls she'd brushed to her shoulders. The green and white striped frock she'd brought from Jamaica was clean, and she'd laced the bodice tightly until it fit her waist to perfection. Not damask, not velvet, not even warm, soft wool, just plain cotton, it would have to do. When she exited the carriage, she'd leave Harry's doublet on the seat. To greet her husband's mother in an unsuitable gown was one thing, in a man's garment quite another.

Her lip trembled as they approached the circular drive, slowing in front of stone steps twice as long and wide as those on the quay.

"I'm terrified, Harry," she said.

"You shouldn't be. My mother is a lady."

"That's why," she retorted.

"As you are," he said, squeezing her hand.

She kissed him. Though the last thing in the world she felt like was a lady, she sat a little straighter. The squeeze did it. It reminded her she was descended from Irish kings and Aiden from the sachems of all his people. They were royalty, too, in a way. The thought stiffened her spine as they came to a halt at the massive double doors of the manor house.

A smile lit Harry's face. "Welcome to Hartford Hall," he said, opening the carriage door and leaping out before the coachman could climb down from his perch. He took the broad stairs two at a time and grasped the heavy brass knocker. As he was about to pound the clapper against the wood, the door swung wide. A tall, stately man dressed in black livery peered out.

"Lord Rushmount," he exclaimed. "What a delightful surprise. Welcome home, your lordship. Welcome home. Lord Ducharme and young Lord Beauchamp are in London on business. But your lady mother and your sister are in residence. They will be most pleased to see you."

"Elizabeth's here? Wonderful, Giles. I can hardly wait to see them,"

"They're in the drawing room, sir." A reserved smile lit Giles's face. "You know the way."

"I certainly do, but I have guests accompanying me. Let me escort them in. And there's a little luggage as well."

"Very good, sir."

FROM HER CARRIAGE SEAT, ABBY CAUGHT a TANTALIZING GLIMPSE of what lay within the open doorway. She stared down at her fingers clutched together in her lap. What little she had seen was opulent beyond her wildest imaginings. She looked over at Aiden. For the first time since his arrival in England, humor glittered in his eyes.

"It would seem my little sister has made quite a marriage for herself."

"Oh, she has, has she? You think that's amusing?"

His hint of a smile disappeared. Instantly contrite, she reached across the seat to take his hand. "Forgive me, Aiden. I'm afraid of what lies within."

"A dragon?"

"Exactly."

"Well, we'll soon find out. Here comes Harry." He patted her hand. "Don't worry overly much. No one will be breathing fire."

"Not even Harry's mother?"

Aiden shook his head. "Not even." The slight smile returned to his lips. "Come. You can't hide in here all day. The horses will get restive." He exited the carriage and held out a hand to assist her.

She shrugged off the doublet and stepped down. Harry, wreathed in smiles and dropping all formality, said, "Abby. Aiden. This is Giles."

The man in black bowed deferentially, a fleeting hint of surprise the only emotion he revealed. Abby surmised he was a serving man of some kind. Maintaining a house of this magnitude would surely require many devoted hands.

"My mother and sister are in the drawing room," Harry said. "What say we surprise them?"

"Harry, would you like us to wait for a bit while you go in first and greet your mother?" Abby asked.

He arched an eyebrow. "Is that timidity I detect?"

She shook her head. "No. Terror."

Harry laughed and tucked her arm in his. "You are my wife, and Aiden is my kinsman. We go in together."

Abby sighed in agreement, trying not to gape as they walked the length of the central hallway on gleaming squares of black and white marble that stretched to a massive carved staircase. As if that alone wasn't enough to capture every eye, a life-sized statue of a nearly naked woman stood under the stairwell, her hips draped in a marble cloth as she bent to an unseen task. On either side, along the dark-paneled walls, stern faces glared down from heavy gilt frames. Beneath the portraits, more gilt gleamed on pierced back settles and chairs carved with a delicacy she could only wonder at.

Abby's heart sank within her. Nothing, absolutely nothing, had prepared her for this. And to think she would be introduced to Harry's family like a waif in a hand-me-down cotton dress. How pathetic her attempts at grooming that morning now seemed. She had thought being shining clean would be enough. Wrong. All wrong. She didn't belong here. Harry had made a terrible mistake in marrying her. She should turn, rush out and never see him again. Even before meeting Harry's mother, she knew in her bones the woman would agree. She took her hand from Harry's arm.

Without missing a step, he placed it back. Grasping it tight, he said, "Oh, no you don't. Square your shoulders, Abby." Poised in front of yet another set of carved, double doors, he bent to kiss her cheek. "If you're really as worried as your expression seems to warrant, think of that ancestress of yours, the one you named the ship after."

"Granuaile."

"Yes, that one. She plundered the seas, did she not? Afraid of no man? Or woman?"

"Aye, she did. Thank you for reminding me."

Harry winked at Aiden who returned it with an ear-to-ear grin. "Shall we?"

Without further ado, he opened the doors and the three of them stepped into a room filled with sunlight and flowers and two of the loveliest women Abby had ever seen.

Absorbed in their needlework, the ladies didn't hear them enter. Harry put a warning finger to his lips.

"Mother?"

The older woman looked up, so startled her fingers let go of her embroidery hoop. It rolled along the floor coming to a stop at Harry's foot.

He picked it up and glanced at it before placing it on a tabletop. "A galleon, how apropos," he said, holding open his arms. Hands on the armrests, she half rose in her chair, then fell back.

"Harry? Is it really you?"

"In the flesh."

"Harry, I can't believe you're here!" An exquisite blonde in blue silk jumped up and rushed to him, a rope of pearls swinging over the bodice of her gown. "Mother, it's Harry. It really is."

Lady Anne fanned herself with a hand, her jeweled fingers catching the light with each flutter of her wrist.

Harry clapped his sister to him and gave her a hearty kiss on the cheek before holding her at arm's length. "Marriage suits you," he said and laughed when she blushed pink from her throat to her temples.

"What a thing to say. You haven't changed a bit, I see."

"Oh, I've changed, all right. In ways you might not recognize."

"Harry?"

Together Harry and Elizabeth turned to Lady Anne.

"My boy." She rose from her chair and held her arms out to him. Harry hurried to embrace her. "My boy. My boy. I'm so glad to have you back with me."

"It's wonderful to be here, mother."

"You've been well this past year?" she asked.

"Of course, I have. As you can see."

She drew herself upright, the gray silk of her gown echoed in the powdered wig that rose, as he remembered, high off her forehead.

"You look wonderful, mother. Exactly the same."

Holding his hands tightly in her own, she studied him intently. "You're older," she finally said.

"And wiser, I trust." He looked over his shoulder to the doorway where Abby and Aiden stood frozen in place. "I'm not alone. There's someone I want you to meet and who's anxious to make your acquaintance as well. Someone very special to me." He beckoned to Abby.

"Come here, darling."

Darling?

Lady Anne let go of Harry's hands. Her glance swept over Abby from her hair with its scrap of green ribbon, to the thin dress three years out of fashion, to the worn, scuffed shoes that had seen better days, to the pale face staring back at her from wide, obsidian eyes.

Except for the dark eyes, the girl reminded her of someone. But of whom?

Her heart stood still. Oh no. She raised a hand to her mouth to stifle an outcry. *Darling?* She was terrified she knew the answer to her own question, terrified, too, of the love light beaming from her son's face as he looked at this creature with the impossible red hair. She had seen that very same look before . . . years ago. How vulgar, how—

"Lady Anne Rushmount . . . Mother . . . may I introduce my wife, Absalom Grace O'Donnell Rushmount? But do call her Abby for short. And this," Harry said with a sweep of his hand, "is my new kinsman, Abby's brother, Aiden O'Donnell."

A savage, his garments befringed and beaded, stepped forward extending his hand as if he expected her to touch him.

Though the clock stood at noon, the room turned black as midnight. Her knees failed her. She fell to the drawing room floor, in her descent striking her head against a marble tabletop, a gush of blood pouring into her wig and trickling down the bodice of her silk gown.

"YOU SHOULDN'T HAVE MARRIED ME, HARRY," Abby said. "I'm all wrong for you. If you don't believe me, just look at this bed chamber."

She flung her arms wide, encompassing the dark green bed hangings, the silver candelabra, the carved mahogany furnishings. She pointed a shaky finger at the many-paned mullioned windows. "There's more glass in here than in the entire village of Providence." She stomped on the carpet. "Look at this. Who has a carpet like this? Where did it come from? Arabia? Persia? Wherever on earth they may be." She caught a glimpse of herself in the wall mirror. "See that mirror? It must have cost a king's ransom. And those chairs. I'm afraid to sit on them." She swatted a gold tassel with a palm. "These things are hanging everywhere. And what about *her*?" She gestured toward the mantel. "Another ancestor." Arms akimbo, she whirled to face him. "And this is only one room. What were you thinking when you took me to wife?"

"I wasn't," he said with a smile. "All thoughts flee my mind when I'm near you."

"But . . . but . . ." she sputtered.

"Are you through?"

"No, I'm not." She sank onto the bed. It was incredibly soft, but she didn't bother to mention the fact, just patted the cover a few times, idly studying the pattern woven into the green damask. "Right along, you knew what I was and what I was not." She looked up at him as he stood watching her, the maddening smile still on his face. "But I didn't have the proper measure of you. Your mother was right to faint at the very sight of me. In her place, I would have done the same."

"You're wrong."

"That's what I've been trying to tell you."

"Don't put words in my mouth, Abby. And don't mistake my meaning. You're wrong in your thinking. The fact is, you're perfect for me."

"Not true."

"Are you telling me I'm a liar?"

She shook her head. "I know you love me, and I love you. With my whole heart. But I'm not at ease with all this." Her arms rose again, only to fall back to her lap. "I'm a colonial girl. There are too many differences between us. Let me go, Harry. Find someone of your own station. Someone who'll be at home in these surroundings." Her shoulders drooped. "I never will be. Nor truth be told, do I want to be."

He crouched before her, the smile gone. "The only difference that matters is I'm a man and you're a woman. A difference I adore. The rest is unimportant."

She eyed him warily.

"What you see here and throughout the estate is not mine, will never be mine. Everything belongs to my uncle. Upon his death, it will pass to his younger brother's son, my cousin, Paul Ducharme."

"Not to you?"

"No, the estate is entailed. It goes to the next male in line, a way of preserving the family name. My name, as you know, is Rushmount." He stood and, leaning over, placed an arm on either side of her. "So is yours."

He meant it. Her heart soaring, she reached up and pulled him to her. Together, they tumbled onto the bed's feathery softness. He kissed her breathless then propped himself on one elbow to gaze down at her.

"Now let's forget about my uncle's estate. I want to talk of our future. Our voyage, as you know, was highly successful."

"So you said, Harry, but what does that mean, exactly?"

"Ah, you are going to be a good merchant woman."

"Do you mind terribly?"

"Mind? I love it. But an exact figure will have to wait until we return to London and I call on my banking house. They're handling the details of the transactions. Their clerks will tally the amount due us down to the last penny. In the meanwhile, the men have been paid. And the *Lady*

Anne's owners have assured me that even after the *Granuaile* expenses are deducted, my share will amount to a goodly sum. Enough, I dare say, to make the needed repairs to my Irish estate.

In addition to that," he tapped the tip of her nose with a finger, "your ship's in sound repair. She's a treasure, Abby. She'll be a source of income for years ahead. Now here's what I propose." He sprang off the bed, pulled up a chair and straddled it, facing her. "Aiden loves the sea. While we were together at the London warehouse, he told me he intends to make it his home. So what say you to giving him half ownership in the *Granuaile*, which means half the profits as well?"

Abby jumped up. "I say yes."

"I thought you would. As soon as he's a skilled enough seaman, he can captain her.

In the meanwhile, Carl Johnson has agreed to stay on and sail with him. And most of the crew as well."

"I love the idea. Let's go and tell him now. Didn't Giles show him to the room next to this one?"

"Yes, but no need to rush to him."

"But he'll be so pleased to hear your plan."

"He already knows."

Abby put her hands on her hips in mock anger. "You discussed this with him without asking me first?"

"I knew you'd agree." He arched a brow. "I trusted you."

"Ah, I see." Despite his bantering tone, she sensed an underlying seriousness in his jest. So all was forgiven, but not, apparently, forgotten. Time heals all, Mam always said, but never had she said how long it took.

A soft tap sounded on the door.

Harry went to open it. "Elizabeth, what a lovely surprise." He bowed from the waist, extending an arm wide in welcome. "Come in, come in."

She stepped into their bed chamber, the crisp silk of her blue skirt whispering like wind-blown leaves.

"How is mother?" Harry asked.

"Resting. The lump on her forehead aches, but I expect she'll be fine by morning. May I sit down?"

"Oh, please," Abby said.

Elizabeth took a seat on one of the delicate, cushioned chairs, and with incomparable grace, arranged her skirts in a circle about her.

I'll never be able to move like that, Abby thought with despair. Or sit down with the poise of a duchess.

Elizabeth glanced at Abby standing motionless in the center of the room. "I ask you to forgive Mother, Abby. Seeing Harry so unexpectedly was a shock for her."

"You're kind to say so. But the truth is she was shocked to hear he had married me."

Elizabeth fingered her pearls and nodded. She didn't voice a denial, Abby noted, liking her the better for her honesty.

"If mother had her way, she'd be the only woman in Harry's life." Elizabeth tossed a mischievous glance at her brother. "No one, the very queen herself, will ever be good enough for her beloved Harry."

"I understand," Abby said. "I feel the same way."

"So be careful, or she'll drive a wedge between you."

"All right, ladies. Enough," Harry said. "I'm sufficiently embarrassed by all this female appraisal." He came up behind Abby and clasped his arms around her waist. "The truth is, little sister, I'm mad in love with this woman. Nothing and no one can separate me from her."

"Lovely. Exactly what I always hoped for you," Elizabeth said, rising from her chair with a smile. "Dinner's in an hour. We'll have the dining room to ourselves tonight. Mother won't join us until tomorrow."

"Ah, one of cook's marvelous feasts." Harry grinned his pleasure. "I can hardly wait. You have no idea what meals are like aboard ship. Let's make it a real celebration. Have Giles raid uncle's wine cellar. A French vintage would be delightful."

Elizabeth's eyes took on a shine. "I'll see to it right away. Four bottles. One each. How does that sound?"

"Excellent. And there's another thing I would ask of you. My lady wife is in need of warm clothing. As I recall, mother keeps a seamstress here at Hartford Hall."

"Yes, Nora Perkins."

"Can you arrange for her to meet with Abby in the morning? She'll want a few warm day gowns and a heavy cloak, and something more formal in silk." He eyed Elizabeth's dress with admiration. "Something like the one you're wearing." He nuzzled Abby's neck. "I plan to take my wife to the London theater."

Abby glanced up at him over a shoulder. "I do need warm clothes, Harry, but not a formal gown for the theater. As soon as your business is finished, I'd prefer to go straight to our new home in Ireland. I'm more curious about that than the plays of this Mister Shakespeare you spoke of."

Harry let go of her waist and turned her around to face him. "No theater? You're certain?"

"Yes. Let's just go home as soon as we can."

"Very well, if you wish. You're sure there's no other reason?" he asked, a worried furrow creasing his brow.

"No." She laughed. "Perhaps my curiosity about London town is waning."

"I doubt that," he said, the shadow of a question lingering in his expression.

How well he knows me, Abby thought. He's closer to guessing at the truth than he realizes. Though she was eager to be in her own home, she hadn't told him she'd been feeling quite ill for the last several days.

Chapter Thirty

In the green and white striped gown, a finely knit shawl covering her shoulders, Abby sat close to the drawing room fire waiting for the ladies to join her. Harry's mother had requested she be present for tea.

As she waited, she took some small comfort in knowing she looked as good as she possibly could. Nora Perkins, it turned out, had many skills, and like Mattie of dear, recent memory, could dress hair beautifully. She had brushed Abby's lengthening tresses until they shone and rubbed in a touch of perfumed unguent. After the curls gleamed to Nora's satisfaction, she'd swept them up at the crown, winding the strands around a finger to form ringlets that cascaded to Abby's shoulders.

Opening a wee pot of what she called rouge, she had whispered, "This will be our secret." A few skillful dabs on Abby's cheekbones and lips, and the wan look of the last several days miraculously disappeared as if it had never been. "Now for your brows."

"What about them?" Abby asked, mystified.

"Just a touch of brown pencil. It will enhance your eyes. They're beautiful, you know, very unusual in one so fair." She rubbed on the pencil and, like an artist judging a painting, studied Abby carefully before picking up a tiny brush. "This is for the lashes. Close your lids for a moment." Several soft, feathery touches, then Nora handed Abby a silver-backed mirror. "Care to have a look at yourself?"

Abby peered into the polished glass. "Oh my, is that really me?"

"Indeed," Nora replied, looking pleased at the impact her handiwork was having.

Stunned, Abby stared at the image in the mirror. Were her eyes really that large and dark? Her lashes that luxuriant? And what of the bones in her cheeks and the slight hollows beneath them? They were accented somehow. Never had the planes of her face seemed so interesting.

"Now if you'll wait a few minutes," Nora said, "I'll fetch you a pale green shawl. Green is your best color, and the shawl will keep you warm till I have the first of your gowns ready."

"Wonderful," Abby said, putting down the mirror. More wonderful that she'd be warm than that the color would be pleasing.

Despite Nora's efforts, for which she was very grateful, she knew her improved appearance wouldn't compare to the perfection of the Rushmount women. As if to confirm what she was thinking, the drawing room door opened and Lady Anne and Elizabeth entered, their silk skirts brushing the pointed tips of their dainty shoes, their hair, their jewels, their gowns all splendid. How, Abby wondered, as they approached the chairs grouped by the fire, did they achieve such utter elegance? It required more than coins spent on lavish fripperies. That innate grace, that effortless, aristocratic ease took a lifetime of training. Of being to the manor born.

Yet thoughts of Mam flooded Abby's mind—her erect bearing, her head held high, her direct, no-nonsense speech softened by the remnants of her Irish lilt. Perhaps there were many forms of elegance, she mused, as Harry's mother came toward her bristling with veiled hostility. Perhaps treating others as equals was one of them.

"You look better this morning," her ladyship said, as Abby rose at her approach.

"Thank you, my lady. I trust you are well today," she replied, resolving in that instant not to curtsey. Mam would be proud.

"Be seated," the older woman ordered.

At the curt instruction, Abby's temper came roaring to life. "I prefer to stand for a while. The fire feels good on my backside."

Her reward was a shocked, in-drawn breath from Harry's mother and a quick wink from Elizabeth.

"Harry will be joining us soon," Abby said, keeping her voice calm. "He's showing Aiden around the stables."

She remained standing while Lady Anne examined her as she had done yesterday, taking in her frock, her shoes, her hair, her ribbon, then saying without preamble, "You remind me of your mother. I remember her well."

"She remembers you as well."

Anne's pale eyes widened. "How surprising. We never met socially. I simply recall her as one of the villagers."

Ah, so the battle lines were drawn. "She spoke of the night your carriage overturned. The night she assisted you as you lay by the side of the road. I believe she met Lord Rushmount on that occasion as well."

Anne's chin turned into marble. "Indeed? It was hardly a formal introduction."

Abby allowed a rippling peal of laughter to escape from her throat. "From what I've heard, I doubt such a thing exists in an Irish village. But I'll soon find out. Harry and I will be leaving for Ireland the moment my new clothes are ready."

"I daresay you'll be right at home there. They're your people, after all."

"You are mistaken, Lady Anne. My people dwell in the New World."

"Whatever." Anne flicked a bejeweled finger at her wrist lace. "Personally, I detested Ballybanree."

"As did my parents. I'm hoping my experience will be different from theirs. What your experience was, I can't even imagine."

Abby took a seat, not caring whether her skirts were tastefully arranged or not. Where was the tea? Sparring with Harry's mother had given her a furious appetite.

With a casual ease Abby admired totally, Elizabeth changed the subject, talking brightly of the latest London gossip until the door opened and Harry and Aiden strode in, bringing with them a breath of fresh air and the odor of straw and stable.

"Ah, Harry, dear. Come sit by me," Lady Anne said. "Giles will be along soon with our tea."

Harry gave Abby a happy grin, kissed his mother's cheek and sat in the chair beside her. They looked much alike, Abby noted, the same long, straight nose and firm jaw, the same long, lean limbs. Harry, though, was dark where Anne was light, his lips full, hers compressed into a thin line.

"Now that you're here, at last, my darling," his mother said, patting his arm, ignoring Aiden as he assumed a seat near Abby, "do tell me what you learned of your father's death in that dreadful Providence place. Were you able to discover any new facts? I've known so little over the years."

Her voice faltered. Surprised, Abby glanced at Aiden poised on the edge of a carved chair. As their eyes met, he shook his head. *No need to warn me,* she thought, her heart beat accelerating. *I know the moment has come.*

Harry cleared his throat. "Except for the location of Father's grave, I learned little, Mother. Governor Williams has passed away, and the only remaining witness to the duel had nothing new to relate."

Abby sent Harry a startled glance. Mam had told him his father had shot at her. By throwing himself in the path of the musket ball, Absalom had saved her life. Surely, such information would be of interest to Harry's mother, but he made no attempt to add anything more to his tale.

With an unsatisfied frown creasing her powdered forehead, Lady Anne asked, "Who is this witness that still lives?"

"Abby's mother. Grace O'Donnell," Harry replied.

Lady Anne went rigid in her chair.

Dear God, I hope she won't faint again, Abby thought. As she watched her, a hot flush of red mounted the woman's cheeks. *No, she's too angry to faint.*

"Why was I never told that woman was present when my husband died?"

Harry shrugged. "Governor Williams must have thought it of no importance."

His mother waved a dismissing hand. "Not so. I know why,"

"You'd only be surmising, Mother. Not a wise course."

"He was protecting her. There could be no other reason."

"How can you make such a statement? You have no knowledge of Governor Williams' motives."

"I have knowledge of this O'Malley person as she used to be called. And of the hold she had on men's minds."

"Mother, you're being outrageous," Elizabeth said. "I'm sorry we lost poor father, but let him rest in peace. He died so many years ago."

"Before I was born," Abby said, hoping to defuse the tension.

Lady Anne swiveled in her seat to stare into Abby's face. "The time matters not at all. You must have heard something over the years, girl. Family members talk among themselves. Mothers tend to tell daughters old, hidden secrets.."

If stares were daggers, she'd have sliced my throat by now, Abby thought. Yet I don't see even the dregs of an old sorrow in her face. Something else lives there. But what?

"It was her red hair and those green eyes and her laugh. It set my teeth on edge that laugh. Your laugh is just like hers, girl."

Jealousy. After all these years, jealousy. Abby remembered what Harry had said: "I love you as much as my father loved your mother." So it was true, after all.

"What do you know of this, girl? Speak up. It seems you're family now."

Yes, I am, More than you realize. "Your husband died before I was born."

"I've already said that matters not. What do you know?"

I know you hate me. "Only one thing."

"Yes?"

"I love your son."

Lady Anne leaned forward in her chair, her eyes glittering. "I care not at all about that. Answer my question. Your loyalty belongs to the Rushmounts now. Not to some peasant."

Abby stood and looked at Harry. "I want to leave this place today."

"That's not possible," Harry said, his voice tight, his words clipped. "My business in London is not yet completed. Until it is, we will remain here, not in a flea-ridden public inn. Must I also remind you this is the dead of winter? Your tropical garments will not suffice on the west coast of Ireland."

"Very well, then. I'll remain in our bed chamber until we're ready to travel." She turned to Lady Anne, who sat gripping the arms of her chair, the knob on her forehead prominent and throbbing. "Please arrange to have my meals served in our room." An impulse out of the blue caused her to add, "Harry will taste every dish, too. He adores your cook's skill with food." To Elizabeth so pretty in pink today, she nodded. "Do feel free to visit me in our chamber. Now I must be excused."

"Well, I never—" Lady Anne began.

Aiden got to his feet. "I'll escort you, Abby."

"I'll be along shortly," Harry said, sending her a troubled look she was all too certain she could decipher.

Abby placed her hand on Aiden's arm, and they left the drawing room together. As soon as they were alone, he asked, "Do you really think she'd poison you?"

"It's not impossible. Hatred of me was oozing from her pores."

"Have you told Harry the truth?"

She froze mid-step then shook her head.

"You won't be able to put him off forever."

"I know. I live in dread of the day when I must tell him."

As they climbed the stairs hand in hand, Aiden said, "Harry is a reasonable man. He knows you had nothing to do with what happened."

Ever the older brother, he was trying to console her. How she loved him for his unfailing care of her. "True, but blood of my blood killed his father." She stopped walking to grasp Aiden's arm. "I didn't confess what I knew before our marriage, as I should have. Can you understand why?"

He nodded, frowning. "You were afraid you'd lose the love of your life."

"Aye. But I may yet, Aiden. I may yet."

HARRY CAME INTO THEIR BEDCHAMBER CALMLY ENOUGH, but his face in the candlelight was a storm cloud about to burst open.

"I'm so sorry," Abby said.

"I know you are. So am I. My apologies for Mother's behavior. Forgive her, Abby. Her mind isn't at rest. She's reliving an old sorrow."

He yanked off his doublet, flung it over a chair then sat to remove his boots.

"Why didn't you tell her your father killed Absalom with the shot meant for my mam?"

The left boot dropped to the floor with a thud. "I want her to think your mother was an eyewitness to the scene, not a participant." The second boot hit the floor. "It's clear my father couldn't, or didn't, conceal his fascination with Grace. I wish for my mother's sake he had."

Harry stood to remove his breeches. "But having met her, I can understand why that might have been difficult or even impossible. No, Mother need not know the full details. Let her salvage what little she's had from life."

"But she's had so much." No, actually, Harry was right. For all her luxuries, his mother led a deprived existence. Abby shivered under her cocoon of pillows and bed covers. The cold barrenness of such a life would be a kind of death.

Stripped naked, Harry blew out the candles and piled into bed, wrapping his arms around her, drawing her close to him. "Mother may be better off without knowing the truth about my father, but I am not. Is there anything at all you can tell me, love? Anything, no matter how small."

She stiffened in his embrace, hoping he hadn't noticed.

Ever intuitive where she was concerned, he must have sensed her withdrawal, for his arms loosened about her. "You're my beloved wife, Abby, tell me what you know."

She rolled onto her back and stared into the dark. "Shouldn't we look to the future, Harry, not to the past?"

"Yes, of course. The future's what matters, but it's built on the past. For that reason, the past can't be denied."

"Lord Rushmount isn't the father I wish to speak of tonight."

"Your own father, then?" he said, his voice tinged with frustration.

She shook her head. "No, another one entirely." Though she couldn't see Harry's face clearly in the flickering firelight, she felt him rise on an elbow to peer at her. "The father of my baby."

A stunned silence clogged the air, a silence Harry shattered with a shout. "A baby? We made a baby?" He sat up, taking the bed covers with him. "Omigod, I can't believe it!"

"Believe," she answered, stretching for the blanket. "It's true."

"How absolutely wonderful," he said, falling back onto the pillows, his breathing coming in short gasps as if he were running up a steep incline.

Abby leaned over him. "Harry?" In the shards of moonlight and pinpricks of stars, she could just make out his face. He was smiling. "So you're happy with my news?"

"Happy? I'm up in the sky with the moon." He turned toward her, and gently as a floating feather, his hand caressed her belly. "It's still concave," he said, laughing.

"Not for long."

"No. Soon you'll be full of him."

"Or of her, perhaps."

"Yes. A her. I'd love that, too."

He gathered Abby close, stroking her hair, her cheek, her breasts, his hand seeking again and again for the silken flesh of her belly where the new life lay.

"Ours," he murmured. "All ours. Our creation. Our little one to love. And I will love him . . . her . . . as I love you."

She caressed his cheek with her finger tips. "I know you will."

"I'll be a good father, though to tell you true, I've had no experience of fathering."

"I think, love, it's a learning experience for every man in turn."

"You comfort me in all ways," he said, kissing the lids of her eyes.

"Which is what I'm longing to do this very minute," she said, reaching for him.

I WAS HASTY IN MY DEALING WITH LADY ANNE, Abby acknowledged to herself the next morning. Always, I speak before thinking and always I act in haste. It's a terrible trait. One I must change. Now that I'm to be a mother, I must learn patience and understanding of others. A measure of wisdom.

Restless, she wandered to the windows. The scene outside the bed chamber sparkled as it had the day they journeyed here—the bare limbs of trees, the dried meadow grass, even the great, stone stairs—gleaming under a covering of hoar frost. With a sigh, Abby walked to the fire and held her hands to its warmth.

I'm a prisoner in here, with no one to blame but myself. How can Harry's mother be different from what she is? How would I react if my beloved son allied himself with one unsuitable in my eyes? With my fierce temper, I'd throw a vixen's fit, alienate everyone, create havoc.

She fisted a hand and pounded it into her palm.

I'm too intemperate. I must change. For the babe's sake and for Harry's . . . I should go to his mother and apologize.

For what?

For marrying her son?

For my parents and their forebears?

For my colonial ways that are not her ways?

No. For reacting to her hostility with hostility of my own. Perhaps for that. But, dear God, I'm human, and the woman hates me. It's better if I stay out of her way, if she doesn't have to see me or speak to me.

Coward. Go to her. It's what Harry would want. You have hours yet before he and Aiden return from their ride. So you have time. Do you also have the will?

A cord hung by the bed chamber door. "Pull it to summon a maid or a footman," Harry had said.

Should she? Nora Perkins hadn't dressed her hair this day, nor had she dipped into the wee pot of rouge. She had simply brushed her hair back at the temples, washed with the lavender soap she'd found near the ewer and bowl and donned the striped gown yet again. That would have to do.

Not stopping to think longer on it, she tugged at the cord. Sooner than she would have thought possible, a knock sounded. A young girl in a simple gray frock curtsied when Abby opened the door.

"You rang, my lady?"

My lady. Mam would die. "Ah, yes. I did. Can you take me to wherever Lady Rushmount is at the moment?"

"Yes, my lady. She's in the morning room."

"Is she alone?"

"I believe so, my lady."

"Then I'll follow you there."

Her heart tripping faster than usual, she walked with the little maid past the rows of stern ancestors, past the marble beauty beneath the stairwell, and through the drawing room into an octagon-shaped chamber with crenellated windows soaring to a vaulted ceiling.

A jewel box of a room, it faced east, the morning sunlight shedding its warmth and cheer onto a dour woman gowned in brilliant peacock blue silk. Though busy with her correspondence at a table by the windows, Lady Anne glanced up when she heard footfalls. At the sight of Abby, she stopped writing. "Humph. So you've emerged, girl."

She knows my name, Abby thought, but I won't ask her to use it—not if she never does. I came to heal not to agitate. She dug the fingernails of her right hand into her left palm, the little crescents of pain forcing her to concentrate on her mission.

"I came to apologize for my hasty leave taking yesterday. Will you forgive me?"

Her head held at a haughty angle, Lady Anne looked at her down her long, aristocratic nose. "Who put you up to this? Harry?"

"Why no. He's out riding. I just wanted to—"

"Save your breath, girl. You and I are oil and water. We will never mix. Do you understand me?"

"Surely you don't mean that."

"Quiet. In marrying you, my son made a tragic error. One I am endeavoring to correct." She dipped her pen in the ink well. "My solicitor is to be informed of your so-called marriage. I'll see that union dissolved or Harry disinherited."

Abby removed the pressure of her fingernails from her palm. No pain could hurt more than the words she'd just heard. "Does Harry know of your intent?"

"Of course not. When a man beds a wench regularly all reason goes out the window. All thought of position, of family, of reputation. He is no different from other men. No different from his father before him." Pen in hand, Lady Anne resumed writing.

"Lady Rushmount, I've come with good tidings," Abby said to the woman's elegant, peacock blue back, to the laces on her gown, to the gray curls cascading from her high-piled wig. "I'm with child. I thought you'd be pleased to know it."

"Pleased?" Lady Anne flung down the pen and rose to her feet, sending her chair teetering onto its rear legs. "Pleased to have my blood mingled with that woman's? Are you mad? I'm outraged, as my husband would be." She stepped closer, her face contorted with fury. "He'd hate the very idea of his son mating with the likes of you. As I do!"

You're wrong. He would have loved the idea. And you know it.

Abby stepped behind a cushioned chair and held up a warning finger. "Don't come any closer. I don't want to touch you. Nor do I want you to touch me. But hear this. If my baby is a boy, he will be named Harry Ross Rushmount, as is his legal right. If a girl, she will be Grace Anne Rushmount."

"You cheap wench, how dare you name your offspring for me? I won't have it."

"But I, Lady Anne, will. And there is nothing on earth you can do to stop me."

Abby walked to the morning room's carved door and flung it open, letting it slam against the wall and echo throughout the manor house, shaking the ancestors in all their gilded frames.

CHAPTER THIRTY-ONE

A STIFF BREEZE BLEW ACROSS THE *GRANUAILE*'S DECK. Beside Harry at the ship's rail, Abby breathed deep of the ocean air, sniffing at the salt, watching the sails swell as the prow dipped and rose in rhythm to the sea.

Aiden stood at the helm listening to Carl Johnson's every word. He's found contentment, Abby thought, watching him. The sorrow she'd seen dulling Aiden's eyes when they'd first met in London had lightened somewhat, and she was glad. She was glad, too, that she and Harry were sailing toward their new home, though she did miss Mam. More each day. It must be because of the coming child. She had heard women underwent strange sensations at such a time, behaved oddly, made unwarranted demands of all about them. She'd be sure not to succumb to any such tendencies. Her body was doing what it was meant to do. No need to be crying for her mam. She was no longer the babe in the family.

She smoothed the fine, leather gloves over her hands. A gift from Elizabeth, they were wonderfully warm as was her green woolen cloak and gown. She loved her new things, but nothing could erase the sight of her mother-in-law's distorted face and worse, the hate-filled venom spewing from her mouth.

When Harry had returned from his ride that day, energized, his skin ruddy from the winter wind, he found Abby spread across their bed, her eyes swollen, her cheeks tear stained. After she sobbed out her story, he strode from the room, white and grim, returning in an hour with a bottle of brandy and two crystal glasses.

"Sit up, love," he said. "This will do you good." He poured a generous tot into one of the glasses and held it out to her.

"She's writing to her solicitor to dissolve our marriage," Abby said, wiping her tears on the hem of the sheet before taking the glass from his hand.

He pulled a chair up to the bed and rested the decanter on the Persian carpet by his foot. "I've just informed Mother she can write till her wrist drops off. Her threats are meaningless. She doesn't have the legal right to deny me my Irish holdings, nor can she dissolve our union. You have the marriage certificate from Captain Tamworth?"

"In my bag."

"Good." He raised his glass. "To us. With the governor as our witness, we're married, fast and true."

"She hates me."

He took a swallow of his brandy. "What she hates is seeing a happiness she never had. We're married for life, you and I. Her railing against that fact will do her no good."

"She loves you, Harry, and wants the best for you. Clearly that's not me."

"I spent the last hour telling her all about you. She can see for herself how beautiful you are, but I wanted her to know of your courage, how your quick thinking saved the ship and the lives of the crew . . . and not incidentally, my life as well. But nothing I said could convince her to change her mind. She's entrenched in old animosities. I doubt she'll ever let them go."

"That's so sad."

He nodded then shrugged. "Sad, aye, but there's naught to be done about it. We must lead our own lives in our own way." He poured himself another finger of brandy and smiled. "As soon as your clothes are ready."

Though a fortnight had passed since that day, she was still heartsick at what had happened. Perhaps after the baby was born, Harry's mother would soften toward her. Abby leaned against the ship's railing and sighed. Or perhaps not.

"You seem lost in thought," Harry said, wrapping an arm around her. "I'm sorry England was a disappointment."

"Yes," she agreed. To say otherwise would be a lie. "But I saw London. I never expected to in this lifetime. And Hartford Hall was beautiful. Very, very beautiful."

"Wait till you see Ireland. You'll love it. From Clew Bay, it's a short carriage ride to Ballybanree."

A vicious gust of wind whipped at her skirts, blowing her cloak into a billowing sail. She shivered. "Shall we go below, Harry? It's so cold here."

HARRY BEAT HIS HAT AGAINST HIS THIGH, knocking the wet drops from its brim. "The best conveyance in Westport's an open hack. Truth be told, it's little more than a cart. We'll be in a sodden state before we get to Ballybanree, but I'd rather not spend a night in what passes for an inn in these parts. And from what I remember of the weather, tomorrow may be much the same."

"Let's press on," Abby said. "I'm anxious to be home."

"You'll get jounced around, love. Can you bear it?"

"It can't be worse than two days of rough seas. Besides, we colonial women are made of stern stuff . . . so are our babes." The slight, unsettled queasiness never seemed to leave her, but no need to mention that. It was only nature's way of telling her life was changing in a new and wondrous way.

Harry hesitated in the doorway. "You're sure?"

"Sure as rain." She went up to him and kissed the mole by his upper lip. "I hope the babe has one of these."

He laughed. "Come then, let's be off."

Waiting on the rough cobbles that served as a pier, Aiden held the reins of a thin-flanked mare. Boxes and bags were piled high next to the driver's seat; others were strapped above the carriage's rear wheels. He peered through the mist that had begun to feel suspiciously like rain. "I guess there's no mystery about which route we take."

""Follow the ruts," Harry said with a grin. "They lead to Ballybanree." He helped Abby into the carriage and climbed in next to her. He held tight to her hand, brimming, she could tell, with excitement. She glanced over at him and smiled, letting his eagerness at what lay ahead lift her mood as well.

In a handful of minutes, the town of Westport, with its quiet, shabbily-dressed people and its stone houses crowded along a single lane, gave way to a narrow cart path. "In summer time this is all so beautiful," Harry said, looking about at the wet countryside.

But Abby well remembered Mam's tales of Ballybanree and suspected all wouldn't be beautiful. Not even in summer. Still, anticipation bubbled within her. She'd soon be seeing her new home—a home she'd have for the rest of her life. She could hardly wait for the first glimpse of it and peered straight ahead as they bumped along the twisting path.

FAR LARGER THAN ANY HOUSE IN PROVIDENCE, though smaller than Hartford Hall, Rushmount Manor stood stark and imposing at the end of a long, rutted drive. Built of gray stone blocks pierced with tall, narrow windows, its roof bristling with chimneys, its heavy double doors carved and closed, it bore a forlorn look as if no one happy had ever dwelt within. Abby's heart sank a little at the sight of the imposing structure. Then, what nonsense I'm thinking she said to herself, we'll soon make this the happiest of places.

Harry peered through the mist. "I see no smoke coming from the chimneys. Well, we weren't expected, so no wonder. But at least we're home, Abby. We'll soon have a fire going."

When the tired mare slowed to a stop at the entrance, Harry leapt out of the carriage, a large bronze key in his hand. Too eager to wait a second longer, Abby jumped down beside him and ran up the stone steps. After a moment of resistance, the door yielded to the key and creaked open on its rusty hinges. They stepped inside.

Hartford Hall had trained Abby's eye to the sight of majestic spaces, so she half knew what to expect. Yet at her first glimpse of the great hall, her breath caught in her throat. In the center of the space, on a floor of black and white marble, rose a dark, carved staircase. Under its curved arch, a life-sized statue of a woman naked to the waist, stood poised, a fold of stone drapery clutched in one hand. Abby's fingers flew to her mouth. "My goodness," she said, her eyes on Harry, judging his reaction.

"My father's idea," he said with a grin. "She makes a fine coat rack."

Abby laughed. "Indeed. She must be chilled straight through."

Twin mahogany doors pierced both sides of the hall. What mysteries lay behind them? She had to know. She ran to the first door on the left and twisted the knob.

As it swung wide, her mouth dropped open. "Oooh." Entirely wood paneled, like the entrance hall, the room contained a massive fireplace and a great, flat-topped desk. Behind the desk stood a high-backed leather chair, and behind that rose an entire wall of books. A round tea table sat under the long windows and through them, the room had an unobstructed view of rolling, rain-soaked meadows.

Abby whirled around to Harry, her damp skirts clutching at her ankles.

"I love it in here."

"It was Father's study," Harry said. "His favorite room, I was told"

"I think it will be my favorite, too."

"Really?" He laughed and pulled her into his arms. "Your preference disappoints me, Lady Rushmount. What of our bed chamber?'"

"Well, of course, that's my favorite of all, but—"

"Anybody home?"

Giving Harry a quick kiss on the cheek, she stepped back from his embrace. "We're in here. In the study, Aiden."

He came in and eased an armload of boxes onto the floor.

"Isn't this room wonderful?" Abby asked.

"Aye, it is, indeed," he said, looking about.

"Wonderful, may be. Cold and musty for certain," Harry said. "We need a fire in here and in the bed chambers. You'll find the peat bricks interesting, Aiden. They're fuel cut out of the earth."

"You're jesting."

"Not at all. You'll see."

"Let's light a fire in the kitchen first, so I can heat some food," Abby said. "I'm starving."

Over her head, Aiden and Harry exchanged an amused glance.

Men, she thought, what do they know? She had a baby to feed, that's what she knew. "Show me where the kitchen lies, Harry, then after we sup, I'd love to have a tour of everything. Absolutely everything."

CROUCHED BEFORE THE KITCHEN HEARTH, Aiden struggled to start a peat fire. "What a strange fuel," he muttered. After several failed attempts, a spark from the tinder box ignited a scrap of moss clinging to one of the bricks, and a tiny flame flared up. He watched the fledgling fire, fascinated. "This will burn slow and steady," he said. "'Tis unlike wood, but one becomes accustomed to what one must, I warrant." He stood, wiping his soiled hands on his breeches.

Abby sent him a quick glance. Is that all he meant? Getting accustomed to a different fuel? Or something else? To her relief, he looked untroubled. Perhaps she was wrong in thinking he nursed a secret sorrow. Still she feared Mattie's death weighed more heavily on him than anyone knew. Perhaps he felt responsible in some way. Though he should not. If anyone were to be faulted she was the one, for her interference in Mattie's life, no one else. She turned from the hearth with a sigh.

They needed water. While Aiden added more peat to the fire, she opened the scullery door . . . another set of creaky hinges . . . and spied a well a short distance away, a bucket beside it tied to a frayed length of hemp rope. She eyed the rope wondering if it would hold, then hoping for the best, dropped the bucket into the well. It landed with a splash. She waited while it filled then tugged it up full of fresh, sweet water. The rope needed to be replaced, and what else she wondered, as she walked past the stubbled plot of what in summer must be a root garden. Or at least it had been some years ago.

With the fire spreading cheer in the cavernous kitchen, she filled a kettle and hung it from a spit over the flames.

"Here's the box of food you wanted," Aiden said, placing it on the thick-legged table in front of the hearth. A puff of dust rose around the box as he laid it down. Abby ran a forefinger over the tabletop.

"Everything's covered with film. I wonder if there's a piece of clean rag anywhere?"

Aiden rattled open several stiff drawers in an old hutch standing against a wall. He held up a scrap of gray linen. "Will this do?"

"Perfect," Abby declared. She poured a little water over the rag and wiped off the table top. "Now let's see what we have. Oatmeal. Cheese. Bread. Salt, too. With our oatmeal, we'll have toasted bread, and I'll melt cheese on top like Mam does. And tea. There must be tea." She rummaged through the packages. "Ah, lots of it."

The kettle began humming. In the scullery, she found a good-sized pot covered with dust, its inside littered with dried insects. She wrung out the linen scrap in a little clean water, scouring and rinsing the pot before adding the dry oats, the water, the salt.

"A feast. Our homecoming feast," she declared. Warmed by the fire and the thought of food, she removed her cloak and carefully hung it on a wall peg to dry.

Harry strode into the kitchen, frowning. "I lit a fire in both bed chambers. The beds are musty. The stuffing in the mattresses needs changing." He rubbed his hands together over the glowing peat. "I'd forgotten how raw this Irish weather can be. The house is like a tomb."

"We're warm and snug in here, Harry," Abby said.

He glanced from the flames to Abby's flushed, radiant face. "You are a wonder," he said, leaving the fireside to take her in his arms. "Always, you surprise me. But I should know by now how extraordinary you are. How—"

"I'll see to the horse," Aiden said. "That tired old nag must be ready to collapse. Your stable looks a little run down, but at least she'll be out of the weather."

"Everything's run down," Harry agreed. "Which is why I voyaged to the New World." He nuzzled Abby's neck. "A good thing, or I wouldn't have met this paragon of womanhood, this—"

"I'll be back," Aiden said. "And I'll make plenty of noise on my way in."

"There should be hay out there," Harry called. "If it hasn't been stolen."

The pot lid rattled, the sound taking Abby from Harry's arms. She gave the porridge a stir with a battered wooden spoon. "Our supper is nearly ready."

"We'll dine then I'll show you around. First thing in the morning, I'll call on my bailiff, Connor Mann. Unless he sees the smoke from our chimneys and honors us with a visit in the meantime. I have more than a few questions for him. Judging from the look of things, no one's been in here since I left a year ago."

"We're here now, Harry. All will soon be well. We'll make it so."

A shout sounded from the direction of the stable. Harry held up a warning hand. "Wait, what was that?"

Another shout, even louder. Harry yanked open the scullery door and raced out into the rear yard. Ringed by three men armed with sticks, Aiden had his fists up ready to swing.

"Who are you, you bloody savage?" demanded a heavy-set, middle-aged man, the oldest of the three. "Come to steal his lordship blind, are you? Explain yourself. How came you here?"

"Con. Connor Mann," Harry shouted over the din.

The man spun around and lowered his stick. "Your lordship." He whipped off his hat. "It's Lord Rushmount, lads, show your respect."

The two striplings snatched off their caps and ducked their heads at Harry. "Your lordship."

"Yes," Harry said. "The same. So put down your clubs." He nodded at Aiden. "This man is Master Aiden O'Donnell. My new brother-in-law."

"Your—" With mouth agape, Con took in Aiden's fringed shirt, his beaded moccasins, his copper skin. "Aiden, you say? An Irish name. But in truth, the look of him is not."

"Indeed," Harry said, not bothering to explain. "We've had a wearisome journey. We're about to sup. Since you're here, Con, take care of the horse. And report to me in the morning. I want an accounting of this last year." Half turned on his heel, he added, "Bring some people with you. Willing workers if you can find such. The house is in need of a thorough cleaning. An hour after sun up will do nicely. Come along, Aiden, food's ready." Without waiting for an answer from Con, his boots digging into the soft rain-soaked earth, Harry strode back to the house.

As Aiden followed him, Connor snapped at his gape-mouthed sons. "Step aside, lads. Let the man through."

They're staring at me like I'm not of this earth, Aiden thought, as he eased past the Irishmen. And they treated Harry as if he were master of that same earth—which he took as his due. They're all wrong, of course. We're just men together. The trouble was, no one would believe him if he said so. Except for Abby.

Chapter Thirty-Two

Connor Mann's wife, Agnes, had an unfortunate affliction. Her left eye drifted sideways, leaving one to guess where she was focusing. The poor thing, Abby thought, going through life like that, though after two days of working side by side with the woman, she got used to the wandering eye. It was simply the way Agnes looked. To aid with the house cleaning, Agnes had brought another woman, Mary Burke by name, reed thin, her face as wizened as a distressed apple. Abby guessed her to be a few years older than Mam, but there the comparison ended, and again Abby was assailed with a longing for her beautiful mother.

While Harry directed Connor Mann and his sons and two village men—who mumbled their names then fell silent—in the scrubbing of the floors and windows in the ground floor rooms, Abby, silently thanking Mam for her practical housewifery training, helped the women clean the upstairs bed chambers. After carrying the straw mattresses outside, they filled a caldron with water and set it over an open fire pit in the rear yard. When the water reached a rolling boil, they split open the mattress tickings and and emptied them.

"After the tickings are washed, we'll lay them in the sun," Abby said, looking at the stained cloth with distaste. "If it should rain, we'll dry them by the kitchen fire. Where did your husband put the fresh straw, Agnes?"

Agnes curtsied before replying, something she and Mary had both been doing for the past two days. "In the stable, your ladyship."

"Good. When the tickings are dry, we'll fill them out here in the air."

Agnes curtsied again. "Sure and that's the way, your ladyship."

"Mistress Mann. Agnes," Abby began, trying not to sigh. "You, too, Mary. I prefer that you not curtsey to me. A curtsey is a bow, you know, and a bow, my mam taught me, is a kind of kneeling."

Agnes's lower lip began to quiver.

"You have no reason to kneel to me," Abby said quickly, afraid the woman would burst into tears.

"Ah, begging your pardon, your ladyship, but I do," Agnes said.

"Why, pray tell?" Abby dropped a spoonful of soft soap into the boiling caldron.

"If I don't show proper respect, 'twill make my Connor worry. He's a great one for the worrying."

Why were these people so fearful? Abby wondered watching Mary, who looked every bit as distressed as Agnes, drop the empty tickings into the caldron.

"What of your man, Mary?" she asked. "Does he share Connor's view?"

"My man was taken with the cough many years ago, your ladyship, and my wee lasses as well."

"Your little girls, too? How sad. I'm so sorry to hear that." Abby smoothed her open palms over her flat stomach, over her child so safe and warm. "Without a man to do for you, how do you manage?"

Mary twisted her fingers over and over as if each hand sought a warm caress from the other. "Two of my lads still live. They help me as best they can."

"I see." What more could she say? And then she thought of something. "My mother comes from here. From Ballybanree village. Do you remember her? She left twenty years ago. Grace O'Malley was her name."

The woman's face turned the color of January snow. Their kneading forgotten, her hands dropped to her sides.

"I knew a Grace O'Malley," she said, forming the words slowly. Forgetting, for once, to lower her eyes, she stood gazing at Abby, the ghost of an unaccustomed smile rising to her lips. "Sure and I see Grace in you. The hair is the same, and your straight carriage with your shoulders flung back like hers, and your direct manner of speaking, though you don't have her Irish way with words. But your eyes, they're dark. Grace's are the color of the sea." Mary drew in a sudden, shocked breath. "Your ladyship, who might your father be?"

"Owen O'Donnell is his name. He was a blacksmith hereabouts."

"Aye. He injured his leg as a lad."

"Yes. You knew him?"

"His forge stood next to our cottage." Mary's whole body sagged as if with relief. "So he's the one. We'd heard rumors, we did. I always knew they ran false. She hated him."

Agnes, busy stirring the boiling ticking with a wooden paddle, drew in a shocked breath. "Hush, Mary Burke," she hissed. "No good will come of speaking of his lordship that way."

HARRY LEANED BACK IN THE STUDY'S LEATHER CHAIR. His bailiff stood in front of the desk, twirling his hat in his hands, sweat beading on his bald scalp. "So what went on in my absence, Connor?"

"What went on, my lord? I don't quite take your meaning."

"Is that so? Then allow me to rephrase for your greater understanding. What in hell did you do all year, Con? Did you fertilize the north field with kelp? Did you rethatch the outbuildings? Did you bring in a peat supply?" Harry pounded his fist on the desk. "Did you, in short, complete a single damn thing?"

"I, I—"

Harry flung the paper knife to the desktop. Connor flinched.

"Did you wash one bloody floor or one grimy window in this entire house?"

"As to the floors and windows, my lord, no. With no one on premise, as it were, that seemed a waste of time and effort." He stood straighter. "But I did let the north field lie fallow. As you instructed."

"I'll warrant you did."

Puzzlement came into Connor's face. "'Twas your express request."

Harry leapt to his feet, gratified to see Connor fall back a step or two. "I said we'd let one fertilized field lie fallow for a year beginning with the north field. I made that point unmistakably clear before I left. Therefore, I will repeat one simple question. Did you, Connor, fertilize the north field?"

Con stared at his hat, studying its soiled brim as if he had never seen its like before. "No, my lord."

"Why the hell not? Planting time's two months away."

Con glanced down at his sorry excuse for a hat. "There was no way of knowing when you'd return. Or if you'd ever return. Fertilizing, without out planting a crop to take advantage of it, seemed like much wasted laboring time, and with my own fields to care for, and my lads without a man's strength between them yet . . ."

Harry dropped back into his chair. "Have a seat, Con." This line of talk would do no good. He'd try a different, an Irish tack. "Would you care for a hair of the dog?"

A gleam came into Connor's eyes. "Aye. 'Twould be a rare treat, indeed."

Harry pulled a key from his breeches pocket and unlocked a lower desk drawer. As he remembered, it was fitted with green baize cubbies, a whiskey bottle and two glasses snugged within them. He poured Connor a generous drink and a mere splash for himself.

"*Slainte*," Con said, raising his *uisce beatha* on high.

Harry lifted his own glass in a silent salute. "It's been difficult for you, Con. Managing the property," he nearly choked on the word managing, "tending to your own acres and the dairy, but I'm here now, and together we'll improve the estate. What say you?"

"Aye, my lord." Con took a hefty swallow.

"You keep the ledgers, so you read and write," Harry said.

"Indeed, my lord. My da taught me well."

"Excellent. Tomorrow at this same hour come by with a list of what's needed in the way of farming supplies. Seeds. Equipment we're lacking. That sort of necessity. I'll winnow the list after I read it. Or add to it, perhaps. Don't skimp on what you think we might require. My brother-in-law has a ship waiting in Clew Bay. He'll fetch what we order from London and have it here in time for the planting."

Narrow eyed, Con took another sip.

Harry watched him, forcing himself not to frown. Con would have to do some thinking this day, and that was so much like work, it threatened to steal the good from his *uisce beatha*. Well, so be it. With an estate to get in order, an heir to provide for, a legacy to establish, he would let nothing and no one stand in his way.

"He's going to work the arse off all of us," Connor said. "Do this. Do that. Fetch this. Fetch that. There'll be no peace, none at all, now that he's back, the high fallutin' lord of the manor."

Agnes set a bowl of boiled eggs before him. "There's cheese, too, Con, and a piece of skillet bread."

He pushed the bowl away. "I've no heart for food. I have to write. Can you believe that? A list he wants. A list. As if a simple telling wouldn't do." Con reached into his doublet and removed a folded sheet of paper. 'He gave me this to use. See if there's any ink left in the inkwell."

Agnes hurried into the room where they slept and came back with a small china pot, her most treasured possession, though she never used it. A quill jutted from a round opening in the domed lid. She removed the quill and the lid and peered inside. "'Tis dry as bone."

"Add a wee drop of warm water and stir it about with the nib. Now let's see. He wants barley and rye in the ground this spring. Barley in the north field and rye in the larger one to the west. Rye should do well in that sandy soil. He's insisting on praities, too. Says the colonists rely on them. Humph. We don't eat the damn things. We're not colonists here. We're Irishmen through and through. Something he's not."

"His wife is," Agnes said, sitting down to eat the eggs Con had refused.

"Oh?" Con looked up from the blank page in front of him. "With all the scrubbing keeping me on me knees like a slave, I've not yet clapped eyes on her. I expect I will some day soon." He dipped the quill into the ink. A watery black drop dripped onto the table top. He wiped it off with his sleeve. "An Irish lass you say?"

"In a way of speaking. She's a colonial. From a place called Providence." Agnes swallowed a lump of yolk. Perhaps she shouldn't have raised the topic, but Con would find out sooner or later, and she couldn't bear to wait for his reaction. Still, her hand holding the half empty shell trembled. "Abby's her name. She says she's the daughter of Grace O'Malley."

Connor's head snapped up. "Grace? My Grace? She had a daughter?"

Agnes crushed the egg shell in her palm. *His?* Grace had never been his. But he had wanted her hadn't he, through all these long, gray years? Ach, she'd always known how he felt, but tonight some evil spirit had bedeviled her into reaching after a proof she didn't need. Using her elbows, she pushed herself up from the table. "I'm that weary tonight, Con. I'll go in to the bed now."

He didn't hear her, filled as he was with the image of Grace sitting here beside him on this very bench the spring he taught her to read, her hair a glory in the firelight, her lips . . . mouthing the words softly . . . her fingers running along the page as she spelled out the meanings. And the time he well remembered, when his hand had stolen to her thigh.

His fingers began to shake. A large wet blob dripped from the quill, sullying the paper. He left it there. What did that matter? He had let her go. He had been too weak to keep her. Aye, weak. No match for Lord Rushmount who had wanted her, too.

Rushmount. Connor threw down the quill and got to his feet. He flung open the door to the second room. "Who's the father?" he asked. No need to mention the name. For certain, Agnes would take his meaning.

From the bed, she murmured, "The blacksmith. Owen O'Donnell."

The cripple. Connor leaned against the door frame, the breath sagging out of him. He'd lost the love of his life to a cripple. Some of the rumors were true, then. Owen had run off with her after beating his lordship black and blue. Once his face healed of its bruises, Rushmount had left as well. Wife and all. Bag and baggage. Never to return. All that came year after year were the letters from his son's guardian, Lord Ducharme, with their demands for the rents.

Con stumbled back to his place by the fire. God, what he'd give for a jug of the spirits tonight. He'd get roaring drunk and forget her. Forget all that had happened in the past. Forget he was tied to a woman he could barely tolerate. He sat, his head in his hands, staring at the paper but not seeing it.

As soon as he could, he'd seek out this daughter and discover if she bore any resemblance to Grace, the Grace of his heart. He picked up the quill. Seeing her lass would be like seeing herself again . . . the most beautiful . . . he began to write on the blotched paper. Foolscap, he'd once heard it called.

"HARRY, WHEN I WENT INTO THE VILLAGE with Agnes and Mary today, I saw people who looked hungry and were dressed in little more than rags. I doubt there's a sturdy garment in all of Ballybanree or a well-fed belly. Worse, everybody scrapes and bows as if they're afraid of me. I've never seen the like. It's as if I hold their lives in my hands."

"As my wife, you do," Harry said.

"But—"

"There's an order to things here, Abby. Every man knows his place and stays within it. This is not the New World. This is an old, old country."

Abby rolled her eyes, vowing never to believe such nonsense. "The whole round earth is of an age, Harry."

"True, but this small place has been peopled since time immemorial."

"Is that the reason they're so poor? So down trodden? Even here in the house, Mary and Agnes bob up and down all day long, calling me "your ladyship" though I've asked them over and over to call me Abby. It does no good. They insist on treating me as if I'm set apart, as if not to do so would rain down some kind of punishment on their heads. Knowing my parents come from here, that they were villagers like themselves, makes no difference. They're afraid, Harry, just like Mattie was afraid. Oh, God." Abby clapped a hand over her mouth. "That's it. They're enslaved like she was."

Knife in hand, Harry severed a leg from the roasted chicken. He placed it on Abby's pewter plate, his eyes as cold as she had ever seen them. "What an odious comparison."

Abby ignored the chicken leg though moments before she'd been ravenous. "Look at the people, Harry, really look. Only your bailiff and his family appear well fed. The rest are hungry—all of them—men, women and children. We must do more for them. At least lower the rents."

With exaggerated care, Harry laid down his carving knife and fork. "It's not that simple. The estate is in shambles. It's been neglected for twenty years and must be put to rights if we . . . and our children . . . are to have any kind of life. That has to be my first and foremost concern."

"But the people—"

"Are you aware that I pay a tax as well? During the years since my father's death, my uncle took the rents Connor Mann collected from the villagers and sent them to the crown to keep the estate clear of debt. I'm thankful to him for doing that. As soon as the estate begins to yield well again, we'll see to the plight of the villagers . . ." Abby jumped up, ready to run around the table and kiss him, ". . . but it might be several years before that's possible."

She slumped back onto the bench. "Years? While a whole village starves?"

"They're not starving. You're exaggerating the situation."

"They're in distress, body and soul. How many dare look you in the eye when you speak? How many take off their caps? How many curtsey? I'm not used to seeing such, Harry. In the colonies, men and women greet others openly as equals. And the land is teeming with life. No one willing to work goes to bed hungry."

Harry sliced off the other chicken leg and put it on his plate. "Is that so? I think you're forgetting."

"What?"

"Your brother's people. What of them? Forced to flee for their very lives to the Great Swamp. They're isolated there. No doubt living in misery."

"They're free to trap and hunt and fish. To grow their own food. They don't give their crops to a lord and master for rent."

"Oh, Abby." Harry reached for her hand, but she snatched it away.

"When Aiden returns from London, ask him about his father's people and how well they fare," she said.

"His answer may surprise you, Abby. I suspect he's more bitter than you realize."

"They abandoned him in the snow. They're strangers to him."

"True as that may be, I'm trying to tell you something, but you refuse to listen."

Devil take the man. She glanced down at the meat on her plate. Drops of blood oozed from the joint, the sight causing bile to rise into her throat. "I acknowledge this is not a perfect world, and neither you nor I can make it so."

"You're admitting the New World is imperfect as well?" he asked, sounding as triumphant as if he had won a joust.

"Yes, but it offers hope, Harry." She spread her arms wide. "Here in Ballybanree, I see only despair."

"You're not—"

Leaping up from the table with a little cry, Abby ran out the scullery door to vomit onto the ice-rimed ground.

CON HAD MADE UP HIS MIND. Today he'd have a look at the lass. Each time he met with young Rushmount in his study, she was upstairs with the women. Putting things to rights as Agnes said—waxing the old mahogany pieces till they shone, washing the bed canopies and the window coverings, replacing the perfectly good mattress tickings. According to Agnes, there was no end to the aggravation.

"Where will she be today?"

"Dunno for certain, Con. We're finished with the bed chambers, thanks be to God. Mayhap she'll be busy in the room set aside for dining. His lordship is tired of taking his meals in the kitchen. So you'll likely find her there. I think she's in the family way. She's drinking tea mainly and taking wee bites of dry toast. Not surprising is it when a lass looks the way she does?"

Con didn't answer. All the more reason to see her soon. A woman swollen with child would not be like the Grace of his dreams. And once, just once more, he had to stoke that fire. He'd never expected to be able to, but now with the opportunity miraculously presented to him, he'd seize the chance. 'Twould help warm him for the rest of his days.

Chapter Thirty-Three

Connor hoped the lass would be where Agnes said she'd be, in the room reserved for the taking of meals. A strange custom, setting aside an entire room for a single usage. Well, the ways of the gentry were past understanding. Except that the lass was not gentry, but one of his own kind. If fate had seen fit to bless him, she might be his very own child. But no good would come of such thinking, and with a sigh that sent up a puff of cold air in front of his nose, he forced the thought out of his mind and plodded across the frozen field. As soon as he delivered the list of needed supplies, he'd seek her out.

Seated behind the big desk in the study, his lordship kept him standing and took his time going over the items one by one as if, for God's sake, he didn't trust his bailiff to know what he was doing. Finally he gave him a curt nod and waved him off.

"I'm sure you have plenty to do, Con."

Aye, that he did as always, but when he left the study, cap in hand, he didn't hurry through the great hall without stopping as usual but cracked open each door as he passed by, peering in until he came to the one nearest the kitchen.

He pushed the door ajar. Someone must have oiled the hinges. They no longer squealed like stuck pigs. There she was at last—Grace but not Grace. Busy rubbing at a sideboard, she had her back to him, not noting his presence. A slim lass, the hair tumbling below her nape the same golden red he remembered, but shorter, not a long, glorious cascade. As she worked, he gazed at the lovely line tapering from her shoulders to the curve of her waist. A hand span of a waist, exactly like her mam's. Her skirt flared around slender ankles, but there the comparison ended. For her feet were clad in smooth, buckled shoes with cunning heels to them. The Grace of his dreams went about barefoot or, in foul weather, in moleskin brogues. He wondered for a fleeting instant, if she had ever desired shoes such as her daughter wore this day.

A cough escaped him. She whirled around at the sound. "Oh, good day, sir. You must be, ah, Connor Mann, my husband's bailiff."

Connor Mann. Coming from her lips, his name was music.

"The same." No need to doff his cap; he already clutched it so hard the shape of the old thing was destroyed entirely.

Oh, she was beautiful. Just as he had known she must be. The same high bones in her cheeks with the faint hollows beneath them, the same small, straight nose, the same rounded chin, and the mouth . . . ah, the mouth . . . his throat went slack and dry.

A cleaning rag in one hand, she walked up to him, as direct as the sun through the clouds. "I'm pleased to meet you," she said, holding out her free hand.

He wiped his palm on his breeches and took her fingers in his own. For all the work Agnes said she'd been doing, her hand was soft and small. He found he had no words in him to give to her. But she seemed not to notice as she went back to her chore, chatting blithely as if they had known each other forever.

Her voice with its curious New World twist to the words poured over him like honey. Finally, a question she asked penetrated his fog. "Did you know my mam? Grace O'Malley she was called then. Everyone else I've spoken to remembers her very well."

He nodded. "Aye, they would. Grace is unforgettable."

Her busy hand stopped, and she looked at him as carefully as he had studied her.

She suspects what I feel. What I always felt. Like her mother before her, she can see below the surface to the truth. Aye, she's much the same, though her eyes are different and the pattern of her speech.

"You're right, Mister Mann," she said. "I find myself thinking of her more and more these days."

"'Tis understandable," he replied then as if he had said too much, a red flush mounted his broad face.

He's embarrassed, Abby thought, studying him under her lashes as she worked. She could swear this bald, corpulent man—the only one in the village whose belly strained at his soiled doublet—spoke of her mother with far more than a neighbor's interest. A few times, Mam had mentioned a village lad she once knew, Connor by name. Was this the man, and was this an accidental meeting? Or had he sought her out, looking for news of her mother? Looking, perhaps, for a resemblance?

Did he see one? She found that she really wanted to know. "Tell me, Mister Mann, do I remind you of my mother?"

His flush darkened. "Sure and I can't recall, your ladyship. The image of her in my mind is a blur like . . . after all these years, don't you know?"

He's lying, Abby thought. He doesn't want to admit what Mam meant to him. Still, she was certain he would know what happened here so many years ago—all the secrets her parents had never revealed. She gave the top of the sideboard a final swipe with the rag and went over to him, standing close enough to see the sweat shining on his face. Leaning in even closer, as if asking a simple request from one old friend to another, she whispered, "What caused my mother to flee from here? I'm sure you could tell me much about her that I don't know. If only," she smiled, "you would try."

He frowned and scratched his bald head with a fingernail. "Ah sure now, mistress, there's no need to stir that old pot of gruel."

"Please, Con, there's no one else I can ask."

A wary, uncertain expression took over his face. "I wasn't here the night she left. My brother Tim and I . . . he's deceased now . . . were in the hills bringing the cattle back from their summer pasturing, so I wasn't witness to—"

She came up to him, still smiling, and put a hand on his arm. She peered into his eyes, locking them to her own.

"You know, Con. You know."

He glanced over his shoulder for an instant, then back at her as if he couldn't get his fill of her face. "His lordship won't like the telling of old tales."

"You're telling me, not him." She kept her gaze fixed on his small eyes and smiled yet again.

He licked his lips. "He was after her."

"Who?"

"His lordship's da. He wanted her. Every man who knew her did as well. But the difference was he could have her with no one to stop him from the taking. Or so he believed. So my da believed. And God help me, so did I. Only one man did not. Owen O'Donnell." Connor's tongue darted out, moistening his lips for the telling. "With Grace's family all dead by then, she was alone, don't you know, and Lord Rushmount came to her cottage. Your mam was holding him off at knife point when Owen found him there and gave him a savage beating, or so I was told.

"After that, there was no way Grace and Owen could stay in Ballybanree, and truth be told, they had no desire to. So they stole Rushmount's horse, a chestnut steed he was particularly fond of. Damn near killed him . . . begging your pardon, my lady . . . losing Grace and that horse into the bargain."

Abby's mouth dropped open. "My mother and father stole a horse? Even in the New World, that's a hanging offense."

"Well stealing's a harsh word, I grant you. They took the chestnut in exchange for the O'Malley crop. 'Twas harvest time when they left. But his lordship called it theft nonetheless, said the crop in no way paid for a horse of that high quality.

"Rumor had it he followed them to the edge of the sea before losing their trail. Never got over it, so the story goes. All I know for sure is soon after that he left Ballybanree with his wife and babe never to return. And there you have it. The whole of the tale as I know it."

"What tale?" Harry asked, pushing open the dining room door and striding in.

"An old tale of Ballybanree," Abby said, hastily stepping away from the bailiff.

Muttering, "I'm late for my chores," Con hurried from the room.

"What lit a fire under Con?" Harry asked, glancing down the hall at his bailiff's retreating back. "I've never seen him move so fast."

"You did, love, walking in on his tale." To change the subject, Abby pointed to the sideboard, agleam from the waxing she'd just given it. "How does this look?"

"Wonderful, better than ever. Ready to display the plate I've hidden away."

"Silver pieces? Hidden away? Like a treasure trove?"

"In a sense, yes."

"Where have you hidden it?"

"Under the stairs in the back passage. In the hollow beneath the first two treads. At least it was there a year ago. I told Con I was taking it with me. I didn't, of course."

"Show me."

"Let's wait until we're alone. I'll need to hammer the treads loose, and once my hiding place is revealed, there'll be no using it again. Besides," he took her hand in his, "I want you to tell me what Connor had to say. I heard something about leaving here and never returning. It had to do with my father, didn't it?"

"It's just an old story that doesn't bear repeating."

"Abby, we've been over this before. Keeping secrets from each other doesn't make for a happy marriage. What did Connor tell you?"

She stared at the far wall. A light rectangle in the wood paneling showed where a painting had once hung. After their babe was born, she'd ask Harry to find an artist to paint their son.

"I'm waiting."

She glanced from the wall into Harry's deep, dark eyes. Perhaps their baby would have those same eyes. She would love that.

He let go of her hand and folded his arms on his chest. "Well?"

She sighed and leaned against the polished sideboard. "Since you insist, Harry, I'll tell you, but please don't blame me if the tale upsets you."

"Why would I blame you for an old story?" he asked, his forehead creasing.

But he would be upset, she knew, no matter how she tried to couch the telling. Well, perhaps there was no softening of such a tale. She'd just have out with it and hope for the best.

She ran a hand along the polished sideboard, the wood cold beneath her fingers. "According to Connor, the last night my mam spent in Ballybanree, your father tried to rape her."

"Connor is a bald-faced liar." A muscle twitched in Harry's jaw.

"She held him off at knife point."

"Go on." Harry demanded. "Spew it all out."

"He didn't harm her for one reason only. My father beat him black and blue."

"What? I don't believe any of this. Con's not to be trusted. He's lied or dissembled in every conversation we've ever had." Harry swept his arms wide. "The condition of this house is proof of that. How can I trust his word, when I can't trust his actions?"

"His story can easily be proven. Mary might know something. Agnes, too."

"I don't want Connor's lies bandied about. All I have of my father is his name and this rundown estate. I intend to polish his estate, and I'll polish his name as well. Hearing that he was beaten by one of his own peasants is not—"

"A peasant? How dare you! My father is a descendant of the O'Donnells and the O'Flahertys. They ruled Connaught for hundreds of years. Long before your people ever placed a foot on their soil."

A red flush swept Harry's face. "How dare *I*? I've given you my father's name. You bear it now and a child of his lineage. I'll not have that name dishonored."

"The truth is not dishonor. It is simply the truth."

"Stop right there, Abby."

"No, you will not hide this like you hid your silver plate. Your father would have raped my mother if my da hadn't been too strong for him."

"You're speaking of the dead."

"And of the living."

"My father is not here to defend himself against—"

"Against what? His own actions? There was a reason my parents left here in the middle of the night. They were fleeing for their very lives. Do you know your father pursued them through Ireland and then across the ocean as well?" Abby banged her fist on the shiny sideboard. "By God, he harassed them half way around the world. No wonder my mother killed him!"

Her hand flew to cover her mouth.

Too late. Like noxious fumes, the words she had spewed hung in the air between them.

The color drained from Harry's face turning it ashen, as if, like the villagers, he had known nothing but hunger and hardship all of his life.

What had she done? Oh God, what had she done? She'd always planned to tell Harry how his father died, one day, years and years from now. But not today. Not like this. Not spat out in anger.

For an eon, silence clotted the poisoned air. Then Harry asked, "Repeat what you just said."

His request was clear enough, but his voice was that of a stranger. Harsh. Ragged. Disbelieving. She couldn't bear the sound of it nor the stricken look on his face. She glanced away from him, seeking refuge from his hurt in the pale rectangle on the opposite wall.

"I spoke in anger. I was wrong."

"Did you tell me your mother killed . . . killed . . . my father?"

"It's not that simple."

Harry thrust his hands behind his back. As though he were afraid he'd reach out and shake her, or strike her, or . . .

"Answer the question."

"Yes," she said, goaded beyond endurance by her own stupidity. "The answer is yes." She reached out to him, but he shook her hand off his arm. "I had nothing to do with his death," she cried. "I wasn't born yet."

"I'm not moronic, Abby. I know you had nothing to do with what happened. But you've known it all along. Before you stowed away on my ship, before we married." His gaze dropped to her belly. "While we made love, while we sailed an ocean in a cabin the size of a closet. You had hundreds of chances to tell me the truth. I longed to know what had happened to the father I never met, and you knew that. Even while you spoke of your love for me, you kept silent. There's no excuse for you. None. Not now. Not ever. A marriage built on deceit is no marriage at all." He took a step closer. For the first time since she'd known him, she recoiled in fear from the black ice in his eyes. "Now you will tell me exactly how my father died. Exactly. And slowly."

Her voice low and halting, she repeated what Mam and Da had told her that day in their cottage in Providence. The day she remembered as golden with summer, the day when Harry first kissed her. The day a thousand years ago.

When she finished what she had to say, he turned on his heel and strode out of the room without a backward glance.

Chapter Thirty-Four

As soon as Harry came to bed, they would heal their breach. She'd disarm him with whispers of love and tender touches, press against him in the way they both loved, caress him. He wouldn't be able to resist, not forever.

She lay on the new mattress covered with clean linen and waited. The window shutters were folded back against the wall so they could see the stars . . . if the night were clear . . . or the rising moon. But this night, fog shrouded the view. For hours, Abby lay staring at thick gray mist, or at the clothes chest, or at the chairs and table dimly outlined by the small, flickering fire.

Gradually, the quiet overcame her tension. She fell into a light, troubled sleep. Later in the fog-swept night, Harry came to bed. His movements woke her as he settled onto the mattress. She hoped his hand would pull her to him, seeking the warmth and comfort she longed to give him. But he curled away from her, and soon she heard the quiet, measured sounds of sleep. On her back, she stared, unseeing, at the bed chamber's coffered ceiling. She could wake Harry as if by accident, let an arm bump against him, or turn about, or cough. But she did none of these. If he'd wanted to caress her, he would have. Or perhaps . . . her heart leapt up a little . . . he hadn't wanted to disturb her. Yes, she thought, letting sleep overtake her again, that was it.

The next morning, the fog had lifted. A thin, wintry light shone through the window glass, but Harry was gone from their bed without a word, or a touch, or a "good morning." She had been wrong to withhold the truth from him, but he was wrong to punish her with such deliberate coldness. She dressed and hurried downstairs; the sooner they resolved their differences the better. In the hall outside the kitchen, she heard animated voices and paused. Visitors so early?

"He's gone for a horse, has he? Bah, I say the marriage is troubled." That was Agnes cackling like a hen.

"'Tis unkind of you to say so," Mary replied.

"Sure and it's the truth. No wonder he regrets marrying her. She's naught but a country lass like us and of no more worth. My lady, indeed." A door creaked open. "Con carried my bundle to the stable. I'll fetch it then be back to help with the scrubbing. Good Lord in heaven, when will it all end?"

Now, Abby thought, walking into the kitchen with a stiffened spine.

Mary, busy preparing a plump quail for roasting, flushed as Abby came into the room. "Isn't he a beauty?" she asked, indicating the bird. "Connor brought him earlier. Just before his lordship left."

"Left?" Abby stood in the middle of the stone floor, stunned.

"Aye, my lady. For Dublin."

So that's what Agnes had been nattering on about. Abby sank onto a stool by the work table, the nausea she had believed over for good rising into her throat.

"My lady?" Mary asked. "Are you well this morning?"

Abby shook her head. "No. My mind is in a whirl and my stomach also." She forced a laugh. "I'm so addled I can't remember what his lordship said to me last evening."

"He's after going to the horse fair. To purchase a mare for the plow and a chestnut steed." Mary reached deep into the bird to pluck out the steaming entrails.

Abby's stomach rolled over, but she swallowed twice and the urge to vomit lessened. "Dublin's far away. Are there no horses to be had nearby?"

Her voice noncommittal, her eyes keeping to the bird, Mary said, "Around these parts, none but sway-backed nags. Dublin's not so far. He'll likely take a trading vessel from Westport landing. 'Tis the quickest way. He said he'll be back as soon as he's finished his business. I expect when he returns he'll have two lovely beasts in tow."

"How long?" Abby's throat hurt to speak.

Mary glanced up quickly and away even quicker. "He didn't say, mistress, but several weeks I'd warrant."

The scullery door banged open. Agnes hustled in carrying a bundle wrapped in a shawl. She dipped into a curtsey. "Morning, my lady."

Abby nodded. *The hypocrite.*

"I'll put my things in the cook's quarters and be back in a trice," Agnes said. "Con will be along as soon as he's through cleaning the stable. If I know him, he'll be hungry for his food by then."

"Agnes, wait," Abby said. "Why are you're bringing your belongings into the cook's quarters?"

Surprise flitted over Agnes's broad features. "Why I'm after carrying out his lordship's orders."

"What orders?"

"Con and me are to remain in the manor house until his return. We're to sleep in the empty cook's room back there behind the kitchen. Sure and I thought you knew."

"I was so tired last night I hardly heard what Lord Rushmont was saying. That's what happens when you're bleary with sleep." Abby stepped forward, blocking Agnes's exit. "But I was wide awake a few minutes ago. I heard your every word."

Agnes's jaw dropped, and her wandering eye glanced about the room as if seeking escape. "I meant no harm. 'Twas idle talk is all. Please don't think ill of me, Ma'am."

Abby fisted her hands at her sides. "What I think is my own business. What you say about me and Lord Rushmount is my business as well. Take this as a warning, Agnes. You'll not be given another one." She pointed to the back room. "Now deposit your bundle. Be quick. Mary needs your help."

"Yes, my lady." Her face the color of burning peat, Agnes fled for the cook's bedroom.

Abby turned to Mary. "What were his lordship's instructions to you?"

"Until he returns, I'm to stay in the bed chamber across the hall from you, my lady. I'm to leave my door open in the night in case you should need me." Mary rubbed suet over the eviscerated bird, then reaching for the skewer, pushed it into the empty cavity.

The sight of the steel rod piercing the quail's flesh made the bile rise in Abby's throat. She forced down the sour taste, pretending all was well. "Harry is ever thoughtful," she said, watching Mary fit the spit over the flames. She'd not be able to eat that bird. Nor would she stomach quail again for the rest of her life.

"Do you think you could make me tea, Mary? And toast a piece of dry bread over the fire?"

"Only that?"

"Yes, my appetite has fled for some reason."

For the rest of the day, Abby wandered about the house, all desire to polish or clean or restore order on the rooms gone from her. Harry's anger must be bone deep. Deep enough to last a lifetime she feared. And oh God, how she missed him—his smile, his voice, his kiss . . . his hands on her body.

Toward late afternoon, she stifled an urge to sob out her grief and forced herself to settle in the study, sitting on the leather chair behind the grand desk. She sat staring into the gathering dark, hardly noticing the light waning all around her. At dusk, Mary came in with a lit candle and placed it on a stand.

"Will you take some food, Ma'am? You've had little today, and in your condition . . ."

Abby glanced into Mary's troubled eyes. She'd said nothing about the forthcoming babe. "What condition?"

Mary twisted her work-worn hands together in her apron hem. "Begging your pardon, Ma'am, but Agnes and I, well, we guessed you're in the family way." Mary looked as if she wanted to cry. "No offense meant, your ladyship."

"And none taken. How did you guess? I'm not rounded yet."

"No, not at all. But his lordship was so concerned for you, we surmised." Mary let go of her apron. "A shame, really that he had to leave you to buy a horse."

Fearing she'd burst into tears if she had to discuss Harry any further, Abby said. "I find I'm hungry after all, Mary. I'll take some food in my room. Anything but quail. "

She left the study and, holding the candle aloft, climbed the stairs to her bed chamber. A cold, lonely night awaited her. At the prospect, her sorrow turned to anger. How dare Harry leave without so much as a fare-thee-well? Abandon her in this run-down estate with strangers for company who curtsied and said "your ladyship" and gossiped behind her back? If only he had let her explain that she had kept her desperate secret out of fear of losing him. *Though dear God, that's what has happened.*

The thought knocked the breath from her body. Halfway up the stairs, she gasped and leaned against the railing for support. Ah no, surely not. He just needed a little time and a bit of distance to sort out his feelings. Yes, that was it. Harry loved her. He'd never leave her or the home they were making together, at least not forever. He'd told Mary to sleep in a hall bed chamber until his return.

But Harry didn't return, not for the remainder of that long, lonely month, nor the following month. Their child was rounding within her, but still he did not come. She spent her days polishing and cleaning, and whenever the infrequent sun shone, its light poured through the starched lace panels she had hung over the sparkling windows. Even the scullery's collection of old pots and pans had been scoured, shined and stacked ready for use. Except for the silver plate still hidden beneath the stairs, the house was in gleaming readiness, awaiting the arrival of its master.

To while away the hours, Abby retreated into the study for longer and longer periods. Sitting on Harry's oversized leather chair behind the massive mahogany desk brought him close somehow and nearby, ensconced in the floor-to-ceiling bookshelves, she had a whole world of reading at her fingertips. One day, she plucked a volume titled *Twelfth Night* by a Master Shakespeare from a shelf, whooping with delight to read of a girl like herself who went about disguised as a boy. In no time, she had devoured it from cover to cover, amused by the twists and turns of the story, grateful that it took her mind from her loneliness and ever expanding belly.

Toward April's end, with a breath-taking swiftness, the damp and rain disappeared. A sun such as she hadn't seen in months flooded the sky. Overnight, the meadow grass turned brilliant green, and wild flowers budded. Whitethorn, Mary told her, primroses, and field daisies. But with each passing day, as the weather grew balmier, she grew more despondent. Where was he? Why did he not return? Did he not want to be with her when their child was born?

Anguished, she spent hours treading the study's worn Persian carpet, its once brilliant colors now faded like her own hopes and dreams until she could no longer deny the truth to herself. He had left her.

Along with that thought came a brand new sensation. A kick. At least, it felt like a kick. Could it have been? She stopped pacing, and holding her hands over her belly, stood quiet, waiting. There it was again. Definitely a kick.

Her baby was alive and telling her so. Maybe he was hungry. She'd had little appetite these past weeks. Mary was ever chiding her for it. Suddenly famished, she flung open the study door and hurried to the kitchen. She'd have boiled eggs and cheese. Some of Mary's fresh bread slathered with butter and mugs full of milk.

In the kitchen, she found Mary and Agnes busy filling two baskets with food—wedges of cheese, eggs, loaves of bread. At the sight of her, they stopped what they were doing, their expressions as guilty as if they'd been caught in a crime.

Abby walked up to the work table and peered into one of the baskets. "Somebody needs food?"

Mary nodded. "Aye, the whole village," she said, a bitter note in her voice. "In early spring, 'tis ever this way when the stores from the last harvest are low. But this year, there's been much sickness as well."

"What kind of sickness?"

"The kind that comes with hunger."

Abby looked from one woman to the other. She knew nothing of sickness in the village. Consumed by her own unhappiness, since Harry left she'd not once walked the mile or so into Ballybanree. She felt her cheeks flush with shame. It was high time she considered someone other than herself. "Finish packing the baskets, and if you wait until I eat something, I'll come with you."

Agnes shook her head. "'Tis a long walk, Ma'am, and in your condition—"

"I'm perfectly healthy. It will do me good." She pressed a hand to her stomach. "He kicked just now," she said, pleased at the happy looks that sprang into the women's faces but sad it wasn't Harry who first heard the news.

CHAPTER THIRTY-FIVE

THE RUTTED LANE, POCK MARKED WITH HOLES and strewn with rocks and pebbles was a sore test for Abby's shoes. Yet she strode toward Ballybanree feeling invigorated by the long walk.

At the edge of the village, a hawk riding the wind and a few wisps of smoke spiraling out of the vent holes in the thatched roofs, were all that moved. No children romped in front of the cottages, no women chatted together, no men busied themselves about their plots.

"Where is everybody?" Abby whispered into the eerie silence.

"Oh, they're near by," Agnes said. "Sitting by their peat fires, no doubt."

"If they have one," Mary retorted.

"Most do," Agnes replied with a sniff.

"Do most have food as well?" Mary asked, her cheeks pink with rising anger.

"As to that, I cannot say."

"Well, I can. The answer is they do not."

Never before had Mary spoken out so boldly. Surprised, Abby glanced from her to Agnes. Busy picking burrs from the hem of her skirt, Agnes didn't respond. She didn't want to, Abby realized. It was far easier to pretend all was well in her world. Well, whether it was or wasn't, they'd soon find out. She brushed the dust from her own skirt. "Let's call on our neighbors and see how they fare."

At the first in a row of stone cottages, she rapped on an unpainted door, little more than rough boards held together with wooden pegs. She wondered what barrier it offered against the damp and cold when it opened a bit and a small girl peeked out. She gazed up at Abby without speaking.

The child had the bluest eyes Abby had ever seen, and beneath them hollows of a different, darker blue.

"What's your name?" Abby asked softly.

The girl lowered her head without answering.

"Is your mam at home?"

A slight nod. "She's ailing."

"Where is she, please?"

Not opening the door any wider, the girl glanced over her shoulder into the room. "By the fire."

"You see Agnes and Mary here?" The girl's attention swiveled back to Abby. "They're with me. We'd like to visit with your mam for a spell. Perhaps we can help her."

By way of welcome, the girl stepped aside. Abby pushed the door open and walked into a chill room filled with smoky, fetid air. Trying not to inhale deeply, she glanced over at a woman lying on a pile of straw near a smoldering peat fire. Her eyes were closed, her breathing raspy and shallow.

Abby glanced at Mary who had come up behind her. "You know her?"

"Aye, she's Ena, Bren Reilly's wife. She lost her babe. Last month it was. Her milk failed."

"The infant *starved* to death?" Abby asked, aghast.

Mary nodded. "My Deirdre went the same way." Her lip trembled. "Many years ago it was but still like yesterday."

"What's the little girl's name?"

"Ena after her mother."

"Her father, where is he?"

"He must be out seeing to his scrap of land."

"Mary, take some food from the basket. Feed the child and her mam."

The woman on the straw stirred and, turning onto her back, stared up at them, her eyes the same blue as the child's and ringed alike with deeper blue shadows.

"Who are ye?" she asked, her voice rusty with disuse.

"I'm Abby Rushmount."

"Is that so?" A frown creased the woman's forehead. "What are you doing in my house?"

"I want to help. I have some food for you."

With a bony arm, Ena Reilly brushed a strand of lank hair from her cheek and raised herself on her elbows. The effort cost her too much and she fell back onto the straw. "Help, ye say? With a basket of food lastin' for a day? Or maybe two. Take it to hell with ye along with the rents." Her hand gripped the hem of Abby's skirt. "Murderer, ye caused my child to die." A fit of coughing seized her in long, racking spasms. Her fingers released their hold on Abby's skirt and, struggling for air, she rolled onto her side away from them.

Agnes drew in a sharp breath, "You've no ri—"

Abby whirled around. "Not a word, Agnes. Ena Reilly said her piece to my face. I admire her for that." She turned to Mary who was hanging back with her mouth agape.

"Keep some of the food here, Mary, and stay as long as you need to. Agnes and I will go on through the village. I want to see more."

In cottage after cottage, she encountered gaunt, quiet children without the will to frolic and play and sick, wan mothers. The men, when she found them at home, bone thin in their ragged garments, invented excuses for being indoors when so much awaited them in the fields. As if she had asked for a reason why they hadn't the desire to work. No need to do so. Their fleshless frames told her everything she needed to know.

She and Agnes distributed the food, far too little despite their overflowing baskets, then wended their way back to the manor house.

The sights and smells of this day were emblazoned in Abby's mind. The quiet, too. Except for Ena, she had met no one consumed with righteous anger, no loud voices protesting their lot or the misery of their loved ones, only a strange, passive acceptance. Over and over, she heard the same: little could be done to relieve their hunger until the crops came in. Some would not survive until then, but it was ever so. All was in God's hands.

But was God the reason? Crops grew in Ballybanree. Early sprouts of barley and rye and wheat were peeping out of the earth. Fed on the green grass, the cattle gave milk in abundance. It seemed to Abby the laws of the land, not God's will, caused the suffering she had witnessed. These people should all be as angry as Ena Reilly. With an anger, like Ena's, directed at the rents that bled them dry.

"Wait." Struck with a fresh thought, Abby stopped in the center of the path. "We didn't see the parish priest, Agnes. I remember my mam speaking of a Father Joyce."

"Ah, the good man went to his reward years ago," Agnes said. "We no longer have a priest in Ballybanree. Without a lord in residence to see to his upkeep, the bishop said he couldn't spare one."

So the people went without food for body or soul. Abby resumed a slow walking.

"Once or twice a year," Agnes went on, "a priest comes to us from Westport. For weddings, don't you know, and baptisms. And to pray for those who died since his last visit."

"I see."

She was sure Harry had no knowledge of the villagers' suffering. He had never spent a bitter winter here, nor a spring filled with sickness. Once he saw the plight of the people, he'd set things aright. She knew he would. But first he had to return. As if he agreed, her baby kicked again, reminding her he was alive and well. She cupped her belly with her hands, cradling him. If the village children were to be kept alive, too, they needed food. From the look of most of them, they couldn't wait until late summer when the crops came in. Or until Harry returned. No, she had to act without delay; her conscience would allow for nothing less.

"Hurry, Agnes. We must find Connor and see what food can be spared. Everything—grains, dairy supplies, root vegetables, meat if there is any—whatever we have."

She increased her pace until Agnes, puffing with effort, laid a restraining hand on her arm. "Slow down a bit, my lady. The breath is gone out of me with the hurrying."

Abby shrugged off Agnes's arm. "There's no time to waste. You saw them."

"Connor cannot give away his lordship's property, my lady. Sure it would be the end of him as bailiff. The end of all of us."

"With his lordship gone, I'm in charge."

"Begging your pardon, Ma'am. When his lordship left, he put Connor in charge. I heard him with my own ears."

"We'll see about that," Abby said, her pace unwavering. Soon Agnes trailed behind her on the rutted path. No matter. Abby plodded on knowing Connor won't refuse to help. No man hearing of the villagers' plight could ignore it.

But he did. Gripping his cap in both hands, bowing and deferential, he said, "Goodies such as you brought today are one thing, but depleting his lordship's estate is another. He'd have my neck should I do so. Then where would my family be? You cannot ask that of me. It's out of the question."

Sweating, implacable, Connor stood his ground. She could see the depth of his refusal in his small, pale eyes. He wouldn't change his mind.

He'd always known hungry children and hadn't seen fit to help them in the past. Why would he do so now? He had even sacrificed Grace, the love of life, to his fear. He'd never give it up.

She sighed and sank onto a stool by the kitchen table. In the coming weeks, as she grew heavy with child, her trips to the village would become more difficult, even with Agnes and Mary's help. Goodie baskets, as Con had called them, were woefully inadequate. But other than the manor house supplies there was no other source of food . . . or was there? Yes! She pounded her fist on the table startling Connor into dropping his hat.

"We'll do as my mam and grand da did. We'll hunt for deer." Elbows on the table, Abby leaned forward, riveting Connor with her glance, not giving him a chance to look away. "I say we, Con, what I really mean is you. You will hunt for deer, butcher them and distribute the meat to the villagers."

Con went white in the face. "'Tis a hanging offense."

"Not if you've been ordered to do so by Lady Rushmount." She was giving herself a title, but even Mam would understand why. And approve.

"Poaching deer in his lordship's forest is against the law of the land. I cannot, my lady. Not even for you."

"Either you will or I will."

He shook his head, bowed and departed the kitchen in silence.

AFTER CON LEFT, SHE PACED THE HOUSE, clenching and unclenching her fists, striding back and forth, the baby kicking more and more until he gained her attention. She paused to press her hands under her belly mound. The baby knew she was troubled and was disturbed by it. For his sake, she had to calm herself. With her hands still supporting her belly, she went into the study and sat on the leather desk chair.

What to do? She wasn't the marksman her mother was, and seven months gone with child, she doubted she'd be effective stalking deer. But with the villagers in such need, she couldn't just wait like a stump for a miracle to drop out of the sky.

A commotion outside the study windows caught her attention. The open cart she remembered from Westport, drawn by the same sway-backed nag, had pulled up at the entrance.

"Aiden!" There in the flesh was her answer. She ran to the front door, down the steps and flung herself into his arms. "Oh Aiden, you're just in time."

Alarmed, he held her at arm's length. "The babe's coming?"

She laughed for the first time in weeks. "Not yet." Looping her arm in his, she said, "I want to hear all your news. Every bit." Did a shadow darken his face? She couldn't be sure.

"There's the horse needing care," he said. "The supplies to be unloaded."

Could it be he didn't want to share his news? "I'll have Agnes send one of her sons to see to the mare and unpack the wagon. You," she said gripping him with both hands, "I won't let go of. Not for any reason."

"Well," he said, kissing her cheek, "'tis lovely to be wanted."

Yes, she thought, willing herself not to cry. When they settled into the study, he said, "I take it Harry hasn't returned yet?"

Her brows gathered together. "You knew he was gone? But you left days before he did."

Mary bustled in with a tray of bread and ham slices and a jug of ale. At the interruption, the relief on Aiden's face was not to be denied. As soon as Mary left them, Abby asked, "What are you hiding from me, Aiden?"

He hesitated, as if weighing how much, if anything, to tell her. Finally, "I met him. Quite by accident."

Abby drew in a breath. "Where?"

"In Dublin. At a dockside tavern."

"I see." She upped her chin. "How fared he?"

Again the hesitation. "Not so well, the night I saw him."

A stab of alarm seized her, pumping her heart faster, causing the baby to stir. "He was ill?"

"No." Aiden poured a mug of ale and held it out. "A sup for you?"

She shook her head. "I'm waiting to hear." He took a swallow of the ale then another. "Aiden?"

"He wasn't ailing, exactly, he just seemed . . . ah . . . disturbed."

"How so?"

"Unhappy, I'd call it."

"Had he found his horse?"

"He didn't mention it. Actually, he didn't talk much."

Abby clutched the edge of the desk. "Was he with a woman?"

"That's not for me to say. Whatever has happened between you is none of my affair."

Abby leapt to her feet. "Was he with a woman?"

Aiden's sigh filled the room. "Two. One on each knee."

"Two?!"

"Calm yourself, Abby. You needn't worry about either one. They were both raddled hags. They came to him while he sat with me. Not he to them."

"Humph." Though angry to the point of outrage, she had to know. "Did he say when he'd return?"

Aiden shook his head. "No. Only that he had unfinished business to complete. After that, I imagine."

From the troubled look in Aiden's eyes, Abby knew he shared her doubts. She'd let him eat and oversee the storing of the supplies. She'd tell him everything tomorrow. After she did, she'd voice her requests. The first would be to hunt for deer. Aiden was an excellent shot both with musket and bow and arrow. As good as Grace, and that was good, indeed. Two full-grown stags should do the villagers until harvest time. Besides, Aiden would enjoy stalking the game.

The second request he'd not enjoy hearing. That one she'd have to think on overnight, so she'd be sure to ask him in a way he couldn't refuse.

Chapter Thirty-Six

"**A**BSOLUTELY NOT. I'LL HUNT DEER FOR YOU, Abby, and enjoy the doing, but as for the other, the answer is 'no.' Don't ask it of me. 'Tisn't right."

"Is it right for a man to leave his wife and her with child?"

"He hasn't left you. He's away on business."

"Business," she scoffed. "You saw him yourself with two doxies on his knees."

"Nonsense. That's all it was."

Abby rose from the dining table. "Look at me, Aiden. Really look. In two months my child will be born. Into what?" She flung her arms wide. "This manor house is an island in a sea of misery. No man holds his head high here or looks you square in the eye or reaches out to shake your hand. People stand in their rags, caps in hand, their heads bowed in submission. And they're hungry, every man, woman and child. From birth to death, Aiden." She jabbed a finger onto the tabletop. "From birth to death."

"Your child will not go hungry."

"No, he won't, but everyone he knows will wait on him, or worse, fawn on him. I don't want my son raised that way. I want him to be a man among men. Not a lord among slaves. I want to go home, Aiden, back to Providence." She gripped the chair back. *He couldn't refuse.*

"Providence is not a paradise. What of King Philip's War? My blood kin fled to the Great Swamp to escape the whites. Are they men among men? Am I?"

Aiden sat facing her, implacable, right in everything he said.

"Your people's suffering has been great." She retook her seat, seeking an answer for him, but doubting any would satisfy. "It's no wonder they went to war . . . they didn't understand selling their land meant losing it forever."

"No." he replied, his voice as sour as she'd ever heard it.

"But they had the courage to fight for what they wanted. They kept their honor."

"They're not fighting now. They're a defeated people."

"Going down in defeat is not the issue. It's the defiance that matters." She leaned forward, elbows on the table. This was an argument she had to win for her child's sake. "If I stay here, my son will grow up as lord of the manor. In Providence, he'll not be so sheltered. He'll grow up seeing other men as his equals. Not as chattel to be used. Give my child that chance, Aiden. Take me with you. Please."

His glance darted over her. "You're in no condition to travel."

Stung, she reared back. "Answer me this. Are your people hanged for hunting deer?"

"Of course not." His tone said he was losing patience.

"Well, they're hanged for it here. Worse, the crops they grow are not for themselves and their children but for rents and taxation. Your people are better off than those in this village. And there's land in the New World, Aiden, a whole continent of unclaimed land . . . enough for all."

He pinned her with a dark glance. "I won't debate my people's fate with you, Abby. But I'll ask you this—if the suffering here is as great as you claim, why don't you stay and help?"

His question cut to her heart. Overwhelmed by the weight of it, she slumped against the chair back. "The bailiff controls the estate. He's too fearful to help. Until Harry returns, there's little can be done, and, oh God, Aiden, he's not going to return any time soon. I've lost him."

Huddled in her chair, she stared at the man she called brother, at his stern, unsmiling face with its high, bronze cheek bones, its hawk nose and strong jaw. "Take me home," she pleaded. "The ship's cargo will surely turn a profit. You can go to your people then. Bring food and clothing—"

"Charity? Bah. That's not what The People want. They want to hunt and fish and seek their own destiny . . . ah . . . I see . . ." He blew out a breath. "There's no such seeking here."

"None. But there is in the New World."

He stared at her, only partly convinced, but she couldn't give up now. She leaned

forward to seize his arm. "The past can't be changed, Aiden, but the future, the future can be shaped."

HER EYES SWOLLEN WITH WEEPING, the end of her nose red from wiping, Mary said, "Is there nothing I can say to keep you?"

Abby shook her head. "No, I must leave. For my babe's sake."

"I don't understand you, my lady."

Truer words were never spoken, Abby thought as she hugged Mary to her and kissed her cheek. All the woman had ever known was this village; not once in her whole life had she traversed the few miles into Westport. No matter, she was a kind, good soul who would faithfully care for the manor house until Harry's return. But when that day would be Abby didn't know. Only that it would be a time in the far distant future when all love between them had dried and blown away like old leaves.

"I left a letter for Lord Rushmount on the desk in the study. It explains everything. See that he gets it, Mary, and take care. This is for you." She pressed a silver coin into Mary's palm and had the pleasure of seeing her face light up at the sight. "This, too."

"A letter for me, but I—"

Mary needn't tell her she couldn't read. "Should anyone challenge you, it gives my permission to take food baskets into the village. Do so as often as you can. Aiden's deer should last a good while, but harvest is still a few months away. There'll be need before then."

"Aye, there always is," Mary said, rubbing at her nose with the hem of her apron.

"God keep you, Mary. I'll tell my mam you sent your love." She turned and walked down the stone stairs of the entrance. Mary raised her apron to her face and wept into it.

Waiting by the cart, Agnes stood next to Connor, her good eye focused on Abby, her wavering eye looking elsewhere, both filled with tears.

The tears mystified Abby. Did the woman regret her leaving?

"Take care, Agnes. Help Mary as much as you can."

"Aye, my lady."

My lady. Ready to climb into the cart, Abby paused. "No, you were right that morning in the kitchen. I'm no lady. I'm just a country lass."

Before Agnes could protest, Abby looked to Connor. Taking his hand, she pressed it between her own. "Aiden told me you helped butcher the deer and carry it into the village. I thank you for that. I'll tell Grace what you did. She'll be happy to hear of it." For a wild instant, she thought he would kiss her, but he only nodded, fingering his cap, his eyes, like his wife's, taking on a suspicious shine.

"We'd best get started," Aiden said, his rigid bearing telling her how much he disliked this leave taking. He helped her onto the plank seat, eyeing her swollen form with misgiving. "The road's rough," he said. "Hold on."

With a flip of the reins over the mare's back, they were off, but slowly, the nag's only pace. As they left the gravel drive to clop down the rutted lane, one look at Aiden's stern profile told Abby he wasn't in the mood for chatting, so she sat in silence on the ride to Westport. From there, the journey would be long and difficult with an uncertain future awaiting at the end. As she formed the thought, the baby stirred. She rested her palms over where he lay nestled within her. "Life is dangerous," she whispered to him, "but only cowards are afraid to live it to the full."

HARRY OPENED HIS EYES. WHERE WAS HE? He could smell the sea. And the stench of his unwashed body. He shivered under the grimy blanket and ran his tongue over his parched lips. Water, he needed water.

"You awake, luv?" a hoarse voice asked. "High time you opened those big, dark eyes. I was beginning to think you never would."

"Where am I?" he asked, his throat aching dry. Despite the chill that made him shiver, he felt hot. How could that be? Hot and cold at one and the same time?

"In Dublin you are, luv, in Josie's care," the woman said. "I've been here day and night keepin' you in the bed. It wasn't easy with you fightin' like a caged animal. 'Had to get back,' you kept sayin'. 'Twas all we could do to hold you down."

"We?" he croaked.

"Aye, me and Sully the innkeeper." Hands on hips, she sniffed. "Don't worry, he'll exact his price."

"Water."

"Here it is, just waitin' for you to take a sip."

She held a mug to his cracked lips. He sucked it dry then dropped back on the mattress.

"What day is this?"

She shrugged. "I dunno."

"What time of year, then?"

"Early summer."

Ignoring the throbbing in his head, Harry calculated the months. July, Abby had said. Early summer meant late May or early June. Another month. He had to get home.

The woman bent over him, her breasts threatening to pour out of her gown. He turned his face from the sour wine on her breath. "How long have I been here?"

"A fortnight, may be. Coughin' and carryin' on somethin' awful."

"My horse?"

"No need to worry. He's stabled below."

"Will you hand me my breeches?"

She sent him an arch glance. "Why? You're not goin' anywhere soon. Weak as a kitten you are. If you're worried about your purse, don't be. Or mayhap you should." She cackled. "The innkeeper took it. 'For safe keepin',' he said."

Harry lifted his head off the pillow. "Ah, Josie, is it?"

She nodded. "You remember."

He remembered nothing. "Fetch the innkeeper, would you? I want a word with him. And tell him to put a caldron of water over the fire before he comes up here."

Josie looked puzzled. "Whatever for?"

"Just tell him."

"All right, I'll fetch him for you, the greedy bugger. He refused to pay me what's my due."

"I'll see you get it. Go now."

She flounced out of the room. He was spent from the effort of speaking. Though he had no appetite, he needed to eat. Meat would be best and spring greens and wheat bread. He had to gain back his strength or at least enough of it to sit a horse.

What a fool he had been these past months. He should never have left Abby. Never. His pride, his stupid, useless pride had kept him away nursing his anger, nursing his hurt, while she carried his child not knowing where her husband was, whether he was sick or well, or would ever come back to her.

She must be frantic with worry. If he could get out of this filthy hole, he'd race back and beg her forgiveness . . . his little wife, his beloved.

He understood now what he had failed to see when she blurted out the truth. She had kept her secret knowing he would react as he did. The heat of shame flared into his face. He had to get to her before it was too late.

He tried to sit. The room spun out of control. He collapsed onto the bare, stained mattress, vowing that in another day, two at the most, he'd will himself into good health. For nothing on earth, not even his own failings, could keep him from Abby any longer. With every fiber of his being, he ached for her and hoped to God he hadn't lost her forever.

A great clatter of heels pounded up the stairs. That must be Josie returning to 'care' for him. He winced, wondering how well he had known her these past few weeks. The question made him shudder. As soon as he had his purse in hand, he'd pay her and tell her to go.

CHAPTER THIRTY-SEVEN

Traveling aboard ship eight months gone with child was a far cry from voyaging slim as a boy. Though the nausea of the early days had disappeared, Abby felt the familiar bile rise in her throat whenever the *Granuaile* ran into summer squalls and was pitched about on mountainous waves by wild, rough winds.

When the seas were crazed, she remained in her cabin, Aiden's by right, listless, heavy and unhappy. Alone for hours, she'd fall into a fitful sleep and dream of Harry or lie awake thinking of him . . . the tantalizing mole above his lip, the brilliance of his smile when he looked at her, the gleam, warm as fire, in his dark eyes.

But that was then, as Mam would say, and this was now. Their brief idyll had come to an end as surely as if they had both gone to their graves.

Weather permitting, she roamed the deck, staring over the rails into the endless deep. Most days, she avoided Aiden at the helm, bronze as metal from the sun, a pipe clenched between his teeth. Where had he acquired that habit? Not so long ago, she would have asked him and stayed chatting by his side. But not now. She had lost him, too. Every time his glance fell on her, all serenity fled from his face and he frowned

Like Mary, he didn't understand. She hadn't left only Harry. She had left a place without hope. Except for a privileged few. That her child would be one of the few had fueled her decision, not extinguished it. She sighed and clung to the rail, her mind weary from reflecting on her choice. She had thrown the dice. The future would unfold as destiny dictated.

Somewhat comforted by the idea, she took what pleasure she could in the cool, blowing breezes. These days she was always warm, tossing a shawl from her shoulders or opening the ties at her throat. Weeks earlier, she had released all the plackets on her skirts, yet the fabric still stretched tight across her girth.

What was that just then? Had someone spoken to her?

She pressed a hand to her belly and listened, straining to hear . . . what? Nothing. She must have been mistaken. Then out of the blue sky came a cawing, a coarse throaty sound she'd not heard since leaving Ireland. A gull!

She hurried to the prow. "Aiden, I saw a bird! We must be near land."

"Aye, we are," he said smiling for the first time in recent memory. "Carl Johnson said we'll reach land tomorrow. You're almost home, Abby."

"And you, too."

He shook his head, tightening his grip on the wheel. "This is home to me."

"You'll not be staying in Providence?"

"No. I'll ship back out with Carl. I told Harry of my intent and he agreed. The *Granuaile* must be kept afloat if she's to turn a profit."

"Yes," she acknowledged, somewhat annoyed that the two men had decided Aiden's future and that of the ship without consulting her. If Harry were here, she'd give him a piece of her mind, for it chaffed that according to law, the ship belonged not to her but to her husband.

Even worse, the worry that had plagued her throughout the voyage rose up again like bile. She feared that in bringing her back to the New World without Harry's consent, Aiden had endangered his future. She hoped to God not, for he had put aside his own misgivings to do as she asked. He loved her and she had taken advantage of that love.

Guilty and disheartened, she plodded away from him to stare at the horizon and listen for the whisper she was certain she had heard just before the gull cawed. Something, someone, was trying to contact her. Was it her son?

The next morning she peered out her cabin porthole and, as Carl had predicted, the hills of Providence thrust into the horizon. Providence. The most beautiful sight she had ever beheld. Dressing with more enthusiasm than she'd had in weeks, she collected her belongings and wrapped them in a shawl. She'd be home this very day.

On deck, Aiden had already launched the skiff over the portside rail. He took her bundle, his glance sweeping over her. "Can you manage the ladder?"

"Of course," she said with an assurance she didn't feel. She'd ignore the sharp jabs that had been stabbing at her belly for hours and let herself down with care.

"I'll go first so I can help you into the skiff," Aiden said.

She stepped onto the wooden crate he had placed next to the railing, grasped the rope ladder with both hands and, though clumsy and burdened, managed to clamber over the ship's side.

"Hold on tight and take your time," Aiden instructed. Though needing no such warning, she did as he said, and at the last rung let go, dropping into the skiff and Aiden's waiting arms.

"Are you aright?" he asked.

"Aye," she lied. Why tell him of the unease nibbling at the edge of her mind, the rhythmic stitch in her side?

At the shore, Aiden jumped into the surf and pushed the boat onto the sand of a sheltered cove. Throughout their short ride, his troubled glance had kept returning to her. He looked worried, and Lord knows, she had given him reason to be.

"It's wonderful to feel the ground again," she said as he helped her step out onto a patch of dry sand.

"Aye," he replied, distracted. He peered up and down the empty beach. "I expected Elder Thayer would be here to offer a greeting, but he must not have spied us." He glanced at her, his brow furrowing. "I'd best speak to him. Carl and the men are awaiting permission to start unloading."

Abby sank onto the sand. "Go to him, Aiden. I'll be fine here. I'll rest till you come back."

"Sure and I won't be long," he said, bending over to kiss her cheek. "Then I'll fetch your bundle from the skiff and walk you home."

"You must be happy," she said, warmed by his affection. "The Irish is coming back to your speech."

"Ah, 'tis true, 'tis true," he said, grinning. "Be back in a trice."

Abby watched him hurry up the hill to the Thayer cottage, his long stride covering the distance with ease. With a sigh of content, she raised her face to the sun. What did a few freckles matter? The off shore breeze felt glorious on her skin. She filtered the fine, white sand through her fingers. It flew into the air, floating away like a dream or a longing for happiness.

Deep within her came a soft prodding. As the sand drifted through her fingertips, she sat still, waiting for another. *There.* The jabs were stronger than a day ago and more persistent. An instinct old as time told her she had better heed their message.

With nothing to grasp to help lift her to her feet, she knelt, and putting both hands on the sand, raised one knee off the ground. Mustering all her strength, she raised the other knee and, panting with effort, forced herself upright. She stood as erect as she could and pressed a hand against the ache in her lower back. She wouldn't wait for Aiden after all.

She waddled along the empty path toward home, seeing no one who would cause her to stop and chat, and she was glad of that. For her swollen body needed to obey the mysterious signal to make haste. Overhead, far above the stone fences and meadows, a hawk lazed on the air currents. Underfoot, the lack of tracks in the dust told her no one had passed this way in a while. No matter. Home is what mattered, being with Mam and Da again.

The sun was at its zenith by the time she spied the cottage sitting on its slight rise. Her pace picked up. Mam would be by the hearth cooking the noon meal. Abby glanced at the chimney, but no puff of smoke spiraled into the flawless blue sky. The coals must be banked, the air too warm for a cook fire. As she stared at the sky, a sharp jab, stronger than any so far, struck her in the midriff. She stood still for a moment, patting her belly back into quiet ease. Then, "Oh no, my bladder again," she muttered and left the path to squat behind a yew shrub. The relief was like a pleasure.

She stood, adjusted her clothing, and eyed the path ahead. The walk from the village center had always been an easy one, but today, out of breath, sweat dripping between her breasts and down the small of her back, the short distance up the rise looked like a mountain climb.

She could call for Da or Mam to come and help her the rest of the way, but how silly with only a few more paces to go. The jab again. She glanced down half expecting to see the outline of a jutting foot but saw only the great rounding as if the baby had balled himself up and shifted position.

In the sticky noon heat, dirt from the path rose around her ankles. The wetness trickling between her legs had to be sweat running down her body into her smallclothes. Drops of it dotted the trail. Another sharp pang, and a torrent of water rushed down her legs, soaking her shift, running into her shoes, puddling on the path which drank it up in an instant leaving only a large, dark stain in the dust.

Feeling the torrent turning into a trickle, she took a few tentative steps.

"You will not panic. You will not. You—"

A stabbing pain stopped her mid-stride, then as fast as it struck, the blade withdrew. She dragged in gulps of air and waited. A second strike. After an endless moment, the contraction eased. She hurried toward the cabin. "Mam, Da, where are you? I'm home."

She stumbled the last few paces. "I'm home, Mam."

No one answered. She lifted the latch and walked inside. As quiet and well ordered as a tomb, the cottage stood empty. *Oh no.* Her glance swept the small space, the bed, the work shelf, the row of clothes on their wall pegs, the stone cold fireplace, all tidy and neat. Everything in its usual place told her Mam and Da would return. But where were they *now?*

Neatly made, her old bed still stood in the corner by the fireplace, a blanket folded at its foot. She'd lie on it for a while and gather her strength. Seduced by its familiar comfort and exhausted from her trek, she soon fell into an uneasy slumber. *Where are you, Harry? Where, my love? I need you. Our son needs you. There's no life without—*

A sudden pain struck deep, its strength yanking her out of her reverie. When it ebbed, she forced herself out of the bed. She wasn't prepared; there were things she'd need. As she stood, uncertain in the center of the room, a gush of watery pink blood oozed along her thighs, and with it came a contraction of such power it knocked her to her knees. In the brief, painless void that followed, she grasped a table leg and clung to it, panting. Then another strike, its thrust familiar, expected. She'd stay on the floor for the next one . . . make a plan . . . she'd have to do this alone.

The ragged sound of her own laughter jolted her out of a mounting panic. She sounded frightened, ready to throw reason away and let fear take over. That mustn't happen. Women had been giving birth forever and surviving. She would, too. She knew what to do. She'd helped Mam at Mistress Harris's lying-in. But the panic returned for a split second. Was the baby full term? Well formed enough to breathe on his own? Dear God, she couldn't remember.

A powerful contraction tore the question away. It passed, and when the wave swept over her again, she began to count. Sixty. Ninety. A hundred and twenty. One fifty . . . two and a half minutes. She panted, expelling shallow, harsh breaths into the eerie quiet.

She had two and a half minutes to find a knife and a piece of twine. No more than two and a half. Maybe less. And she'd need something to wrap the baby in and to soak up the blood.

Using the table leg as a crutch, she struggled to her feet. A spasm swept through her. She gripped the table edge holding on so tight she thought the wood would crack under her fingers.

The pains were speeding up.

Reining in the simmering fear, she glanced about the room. There had to be a knife somewhere. Her muscles tensed. She clung to the table not moving. When the pain struck, the scream she heard didn't count for a thing. She was in control. A knife. She had to find a knife. There, on Mam's work bench as always. How could she have forgotten?

A lightning bolt ripped through her. She dropped the knife. Less than two minutes since the last one. Another. Then another in rapid succession, no time in between.

"AHHHHH, SWEET JESUS, AHHHHH."

Breathe, breathe, breathe. Short swallows of air . . . short . . . pant, pant, pant. An instant of blessed relief. Cloth. She needed a cloth.

In the sea chest. Don't try to walk. Crawl. Slide. Pick up the knife. Keep it in hand. But dear God, what can I use to tie off the umbilical cord?

Inch by inch, she crawled along the floor, a damp stain on the wooden boards marking her trail. Da had twine somewhere, but where? She had no time to search . . . she had to find something soon or her baby would bleed to death . . . no, that wouldn't happen. She'd squeeze the umbilical between her fingers, pinch it off and hold it till it healed. By God, they would live—both of them.

At the foot of the bed, she knelt in front of the sea chest. Before she could fling open its top, a violent spasm, the worst yet, ripped through her belly. A scream shredded the air.

The hawk must have heard me.

The room spun out of control and turned black.

How long had she fainted. . . a minute . . . an hour? She shivered despite the heat. Her shift and petticoat, her skirt, shoes and stockings, all were soaked through. The sharp acrid odor of blood filled her nostrils. She eased off her shoes, released the tie on her wet skirt and kicked it aside. Her hand, reaching up to pull the bodice over her head, brushed against the ribbon in her hair. Yes, that would do as well as twine.

Beads of sweat popped out on her forehead and ran down her face.

With her arm, she rubbed them out of her eyes then lay back as an enormous calm descended upon her.

"We have what we need now. . . everything we need."

The rhythm increased. *High tide. High tide.*

How open was she? She reached down to finger herself. That hard roundness between her thighs had to be the head.

Not much longer. Not much longer . . . The tide is full now and rushing to shore, a constant wave of pain. No ebb tide. No receding . . . a violent storm coming . . . coming . . . coming.

She pushed and pushed again. The head slipped out. Her muscles caught up in their work struggled beyond her will. A final push, a final scream then silence.

The cries, when they began anew, belonged to someone else, a bloodied, angry little person.

Abby bent over, picked the infant up from the stained cloth between her legs and lay back on the floor. With the baby on her abdomen, she watched the umbilical's slow throbbing.

"We're still attached, love, but not for long. When the pulsing stops, I'll tie a ribbon on you."

The little mouth opened and howled.

"To think I worried you might not breathe," Abby murmured.

She closed her eyes and stroked her baby's head. The howls softened to mewlings. Abby smiled. She could lie like this forever, her whole body at peace, clear down to her toes.

Her eyes snapped open. She mustn't succumb now. She glanced at the cord still joining them. The pulsing had stopped.

"Sorry," she said, laying the baby back on the cloth between her legs. An outraged yell split the air. Abby grinned. "So passionate, little one."

She found the knife by her side and reached up to pull the ribbon from her hair, praying it would be long enough for two knots then sighing in relief that it was.

She sliced the ribbon, then lowering the knife, she worked quickly and tied off the cord near the baby's navel—one firm, tight knot. With the remaining scrap of ribbon, she tied a second knot farther down on the cord. Trembling with effort, she picked up the knife again. Worn though the handle might be, Mam's blade had been honed to a hunter's edge. Her hand couldn't slip. No mistakes allowed. Steady, steady . . . she tightened her grip. A single quick slice severed the cord midway between the two knots.

The knife dropped from her fingers and struck the floor boards. Fearful, she peered at the baby's navel. Except for a drop or two of blood, the knot held fast.

"Easy now, easy." She tugged a clean cloth from the sea chest to use as a swaddling blanket.

They lay back together, the baby rooting for her nipple, finding it and beginning a determined gnawing, the soft, tiny mouth pulling at life. Exhausted, Abby slid the quilt off the foot of the bed and covered them both. This time she could doze off without worry.

The baby still cradled in her arms, she woke to a pulsing rhythm, the pain of it sharp enough to make her gasp. She lay quiet, letting the steady movement course through her body. In minutes, an amorphous, purple-blue mass slid onto the floor.

Somehow she found the strength to reach down and bundle it into the blood-soaked cloth. Soon, very soon, she'd have to find an old shift of Mam's for herself and a diaper cloth for the baby. But not yet . . .

"ABBY, ABBY, OPEN YOUR EYES. FOR GOD'S SAKE, OPEN YOUR EYES."

She knew that voice. She'd heard it calling to her before, a long, long time ago. Her lids, slow and heavy, parted to the sight of Aiden kneeling beside her, his face more anguished than she'd ever seen it. He took her hand and rubbed it between his own.

"Mam?" she whispered.

"She's not here." His glance fell on the baby wrapped in her arms. "I'm so sorry you had to go through this alone."

"Where is she? And Da?"

"In Newport. Their old friend, Sara, is dying. They went to say farewell. As soon as I heard, I hurried here, for I feared for you."

He sounded so distraught she tried to smile, to reassure him. "All's well, Aiden. But I need a woman's aid. The baby should be bathed and so should I. Can you find—"

"Emma Harris?"

She nodded. "Yes, Emma. I have a surprise for her. Silk stockings."

He slid his arms underneath Abby and lifted both her and the baby from the floor. Placing them gently onto the bed, he said, "Emma's in for more than one surprise, I warrant."

CHAPTER THIRTY-EIGHT

"**S**HE'S *WHAT*?"

"Gone, sir," Connor repeated, "on the ship with her brother." He shifted from one foot to the other, shivering in the face of Harry's anger. "Determined she was. Nothing I could do to prevent her, my lord."

"Sir?"

Harry swiveled his attention from the bailiff to the haggard woman named Mary.

"Yes?"

"Her ladyship left you a letter. 'Tis on the desk in the study. She said—"

Not waiting to hear, he dashed through the house, flung the study door wide and grasped the piece of folded paper propped against the ink well. Fingers trembling, he broke the seal.

> *My dearest husband,*
> *If you are reading this, then you have returned to your home if not to me.*
> *Please know I will love you forever. Nothing you say or do can ever change that, for my love depends not on your actions or your words but is a gift I freely bestow. A gift, I fear, you no longer desire.*
> *In the months I have been in Ballybanree, I have come to know there is no future here for me or for our son. At least none that makes the heart soar with joy for what may lie ahead.*

I am a colonial girl, Harry, a wild girl your mother would call me, and I'm returning to my wilderness home. Our child will grow to adulthood there as a man among men in a way that is impossible here, and this is what I want for him, nothing more, nothing less.

Feed your people, Harry, and take care of the man I love,

Your wife forever,

Absalom O'Donnell Rushmount

God, he'd forgotten about her given name. Absalom, indeed. He crumpled the sheet of paper in his fist, and in the next instant, smoothed it out on the desktop. If he didn't know better, he'd swear he was about to cry.

Or laugh. *Our son.* How could she be so damned sure the child she carried was male? But Abby was ever certain of what she wanted.

He perused the wrinkled sheet once more. Not a word of recrimination. He clutched the letter in his fingers—she had held it, poured her heart into it—he would keep it forever

Fatigued beyond reason, Harry leaned back in the leather chair and closed his eyes. Fever had robbed his strength. The long ride from Dublin with little sleep or food had taken a further toll. He had to fight the fog threatening to descend upon him. He needed to think and plan.

A slight cough broke the silence. He looked up to see Mary standing in the open doorway.

She curtsied. "I've a roasted bird on the spit, sir. And fresh baked bread to go with it."

He was about to wave her away but thought better of it. He needed to regain his strength. "I'll be along, Mary. I'll eat in the kitchen."

Another curtsey. "Very good, sir."

She left, the poor soul, silent as a wraith. After he ate, he'd sleep, if he could, and do his planning in the morning. He got up from the chair, the letter still in his hand. He couldn't bear to part with it. His glance fell on the last line. "Feed your people, Harry." The meaning of that he'd have to look into.

He slept after all, dreamless until the early hours when desire for Abby flooded his mind and woke him into the chill, predawn darkness. He lay there alone, waiting for the sun's slow rise, longing for her.

It was July. High summer, the crops green and healthy, the fields burgeoning. Had his son been born? Women died giving birth. Had Abby and the babe survived? He flung an arm over his eyes to blind himself from the thought of the unthinkable, but to no avail.

Before dawn's first fingering, he rose from his bed and dressed. It would do Abby and his son no good to go mad. He gritted his jaw. As soon as Aiden arrived with the *Granuaile*, he'd set sail for the New World. The whole round earth wasn't big enough to keep him from his family.

Connor said the ship had left Westport six weeks ago. By rough reckoning, it would be three months or more before Aiden made it back across the Atlantic. With eager markets in Providence, Newport and Boston, he should have no trouble disposing of the goods he'd brought from England. Pottery, fine woolens, steel farm implements, tea and spices, all items not easily obtained in the colonies. In return, the *Granuaile* would take on furs, lumber, and grains from America's deep, rich soil. Harry smashed a fist into his open palm. And molasses and rum if the New England trade goods didn't fill the ship's hull. He hoped to God they did. Otherwise, with a detour to the tropics, Aiden might not return until spring.

Yet as long as he'd known the man, Aiden had exercised good judgment in matters both large and small. He would sense Harry's need and know enough to tell Carl Johnson not to delay. The certainty calmed him as he went down to the kitchen for breakfast. He'd eat whether he felt hunger or not, then tour the estate with Connor.

"Three boiled eggs this morning, Mary, and some of your good bread."

"Yes, sir," she said, hurrying to do his bidding.

"Mary," he said, as she placed a bowl of boiled eggs before him, "Mistress Abby said something in her letter you might be able to answer for me."

"If I can, sir." she said, pausing to wipe her hands on her apron.

"It's about the people. Are they not fed?"

"Ah." The breath left Mary's body in one long, exhaled sigh. "Not surprised I am she wrote of that. The plight of the villagers troubled her greatly, but there was little she could do to help them. 'Tis an old story."

"Tell it to me, Mary. I have much to learn."

"In that case, my lord, the best teacher is the village itself."

IT'S A REVELATION. A GODDAM REVELATION. No wonder Abby told me to feed my people.

Not a man, woman or child appeared robust. The mothers and their children affected him the most. He suspected the women seemed aged beyond their years, the children often rheumy eyed and coughing. Yet the fields surrounding the village, even the smallest holdings, were thriving. By the look of them, no one should be in dire need.

Mary had told him true. In one day, he'd learned much. Having seen his fill, he swung up on the stallion and left Ballybanree for the manor house. He'd seek out Connor wherever he might be working, tour the farm, the dairy and the crops in the ground. Then have a good, long look at the ledgers.

"SO THIS HAS BEEN GOING ON FOR YEARS? Since Lord Ducharme took control of the estate? Or longer? While my father was alive as well?"

Connor nodded, only one reluctant dip of his head, but that one was enough. Look at the man, Harry thought, quaking before me like all of Ballybanree—except for babes in arms who hadn't yet learned to bow and scrape for survival.

"Last year, when I first came as lord to Rushmount Manor, why didn't you tell me my uncle's demands were so harsh?"

"Sure and I thought you were well aware of the business details. And if you pardon my saying so, my lord, you weren't here overly long . . . for conversations like."

"True enough, Con." For once, Harry was in complete agreement with his bailiff. He hadn't spent much time here; still, he should have known. Along with the legal documents and a ring of keys, his uncle had offered advice. "The estate is now yours to rule, my boy. Tap it for what it's worth."

Where all the monies had gone, he wouldn't inquire. Uncle Ducharme had cared for his mother and sister and himself as well for twenty years. But at what cost? With a sinking realization, Harry knew the conditions in Ballybanree weren't unique but repeated throughout Ireland. *Christ.*

"That will be all for today," he said, dismissing Connor. He needed to think. That would be done more effectively without his bailiff quivering in front of him.

Later today, he'd have Connor and his sons load a cart with food from the estate and haul it into the village. But that would be stop gap at best. Then what? Frustrated, he ran a hand through his hair, puzzled as to how to proceed. The people needed a steady source of nourishment . . . two of the dairy cows could be brought to the village . . . one of the abandoned huts could be repaired and used to house them.

Still, crops were the main source of food; yet most of the annual yield was paid into the estate as rent. He flipped open a ledger. Could he do with half the current assessment and still keep the manor in general good repair? To turn the house into a showplace—as he had planned to do—while his neighbors starved would be unconscionable. Elizabeth was her husband's responsibility now. As long as he could provide decently for his mother, and Abby and the child, that's all that mattered.

He stayed closeted in the study, pouring over the figures, testing one plan after another until he arrived at what might be a viable solution, but dammit, to succeed, it would require Aiden's cooperation. Harry flung down his pen. The need was too great to wait for any man's approval. He'd assume he had it.

Getting to his feet, he headed for the kitchen. He found Mary at the work table kneading bread dough. "Mary, other than Connor, can anyone in the village read and write?"

She stopped kneading for a moment. "Con's son, Neil, can cipher, but no one else I heard tell of."

"That's what I thought. Where does the bishop reside?"

Her eyes widened. "The great man himself?"

"Yes."

"In Westport, my lord. In a grand house, 'tis said."

THE HOUSE WASN'T GRAND BUT STURDY, built of local stone and topped with a gray slate roof. A small fire burned in Bishop McVinney's study. Even in high summer, the air by the Atlantic was damp and chill, and from the lean, ascetic look of the man, he needed a bit of warmth.

"I know Ballybanree village well," he said, peering at Harry over tented fingers. "I've deplored not being able to send a man there, but as you're aware, we are a poor diocese."

He's blaming me for the poverty of the people. How can I fault him?

"Well aware, Your Excellency. That's why I'm here. To ask you to send a priest there. I will, of course, see to his upkeep."

The bishop's hands relaxed on his desktop. "Ah, that makes an enormous difference."

"I'll provide housing, clothing, food, and an annual sum. There's just one restriction."

The bishop leaned back in his chair, the chill in the room coming into his eyes. "A restriction?"

"The man must be able to read and write in English and be good with figures."

"'Tis a scholar you're after," the bishop said. The chill had reached his voice.

"What has that to do with the people's needs?

Harry leaned forward. "Let me explain."

"YOU'RE A CLEVER MAN, LORD RUSHMOUNT. And a principled one, to boot," the bishop said when Harry had finished. "Are you sure you can't stay in Ireland?"

"No, Excellency. My wife and son await me in the New World. But I can assure you her brother, Aiden, will be back at the end of each voyage to consult with my bailiff and the priest you send. The villagers' welfare will be their priority. All I ask in return is that the manor house be kept in decent repair."

"I'll send a young curate to you within a fortnight."

"Good. That's what I hoped for."

He stood and grasped Bishop McVinney's hand. To his dismay, the old man winced. The damp had gotten to his bones, but from the warmth of the smile returning to his face, not to his spirit. Rushmount Manor would be in good hands until the day his son could decide where he chose to live, in the Old World or the New. As for himself, the decision was made. He would spend his days building a new world . . . and convincing his wife he loved her beyond anyone or anything else on earth.

THOUGH THE DAY WAS BRIGHT AND WARM FOR NOVEMBER, the maple tree had lost most of its glory. Only a few dry leaves clung to its branches. The rest lay strewn like a carpet on the surrounding ground. Abby had just settled down, her back against the tree trunk, the baby on her lap when, like a dream fulfilled, she spied Harry striding through the meadow. The breeze riffled his dark hair and sent fallen leaves whirling about his polished boots. Even from a distance, she could see his jaw clenched tight, no smile lifting his lips.

He strode as erect and arrogant as ever, shoulders back, purpose in every step. How like the first time she'd seen him by the shore when he had leapt to the sand looking like a beautiful creature from another world. She couldn't tear her eyes from him then, and she couldn't now.

He was still beautiful, would always be beautiful, but something new, something not there two summers ago, had changed him. *What?* she wondered, as with limbs turned to jelly she sat among the leaves with her sleeping baby and watched him come near.

A few paces away from her he stopped, his eyes searing her, pinning her where she sat. He was older. Thinner. Unhappy.

"How many countries are you going to flee from?" he demanded, giving her no greeting, no bow, no smile.

"Don't wake the baby."

He smiled then, but only at the quiet bundle on her lap. "Our child? May I hold him?"

"Of course it's our child. And no you may not."

His glance snapped back to her face. "Answer my question."

"No, I have one of my own to ask. How many manor houses will *you* flee from?"

"I didn't flee. I left to buy a horse."

"Without saying farewell?"

"I informed the staff."

"Oh really? Does it take nigh on eight months to buy a bloody horse?"

"I was unaccountably delayed."

"What does that mean, your lordship? You couldn't brush the doxies off your knees?"

A puzzled expression flitted across Harry's face before he burst out laughing. "You're jealous."

"Of two raddled old hags, certainly not."

"Your hair's grown long," he said.

"And my patience short."

"You were never overly patient as I recall." He stepped closer. "I understand why you didn't tell me how my father died."

About to lift the baby to her shoulder, she paused and peered into his eyes. "What do you understand?"

"You knew I would react as I did. You know me better than I know myself."

"True," she replied tartly.

"You haven't changed an iota," he said with a wry smile. "I like that." He stooped before her and, with a single finger, stroked the sleeping baby's cheek. "Like velvet," he murmured. "Lovely."

"Aye," she agreed, glancing at the child they had created, the child who looked so much like Harry. The same little mole above the lip, the dark hair, the same temper when thwarted . . . well, perhaps in that both parents had contributed something.

"I don't blame you for leaving me," Harry said, looking up from the baby to search Abby's face. "I failed you."

She shook her head. "Don't fault yourself, Harry. I didn't leave only because you regretted marrying me."

"I never did. I never will."

She put a quieting finger to his lips. "What I said in my letter, I meant. I want my son to grow up believing all men have the right to strive for their dreams. I saw no such belief in the Old World." She rested a palm on the warm, autumnal earth. "This is not a perfect place, Harry. Aiden would be the first to agree. But it's the best our flawed world has to offer, and it's my home and our child's home. Will you make it yours?"

"If you'll have me," he said, his eyes never leaving her face.

"Oh Harry, my love."

The tears welling under her lids gave him all the answer he would ever need. That and the lingering kiss she bestowed. A kiss like those he remembered so well, but with a new tenderness, a new knowledge. Careful of the sleeping baby on her lap, he sat beside her and wrapped an arm around her shoulders.

"We'll buy land and build a home here in this Providence."

"We have the means to do so?"

He nodded. "Remember the plate I hid beneath the manor house stairs? Well, I sold it in London. It's now gold coin. And Aiden, it turns out, is a skilled trader, though most of the profits from the ship should be his by right. Still, overall, we'll be able to secure a good-sized holding for our son."

"Our future son."

He looked at the sleeping baby. "But we already—"

Kissing the baby's cheek, she handed the swaddled bundle to Harry. The infant's eyes opened, two glowing onyx gems.

"The eyes are yours," Harry said.

"Aye, but look, just above the lip. A little mole placed exactly like yours." She reached out and with a single finger touched Harry's face.

"We've both put our mark on him."

"Her."

Harry's eyes narrowed. "What did you say?"

Abby smiled. "Meet your daughter, Harry. Mistress Grace Anne Rushmount."

With a whoop, he lofted the baby on high and kissed her cheek. Startled by his outburst, she stiffened and screamed in protest. Harry grinned at her wriggling in his embrace, knowing with a leap of his heart that yet another strong woman had entered his life.

As Abby watched him delight in their child, her cup runneth over, filling her with joy, spilling its promise onto this great, good earth that together they would honor forever.

Sharon Yanish

AFTER A STINT AS AN ADVERTISING COPYWRITER, Jean Harrington taught writing and literature for sixteen years at Becker College in Worcester, Massachusetts. She enjoyed teaching tremendously, but always simmering on the back burner of her brain was the desire to write a book of her own. So when her two children were grown and launched, Jean left Becker and moved to Florida with husband John and began writing in earnest—both historicals and tongue-in-cheek cozy mysteries. Ten novels later, and now an Ohio resident, Jean is still busy writing, and is very happy with the publication of this third book in her Irish historical saga—*A Wild Colonial Girl.*

Slainte!